A NOVEL

A THRILLER

BUILT ON

LIES, DECEIT

AND MURDER

LUCINDA MICHALSKI

I dedicate this work to my loving parents,
who instilled in me the determination to pursue
my dreams wherever they lead me.

ACKNOWLEDGEMENTS

I want to acknowledge Tara Majuta. Without her talent and skills, this book would not have made it into your hands. She was my mentor and my constant cheerleader. Thank you, Tara, for never losing faith in me during this arduous process.

I am grateful to Asya Blue for her creative cover design and her guidance in the publishing world. Thanks, too, to Ruby Pucillo. Her editing skills helped raise my story to a greater standard. I am forever thankful for all my friends and family, whose constant support gave me the courage to continue even when doubts threatened to overwhelm me.

And above all, I want to thank my husband, Jerry, for his undying support.

SOS

CHAPTER ONE

Tiny flecks of light seeped between the wooden blinds and
threaded their way through the darkness. A ceiling fan
circled above, its slow rotation caressing Lucy's damp face.
She clutched the down comforter and tucked it securely under her
chin. Angling her head from side to side, she scanned the shadows
for something, anything, that would tell her where she was.

A distant thud penetrated the silence. Three more followed
in clipped sequence. *Thump...thump...thump...* "I know you're in
there," a harsh voice intoned. "Open the damn door!"

Lucy struggled to a sitting position and draped her long legs
over the edge of the bed.

"Sylvia, I need to talk to you!"

A smile edged across Lucy's lips as the pieces of the puzzle
melded together. She had arrived at her aunt's lake house late
the prior night. The man at the door wanted her Aunt Sylvia, and
Sylvia was not home. Surely, he would leave when his pleas went
unheeded. Yet: he didn't. The obstinate hammering persisted.

Lucy pushed herself out of bed and grabbed her robe, tugging
the belt snugly around her waist. She marched from the room,
intending to rid herself of the ill-mannered interloper. The image

of a tall man materialized on the other side of the front door's panes of glass. His fist hovered, ready to batter.

Lucy seized the knob and yanked the door open. Her line of vision traveled upward until their eyes locked. The spell broke when he looked past her in an apparent attempt to catch sight of the woman he sought.

"I'm Detective RJ Rafferty. I need to talk to Sylvia Masterson."

His abrasive tone renewed Lucy's resolve. "What the hell are you doing pounding on the door like that at this hour of the morning?"

He leveled his full consideration back to her. "I'm here on official business. Please tell Sylvia to come to the door."

"She's not here."

"What do you mean she's not here? She didn't tell me she was going anywhere."

Lucy's brows furrowed. "I can't imagine my aunt is in the habit of sharing her personal agenda with just anybody."

The ping of the detective's phone diverted his attention. He held up his finger, signaling to her that he had to take the call. Keeping eye contact, he barked into the receiver, "I'm busy right now. What do you need?" Lucy held his gaze, refusing to be intimidated. He ended the conversation with a curt "I'll be there as soon as I can," replaced the phone inside a pocket on his belt, and said, "Sorry I disturbed you, Miss..."

"Lucy. Lucy Rydell."

"Well, Miss Rydell, when you talk to Sylvia, tell her to contact me." He reached into his breast pocket and handed her a card, his eyes probing hers. He shifted his weight from one foot to the other, and then, with a slight dip of his head, took his leave.

Lucy closed the door and stared at the card: *RJ Rafferty, Detective, Otter Tail County Sheriff's Office.*

The sight of the police logo thrust Lucy into the past. Her father, a man she hadn't seen or heard from in almost three decades, had also promised to protect and serve. The malice within his soul, however, had led him to forsake the sacred oath to which he had subscribed. Lucy's fingers moved to massage the side of her face—the burning sensation from the back of his hand lingered to this day.

Aunt Sylvia had earned her niece's unwavering devotion for her role in Lucy's father's permanent withdrawal from their family. An investigator knocking at the door certainly gave pause. But, if Sylvia were in any kind of trouble, Lucy would move heaven and earth to protect her.

Slipping the detective's card into the side pocket of her robe, she retraced her steps to the bedroom. It occurred to her that she should have probed deeper into the motive behind her aunt's last-minute trip to Europe. "Too late now," she muttered.

CHAPTER TWO

Located in one of Minnesota's prestigious retreat areas, Sylvia Masterson's cottage sat on a parcel of land on Rose Lake's south shore. Deep, clear water surrounded by hillsides of dense forest lent a backdrop that rivaled most five-star resorts.

A twenty-minute drive east on Highway 60 led to Vergas, a small, trendy community where tourism soared in the summer months and again throughout the winter season. Arthur's Corner Bar & Grill was one of the first structures built in the small town. Today, it still stood proud, having survived two major fires and a tornado in 1952 that had almost leveled the building.

Jan Coin and Dick Manly sauntered into the establishment. Coin, a demure woman with a pinched nose and teeth whitened a shade too light, slid into a booth. Manly, her Man Friday, sat opposite her.

Jan nudged her heavy, dark-rimmed glasses up the bridge of her pointed nose with her index finger. "You won't believe the call I got this morning. Marv Noble wanted me to check out his neighbor's place, claiming that there's strange activity going on there. He expected me to go over and search the guy's house. Like that's my job."

"What did you tell him?"

"I told him to call the Sheriff, for God's sake. I'm the mayor of this town, not goddamn law enforcement."

Dick's large frame jiggled slightly. "Go easy on him. He's not the smartest guy in town."

Art Mason, the proprietor of the bar, casually dropped off lunch menus and then busied himself clearing a nearby table. The third generation of Masons to own and operate Arthur's Bar, Art was practically part of the joint's upholstery, his unassuming demeanor allowing him to keep tabs on the place and eavesdrop on hushed conversations.

When Art came back to take their orders, Jan said, "Did you hear what happened in Brainerd two days ago? Everyone up there's in a panic. It seems a fight erupted in Digger's Bar when a man accused the waiter of ogling his fourteen-year-old daughter. They actually came to blows. Had to call the sheriff to break it up."

Dick moved his arm to the back of the bench and gave Art a conspiratorial wink. "What have you learned?"

"Everyone's nervous." Art glanced over his shoulder and back at Dick. "I did hear an interesting tidbit the other day. Apparently, the FBI is narrowing their investigation to this area."

Both men turned to see Coin's reaction.

A frown creased her brow. "I'm not able to speak to what the FBI is doing or not doing. I do know that misguided gossip won't help the citizens of our fine community. They've got enough to worry about without rumormongers stirring up more discord."

Art shrugged. "Say what you will, Jan, but much of what I pick up in here winds up being true. And until those missing girls are found and returned to their families unharmed, no one around here will feel safe."

The mayor stopped as if to ponder the issue further and then said to Art, "Sylvia's neighbor informed me that she left town. Just packed her bags and disappeared." Jan held Art's gaze. "Are you aware that her niece is spending the summer at the cottage?"

"Uh, no. I had no idea." No one noticed the faint tic below Art's right eye. "I've got to get back to work."

CHAPTER THREE

Lucy walked into Arthur's later that afternoon. Her vision adjusted and the dimly lit room took on a life of its own. "Swanky" would never be a term used to describe the bar; its quaint charm, however, aided in making it one of the area's favorite gathering places. It was as if she had stepped into a time warp. The heavy wooden tables and chairs, the huge beveled mirror suspended behind the bar, the marred planked floorboards and stuffed animal heads mounted on dark paneled walls all added their own special touch.

She envisioned an old gunslinger walking through the door, stepping up to the massive mahogany bar, and ordering a whiskey straight up. The one thing missing was an old player piano. In its stead was a flashy new jukebox.

It wouldn't be long before the place buzzed with activity. Currently, only a few patrons occupied the tables. Two young men stood at the back of the bar next to a pool table. One laughed gingerly. The other raised his mug, saluted, and guzzled the entire drink in one gulp. Nearby, in a corner booth, a middle-aged couple sat with their heads bowed closely together, talking in hushed tones.

Several elderly men congregated around a large table in the middle of the room. Lucy knew from past visits that these same men gathered like clockwork every day to argue and debate the world's issues. Three nearly empty pitchers of beer positioned in the center of the table served as honorary tributes to the day's discussion. The men's weary expressions reflected their concerns while they weighed in on the events that were tearing their community apart.

Art glanced up from behind the bar at the sound of the front door opening and appreciatively took in every inch of Lucy's 5'6" frame. Her lacy white peasant blouse heightened the natural bronze tone of her soft skin, while knee-length shorts emphasized her shapely legs. He waved, inviting Lucy to sit at the bar, where he poured a glass of her favorite white wine over ice. "I heard you were here for the summer. What's up?" Art said.

"I got in last night. News travels the circuit fast around here."

Art laughed. "It's one of the things we're most proud of."

"I'll be in town for at least a few weeks. Maybe through the summer. Depends on what Aunt Sylvia decides to do."

"Where is Sylvia, anyway? Haven't seen her around lately."

Lucy brought the wine to her lips, stalling until she could decide how much to share with Art. Common wisdom said he was front and center in the rumor mill. She wanted to keep her aunt's private life just that: private. She set the wine glass back on the bar. "You've seen how unpredictable she can be. It's nothing for her to take off to places unknown."

He tilted his head slightly. "Is Jack joining you on this trip?"

Lucy stared at the cubes floating aimlessly in her drink. "No, not this time."

"His job keeping him busy, huh?"

"Something like that." Lucy sucked on her lower lip. "I suppose

I might as well tell you. It'll get out soon enough. Jack and I are separated."

"I'm sorry to hear that. You two seemed to have it all together."

"I thought we did, too—until I found him in the arms of another woman."

"Ouch. I didn't think Jack was *that* kind of guy."

The cook ambled over to recruit Art's help. Lucy watched them weave past the tables on their way to the kitchen. In all the years that she had known Art, he had exhibited traits that were often at odds with each other. The one thing that came to mind was his jovial personality. His constant grin facilitated his easy-going, small-town persona. In contrast, his strong build and purposeful stride suggested a much different temperament.

Lucy shifted her thoughts in another direction: the anticipated Friday night crowd. There would be the predictable number of patrons who simply dropped by for a bite to eat before heading home after a hard week of work. Others would come to meet a friend or two for a night of socializing. Then there would be the optimists—those who arrived with a desire to encounter someone new and special.

Lucy couldn't decide which group best described her current situation. If she were honest, she would concede that she fit into all of these categories. Sighing audibly, she looked up to find Art back behind the bar. She drank the last of her wine and asked for a margarita, a specialty of his.

"I can't help reminiscing about the day we met," Art confessed.

"I believe it was the summer before I headed off to college," she reflected. "That was the year before I met Jack."

"We were so young back then. Good times, huh? Remember the graduation party Sylvia threw for you?"

Lucy laughed. "Yeah. Aunt Sylvia was always so cool. More

of a friend. An equal. I couldn't have survived Jack's affair if it weren't for her."

Art's expression sobered. "Is there a chance you two can work it out?"

"That's why I'm here. Sylvia insisted it would be best to put distance between Jack and me. Since she was looking for a house-sitter for the summer, we agreed I would come up here for at least a month, longer if I can talk my boss into letting me have an extended leave of absence."

There were days when she questioned the wisdom of throwing away ten years of marriage. The notion of being single terrified Lucy, but staying with a man she could not trust was not a viable option.

"In Jack's defense," Lucy said, "he was going through a rough time. His father passed away without warning last year."

Art nodded. "Losing a parent is always tough."

"Jack and his dad didn't always see eye to eye, but Jack assumed that given time, they would overcome their differences. When he realized he would never get the chance to repair their relationship, he became angry." Lucy sat quietly for a minute. "Enough about me. Let's talk about something else. I'm thinking food."

"*That* I can help you with. What would you like?"

"Everything is good here. Why don't you surprise me?"

Art reappeared fifteen minutes later toting a large plate topped with eight ounces of perfectly seasoned corn-fed ground beef and a mound of crispy sweet potato fries. "If this doesn't lift your spirits, nothing will."

They chatted idly until Lucy heard the stool next to her shuffle. Art nodded to Lucy and said, "Let me introduce you to Detective RJ Rafferty."

She angled her chin downward and folded her arms in front of her body. "We've already met."

Rafferty's mischievous nature took the lead. "Sure, we had that pleasure this morning."

She caught his reflection in the mirror. No doubt, he could be trouble. Despite their nettling interaction earlier that day, she was drawn to him—and street clothes suited him. His sculpted abs and bulging arms, tucked snugly into a well-fitting polo shirt, made it abundantly clear that he spent a good share of his time working out. He appeared to be in his early forties. Thick, sandy-colored hair and a roguish smile enhanced his sex appeal. But what really commanded her interest were the same deep-set hazel eyes she had stared into that morning.

When a server signaled Art from the other end of the bar, Detective Rafferty leaned into Lucy. "I think we got off on the wrong foot. I want to correct that." He held out his right hand as a peace offering. "I'm RJ Rafferty. Pleased to meet you."

Lucy faltered slightly before placing her hand in his. The heat emanating between them reminded her that playing with fire could be dangerous. She gracefully pulled her fingers from his grasp, and he nodded. "Let me show you my better side. Can I buy you a drink?"

His boyish manner edged her toward leniency, but she placed her hand on top of her glass. "I'm fine, thank you." She smiled. "There is something I'd like to know. Why are you looking for my aunt? You inferred it was something serious."

"It turned out to be nothing." His raised shoulders told Lucy that he couldn't or wouldn't share information about Sylvia. Twisting in his chair, RJ glanced around the room, before casually asking, "So, what brings you to this fine establishment tonight?"

"I'm a friend of Art's. I try to stop by when I'm in town to catch up on the local gossip. He's been busy tonight, so we haven't had much time to talk."

"This is my lucky day. I'd be happy to be our town ambassador." RJ's features took on the sheen of a newly minted coin. "I was born and raised here. After attending college in St. Paul, I moved to Arizona with big dreams of success." He lowered his chin. "The pull of home proved stronger than I had anticipated. I guess this is where I belong."

Lucy fidgeted with her glass. "So…did a lost love bring you back?"

"No, nothing like that. Don't get me wrong—life in the big city was great. It's the superficial crap that got to me. I missed small-town living." Dimples creased the center of his cheeks. "I'm not sure where that came from, but if you tell anyone I said it, I'll deny it. Can't have people around here thinking I have a soft spot for them."

"Tough guy, huh? Don't worry. Your secret is safe with me."

She gazed at him through the mirror again. He leaned back, connecting with her via the glass, and winked. "So how about you? Any past indiscretions you can share with me?"

"My secrets are mine to keep. Besides, I barely know you."

"You can't blame a guy for trying. Most women I've met are dying to tell their story to anyone who will listen."

"And is this knowledge based on a large number polled?"

"Let's say I tend to attract the wrong women, but I'll keep the count to myself." He paused. "Tell me something about yourself."

"There's not much to tell. I'm here housesitting for my aunt."

He knocked back the rest of his beer. "When you talk to Sylvia, please ask her to call me."

Lucy didn't miss the dark flicker that crossed his eyes. The moment passed, leaving her staring at a devilish grin. She agreed to another drink, and their light banter continued. It all ended abruptly when his cell phone rang and he politely excused himself, bidding her adieu.

Lucy sensed that this would not be her last encounter with Detective Rafferty.

Art swooped in, wiping the bar top in front of her. "I don't get why women find RJ so irresistible. I can't tell you how many women have come in here to drown their sorrows after he inevitably broke their hearts." His expression hinted at sarcasm. "He's a restless man. I think it's hopeless for any female to think she can tame him."

She was careful not to encourage Art's pursuit. The last thing Lucy wanted was to reject his advances and make things awkward between them. She stifled a yawn. "It's late. I think I'll call it a night." They said their goodbyes, and she left.

Lucy pulled into the garage to the beat of distant thunder rumbling in the thick, humid air. There were no streetlamps to illuminate the country road; no moon to cast its glow over the surrounding area. She shuffled down the darkened cobblestone walkway, her head swiveling left and then right, searching for real or imaginary dangers.

The remoteness of the area had not been a consideration when she had agreed to housesit. She looked forward to spending the days on her own, but the mere thought of the isolation she would encounter each night remained daunting. Lucy entered the house and slid the deadbolt into place before decisively switching on the lights in every room.

She slipped into a pair of sweatpants and a t-shirt and made her way to the kitchen. With a warm mug of hot chocolate in one hand and a book in the other, Lucy curled up in the leather chair near the window, hoping keep the loneliness at bay by burying herself in the plot of a good novel.

Her eyelids soon grew heavy. A glance at the clock told her it was almost 2 a.m. The storm had passed, leaving only a hint of rain. Lucy walked back through the cottage, this time to assure herself that the doors and windows were securely locked, reluctantly flipping off the lights as she went. Lingering insecurity compelled her to leave the light in the hallway on.

As Lucy snuggled under the comforter, a sense of dread washed over her. It started as a tiny seed of doubt, took root, and grew during the night, casting suspicions in every direction.

CHAPTER FOUR

Lucy woke the next morning and did what came naturally: she buried her fears. Amid the soft folds of bedding, she leisurely pondered the many complexities of RJ Rafferty. By the time she rolled out of bed, breakfast was her focus.

Passing the front door, she froze. Through the hazy light entering through the window pain, she spied RJ exiting the side entrance of the garage. A well-dressed woman approached him from behind. Lucy fumed over the idea that the two had unlawfully entered her aunt's property. She held the door slightly ajar to afford eavesdropping, ducking to one side when the woman spun around. Holding her breath, she peered back around the doorframe. The trespassers had their backs to her. The woman held a plastic bag in her hand; its contents had their full attention.

Lucy strained to hear the context of their conversation. She thought RJ said, "This could be a game-changer. I need to get in touch with Boris right away."

"Do you plan to show this to him?" the woman asked. Lucy could not make out RJ's answer. She did catch the woman's reply: "I'm glad I'm not in your shoes."

RJ's fleeting glance around the yard sent Lucy back behind the door. She heard him declare, "We better get out of here before someone catches us."

Lucy grimaced. *It's a little late for that.* The click of car doors opening and closing encouraged her to peek around the frame one more time. Spying the taillights of RJ's truck, she closed the door and headed to the kitchen, wondering what RJ was up to and why he had taken an interest in Sylvia.

Her nerves screamed for caffeine. The brand-new coffee maker perched on the countertop presented a bit of levity. Sylvia always had the newest and best of everything. Why shouldn't she? The woman had more money than anyone really needed. When asked, she credited much of her wealth to her late husband's knack for playing the stock market. This could be true. But her aunt had had money long before she met and married Lloyd Masterson.

Sylvia had a valid point, though. Lloyd Masterson had been a shrewd businessman. He had once convinced Lucy to let him invest some of her money and had doubled it in less than a month. When she voiced her concerns, Lloyd had advised her to contact a professional broker if she required an education on the wisdom of good investing, his taunting glare daring her to object. Lucy had let the conversation drop and quietly deposited the money, vowing to avoid further financial endeavors with him.

Lucy sat at the table and gnawed gently on her fingertip. The sweeping grade of the yard drew her gaze to the water's edge. Two boats sat moored at the dock: a small Larson sport boat and a Hobie catamaran sailboat. Normally, Lucy would take advantage of the Hobie Cat, but today, more important issues summoned her.

Strangers illegally snooping around was not a good sign. The idea that RJ had removed something that belonged to her aunt disturbed her even more. Her number one priority today was to search the garage for any clues left behind.

Upon entering, Lucy took stock of the room. She walked over to the cabinets that stretched the length of the opposite wall and opened every door and drawer. The back wall supported a pegged board that held a scattering of household tools and lawn equipment. Nothing looked out of order.

Lucy went back into the house and sat down at the desk in the kitchen to check her email for messages. The loud trill of the phone left her flushed. Her arm brushed against the vase of fresh-cut flowers left by her aunt, sending it downward with a loud crash, shards of glass scattering across the tiled floor. Lucy scowled at the debris as she snatched up the phone, "What?"

"May I speak with Lucy Rydell?" a calm voice responded.

"Who's calling?"

"This is FBI Agent Russell Hunter. Are you Lucy?"

"How did you know to reach me here?"

"It would be better if we spoke in person. Can you meet me at the Lakeside Grill in Detroit Lakes, say, in an hour?"

Ignoring the potential danger, she agreed to meet. As Lucy swept up the mess, suspicions ran amok in her mind. She had to uncover exactly what was going on, and to do that, she needed facts. If the man on the phone was who he said he was, he would have answers to her questions. That decided, she grabbed her purse and keys, and scurried out the door.

CHAPTER FIVE

L ucy entered the Lakeside Grill early and settled into a booth facing the door. It occurred to her that the agent had not asked for a description of her appearance. One glance around the room told her it wouldn't take much detective work to pick her out of the crowd.

A server approached with a menu. Lucy ordered a tuna melt and an iced tea.

Soon after the food arrived, a rather short man in his mid-fifties walked into the establishment. He was of medium build with dark hair cut close to his head. His attire of Dockers and a well-fitted pastel shirt suggested he had come from a family picnic or was on his way to the country club. He approached her table.

"Are you Lucy Rydell?"

Lucy nodded. He edged into the bench across from her. "Thank you for meeting me today."

He did not fit the criteria she expected of an FBI agent. "May I see your ID?"

He dug into his pocket, pulled out his identification, and discreetly passed it to her. Lucy scrutinized it before handing the badge back. She trusted that it was as authentic as it looked. The waitress arrived and took his order of coffee. When she left, the agent got right to the heart of the matter. "I think this is a mistake—me talking to you."

"If that's true, why are we here?"

His shoulders leveled when he leaned back into the booth. "My superiors think you can be of assistance. It is my opinion that you should pack your bags and go back to Des Moines."

Anger flashed. Here was another man trying to bully her into doing things his way. "That's not going to happen."

A deep divide filled the space between them. "I figured that, but I had to make an attempt."

"What exactly is happening here?"

He scanned the room, sizing up the few people in the bar, and turned back, patting his lips with his index finger. "We've had Sylvia's place under surveillance for some time. Unfortunately, she managed to get away. She thinks she can run from this, but she can't. She is in grave danger." His eyes held steady contact. "Did Sylvia give you any hint that she's been working with us?"

Lucy refused to give him the upper hand.

Agent Hunter resumed his narrative. "A couple years ago, Sylvia suspected that her husband, Lloyd, was mixed up in some illicit activities. She took it upon herself to do some investigating."

"I can't believe Sylvia didn't confide in me."

"She's a strong-minded woman."

Lucy could not argue the matter.

"In Sylvia's hunt for evidence," Hunter said, "she discovered a safety deposit box full of cash and damaging documents that could put Lloyd away for a long time. There were also bank statements detailing various overseas accounts."

A chill washed over Lucy. "Was my aunt in danger during any of this?"

"To her credit, she apparently left everything exactly as she found it. Our research suggests that Lloyd never suspected a thing. By the time Sylvia contacted us, she was willing to do anything to bring him to justice. That's when Lloyd disappeared in that fishing accident."

Lucy recalled the day. Lloyd had gone fishing on Rose Lake when an unexpected storm blew in. When he didn't come home, a search party located the remnants of his charred boat. The depth of the lake hindered divers from locating his body, and authorities called off the search after two grueling weeks. With no new evidence, they eventually relegated the case to the cold files.

"We uncovered reliable evidence two months ago that confirms Masterson survived the accident," Agent Hunter said.

"You think he's alive? Have you told Sylvia?"

"She's privy to it now. But during Lloyd's funeral, a detective with the Otter Tail Sheriff's Office insinuated himself into her life. We are pretty sure he's mixed up with Masterson."

"Why do you think this guy is involved?"

"You met him yesterday. His name is RJ Rafferty, and I'm not at liberty to discuss any details regarding him."

"Then why did you bring him up? Also, how do you know I talked to him?" She rolled her eyes. "You're still watching the cabin, aren't you?"

"Our investigation extends to anyone linked to Lloyd Masterson. Please tell me what Rafferty said to you."

"He was looking for Sylvia. When I told him she wasn't there, he left." Heat rose to Lucy's cheeks. If Agent Hunter noticed, he didn't let on.

He continued, "Two weeks ago, Sylvia severed all contact with us. Now, she's gone, leaving us with two questions: is she back in Masterson's pocket? Or is she trying to put distance between herself and his activities? Either way, your entry into the equation complicates things further."

"I'm not sure how I fit into all this. I wasn't particularly fond of Lloyd, but out of respect for my aunt, I tried to get along with him. I had no clue he might be mixed up in anything illegal."

The agent stared at her from under lowered brows. "I can assure you it's in your best interest to tell us everything you've learned."

"I don't know anything—I swear."

Someone filled the entryway, distracting both Lucy and Hunter. A bright stream of sunlight backlit RJ's silhouette. He strolled in and took a seat at the bar.

Agent Hunter raised his menu to shield his face. At the same time, he reached for his phone and punched in a number. "Maggie, meet us in the parking lot." He disconnected and addressed Lucy. "I don't think RJ being here is a coincidence." The agent took a twenty from his billfold and placed it on the table. "Let's see if we can get out of here without attracting his interest. If he approaches you, let me handle the conversation."

He motioned for Lucy to go first. When they got to the parking lot, a slim woman in khakis and a loose-fitting sweater walked up. "Sorry, I didn't see him until he walked in the door. He must've parked his truck down the street." She addressed Lucy. "Ms. Rydell? I'm Agent Margaret Peterson." They shook hands.

Agent Peterson had a star quality about her. Her thick auburn hair and perfectly applied makeup highlighted smooth alabaster skin. Her soft green eyes and million-dollar smile could undoubtedly charm the most hardened criminal.

"Let's get back to Sylvia's place," Agent Hunter said. "I think there's a chance Rafferty has it bugged."

"Lucy, if you don't mind," Agent Peterson interjected before she could respond, "I'll ride with you. Agent Hunter will follow us in his car."

<hr>

During the ride back to the cabin, Lucy's mind reeled with the information she had gleaned from Agent Hunter. She'd ventured to the lake for peace and quiet, and so far, she hadn't seen any of it. In over her head, she needed to come up with a plan.

They approached Highway 60 and made a right. The rearview mirror showed that Hunter went the opposite direction. "Where is Agent Hunter going?"

"He's circling around to make sure no one's tailing us."

"I don't understand why Detective Rafferty would keep tabs on me. I told him I don't know where Sylvia is. She didn't leave her itinerary or any contact numbers for me. If she had, I would have contacted her by now and gotten answers for myself." Lucy tilted her head slightly. "I don't think Sylvia considered the ramifications when she took off." She pulled into the driveway and parked in the garage. "If you knew my aunt, you'd know she's not the type to run away from anything. There has got to be a reasonable explanation for her trip." Both women exited the car.

Lucy stood to the side as the agent conducted an inspection of the garage's interior. When she finished, Agent Peterson said, "I don't see anything. We'll get a tech in here, just in case I missed something. If you don't mind, let's check out the house."

Together, they walked to the door, and Lucy ushered Agent Peterson in. Beginning in the bedroom, the agent systematically peered into, under, and around every piece of furniture, looking for anything suspicious. Lucy quickly tired of monitoring her and slipped away to the kitchen to tidy up.

Agent Peterson entered and swept the room. "As far as I can tell, the house is clear."

Lucy studied Peterson for a moment. Realizing the agent may have planted her own bugs, she said, "I should have asked earlier. May I see your ID?" The agent retrieved the badge from her pocket and handed it to Lucy. After examining it, Lucy passed it back, privately vowing to be more careful in the future.

Agent Peterson spied the Hobie moored at the dock and inquired, "How long have you been sailing?"

"My husband introduced me to it when we were in college. I was instantly hooked."

"My parents are avid sailors. Much of my youth was spent on Lake Michigan."

A knock on the door prompted Agent Peterson to rise and move into the shadows.

"Lucy?" Agent Hunter's voice flowed down the hallway and into the kitchen.

Agent Peterson stepped back to the table as her partner came into the room, his gaze fixed on Lucy. "From now on, you keep your doors locked at all times." Eye contact with his partner exposed his disappointment. She should have known better.

"It won't happen again," she replied.

Agent Hunter quizzed Peterson on her preliminary analysis of the cottage. She delivered her report and then queried him on what he had observed.

He shook his head. "No one followed us here. I put in an order for the tech department. They should be here within the hour." To Lucy, he said, "It could be a coincidence that RJ showed up at the Lakeside Grill today. It's also possible he tailed you there. I don't think he knows who I am, but we can't be sure of that. We have to be very careful from now on."

Lucy didn't try to hide her irritation. "I've had enough of this! You either fill me in on everything, or I'm going to have to ask both of you to leave."

"Let's sit for a minute," Agent Hunter said, taking a seat at the table. "I doubt your aunt calculated the risks before she ran. Nevertheless, the fact is that she put you in a very dangerous situation. I've already told you about her not-so-late husband Lloyd. The one thing I haven't explained is Lloyd's participation in a kidnapping ring dealing in human trafficking. We were close to making an arrest when Sylvia fled the country."

CHAPTER SIX

As a young boy, Wayne Johanson had yearned for a better life. The abusive hand of his father and the loveless care of his mother had created an enormous void in his heart. Early experience taught him the value of a low profile. That lesson served him well whenever his dad was in the picture. Sheer luck aided him in dodging the family's criminal activities until the ripe age of fourteen.

One cold October night, gruff hands yanked him from a sound sleep. His father's harsh voice ordered him to get dressed. Wayne stumbled to find his jeans and a shirt and wasn't allowed enough time to tie his shoes before the old man took hold of his collar and dragged him down the stairs and out to the barn.

"Deliver this truck to the Anderson farm and get yer ass back here by dawn."

Wayne kept his eyes on the ground and shuffled his feet to knot his laces. "Sure, Pa, but how do I get back? Is someone gonna pick me up?"

With no warning, Wayne was laid flat on his back, blood gushing from his lower lip. The dark form of his father loomed over him. Wayne eased himself into a sitting position, confusion and anger simmering just below boiling point. The old man's foot took aim, but Wayne was ready. He rolled to the left, narrowly dodging the steel-toed boot.

A growl skirted past his pa's stained teeth. "You worthless piece of shit. Git yer ass up off that ground, or I'll give you the beating of yer life."

Acting on adrenaline, Wayne jumped into the truck and shoved the gear into reverse. Gravel flew into the air as he backed around and took off for destinations unknown.

The little sister he had left behind tugged sharply at his heart. Sadly, fear kept him from going back. He spent the next sixteen years trying to get as far away from the past as he could, only to find himself back on the family farm when he got word of his parents' demise. Authorities had discovered their charred bodies among the ashes of the old barn. Although the fire triggered much speculation in the small community, the fire chief found no evidence of foul play.

The shabby homestead brought back everything Wayne had worked so hard to forget. The last thing he needed was to put down roots in a place that represented a lifetime of pain. He couldn't, however, bring himself to forsake his young nephew, abandoned as a baby by his sister and then orphaned by the loss of his grandparents at a very young age.

Wayne Johanson was no longer the scrawny kid his father had bid goodbye to. He now stood 6'2" and weighed over 210 pounds. Known to be a hard-ass, he tucked his gentler side behind a bastion of bravado. His father's utterances forever echoed inside his head: "The seed don't fall too far from the tree." Following his example, Wayne found trouble wherever he went.

Word traveled fast, and the wrong people quickly learned that Wayne would take substantial risks for the right price. In time, it was business as usual on the Johanson farm.

When the time came to groom his nephew, Hal, for the family business, Wayne woke him in the middle of the night and handed him a package. "Put this in the trash can outside the gate at St. Adalbert's." The ironies didn't escape Wayne. First, he was introducing Hal to the business in the same manner in which he had been inducted. Second, St. Adalbert's Cemetery housed the graves of his parents—Hal's grandparents. "Don't make any stops on the way. And get back here as soon as you complete the job."

It was Hal's first drug run. *He was fourteen years old.*

CHAPTER SEVEN

Hal Johanson had become the ward of his grandparents at age five. By age eleven, he was an orphan. Young Hal's downtrodden gaze took in the meager crowd gathered at the burial site in St. Adalbert's Cemetery and wondered what would become of him now that his grandparents were dead.

His Uncle Wayne returned to the farm in due time, bringing with him a new kind of life.

Although no one knew the identity of Hal's father, it was plain to see that the young man had inherited his good looks from that side of the gene pool. Wise beyond his years, he saw the world through narrow, poignant eyes. His earnest stare, curved nose, and pencil-thin lips intimated a sense of acceptance for things he could not control. His natural ability in sports gained the attention of school coaches. Many felt he had the talent to become the next track or basketball star—but life had other plans for him.

Hal never questioned his uncle's demands over the years; he simply did as he was told. But one night, curiosity got the better of him: he delivered a package per instructions, drove the car a mile up the road, and parked, choosing to hoof it back to the drop-off point. Hal hid behind nearby shrubbery for more than an hour.

He was about to leave when he saw headlights veering onto the lane leading to the cemetery. His heart quickened when the car halted in front of the gate.

With the aid of the moon's glow, he recognized the Otter Tail County Sheriff decal displayed on the side of the SUV. An officer got out, walked to the trash can and commandeered the package. When the taillights glided out of sight, Hal scurried back to his car and sped home.

He flicked off the lights and rolled up his driveway, killing the engine when the car came to a stop. The typically well-lit house was now dark and foreboding as if haunted by veiled demons. Shadowy windows looked down on him like sentinels. Hal crawled out from behind the steering wheel and mounted the wooden porch stairs, avoiding known boards that creaked from years of disrepair. A heavy screen door blocked his entrance to the kitchen. He slowly edged the door toward him, careful to hush its squeaky hinges.

Hal stepped inside and noticed a sliver of light wafting from the adjoining room. He tiptoed to the doorway and peeked inside. Wayne had always stayed up for a report after every delivery, but tonight he was fast asleep on the couch. Hal scooted around the prone man, trotted up the back steps to his bedroom, stripped naked, and jumped into bed. When Wayne said nothing the next morning, Hal chose to let sleeping dogs lie.

Jared Lawson was Hal's one true friend in high school. Jared's charm opened a lot of doors—though not always the right ones. Whether drinking, racing cars or chasing girls, the duo was inseparable. When trouble arose, Uncle Wayne came to their rescue. If the police got involved, Wayne bailed them out. For Jared, life on the Johanson farm was fun and exciting. He often referred to Hal as the brother he never had.

Wayne gave the boys jobs at his auto repair shop when they graduated high school. Hal and Jared learned everything, from engine repair to bodywork, and rapidly earned reputations for being the best mechanics in the area. They worked hard. They also played hard, spending most of their free time carousing local bars. With their bad-boy images and pockets full of cash, they took full advantage of their lifestyle, attracting a wide variety of women.

The first year on the job flew by with minimal problems. Early into their second year, Wayne called them in the wee hours of the morning and told them to get to the shop immediately. When they arrived, they were ordered to repaint the Mercedes sitting in the last bay. Hal took one look at the shiny new car and innocently asked why the owner had requested a paint job.

Wayne saw red. "That's none of your damn business! You're not paid to ask questions."

A week later, Wayne told them to drive the newly painted sedan to the rest area at mile marker 26 on Highway 59. "Leave the keys in the glove box, lock the doors, and walk away. I'll pick you up a mile down the road." He dared either of them to challenge his authority. "Under no circumstances are you to talk to anyone. Do you understand me?"

Hal and Jared nodded.

Wayne called on them regularly over the next two years to perform the same job on a variety of automobiles, almost all of them brand new. Hal convinced himself that there were no draw-backs to their illegal activities. The owners collected from their insurance policies, and he collected a fat paycheck that afforded him a standard of living most young men only dreamed about. In truth, Hal knew his luck would not last forever.

It came to pass one night.

They were in a freshly painted Lexus, ready to deliver it to the designated location, when a black SUV drove up behind them and blocked their exit. A huge man rolled out of the driver's seat, his beefy fist waving Hal and Jared out of the car. Even in the darkness, his menacing frame cast a sinister silhouette. "You boys hang tight till I talk to Wayne." He lumbered into the shop.

Wayne accompanied the man back to the SUV. The rear hatch popped open, and together, the two men dragged a large bundle from its rear compartment. The man hoisted it over his shoulder and walked toward the car. Wayne, two steps behind him, gestured for Hal to open the trunk. The man dropped the bundle in, slammed the lid shut, and strolled back to his SUV. He plopped his burly frame into the driver's seat and drove off without any further communication.

Wayne audibly grappled to keep an even tone. "Time to roll. Do not veer from the plan. I'll pick you up two miles north of the drop-off point."

No one moved.

"Well? What are you waiting for?"

Hal started to walk away in defiance.

Wayne grabbed his arm and swung him around. "You do as you're told, boy, or there'll be hell to pay."

Hal marched back to the Lexus with his eyes staring straight ahead. Ever the obedient subordinate, Jared trailed like a lost dog.

They drove in silence until Hal had the courage to speak up. "What do you think is in that bundle?"

"Hell, I don't know, and I don't want to guess."

Hal nosed the Lexus onto the entrance ramp of the rest area. His pulse raced. He searched the site for anything that might be construed as out of place as Jared sat rigid in his seat. Both exhaled audibly when they determined that the parking lot was empty. Hal parked the vehicle in the end space, pushed himself out of the driver's seat, and used the key fob to open the trunk.

Jared scrambled out of the car. "What the hell are you doing?"

"I'm not playing dumb anymore. If this is what I think it is, we are getting in way over our heads."

The light from the trunk splattered onto the pavement. Beyond that, the night was blacker than black. Hal took several deep breaths. Steadying his legs against the bumper, he reached into the trunk and tugged at the heavy blanket. The shroud unfurled, revealing the embodiment of pure evil. He spun on his heels and spewed vomit where he stood.

Sweat dripping from his forehead, Hal shivered and turned back, unable to tear his eyes away from the macabre young girl who now took center stage in his narrowing world. She couldn't be more than fourteen or fifteen years old. A deep gash stretched jaggedly across her delicate throat.

Jared seemed unable to divert his eyes from the gruesome scene. "Jesus!" he moaned. "Let's get the hell out of here before someone drives up and sees us!"

"I'm surprised there's not more blood." The words tasted like dung on Hal's tongue. His gaze lingered on the girl's pale, bruised face. Gently, he re-tucked the blanket around her and lowered the trunk's lid.

Jared grabbed Hal's arm and guided him across the parking lot to the exit ramp. "Come on. We've got to get outta here."

Hal stopped short when they reached the highway and opened his hand, palm up, to show Jared the contents. "I forgot to leave the keys in the car. Do you think I should take them back?"

"I'll do it." Jared grabbed the keys and stuffed them in his jean pocket. "You stay here. I'll run back and put them in the glove box."

Hal ducked behind a row of trees and sank to the ground with a thud. An eternity passed before he watched the Lexus and another car race by, followed by Jared's jogging figure coming into view not far behind. Hal struggled to his feet. "Hey, wait up! I'm here." He moved in front of the tree. "What took you so long?"

"You scared the shit outta me."

"Fuck you! What happened back there?"

Jared bent over and put his hands on his knees. He inhaled deeply and then righted himself. "The minute I got to the car, I saw headlights approaching, so I hid behind the hedges. A man jumped out of the passenger side. He was inside the car in a nanosecond." Jared reached into his pocket and pulled out the set of keys. "The guy was really pissed when he couldn't find these, but like a pro, he had the car running in seconds. I laid low until they were gone before heading back." He paused and wheezed, "You're not gonna believe this. I think I recognized the driver."

CHAPTER EIGHT

Jared was about to tell Hal who was driving the second car when Wayne drove up and stopped long enough for the two to get in. The truck lurched forward. Wayne gave the boys time to catch their breaths and then said, "I don't know about you two, but I need a drink."

He drove straight to Vergas, pulling up behind Arthur's Corner Bar. Wayne had a standing agreement with Art Mason. Provided he was discreet, he could entertain "friends" beyond business hours. A public establishment was not the ideal place to carry on a conversation of tonight's magnitude. Even so, Wayne anticipated he would have a better chance of managing the situation if everyone had to keep their anger in check.

The silence that ensued spoke volumes. The consequences of the evening's events had begun to sink in. "Okay," Wayne said. "We need to stay calm, get some perspective, and decide what to do next. I always think better after a couple of beers." He clambered out of the truck and led the way to the back entrance of the bar. Hal and Jared moved like zombies in his wake.

Art strolled out from the back room. "You're out late tonight."

Wayne was not interested in small talk. "Bring us a pitcher of beer and some privacy."

"You got it."

Art came back with the beer, three chilled mugs, and a bowl of peanuts. "The kitchen is closed, so no food tonight. I'll be in the back if you need anything else."

Wayne bided his time until Art left the room before pouring beer into the mugs. He doled one out to each boy, tossed down his first glass, and refilled it before shoving a handful of peanuts into his mouth. His focus flitted around the room and eventually landed on the bubbly head of foam in front of him.

Hal fidgeted in his seat. "Did you know this was happening tonight?"

Wayne shook his head. "Hell, I'm a petty thief, a con man. I'm not into murder. I'm as in over my head as you two are."

Hal moved to the edge of his chair. "We," he waved his thumb toward Jared and back at himself, "are not involved in this! We didn't know there was a dead body rolled up in that carpet." His voice escalated. "If we go to the cops now, we won't be held responsible for the murder of that girl!"

"Shhh!" Wayne eyed the kitchen door. "We can't let Art catch wind of our conversation." He gulped his beer and slammed the glass on the table. "We can't go to the cops, and that's final!"

Hal rolled his head back. "This is crazy. We have no other options. We have to report it."

"There are dirty cops who have their fingers in this. If we tell anyone, we're dead men." He pushed his glass to the side and leaned over the table. His bared teeth reminded Hal of an angry bear he had encountered during hunting season a few years earlier.

Hal's mind slipped back to that day. He had spent the afternoon in a deer blind with no success. As evening set in, he had gathered his gear, shouldered his .30-06 Winchester rifle, and descended the ladder. Movement from behind had raised an alarm. Hal pivoted to see a large black bear staring straight at him.

He brought his firearm up to his shoulder and aimed. His finger twitched. The bear pawed the ground, his huge head swinging from side to side, saliva spilling from his jaws. Hal lowered the rifle. He couldn't bring himself to fire the gun. The creature emitted one last snarl, did an about-face, and sauntered off into the woods.

Hal sank back against the ladder. He had come face-to-face with a black bear and lived to tell the story. It served as a valuable lesson. Nothing could stand in his way if he remained true to himself.

Wayne's words jolted Hal back to the present. "Be a man, will ya? You two have been reaping the benefits from my contacts with no complaints. Suddenly, a little ripple in the action has you whimpering like babies. Suck it up!" He sat back. "Trust me. Everything will be fine."

Hal stiffened. "Can you assure us that this will never happen again?"

"There is no way I can make that kind of promise. I'm not the boss here. I've been in business with these people for years. They do favors for me; I do favors for them. You're a smart kid, you know there's a chain of command here. I'm stuck in the middle, same as you."

Hal's fist hit the table hard, making the glasses dance in place. "I'm not stuck, and I refuse to go down this road." His bearing evolved into something cold and unyielding. "I'm telling you right now, I'm done working for you." He rose, upsetting the chair behind him. "I won't go to the police, but I won't be a part of anything this ugly. You do what you have to do, but keep me out of it."

Hal stomped out the back exit.

No one noticed Art's bulky frame stepping back from the kitchen doorway.

CHAPTER NINE

Hal set off on foot, hoping to clear his head. He took no note of where he walked to or how far he went. By the time he got back to his apartment, he had a rough plan sketched in his head.

The early morning sunlight filtered through the kitchen window, bathing the room in pale shades of pink. Jared sat slumped over the table.

"You look like shit," Hal said, guessing he probably didn't look much better himself.

"Where've you been?"

"I think I walked about a hundred miles. My feet are killing me." Hal pulled out the chair across from Jared and sat down. "Did you and Wayne reach any kind of decision?"

"Yeah. No. Well, I don't think there's any way out of this. Wayne said he would protect us, and he'll do his best to make sure this kinda thing never happens again."

"You know he can't keep that promise. He told us that himself. And how is he going to protect us? I'm warning you: things will only get worse."

Hal got up and paced the short distance across the room. "This is bad. Really bad." He massaged his temples. "I don't intend to spend the rest of my life losing sleep over a possible prison sentence. I know I haven't been a model citizen up to now, of course. I always knew what we were doing was wrong and that someday it would probably come back to bite me in the ass. But I never anticipated this." His concentration lingered on a squirrel zipping across the yard outside the kitchen window. He turned back to Jared. "Well, today I'm making a change."

Jared blinked several times. "What do you plan to do?"

"I need to get some sleep. Tonight, we'll go out for drinks, hit some bars for one last hurrah, because tomorrow, things will be different around here." His confidence surged. "The first thing on my list is finding a job that won't land me in jail." Hal marched down the length of the hall and into his bedroom. Closing the door, he collapsed onto the bed and fell fast asleep.

Snapping awake, Hal felt better than he had in years. Evening shadows cascading throughout the room hinted that he had slept more than twelve hours. He rolled out of bed and went to the bathroom to relieve himself. After a hot shower, he proceeded to the kitchen.

Jared sat at the table, looking worn and tired. They eyed each other warily. "Did you get any sleep?" Hal asked. Jared shook his head.

"Did you eat? I'm starving." Hal pulled two slices of white bread from a bag and smeared them with peanut butter and jelly before pouring himself a tall glass of milk. He sat at the table and slid half of the sandwich across to his friend. Jared took a bite and then helped himself to a healthy swig of Hal's milk. "You could've poured me a glass, you know."

A small smile broke the ice. "Yeah, and who was your maid yesterday?"

———◆———

Hal and Jared drove separately to Arthur's Bar. The first beer eased their anxiety. The second boosted their morale. They continued to dance around the subject most on their minds. Emon Franken, a drinking buddy, joined them, and the three took their festivities to the Pizza Ranch in Perham.

They seated themselves at a table in the back of the room and carried on as if it were any normal day. Hal had just bet them a round of beers that he could eat more pizza than they could when suddenly, a strange expression crossed his face. His comrades twisted in their seats to see what, or who, had captured Hal's fascination.

"See that redhead near the front door?" Hal whispered. "That's the girl I'm going to marry." Jared and Emon erupted like hyenas.

"That's the beer talking," Emon counseled.

"Don't you think she's a little young for you?" Jared queried, shaking his head. "You've got enough turmoil in your life. Don't be stupid."

Hal shrugged. It was a watershed moment. He had to change his ways, and change them fast, if he had any chance of a normal life. For the first time ever, he wanted to make plans for the future—bright, promising plans.

CHAPTER TEN

Becca Banks, at the tender age of sixteen, did not fully comprehend that present-day decisions could have dire consequences in the future. As with most teenagers, her narrow view of the world centered around herself, her family, and, more importantly, her school activities. She was an honor student, well-liked by her peers. Her lifetime dream had become a reality during her junior year, when she won a place on the cheerleading squad at Perham High School. To top that, her schoolmates had crowned her Miss Perham.

Becca's parents had moved her and her younger siblings from Fargo, North Dakota to Perham, Minnesota with the belief that a small town would be a safer place to raise their family. Dan and Mary Ann Banks doted on their three children, taking daily pride in their development. They assumed that with the proper guidance, the girls would lead happy, productive lives. Everything fit into place until the fateful day Becca met twenty-one-year-old Hal Johanson.

The chance meeting took place following the first football game of the season. Becca and four of her girlfriends had agreed to meet up with some of the boys on the team at the local pizza parlor.

No one in her group had noticed Hal sitting at a table with two of his pals until he approached Becca. In front of everyone, he asked her if she would accompany him to a movie sometime. The girls giggled and the boys snickered. They all sobered up when Becca responded, "I'd love to, except my parents won't let me date yet."

"I understand." Hal flashed her a warm smile. "Will you join me for a pizza here tonight?"

Becca sought assurance from the other girls. They all nodded in unison. Hal took hold of her hand and led her to an empty booth in the corner, sliding in across from her. She blushed as his gaze traced the shape of her curls before staring admiringly into her eyes. They dined on pepperoni pizza, which they learned was a favorite of both, and chatted as if they had known each other their entire lives.

At ten-thirty, Olivia Howard, one of Becca's confidants, gingerly approached and tapped her finger against the watch on her wrist. They had to leave immediately if they expected to be home by their eleven o'clock curfew. The group of girls weaved their way to the exit, their laughter reminiscent of a gaggle of geese ambling across an open field.

Standing in the parking lot next to Izzie's car, Becca felt as if she were part of an inquisition.

"Who was that guy?" Sophia, a fellow cheerleader, asked.

"He's so cute! Are you going to see him again?" Izzie followed.

"How old is he? He looked old." Olivia sucked on a strand of her hair.

"Your dad will have a heart attack if he finds out you were talking to a guy that old," Izzie added.

Becca scrunched her nose until it wrinkled. "He's the most wonderful man I've ever known." She whispered, "I gave him my number."

The girls piled into the car. "What will you do if he calls you?" A tinge of jealousy colored the words of her best friend, Betsy. "Your parents won't let you date him."

Bookended in the backseat by Sophia and Olivia, Becca hugged herself. "I'll worry about that later."

Her confidence waned as the days passed. *Why hasn't he called?* Maybe he had lost her number. Or were her friends right?—had he decided she was too young for him? Unfortunately, she couldn't call him. She hadn't even thought to ask for his last name.

Locked in her room, she threw herself on the bed and buried her head under the pillow. When her cell buzzed, she rolled over and grabbed it from the nightstand. An unfamiliar number flashing across the screen quickened her heartbeat. "Hello?" she nearly sobbed.

From that day forward, not a day went by that Hal and Becca didn't talk on the phone.

CHAPTER ELEVEN

al paid the bill after Becca and her friends left the Pizza Ranch. A scan around the room told him that his friends had already gone. That was fine by him. He was on a high and wasn't going to let anyone spoil a perfect evening. Hal drove home with visions of a new life taking shape. Upon entering his apartment, he grabbed a pen and paper and compiled a to-do list. The telephone on the wall rang. He opted to let the machine answer.

"I know you're there. Pick up the phone!"

Hal had anticipated Jared's voice coming through from the other end, not the slurred words of a lunatic. His veins filled with ice. He couldn't bring himself to reach for the receiver.

The fiendish voice sounded more like the snarl of a wild animal than that of a sane man. "I know you're listening, so pay close attention. Wayne pledged on his life that you won't talk. You better not. If you do, we will find you and your two-bit uncle. When we're done, there won't be enough of either of you for anyone to identify. You won't get another warning. Don't mess it up."

The room began to spin. Hal's body slid from the chair and landed hard on the floor, tears streaking down the sides of his face. He couldn't say for sure if they were the result of fear or relief, but it didn't matter. He had a second chance. Tonight, he had met the love of his life, and he planned to do everything in his power to see that he had a happy ending.

With renewed purpose, he got up and went to the basement to retrieve several storage containers. He gathered his belongings, filling the boxes as he went. First thing tomorrow, he would look for a new place to live. Next, Hal planned to find a different job.

He had a new place to call home within days. Finding a legitimate job was a bit trickier. Most businessmen in town wanted nothing to do with him. In their minds, he was guilty by association, with respect to his uncle and the gossip that shadowed the family. Fortunately, Doug Brown, the owner of the local marina, was in dire need of an experienced mechanic. Doug hired Hal on the promise that he and Wayne had permanently parted ways.

Hal spent another three nights mustering up the courage to call Becca. He finally picked up the napkin bearing her number and dialed. The sound of her voice caused his throat to constrict, but he talked through the nerves. "Hi. This is Hal. Remember me?"

She sighed. "I was afraid you lost my number."

Seconds ticked by. Hal swallowed hard. "I've been thinking a lot about you." He felt his courage slipping. "Um, so much has changed since I met you. I got a new job and a new apartment, and I signed up for classes at Minnesota Tech for next semester. All because of you."

"You did all that for me?"

They chatted for over an hour until Becca suddenly went quiet. Hal held his breath. "I have to hang up now," she whispered. "My mom needs help with dinner."

Afraid he might not get another chance, he blurted out, "Can we get together sometime?"

He barely heard her answer over the pounding in his head.

"I'm so embarrassed to admit that I have to ask my parents."

"Don't worry. I think we should get their permission. I don't want them to have the wrong impression of me." He agreed to call her back the next day at the same time.

Hal dialed her number at exactly four o'clock. She answered on the first ring and informed him that she had not convinced her parents that she was old enough to date.

"We'll have to be content to talk on the phone until they agree to let you go out with me."

"You're okay with that?" she asked.

"I'll wait for you forever if I have to."

They talked for another hour. When it came time for her to hang up, Becca confided that she had a plan. "Why don't we meet again at the Pizza Ranch after the football game next Friday? I'll be there with my friends. And since it's a public place, it won't officially be a date if we randomly show up at the same time."

Things progressed from there. Becca introduced Hal to her friends. He dazzled the young girls with his handsome physique and captivated them with what they perceived as worldliness. He, in turn, maintained that he was the luckiest man alive. It amazed him how much the girls' lives differed from what he had experienced when he was their age.

The daily tightrope he walked between his past and his future kept him awake most nights. He wanted to fit into Becca's world more than anything. To do that, he had to find a way to erase his past. How was that even possible, given the fact that Wayne could rat him out at any time if he was so inclined?

CHAPTER TWELVE

Agent Hunter and Agent Peterson had been in the cottage for over an hour and a half. Brian, their tech guy, detected no evidence of wiretapping. Even so, Agent Hunter refused to believe that Detective Rafferty's hands were clean. The agent's typical calm veneer showed signs of cracking when he shifted his interrogation back to Lucy.

"We know from our surveillance that Sylvia and Rafferty were acquainted with each other. Did Sylvia ever give you any clue concerning the extent of their association?"

"No. Actually, my aunt never mentioned his name to me. That's why I had reservations when he insinuated that he knew her well."

Lucy outlined her conversation with Rafferty and finally confessed that she had witnessed him and a woman exiting her aunt's garage earlier that morning. "They apparently located something of value. Whatever it was, they took it with them when they left."

"I hope to God you didn't confront them."

Lucy shook her head. "No. Even though I was outraged at their intrusion, something urged me to hold back. Instead, I attempted to eavesdrop on their conversation. I wasn't able to hear much."

"Did you get a look at what it was that they took with them? Can you describe it at all?"

"Not really." Lucy took a moment to recall the item. "It was rolled up inside a plastic bag."

Agent Hunter laced his hands together on top of the table. "Did you notice anything else? Even the smallest detail could be important."

Lucy nibbled the top of her finger while organizing her thoughts. "I heard RJ—I mean Detective Rafferty—say he had to talk to someone named Boris. He sounded alarmed." Lucy leaned back into her chair. "That's all I know."

Agent Hunter mimicked her pose. "Well, if you're sure there's nothing else you can tell us, I think we're done here." He leaned forward again. His intensity drew Lucy toward him. "If you have any contact with your aunt, or if you gain any knowledge as to where she is, call us immediately. We are dealing with very dangerous people here."

Lucy's nod belied the defiance amassing at the back of her throat.

Agent Hunter frowned. "Don't try to be a hero. You won't be able to save your aunt on your own, and there's a good chance you could end up getting her killed."

Lucy stood. "When I talk to Sylvia, I'll let her know you want to talk to her."

Apprehension set in as soon as she was alone. Lucy retraced Peterson's earlier steps, in search of anything that appeared suspicious. Nothing popped out. A headache settled in behind her brows. Normally, the Hobie Cat would provide the perfect stress relief, but Mother Nature did not oblige her with enough wind to achieve much of a workout. A good run was a better choice. She changed clothes and stepped out the door.

Familiar with the area, she considered which course to take. If she proceeded left at the end of the driveway, the road would circle the perimeter of the lake before running into the main highway. At least a dozen homes occupied properties in that direction. She opted for the less populated route. The run would give her a four-mile workout, dead-ending two miles west at the edge of the Penalton farm.

It was a beautiful mid-June day, so she paced herself, soaking in the late afternoon sun. To the south, regal mounds of hay dotted the adjacent field. The sweet, pungent smell of freshly cut fodder penetrated her nostrils, enhanced her senses, and breathed energy into her body.

She quickened her stride as the sun tracked its westerly descent. A thick grove of trees bent close to the road, blocking the view of the lake. There would be no more houses until the Penalton Farm. Isolation closed in around her, pushing her harder. Lucy's feet slapped the road's surface, her knees absorbing the shock while beads of sweat streamed down the sides of her face. A fixed mantra echoed in her head. *Feel the run. Feel the run.*

Tires crunched on the loose gravel behind her. She slowed and moved to the edge of the road, allowing the old Ford pickup to pass on the left. Sean Penalton's dark stare appraised her from the passenger's seat.

Lucy had encountered Sean on several occasions over the past few years, usually when jogging. At age twenty-seven, he continued to live with his parents on the family farm. His six-foot-two stature provided an intimidating persona. Add the tousled hair, the consistently bedraggled attire, and the constant scowl he wore, and one could easily understand why people preferred to keep their distance from him. Lucy, however, found him intriguing.

Sean never initiated a conversation. If she engaged him, he answered politely in short, precise sentences. Over time, she had discerned that he had many passions.

Lucy resumed her run after the truck carrying Sean rounded the bend. She arrived at the Penalton farm ten minutes later, did a one-eighty, and jogged back to the cottage. After a brisk shower, she dressed and stepped out onto the deck. A group of purple martins fluttered playfully in and around a large birdhouse that balanced precariously atop a tall pole at the shore's edge. Lucy chuckled when she heard the scold of a blue jay from a nearby maple tree. The sound of her own laughter made her realize how long it had been since she'd been truly happy.

She walked out to the dock and strolled to the end. A slight breeze, combined with the warmth of the evening sun, caressed her lightly suntanned skin. She slipped off her shoes and dropped to a sitting position on the wood decking. Her feet dangled over the edge, her toes barely dipping into the cool water. The gentle slap of waves against the sandy shore lulled her into a sense of calm.

Straight across from where she sat was a secluded strip of land known as Kleins Point, named after one of the area's first settlers. Per local lore, a gruesome event had taken place on the property more than a century and a half earlier. Joseph Kleins, the local doctor, had returned home after spending several days tending to a sick neighbor. Woefully, he discovered that his wife, Isabel, had been brutally raped and murdered. The two men guilty of the crime laid drunk and passed out next to her body. Joseph seized a nearby axe and savagely beheaded both men. He left their carcasses where they lay, exposed to the elements, hapless prey for the buzzards.

After Dr. Kleins carefully buried his beloved wife, he wandered the area for weeks, crying out her name in anguish. He died shortly thereafter, allegedly the victim of a broken heart. It's rumored that Joseph and Isabel Kleins remain on constant watch, seeking revenge on anyone who dares to desecrate their hallowed realm.

Lucy's aunt gave no credence to the folklore when she sought to purchase the parcel of land. She had had plans to build a small bed and breakfast but had abruptly backed out of the deal for no apparent reason. Lucy's inquiries into her aunt's decision were met with a fierce wall of silence. To this day, Sylvia refused to discuss the details of the property or its ownership.

Lucy could barely remember a day when Sylvia hadn't been a driving force in her life. Together, they had overcome a myriad of obstacles. Admittedly, it had not always been easy for Lucy. Residual effects of abuse and abandonment shadowed her, ready to ambush her whenever she let down her guard. Sylvia was supportive through it all. Bonded to her aunt by blood, loyal to her by circumstance, Lucy could never be convinced that Sylvia was entangled in something as heinous as kidnapping.

Yet, Sylvia's last-minute Houdini act was a thorn in Lucy's side. Had her aunt taken a European vacation, per her explanation on the phone? Or had she really fled the country, as the FBI asserted? Either way, Lucy had to find the truth. Rising to her feet, she walked back to the cottage.

It was June 21st, summer solstice, the longest day of the year. By Lucy's estimations, she had at least an hour until dusk descended and unleashed a torrent of mosquitoes eager to feed on any warm-blooded creature.

Lucy grabbed a notepad and pen and sunk into a brightly cushioned deck chair. Her mind wandered while she massaged her index finger against her teeth. She began by listing everything in sequence as it had occurred since her arrival at the cottage. On a separate sheet of paper, Lucy noted every detail she had gathered since her arrival.

She filled two pages within an hour's time. She had essentially noted four important factors: Rafferty's mysterious relationship with her aunt; the FBI's account of Lloyd's staged accident and subsequent revival, and their assessment regarding his involvement with the missing girls; and, last but not least mystifying, Sylvia's role in all of it. None of it made sense, but she had to keep faith that it would eventually come together.

The temperature had dropped several degrees, the air thick with humidity. Lucy got to her feet and walked the perimeter of the property to ensure that everything was in order. She swatted the first mosquito of the evening, picking up her pace as she rounded the corner of the house, and was surprised to find the side garage door slightly ajar.

Guardedly reaching inside, Lucy flipped the light switch on and stepped over the threshold. A short search revealed nothing to be out of place. She exited, pulling the locked door closed behind her.

An unexpected gust of wind raked the tree leaves as distant thunder rumbled across the skyline. Her skin crawled with the sensation that someone, or something, watched her from afar. Nerves bordering on fear sent her rushing into the house. The clank of the deadbolt sliding into place gave her little relief. For the second time in as many days, she walked through the rooms, making sure every window and door was securely locked.

CHAPTER THIRTEEN

I f Sean Penalton hadn't exited the garage when he did, he would have run smack into Lucy when she came around the corner of the house. As it was, he knelt close to the ground, his breathing erratic while he observed his quarry with intense interest. From the other side of the road, he noted her staccato movements and knew she was frightened.

He leapt to his feet and jogged home after Lucy ducked safely inside the cottage. The threat of the looming storm didn't send him scurrying home; it was his mother's impending wrath. Her anger would rain upon him like a pox if he wasn't home before she locked up for the night.

He had tried to placate her for years. Nothing ever worked. In his youth, Sean used to creep from his bedroom to sit at the top of the stairs and listen to his parents argue, their fights usually centering around him. His mother's bitter words essentially served as a fist punch to his gut.

Over time, he had abandoned the prospect of ever gaining her love. When the tears ran dry, resentment took over. Isolation became his refuge, creating a safe harbor in the wake of family turbulence.

CHAPTER FOURTEEN

Lucy secured the house and proceeded to the kitchen to fix herself a snack. She reached for the TV remote and hit the on button. A perky weather girl forecasted strong winds accompanied by two to four inches of precipitation for the night. The raindrops pummeling the exterior of the house confirmed those predictions.

The landline sounded sometime after eleven o'clock. Lucy let it ring, readying herself to grab the handset on the off chance it was Sylvia. The caller's voice generated a scowl.

"Hey, it's me. Just wanted to see how your day went."

With an exhausted sigh, Lucy reached for the phone. "Hi, Jack. I'm here. I couldn't get to the phone before the answering machine kicked on."

To her astonishment, she chatted with her estranged husband easily about nothing and everything. Nostalgia set in, and before she could stop herself, she let her emotions get the better of her. She told him of the day's events and confided some of her fears—a mistake she immediately regretted.

"I don't understand why you let Sylvia put you in these situations. I insist you come home. You have no idea of the danger you could be facing."

Lucy bristled. "I can take care of myself. Besides, Sylvia wouldn't let me stay here if she thought I'd be in danger."

"I'm only looking out for your best interest," he said, his approach softening. "I worry about you, especially when you're so far away." He hesitated. "Maybe I should come up there."

"It's nice of you to offer, but I don't think I require a knight in shining armor just yet."

"Seriously, I have a meeting on Monday that I can't miss, but I can drive up on Tuesday and be there by dinner."

"Let me see what happens in the next few days."

Experience had evidently taught him not to push too hard. "Of course. Call me if things get out of hand." She promised she would. He ended the conversation with, "I love you."

"I know you do." Lucy hung up and paused; she hadn't told Jack about the FBI's suspicions that Lloyd Masterson was alive.

She shrugged. Their conversation had gone better than she had expected, but she would be wise to keep Jack at arm's length. If she gave him an inch, he would take a mile—meaning he would try to govern every move she made, and Lucy had no desire to let that happen.

Wide awake, she sank onto the sofa and buried her nose in the novel she had started the night before, but her concentration faltered. The lack of window coverings facing the lake left her feeling naked and exposed.

She had raised the issue with her aunt on more than one occasion. Sylvia, as always, had a different attitude. "Why would I block out such a great view?" Lucy pictured her aunt's arms extending to emphasize her words. "I love blending this part of the house with the yard and the lake."

"What about at night? Someone could be out there looking in, and you would never know it."

"Dear, Lucy. Let the would-be voyeurs see what they can. Besides, I love getting up in the middle of the night when it's so black out there. You can almost imagine life on Earth in the dark ages." Her aunt could barely contain her excitement. "And the lightning storms—there's absolutely no way to describe the beauty nature conjures up when wielding its anger at the world. The best part is that I can witness all of it from the comfort of my own living room."

Now, as Lucy faced the wall of windows suspended in the dark shroud of night, a lone streak of lightning glided over the distant skyline, giving substance to Sylvia's words. Lucy put aside her book and doused the interior lights. An extravagant light show, enhanced by heavy rain, produced a magical performance.

Too soon, the day's activities caught up with her. She glanced out over the lake one last time. A sporadic light flickered on the north shore, the pouring rain making it impossible to establish its source. Lucy was sure her uneasiness was due to an overactive imagination. A good night's sleep would give her a better perspective in the morning. She padded to the bedroom, vowing to track down her truant aunt first thing in the morning.

CHAPTER FIFTEEN

Fourteen-year-old Jenny Larson shivered in the pouring rain. Her small hands gripped the flashlight as if it were her most prized possession. It was, in fact, her last hope. With aching arms, she persisted: three times fast and three times slow. She repeated the sequence until she collapsed with exhaustion. Time was running out. She had to get back in case they discovered her missing. They had threatened to kill her if she tried to escape again.

Jenny did not want to die, not like this. She had fought with her mother the last time they were together, and she had said things she regretted. The fact that those words would be the last thing her mom remembered drove Jenny to keep going. She dreamed of being back home, back with her mom, snuggled together on the couch, catching a late-night sci-fi movie. More than anything, she wanted to make sure her mom knew how much she loved her.

Jenny lifted her arms with renewed energy and pressed the button again, three times fast and three times slow. If no one saw her distress signal tonight, she didn't know when, if ever, she would get another chance. "Please, God, let someone see this and come to my rescue. I promise, if you let me go back home, I will never hitchhike again. Please, help me get back home."

She angrily hurled the flashlight into the darkness. She didn't dare take it with her for fear that they would learn what she had used it for. Jenny trudged back to the shack where she'd been held captive for several days. She dried off the best she could, wrapped herself in the dirty blanket, and curled up into a small ball on the floor.

The door behind her creaked open. Jenny stayed quiet, her body tensing as footsteps drew near. The toe of a boot nudged her thigh. When she didn't move, the footsteps retreated. The door's hinges let out another mournful groan in conjunction with his whispered declaration: "Sleep tight, little girl, 'cause tomorrow, you're destined for a new home."

CHAPTER SIXTEEN

Lucy snapped awake. She listened to the sounds of the night. Blackness closed in around her, forcing her deeper beneath the sheets. Had a bad dream awakened her? She didn't think so. Whatever the cause, she could not rationalize the sense of trepidation descending around her. She slipped back in time to where, as a child, she had experienced the same deep fear. She sank deeper. Her eyelids, now heavy as molasses, fluttered shut.

By morning, the incident had receded into the far reaches of her memory. She dragged herself out of bed, showered, and ate breakfast. Lucy didn't know why she had consented to another meeting with Agents Hunter and Peterson. It didn't matter. If she planned to be on time, she had to leave now.

The drive to Detroit Lakes Public Library took forty-five minutes. A dank odor of aged wood, mingled with the scent of newly painted walls, crinkled her nose when she entered. Strategically placed floor fans worked hard to cool patrons on this hot summer day.

Lucy found no sign of Hunter or Peterson on the first floor. She ascended a narrow staircase and spotted them seated well away from prying eyes. Strewn papers and file folders covered much of the tabletop. Their noses buried in a computer screen, neither agent acknowledged her approach.

"Good morning," Lucy said in a hushed tone.

Hunter rose and offered Lucy his chair. Peterson got right to business. She hit a few buttons on the keyboard. Lucy took the seat extended to her and scanned an article from the Minneapolis *Star Tribune*. The editorial dated back thirteen months. A young girl had gone missing from a campsite near Whitefish Lake after her parents had taken their three children camping for the weekend. The morning after their arrival, their eldest daughter was not in the tent she shared with her siblings. Under the assumption she had gone for an early hike, they waited an hour before contacting the authorities.

The police questioned everyone: the girl's parents, her siblings, fellow campers, neighbors and friends, schoolmates, teachers. They uncovered nothing that led them to presume the young girl had run away. On the other hand, there was no evidence of foul play. Days evolved into weeks. The FBI got involved when the girl's cell phone showed up in a drug bust in Arizona. The case attracted national news, and the girl's picture flashed on TV screens in living rooms across the country.

Lucy closed her eyes and exhaled.

She immersed herself in another article after Peterson pushed a few more buttons on the keyboard. A teenage girl had disappeared while walking home from a party a block away from her house in Maynard, a small town in southern Minnesota. Lucy read five different news articles referencing five different girls who had disappeared from various cities and communities within the state of Minnesota, all within the last two years.

Agent Peterson fingered the band on her watch. "We have no solid leads to suggest what happened to any of them."

Lucy pushed her chair away from the desk. "Is there proof that my aunt has ties to any of these girls?"

Hunter gave his partner a quick nod. "No. We have no concrete evidence that links Sylvia to any of the girls." He remained standing with his arms crossed in front of his chest. "What I can tell you is that Agent Peterson and I have uncovered evidence to suggest that at least three of these girls were not runaways. They are kidnapped victims, and it's our opinion that the kidnappers are the same in all three cases."

Lucy's shoulders sagged.

Peterson nodded. "As you know, we suspect Lloyd Masterson is running a cartel dealing in slave trades."

"You mentioned that yesterday. I've been thinking a lot about it. Lloyd was overbearing, and sometimes too crude for my taste, but I don't think he'd be embroiled in something so vile. Money laundering, maybe. But kidnapping..." The possibility that Lloyd could have used the money Lucy had invested with him for illicit activities knitted her stomach into tight knots.

Hunter cleared the screen. He took the chair next to Lucy and leaned in close enough that she could smell the garlic on his breath. "Sylvia contacted us two years ago because she suspected her husband was engaged in illegal activities. We were close to an arrest when he staged his death. We agree: if he was on that boat when lightning struck it, he would certainly be dead. But we're betting he was long gone before the accident. Dumb luck, I guess."

"Do you have any proof that he is tied to these girls?"

"I can't divulge the specifics at this time. What I can tell you is that another girl has disappeared. There was alleged abuse in her home, and our sources say she had reached out to Sylvia for support."

"You told me you don't think Sylvia is working with Lloyd."

Hunter eyed Peterson. Lucy had noticed that they often played touch tag.

Peterson took her turn. "We're not really sure how things went down, but we believe Sylvia rescued the girl from the kidnappers and then somehow hid her for over a week. We don't know how she was able to keep the girl away from her parents, the authorities, and even the abductors."

Lucy rubbed her damp palms over her denim-clad thighs. "And you think Sylvia took this girl to Europe with her?"

"Yes. Two days before she left, your aunt used her credit card to purchase one roundtrip ticket for herself. The day she flew out, a young girl named Melissa Mills boarded the same flight. We have no way of tracing the ticket because it was paid for with cash. The video surveillance at the airport was too grainy to give us a positive identification, so we're not a hundred percent sure we are talking about the same girl. Having said that, the description the ticket agent gave us matches the description of the girl we're seeking. If it is our girl, that means someone supplied her with an ID and passport that allowed her to travel outside the country. We're trying to figure out how that was accomplished."

Hunter picked up the narrative. "Both tickets have return dates of July 19th. Of course, those dates could be changed at any time. We lost Sylvia's trail in Rome. As far as we can tell, she hasn't checked into a hotel, unless she's using an alias we're unaware of. Do you know of anyone she might have contacted over there? Anyone who might provide her with housing?"

Lucy shook her head, belying her thoughts. Sylvia's recounting of her escapades abroad had entertained many partygoers. If Lucy were inclined, she would tell the agents that she had tagged along with her aunt to Europe on two separate jaunts. During Lucy's freshman year of college, Sylvia had chaperoned her on a retreat in

Switzerland. During her senior year, they had ventured to Norway to locate distant relatives. Lucy knew from those trips that it was quite possible that Sylvia had taken refuge with family members. Again, she kept her opinions to herself. Instead, she said, "Who is the girl you think is traveling with my aunt?"

"Her name is Kelly Grant."

Pushing a few buttons on the keyboard, Peterson brought up another picture. It depicted a young girl seated on the front steps of a well-manicured farmhouse, presumably with her parents and four older brothers.

"She is fifteen years old. Don't let the picture fool you. It looks as if she has the perfect family life, but it's far from that. We can't go into the details. Arguably, she had legitimate reasons to flee from home."

Lucy peered closer. The girl's eyes seemed devoid of emotion.

"At this time, we are treating her as a runaway. That could change, though."

Lucy flinched under Hunter's judgmental stare. She had withheld essential data, and she suspected he was on to her. Her determination weakened. "Do you think my aunt kidnapped this girl?"

"We think Sylvia is doing her best to assist Kelly, but if she took a minor out of the country without her parents' consent, she is facing kidnapping charges. She's in a hell of a lot of trouble, regardless of her objective. However, our bigger concern is Masterson and what he might do if he finds out your aunt is working against him."

There it was: their trump card. Masterson's threat to Sylvia. Lucy could not think about that now—she wasn't ready to join forces with the FBI. She donned her poker face as she tried to rationalize her intentions. Her aunt was one tough lady, capable of taking care of herself. Then again, if Lloyd was as evil as they said he was, it was possible that Sylvia was in over her head.

Hunter straightened his posture and spoke slowly. "I know this is a lot of information for you to absorb in such a short amount of time. You have to trust us if you intend to help your aunt. What can we do to assure you that we are who we say we are and that we are telling you the truth?"

Lucy looked from one agent to the other before answering, "I've been asking myself the same questions. Everything I know about the CIA and the FBI is what I see in the movies and read in the news. These days, it's hard to believe anybody."

Agent Hunter countered, "A lot of our training teaches us to rely on our instincts."

"That's the problem."

Hunter snapped his head back. "It seems we're at a stalemate."

Peterson intervened: "We had hoped that the pictures and stories of the victims would alleviate your doubts and help you understand the time limits we are under. Russell, I think the best thing for us to do is to let Lucy go home and think things over. She can't be our advocate if she doesn't have faith in our abilities."

"You're absolutely right, Margaret." Hunter's next comment spoke to the true issue. "If you talk to Sylvia, please ask her to contact us. Her life may depend on it." He wheeled back to the computer.

The hasty dismissal had Lucy rethinking her strategy. At the very least, she had expected them to attempt to coax her into partnering with them. The enormity of her plight finally hit home. If she joined forces with the FBI in the search for her aunt, it was quite possible Sylvia would end up in prison. If she didn't cooperate, the girls, the ones with their pictures spread across the computer screen, might never see their families again.

Lucy stewed over her aunt's safety; yet she would not be able to live with herself if she didn't do everything in her power to bring those girls home.

She pivoted back to the agents. They were bent over the table, absorbed in the data before them. Lucy cleared her throat. "I want to do my part."

Both agents met her gaze straight on, their expressions unreadable.

Lucy grimaced, "I don't know what I can do, but I have an obligation to help find those girls." She took a deep breath. "Before I go any further, I have to talk to Sylvia and confirm that she is on the same page with you two. I'll contact you after I've talked with her."

Hunter gave her a brisk nod. The conversation was over.

Lucy pushed herself up from the chair and left.

CHAPTER SEVENTEEN

L ucy's eyes rested on the answering machine the minute she entered the cottage. Three new messages awaited. The first caller's voice brought a frown to her face. Jack was nothing if not persistent. Lucy hit fast forward, anxious that one of the other messages might be from Sylvia.

The second voice was not one she had expected. All the same, her stomach knotted as RJ's deep baritone invited her to meet him at Arthur's for dinner. No need to call him back, he added. He would be there around six o'clock.

Lucy fast forwarded to the third message. The lonely drone of the dial tone greeted her.

Her Rolex, a gift from Jack for their tenth anniversary, showed it was two-thirty. She had plenty of time to decide if she wanted to meet RJ. Who was she kidding? This was the perfect opportunity to gain information from him. Tonight, she would be the one in charge. He would be putty in her hands.

A clear head was vital if she intended to coax a detective into sharing information. Besides, a steady wind called to her. She fixed herself a bologna sandwich and proceeded to the bedroom to change into her swimsuit. Grabbing a t-shirt and a baseball cap, Lucy scooted out the door and down to the dock.

She planted her feet firmly in the sand and nudged the boat gently off the lift and into the water, hoisted herself onto the tarp, and raised the Hobie's main sail and jib. Her practiced hands tugged at the lines until the sails caught the wind and the boat eased away from the shoreline.

The northerly breeze wasn't strong enough to allow for fancy maneuvering. Most days, Lucy would have preferred the workout required to sail a Hobie on a gusty day. Today, she was content to calmly tack back and forth over the water. The heat from the sun melted some of the icy tension that had accumulated during the past thirty-six hours.

As the Hobie drew near the north shore, Lucy noticed that the wind had carried her to the approximate location where she had seen the flickering light the night before. She steered the catamaran to a small sandy area and jumped to the ground as the pontoons skidded effortlessly up and over the sand. Using all her strength, she thrust the pontoons leeward to keep the wind from catching the sail and tipping the boat over, or worse, pushing it back into the water.

Lucy had never walked the beachfront at Kleins Point. The heavily treed slope showed no indication of human habitation, so she set off on foot along the shoreline in search of a path that would lead her up the steep grade. She was about to turn back when her gaze fell on a narrow trail flanked by dense trees. A small clearing came into view halfway up the hill. In the center was an old decrepit log cabin hidden amid thick undergrowth.

Steps leading to the front door sagged in despair. She placed her foot on the lowest board and climbed timidly. The door swung inward when she tapped it lightly with her knuckles. "Hello? Is anyone here?"

No answer came. Dirty windows on either side of the room let in enough light for her to see the tattered sofa that sat against one wall. Nearby was an old metal table surrounded by three grimy chairs. Tucked into one corner, lying on the floor, was a badly stained mattress topped with a dirty, crumpled blanket. Everything about the place rubbed her the wrong way. She spun around and retraced her route back down the stairs.

Lucy squashed her inner voice's urges to flee and made her way along a well-trodden footpath leading further up the hill. Spotting a large mound of fresh dirt, she stepped closer to investigate. A raised tree root caught the toe of her shoe and sent her tumbling headfirst into the soft pile of soil. The thought that the hole beside the dirt resembled that of a grave sent a chill through her body.

Lucy decided she'd seen enough. She moved down the hillside to the Hobie, jostled it into the water, and hurled herself onto the tarp. Grabbing the guideline, she adjusted the boom until the wind took hold of the mainsail and propelled the pontoons across the water.

Glancing back when she had put enough distance between herself and the shoreline, she saw nothing out of order nor anything that would suggest that this was the exact location where she'd seen the signal. Despite the eerie hole in the ground, the area appeared to be abandoned.

She reworked the jib and plotted a course for home. The wind blew from the north at approximately fifteen miles per hour, allowing the catamaran to cross the lake in less than twenty minutes. She tacked twice to correct her heading. Lucy lowered the main sail as she neared the shore and jumped into the shallow water, pushing the pontoons up onto the mooring station and stowing the gear.

Lucy jabbed at the button on the answering machine when she entered the kitchen, and Sylvia's voice filled the room. "Hi, dear. I hope that you have settled in by now and are out enjoying the sailboat. I've arrived in Rome. Everything is fine here. I will be out of touch for a few days. I trust you can handle everything at the house. Feel free to contact my attorney, Chris Foley, at the bank—you met him at last year's barbecue. He should be able to assist you with anything that might come up, and as a precaution, he has signed papers giving you access to all my accounts. Hugs and kisses and happy sailing."

Anger colored Lucy's cheeks. *Why would Sylvia entrust her accounts to me? And why in the world didn't she leave a number where I can reach her?* Lucy glanced at the clock. Was the bank even open on Saturdays? A call confirmed it was. She had to get moving if she intended to confer with Mr. Foley before meeting RJ at Arthur's Bar.

Lucy headed to the bathroom, twisted her hair into a knot and stepped into the shower. Emerging refreshed, she toweled off and ran a comb through her hair, letting it fall loosely about her shoulders.

The telephone ringing sent her rushing into the bedroom. "Hello," she gasped. The click on the other end made her brow pucker. Lucy slammed the phone back into its cradle and moved to the closet. She pulled out a pair of slim-fitting jeans and her favorite blue sweater. Her eyes danced. RJ didn't stand a chance tonight.

Lucy jockeyed her car into the last available parking space on Main Street and ventured onto the crowded sidewalk, unaware of the man who furtively watched her enter the bank.

Sue, the head teller, greeted her. "I haven't seen you in a while. How have you been?"

Lucy knew Sue, as she did many residents of Vergas, from Sylvia's sphere of influence. The two endeavored in small talk until Lucy inquired, "Is Mr. Foley available?"

Sue nodded toward the attorney's office. "He's on the phone, but you can go on in."

Chris Foley sat typing on his computer with the phone cradled against his left shoulder. "Boris, I have the figures you are looking for on my screen. According to this, that account was closed two weeks ago."

Distracted, the attorney moved the handset away from his ear in an apparent effort to avoid the loud cackle emanating from the earpiece. His hand twisted into an apologetic gesture when he spied Lucy, his computer screen going blank with one deft move.

Chris extended an invitation for Lucy to take a seat in one of the large armchairs facing his desk and resumed his conversation with the caller. "Someone just walked into my office." A pause. "No, I'm going to have to get back to you." Another stretch of silence. "No." Chris's voice grew firmer with each reply. "I'll call you before I leave the office."

Lucy sank into the chair and sat quietly. An ancient overhead fixture bathed the office in a yellow haze. Heavy draperies, drawn to block out the afternoon heat, darkened the room further. Neither the lighting nor the window coverings lessened the effects of years of foot traffic on the dull, beige carpeting.

Lucy caught Chris scrutinizing her when she looked back in his direction. A hint of pink dotted his cheeks. His bushy brows slanted upwards. The same index finger he had used to blacken his computer screen signaled that he would be with her shortly.

Chris Foley ended his call, stood, and came around the corner of his desk. He took Lucy's hand and held it snugly between his huge paws. His eyes were welcoming, his touch warm and sincere. "What a lovely surprise!" he said.

CHAPTER EIGHTEEN

C ecil Foley, Chris's great grandfather, had founded Midwest Bank in Vergas in 1932, and the business had passed from one generation to the next. Tom, Chris's older brother, took over management of the bank upon the death of his father, while Chris maintained his position as local attorney. Both brothers had a strong reputation for honesty and integrity.

Chris's Scandinavian ancestry boosted his boy-next-door manner. He saw the world through wire-rimmed glasses perched on a solid nose above a square jawline.

Aware of his gift of gab, Chris eased his bulky frame into the chair next to Lucy and endowed her with a warm smile. "I wondered when you'd be in to see me," he said. "Sylvia has left you with quite a bag of worms, hasn't she?"

Lucy folded her hands in her lap. "I must admit, I am somewhat confused and a little more than upset about what my aunt may be up to. I don't have a phone number where I can reach her, and I really have to talk to her."

Chris shifted his weight. "Let me start by saying that your aunt is a very unique individual. But she doesn't always make things easy for the people around her—I know that from my own experience. She was devastated when her husband died in that horrible boating accident." He bowed his head to give the appearance of respect and then added, "We all were."

Something about this doleful performance was unconvincing. Lucy stiffened. "When Sylvia asked me to housesit, she said she was under a lot of stress and planned to take a holiday. At the time, I assumed she was exaggerating. Now I'm not so sure. Do you have any clue as to why she went to Europe?"

"All I know is what your aunt told me. She desperately needed to get away for a few weeks. She gave me her itinerary, so I have a number where I can contact her." Foley tossed Lucy a cloaked look. "Sylvia asked me not to call her unless it was absolutely necessary. She said it was imperative that I tell no one—except you, of course—that I know how to reach her."

Sue appeared in the doorway. "Chris, I've locked everything up, and I'm heading home."

Chris held his breath until he heard the front door swing shut and the deadbolt click into place. He replayed his conversation with Lucy in his head. It was doubtful that Sue had overheard anything of consequence, yet he couldn't be sure. "Will you excuse me for one moment?" he said. "I have to make sure everything is locked up properly." He strolled from the room.

Chris's face was somber as he stepped back into his office and sank heavily into the chair behind the desk. "As I was saying, Sylvia doesn't want to be contacted unless it's an emergency."

"Do you know if she is traveling alone?" Lucy asked.

"I don't know. She didn't say one way or the other, though I'm not aware of any traveling companions."

"Why don't you give me her contact information? That way I can get in touch with her without having to bother you again."

Chris stood and paced the distance of the room, and then retraced his steps. His mass shifted when he lowered the bulk of his 215 pounds onto the edge of the desk, crossing his arms soberly. Chris had lost so much the day Lloyd Masterson waltzed into his life. At the heart of it was his self-respect. An opportunity now arose for him to atone for his unseemly choices. He worried that he didn't have the courage to move forward.

"Lucy." He voiced her name so softly that he wasn't sure he'd said it out loud. He leaned forward, Lucy mirroring his lead. Looking deep into her eyes, Chris started, "Your aunt has gotten herself into a real mess." He hadn't expected the rush that washed over him. Those simple words, spoken candidly, breathed new life into him.

There it is, he thought. *I went back on my word, but I know it's the right thing to do.* He had promised Sylvia he wouldn't involve Lucy. Nevertheless, that was exactly what he intended to do. He had warned Sylvia repeatedly that she was in over her head. She should have listened to him. Instead, she insisted on doing things her way. Well, her way was going to get someone killed. Besides, he had a wife and two kids to consider. Chris would do everything in his power to protect Lucy, but the safety of his own family had to come first.

Foley couldn't change the past. He had a duty, however, to confront the present. Lucy could be in real danger. She had to know the facts in order to make her own decisions on how to proceed.

Chris glanced at his watch and spoke with a steady voice. "I'm running behind schedule and might be tied up until maybe eight or nine this evening. If you're available then, I'd like to swing by your place. I promise I will explain everything to you."

"It must be important if you're willing to come out that late."

Chris ushered her from his office and out the front door without further explanation. "I'll see you tonight."

With that, he pulled the door shut and slid the deadbolt back into place.

CHAPTER NINETEEN

L ucy stood outside the bank and mulled over Chris Foley's comments. What possible motive could he have for a late-night house call? Plausible explanations evaded her like errant soap bubbles bursting in thin air. She warned herself that speculation would get her nowhere and set her sights on RJ. It was time to find out exactly what he knew.

Arthur's Bar was abuzz with activity when she entered. Lucy elbowed her way in, sandwiching herself between the crowd, until she spotted an empty table at the back of the bar. Marti, the manager, cruised by to say hi and take her order. A striking young woman with stylish black hair and fine facial features, Marti had the patience of a saint, but had no difficulty standing firm when anyone, drunk or otherwise, threatened the peaceful patronage of her everyday customers. Always cheerful, Marti had time for everyone, especially old friends.

She leaned in closer to be heard above the din of the crowd. "Hey, Lucy. Art said you were in town. I've been meaning to call you all day. We've just been so busy here. How long are you visiting?"

Never one to let others see her squirm, Lucy adopted an affable posture. "Things are kind of up in the air right now. I'm housesitting for Aunt Sylvia, so it depends on her schedule."

"Yeah, I heard she was out of town. Someone told me she went to Europe. Lucky her. Are you up here by yourself or is Jack joining you?"

"Actually, Jack and I are trying to work out some issues, so I'm here on a hiatus."

"I hope you two can figure it out."

"Time will tell."

"I hear you. Are you expecting anyone, or is one menu enough?"

"Not sure. I might have company."

Marti laid two menus on the table. "Can I get you something to drink while you wait?"

"A Blue Moon sounds great."

"I'll get it right out."

Lucy scanned the crowded room. RJ wasn't due to arrive for another thirty minutes, but there he was, studying her from the other side of the bar. He sauntered toward her, his penetrating gaze challenging the tough façade she worked so hard to maintain. Heat rose from her toes, ascending upwards until it colored her cheeks.

He reached the table, pulled out a chair, and sat facing her. "I wasn't sure you would show tonight."

Lucy studied him as if he were a specimen under a microscope, her head angling slightly. His appearance did not suggest a hardened criminal. That said, one fact remained; he had revealed his character when he unlawfully searched her aunt's garage.

She put aside her misgivings. "A girl has to eat, and dinner out sure beats cooking for myself."

"Ouch. So, you're telling me it isn't my irresistible personality that brought you here tonight?"

She grinned. "In all honesty, it wasn't."

He leaned back and appraised her in the same way a gem dealer examines fine jewels. "I have to admit something to you." He halted briefly, as if organizing his thoughts. Lucy held her breath. She hadn't expected a confession from him without some tactical persuasion on her part. RJ stated flatly, "Even though I had a very busy day, your face kept popping into my head."

"I'm sorry, what did you say?"

"I said your face kept popping into my head today."

"What's that supposed to mean?"

"I don't know what to make of it myself. If we spend a little more time together, I might be able to figure it out."

So much for an easy go of it. Lucy tucked a loose strand of hair behind her ear and said, "Well, here's to new discoveries."

RJ picked up the menus and handed her one. "Are you hungry? I missed lunch, and I'm starved."

Marti stopped by with Lucy's beer order and nodded at RJ. "What can I get you?"

"I'll take what she's drinking and an order of nachos?" He said to Lucy, "Shall we share them, or would you care for something else?"

"Nachos are good."

Marti winked at Lucy, who nodded in return—girl talk for "You could lose your heart over this one" and "I'm simply here to check out the merchandise."

"I'll get your order right out," Marti said as she left.

RJ leaned to one side. "Dare I ask what that was all about?"

Lucy picked up her glass of beer and saluted him. "Nothing to trouble your pretty head about."

His face lit up. "So you think my head's pretty, huh?"

Lucy looked him over. "Well, now that I see it in this light, some women might deem it attractive." The hint of flirtation in her voice startled her. She reminded herself that she was here on a hunting expedition, not to play with a possible adversary. "So, what kept you so busy today that you missed lunch?"

"Let me be frank. I had a bad day. If you don't mind, let's sit back and enjoy each other's company." Absent a response, he stood and reached into his jean pocket. Pulling out some dollar bills, he said, "I'll be right back."

He weaved his way to the jukebox, where he took ample time studying the song selection. She watched him feed money into the slot and punch several buttons.

As he turned to rejoin her, a man rushed up and grabbed him from behind. In a blink, RJ twisted free and within seconds had the man pushed up against the jukebox, an elbow jammed deep into his throat. A hush fell over the crowd until the only sound to be heard was Crystal Gayle's rendition of *We Must Believe in Magic*, vibrating eerily through the overhead speakers.

Marti appeared out of nowhere and jostled her petite frame between the two men. Pressing her hands flat against RJ's chest, she shoved him with all her might. RJ, in tantrum mode, threw his arms into the air. He swung in a complete circle and then squared off with her, only to find Marti with her hands on her hips and her best disappointed-mother's pout staring back at him, daring him to challenge her. Grins on the faces of onlookers told Lucy that all bets were on Marti Wells. While everyone's attention was on them, Lucy watched as the assailant ducked through the crowd and exited the bar.

78

RJ puffed out his chest, lifted his head high, and pushed his way back to the table to rejoin Lucy. "There's never a dull moment around here," he said.

Lucy exhaled. "Care to fill me in on what that was about?"

RJ shrugged. "In my job, I sometimes piss people off. People think they can intimidate me. I have to set them straight. Usually, from then on, they show me respect." His boyish charm reappeared. "Don't you think I should demand respect?"

"I don't think you can demand it. You have to earn it. Who was that man? And what did he want?"

RJ gave her a tight nod. "That's a conversation for another time. As I said before, let's keep things light tonight. I don't want to talk about disagreeable people or unpleasant things. Can we do that?"

Lucy relented. It was better to be here in his company than sitting alone at the cottage waiting for Chris Foley to show up. She checked her wrist for the time.

RJ's chin jutted outward. "Do you have a late date tonight?"

She ignored his inquiry. "Didn't you order nachos?"

Marti showed up toting a plate heaped high with tortilla chips and all the fixings, plus two more beers. Lucy helped herself to a chip piled high with melted cheese, ground beef, beans, and chopped jalapeños. "Wow. These are really good." RJ had a far-away expression on his face. "A penny for your thoughts," she said.

"Sorry. I was thinking about something I need to take care of tomorrow."

She gave him a wry smile. "Does it have anything to do with my aunt?"

They locked eyes. "As a matter of fact, it does." Lucy held her breath. "When did you say Sylvia was coming back?" he asked.

Lucy didn't try to mask her frustration. "Actually, I don't have any idea." The conversation was not heading in the direction she had planned. She was here to get answers, not give them. Time to get things back on track. She leaned forward. "Just how do you know Sylvia? Were you friends? Lovers, maybe? I don't care about your personal life. I'm terribly worried about my aunt, considering the rumors I've heard since my arrival. Something terrible is going on around here, and I'm pretty sure you know more than you're letting on."

"You've heard about the missing girls?"

Lucy gave him a curt nod.

RJ glanced at the customers occupying the nearby tables and lowered his voice. "I guess you deserve the truth," he murmured, reflexively cracking the knuckles in both hands. "Sylvia and I had a short fling. Soon after we started seeing each other, she told me she suspected Lloyd was somehow associated with one of the missing girls. The story she gave me sounded plausible, so I agreed to sort out the leads for her. In the end, she had nothing that led me to believe Masterson was linked to any of the girls." Rafferty clicked his tongue. "Funny thing, though: Sylvia's determination to establish Lloyd's culpability in the illicit activities went beyond normal. I mean, the guy's dead, and she was still all fired up to prove his guilt. As the days evolved into weeks, her theories stretched into paranoia."

Lucy ignored RJ's reference to Lloyd's death. "What exactly did Sylvia have on him?"

"I don't know. She claimed she had all this incriminating evidence, and like I said, she never shared anything useful with me. Whenever I quizzed her about her storyline, she'd go all soft and seductive. Before I knew it, we were in bed, and I'd forget all about Lloyd."

"When was the last time you saw her?"

"A few days before you arrived. We had dinner together."

"What did you two talk about?"

"She was in one of her funky moods. Distant, really."

"Did she say anything as to why she decided to travel to Europe at this particular time?"

"Not a word."

"Did you ever check into Lloyd's background?"

"I'm sorry, but now you're seeking information that I'm not at liberty to divulge." His gravelly voice exposed the tension behind his calm front. "If you're up for it, we can enjoy the rest of the evening on a lighter note. Or we can call it a night. It's up to you."

Lucy sensed she had hit a brick wall. "I can stay awhile. It would be a shame to waste the nachos and beer."

He beamed. "You're my kind of gal."

Lucy helped herself to a couple of chips while she composed her thoughts. For reasons unclear, the mystery of RJ's personal life ate at her. "I'm curious," she started, "what was it like growing up in such a small town?"

"That's an easy one. I suspect it's pretty much the same as any other place. The difference, in my humble opinion, has to do with the values one learns as they go through life." He proceeded with no further encouragement from her. "We lived about thirty miles south of here. My parents worked hard their entire lives trying to make ends meet while raising me, my brother, and my two sisters."

"Do your siblings live nearby?"

"My younger sister, her husband and their two children live on the family farm and assist my parents in its management."

"Did you ever have any interest in farming?"

"Me? No. That business calls for long hours and hard labor, and I've done my time. We were always up at the crack of dawn.

Cows had to be milked before school and a long list of chores greeted us when we got home. Not enough excitement in it for me. I followed my older sister into law enforcement."

"Really? Do you two work together?"

"No. She moved to Billings, Montana. We miss her, but she's happy where she's at, so that's all that counts." RJ stared off into the room and rubbed the back of his neck. His voice turned somber: "I mentioned I had a brother." His eyes closed for a second before he continued, "He was killed in a snowmobile accident when he was sixteen. The day before my eleventh birthday."

Lucy sat back and took time to reevaluate him. She had originally pegged him to be brash and conceited, but during the past hour, he had proved that assumption wrong. He'd kept her on her toes with his humor and disarmed her with his charm. His loyalty to his family had gained her admiration, and the pain RJ visibly suffered while eulogizing his brother touched Lucy's heart. She could only imagine the impact the loss had had on him at that young age. Knowledge of RJ's loving family and his experience with his brother raised doubt in her mind that he could participate in anything as contemptible as child kidnapping. When Lucy looked deep into his eyes, she saw something she hadn't seen before: behind that tough exterior was a sensitive, caring man.

Neither spoke. It was as if they didn't need words to communicate.

Soon, though, the moment passed. RJ cleared his throat.

Lucy caught sight of the clock on the wall and sighed. "I hate to be a party pooper, but I really should be going."

RJ started to object and then changed his mind, gracefully acquiescing. "I'll walk you to your car." He signaled to Marti that they were ready for the bill.

Lucy reached for her purse.

"I'll get this," he said. "You can pay next time."

"How do you know there will be a next time?"

He smiled. "I'm a betting man."

Lucy stood. RJ rose in unison and led the way. Outside, the cool night air enveloped them, heightening their senses. RJ took the liberty to encircle her shoulders with his left arm. She felt a little uneasy but didn't pull away. Strangely, she drew some solace from his company.

They walked together silently, each caught up in their own thoughts. As they neared her car, Lucy tilted her head ever so slightly. RJ apparently deemed it an invitation and leaned in to her, bringing his lips to meet hers. Out of nowhere, a shadowy figure danced across her peripheral vision. She spun around quickly, his kiss lightly brushing her cheek. The surrounding darkness made it impossible to confirm her suspicions. Had she imagined the ghostly apparition?

Lucy stalled briefly. RJ likely viewed her evasive tactic as a rejection. Would he try to kiss her again? What if he didn't? Unable to put it off any longer, she faced him.

The moment had passed. Too bad. She envisioned his mouth against hers. Would it be warm and supple or firm and sensuous? Seemingly mistaking her shiver for a chill, RJ reached to open the car door for her. She slid in behind the wheel, said goodnight, and pulled the door shut. With a slight wave of her hand, she drove off.

CHAPTER TWENTY

RJ had done little to correct his corruptive ways in the year since he'd left his previous girlfriend, Mindy, standing on the curb. Mindy had repeatedly tested RJ's limits and one day, he hit her. He regretted that he'd allowed their relationship to spiral into such depths. The memory of her bruise cheek remained a constant reminder that he had crossed a line he planned never to cross again.

To his amazement, Lucy had him taking a good, solid look at himself after only a few hours in her company. His shoulders sagged. It felt as if he were speeding along a one-way street in the wrong direction. Uncertainty filled him with self-doubt, an affliction he had not suffered since the fifth grade. Not since Melissa von Ruden.

The sound of laughter nudged RJ back to the present. A group of patrons had exited Arthur's Bar and gathered at the corner to say goodbye. Rafferty walked to his truck and got in. He reached to adjust the rearview mirror and came face-to-face with his own reflection. "What do you think, buddy? Is it too late for us?"

The image in the mirror sneered at him. He hadn't asked the right question. What RJ truly wanted to know was: did he have the courage to confront and rise above his demons? If not, there was little chance of redemption.

RJ started his truck. As he pulled away from the curb, he spied a late model Volvo parked several spaces in front of him. The man in the driver's seat was the same man he had seen eyeing Lucy when she had entered Arthur's Bar earlier that evening. RJ radioed the station for a DMV update and then made a U-turn. He took a left at the end of the block. Circling around town, he came back out on Highway 60, a half mile east of Vergas.

Dispatch called back with the requested information. Recognizing the name of the perp, Rafferty stepped on the gas pedal. He pulled onto South Rose Lake Road and drove slowly up the lane until he reached a turn-off leading to the adjacent farmland. He parked his truck behind a row of trees a mile from Sylvia's cottage and hoofed it the rest of the way.

Nearing the residence, RJ noted several lights lit within. The sleuth in him concluded that Lucy was inside. He confirmed that there were no parked cars in the driveway and then tested the side garage door. It was locked. He dashed around the house to the lakeside.

That's where he finally gleaned a bit of luck. There were no window coverings to restrict his view of the interior. Lucy moved gracefully about the kitchen while preparing a pot of coffee, a phone resting against her ear. RJ wished now that he had bugged the house. Without it, he could only guess who was on the other end of the line. If it wasn't Sylvia, then who?

The sound of tires on gravel sent him racing back around the house in time to see the Volvo moving slowly past the cabin. Since the road was a dead end, the driver had no choice but to head back this way. RJ ducked behind the underbrush on the far side of the road and stood in the exact spot where Sean Penalton had crouched the previous night.

RJ soon observed a man dressed in dark clothing making his way toward the cottage. The man vanished behind the garage and then reemerged on the porch steps. He surprised Rafferty by rapping his knuckles on the door. The porch light flickered, and Lucy appeared in the doorway. The two exchanged words until she stepped back and allowed the stranger to enter.

RJ jogged back to the lakeside to witness Lucy pouring her guest a cup of coffee before joining him at the table. His attention rested solely on the two inside, to the exclusion of the footsteps approaching him from behind.

The scent of damp grass filled RJ's nostrils as he came to. Carefully, he rolled onto his back and looked skyward. The position of the moon confirmed his suspicions: he had been unconscious for a lengthy amount of time. RJ was no stranger to fights. Still, no one had ever knocked him out cold. There was no mistake—the wielder of the bat had intended him great harm.

RJ thrust himself up to a sitting position and took stock of his surroundings. His heart stopped. The dark cottage melted into the night, revealing no clue as to whether Lucy was inside. Had the stranger whisked her away for reasons he did not care to think about? He would never forgive himself if something had happened to her while she was under his watch. Stumbling, he climbed the steps to the deck and fell heavily into one of the Adirondack chairs. Exotic diamonds glittered overhead. RJ couldn't discern if they were stars or merely the result of a concussion, but there was no time to dwell on conjectures. He had to find Lucy and make sure she was safe.

He jumped at the unexpected vibration of his cell phone. Digging it out of his jeans pocket, he glanced at the clock prior to answering. "Yeah?" His raspy voice was barely more than a whisper.

"Where are you?" his partner, Cassie, demanded.

"It's a long story. I'll fill you in later. Why are you calling?"

"I've been trying to reach you for the past two hours. It's not like you to let your calls go unanswered."

"Sorry about that. I guess you could say I was indisposed. Someone smacked me upside the head with a baseball bat."

"Oh, my God. Are you alright? Do you have any idea who did it?"

RJ thought her inflection sounded strange, like she might be holding back something, but he let it slide. "I'll live." He groaned and moved the phone to his other ear. "I'll explain everything when I see you. You haven't told me what you're calling about."

"Oh, yeah, it's nothing really. I just wanted to go over some of the details on this kidnapping case, but it can wait until morning."

Rafferty heard the door behind him creak open. "I'll see you in the morning." Ignoring Cassie's follow-up query, he disconnected and stuffed the phone back into his pocket, easing himself out of the chair only to tumble back into it. A razor-sharp pain shot from his head straight down his spine, reaching all the way to his toes.

The throbbing ebbed substantially when he spied Lucy's robe-clad body hovering over him. Three blurry images made him reach out to determine which one was real.

She brushed his hand aside and aimed her flashlight at him. "What are you doing here at this hour?" Her attitude tempered at the sight of blood on his face. "What in the world happened to you?"

She knelt next to him and gently touched his cheek. The massive knot on the side of his head flared in the dim light, a jagged cut zigzagging from end to end. She stood, wrapped his arm around her shoulders, and helped him to his feet. RJ leaned into her as she led him into the kitchen, where she gently eased him into a chair.

She hurriedly switched on the overhead light, grabbed a towel from a kitchen drawer, and filled it with ice cubes from the freezer. In an instant, she was back at his side, gently applying the compress to his wound. "I think you better have a doctor look at this. You need stitches."

He tried not to wince. "I'll be okay. I've had worse."

Lucy retrieved a clean dishtowel, ran warm water over the cloth, and used it to gently wipe caked blood from his face and neck. The tightness in his shoulders evaporated under her tender touch. Maybe taking a bat to the head wasn't so bad if this was the result. Sadly, the moment passed. She finished cleaning the wound and sat in the chair next to him, where she waited quietly.

RJ saw something in Lucy that he had not seen in a very long time. She deserved the truth. He took a deep breath and exhaled. "I'm not a stalker, if that's what you're thinking. Earlier tonight, I saw a man watching you when you entered Arthur's Bar. I noticed him again when you drove off, and I came out here to make sure he didn't have bad intentions. Imagine my surprise when you invited him inside. I couldn't leave until I was sure you were safe. While I was trying to be a hero, someone snuck up behind me and hit me over the head with a baseball bat." RJ stopped to catch his breath. "And no, I didn't get a good look at the person." His mind went back to the moment before he blacked out. "He, or she, was wearing a hoodie pulled over their head. After that, I was out cold on your lawn." He swallowed hard. "What was that man doing here?"

"He said his name was Malcolm Bremer. His daughter went missing six months ago. He's hired a private detective to find her. Their search led him to Sylvia, and he came out here to talk to her."

RJ did not let on that he was aware of Bremer and his daughter's plight. Instead, he quizzed, "Why would you let a man you don't know waltz into your house?"

"I felt sorry for him. He was so distraught. He told me he's spent his entire life's savings trying to find his daughter. He only got angry when I couldn't give him what he requested. He finally left, screaming that he would be back and that I better get the information he needed."

"What information, exactly, was that?"

"He wants to know where Sylvia is."

"That's the million-dollar question. I cannot believe she left the country. And I certainly don't understand why she put you in the middle of this."

Lucy leaned back in her chair, her arms forming a barrier across her chest. She had no intention of showing him her cards.

Despite their discord, the attraction was tangible. RJ bit his lower lip to ebb his desire, his imagination wandering briefly. He yearned to scoop her up in his arms and carry her to the bedroom. He pondered how her body would feel under his weight. He saw himself kissing her, his tongue lapping up every inch of her yielding body.

Abruptly, he reined in his self-indulgent notions. He leaned forward and placed his hand over hers in fear that she might notice the spontaneous bulge in his jeans.

He wished he could tell her what he knew about Sylvia and that his affair with her aunt had been a mistake. More importantly, he was duty-bound to warn Lucy of the danger she was about to encounter. Even though rationale dictated that he disclose his misgivings, he opted to remain silent.

———◦◉◦———

Lucy's blood ran hot at the touch of RJ's hand. She lost herself in his gaze, secretly admiring his salient good looks. The chiseled contours of his cheekbones prevailed even when half of his face bore the resemblance of a swollen balloon. Memory of his earlier quest to kiss her quickened her heart. The absurdity of these musings caused her to sit up and take note of her situation.

Technically, she was still a married woman. Lucy had been faithful during her marriage, which was more than she could say for her husband, Jack. Sleeping with RJ would only muddy the waters and cloud her judgment. She eased her hand from under his fingers.

Lucy didn't know what to make of Chris Foley's no-show earlier that night. She contemplated telling RJ that the attorney was privy to her aunt's itinerary, but skepticism compelled her to keep her thoughts to herself until she knew exactly what Rafferty was up to.

They sat staring at each other until RJ stood. He limped to the front door, each step eliciting a shallow moan. Lucy trailed behind.

He faced her. "It's late," his voice echoed exhaustion. "Try to get some sleep. I'll do some checking on your Malcolm Bremer and call you when I know more."

CHAPTER TWENTY-ONE

It was only a matter of time until Hal Johanson's transgressions brought him down. The image of the dead girl lying in the trunk of the car haunted him mercilessly, ripping him from sleep more times than he cared to admit. Shrouded in the soiled blanket, she beckoned him to follow her into the murk and gloom where he feared he belonged.

The nightmares haunted him. Yet, every time he survived the night, Hal reminded himself to be thankful for everything he had. He woke each morning grateful for the opportunity to prove that he deserved a second chance.

Three weeks after their first date, Becca had talked her parents into meeting Hal. Hal slowly won their favor, and over time, Dan and Mary Ann Banks softened to the idea of the two together.

Eventually, things began to stabilize, and Hal could breathe a little easier. That's when reality swooped in like an eagle descending on vulnerable prey.

It was a cold, mid-April night. Hal and Becca had taken in a movie and then gone for a bite to eat. He dropped her off at her parents' house, went back to his apartment with a spring in his step, and headed to the fridge for a beer. Plopping onto the sofa, he dug his cell phone from his pocket. One unheard message appeared. He tried to shake off the doom closing in around him as he stared at the unfamiliar number. Not knowing what else to do, he pushed the playback button.

He recognized the malicious voice from months earlier. "We'll be collecting on that debt you owe us real soon."

———◉———

Hal nose-dived into his own personal hell. Locked in the apartment for days, he idled away the time, slumped in the recliner, staring at a blank TV screen. At night, he'd lay awake searching for a happy ending to this God-awful quagmire. Loss of sleep dulled his senses, leaving him vulnerable to mistakes. *Pull yourself together, man.* The words filtered through his head day and night. "If I don't figure this out, I could lose everything I've worked so hard to gain."

He forced himself to call Becca at least once a day. If he didn't, she would worry, and if she suspected any trouble, she'd be by his side in a second. That, of course, could not happen. He couldn't bear the thought of her being anywhere near him if the walls came tumbling down. Time slowed to a crawl, but nine days later, he forced himself to pop his head out of the sand and go about his life.

Spring melded into summer. One evening after dinner at the Bankses' home, Becca's father cornered Hal. "Grab a soda from the refrigerator, and let's go outside. I have something important to talk to you about."

Hal held his breath as he followed Dan to the backyard.

Dan rested his elbows on the patio table and formed a steeple with his fingers. "There's no easy way to broach this subject, so I'm telling you straight out." He lowered his hands and focused on Hal with the intensity of a grizzly bear protecting its cub. "I'm very uncomfortable with the amount of time Becca spends at your apartment."

Hal choked back some coke and wiped the spittle from his chin. "Sir?"

Dan showed no hint of caving. "Becca has her whole life ahead of her. She's much too young to be sexually active."

Hal could not fault Mr. Banks's concern, and he certainly understood the premise of the conversation. He had had the same dialogue with himself many times over the course of the past year.

Dan persisted, "Mary Ann and I have faith that you will do what's right for our daughter. We expect you to abide by our wishes and wait until Becca is mature enough to enter into a physical relationship. In short, we request that you abstain from any physical activities with her."

Hal lowered his head. "I understand, sir."

Dan rose. "No need to make small talk. We'd better get back inside before the girls start to wonder what we're up to." He firmly clasped Hal's shoulder. "I trust this conversation will remain between the two of us."

"Yes, sir."

It wasn't an easy request to honor. Prior to meeting Becca, his goal had been to bed as many women as possible. And why not? He was young, single, and attractive. A variety of women had crossed his path over the years, and he had become very deft at pleasing every one of them. Hal wanted to share his expertise with Becca more than anything in the world; but after Dan's talk, he knew that this was not going to happen anytime soon. He questioned how long he could go without a woman's intimate touch.

He convinced himself that everything was under control—until a new development emerged. He and Becca were snuggling when, out of the blue, she placed her hand on top of his leg, massaged his inner thigh and cooed, "I think it's time we move to the next step."

Hal jumped up so fast, he nearly knocked her to the floor. "What the hell are you trying to do to me?" he screamed.

Becca didn't try to reason with Hal. She merely grabbed her sweater and purse and ran out the door.

CHAPTER TWENTY-TWO

Hal struggled to understand what had transpired. He debated going after Becca. Instead, he flopped onto the couch and stared blankly at the door she had slammed on her way out.

A bleating noise jolted him back to consciousness. He stumbled to his phone and brought it to his ear. The same raspy voice that had assailed him previously erupted from the receiver: "Do you know where your little girlfriend is?"

"Who the fuck is this?"

"More importantly, you should ask yourself: what's the worst thing you can imagine happening in your life?" The line went dead.

Shouting Becca's name, Hal retraced his steps, knowing he wouldn't find her. He punched in her number and was woefully greeted by her voicemail. Hal left a message begging her to call him as soon as possible.

He had to act fast—Becca's life depended on it. Few options sprang to mind. Calling her parents was not one of them. What could they do? He thought about calling the police but didn't think that should be the first resort. He hated to admit it, but his uncle was his best bet. Dialing the number, he felt the color drain from his face as Wayne's prerecorded message crackled to life. Hal disconnected. He closed his eyes and leaned back against the cushion. "Think," he demanded. His eyes popped open.

Car keys in hand, he raced out the door. The tires squealed as he made a sharp right into the driveway, the old homestead rising in the distance, triggering a sentiment that Hal had not acknowledged in quite some time. Namely: his life had not been that bad on the farm, nor was his uncle likely the demon he had condemned so many months earlier.

Hal pulled up behind a shiny new pickup, cut the engine and hightailed it to the house. Mounting the stairs, he entered through the back door. Seated at the kitchen table were two men, one of whom Hal recognized as Jason Holmes, a longtime associate of his uncle. The identity of the second man drew a blank.

"Well, look what the cat dragged in," Holmes chimed.

"Where's Wayne? I need to talk to him."

The stranger leaned forward and put his hands on his knees. "He's not here. Something we can help you with?"

Holmes slid a glob of chew from one side of his mouth to the other. "You got nerve comin' 'round demanding anything."

Hal grabbed Holmes's shirt collar and pulled him out of his chair. "I don't have time for this! Tell me where Wayne is or so help me, I'll beat the shit out of you!"

The stranger pushed back from the table and got to his feet. "Everyone stay calm. Wayne should be here any minute." Hal released Holmes and studied the stranger with hostility. The man reached out to shake Hal's hand. "You must be Wayne's nephew. I've heard about you. My name's Boris, Boris Krause."

"I don't care who you are."

Boris rocked back on his heels. "If you don't mind me asking, what's got you so riled up?"

"That's none of your damn business."

The verbal volley came to a halt when the hinges on the screen door screeched loudly. Juggling a case of beer in one hand and a bag of groceries in the other, a t-shirt-clad Wayne greeted Hal. "Thought that was your car in the driveway." He nodded to the other men. "Everyone, sit." Wayne motioned to the empty chair sitting next to the wall on the other side of the kitchen. "Hal, pull up a seat and tell us what brings you back to this side of the tracks."

Anyone acquainted with Wayne knew his smile could charm a raging bull. Those same people often underestimated the storm that brewed behind it and the capacity it had to destroy whatever stood in its path.

Hal took a step backward and nodded toward the door. "I need to speak to you in private."

"Hell, whatever you have to say, you can say it in front of my friends." Wayne set his bags on the counter, grabbed a beer, popped the cap, and handed it to Holmes. He did the same for Boris, then for himself. "Cheers!"

Boris took a swig from his bottle. "Are we celebrating something?"

"I finalized a deal that I've been negotiating, and it looks to be very lucrative for all of us." Wayne set his half-empty bottle on the countertop. "You boys drink up while I see Hal to his car. He's sorry he can't stay. Do you want a beer to go?" Wayne didn't wait for Hal to answer. He took a fourth bottle from the box, shoved it into his nephew's hand, and pushed him out the door.

"You've got a lot of nerve showing up here," Wayne said loudly. He walked a few steps from the house and then quietly inquired, "You look like shit. Why are you here?"

Hal hurled the bottle of beer at the new truck parked in the driveway. It bounced against the gravel and shattered within inches from the rear bumper. "You damn well know why I'm here."

"How the hell would I know? I haven't been blessed with your presence for, what, over a year now? Did you have a fight with your little girlfriend? Did she finally find out who you are?" Wayne spit a wad and grinned. "She kicked your sorry ass out, didn't she?"

Hal leaned in close, their noses no more than millimeters apart. "Becca's missing, and considering your past, I suspect you had something to do with it."

"Why would I want to hurt Becca?"

"Oh, I don't know. Maybe because you hate me. Or maybe it's because you're in that type of business. You tell me." His voice rose. "What did you do to her?"

"Keep your voice down, you idiot." Wayne grabbed Hal by the arm and elbowed him up against his car. "I'll see what I can find out. Now, get the hell out of here. And don't do anything stupid. I'll be in touch."

"What do I do in the meantime? I can't sit around doing nothing. I have to find her."

"If you're smart, you won't do a thing. Go back to your apartment and stay there 'til I contact you. And whatever you do, do not call the police." Raising his voice, Wayne shouted, "Go on, get out of here. You're not welcome." He reached out with his left hand, opened the car door, and shoved Hal into the driver's seat. "Don't call the police," he growled again under his breath.

Dread escalated to panic as Hal's uncle retreated into the house. His hands shook so bad it took him three tries to fit the key into the ignition. He backed the car around and headed up the driveway, only to come to an abrupt stop.

The reappearance of the young girl wrapped in the shroud taunted him from where she stood in the middle of the road. Her finger urged him forward. He blinked several times to expunge the vision. "It can't be her," he moaned. *It's just my imagination.* His foot pushed against the gas pedal.

Hal realized his error the instant he pulled onto the highway. The blaring horn and screeching tires registered too late. A huge Hummer bore down on him with the speed of a bullet. The horrendous squeal of metal on metal overwhelmed his senses as the giant piece of machinery hammered into the passenger side of his car.

CHAPTER TWENTY-THREE

L ucy couldn't sleep after the trauma of finding RJ on her deck with a huge welt on the side of his head. Who would do such a thing, and why? She brewed a cup of herbal tea, gathered the throw blanket from the back of the sofa and exited through the patio door. Unable to shake the feeling of doom settling around her, Lucy crossed the yard, walked out on the dock, and lowered herself onto the wooden bench.

Her life had gone from bad to worse, starting with her husband. Lucy's concerns regarding Jack were nothing new. She had come to understand through the years that although he wasn't physically abusive, Lucy had to admit that a small part of her feared him. Given everything she'd been through, past and present, she wondered if she would ever be able to trust anyone again.

She cupped the warm mug between the palms of her hands and sipped languidly. The silence around her eventually gave way to the chatter of birds announcing a new day, while tiny traces of pink unfolded across the sky like yards of soft chambray flapping effortlessly in the breeze.

Nature's lavish display did not ease her trepidation. She took another sip of tea and pondered: had she actually witnessed a blinking light the other night, or had it been the product of an overactive imagination? Her eyes widened in disbelief as she scanned the far shoreline. There it was! No wind or rain to obscure her vision. The telltale flicker summoned help—three times fast and then three times slow.

Lucy jumped to her feet, grabbed the blanket as it slipped from her shoulders and ran into the house. She hurriedly donned a pair of jeans and a sweatshirt. With keys to the motorboat in hand, she raced back to the dock, lowered the boat into the water, and jumped aboard. Backing far enough out to clear the end of the dock, she slammed the boat into full throttle. The elusive light vanished without warning.

The boat, though equipped with a forty-horsepower motor, seemed to travel at a snail's pace. Lucy switched the key to the off position as she finally drew near the north shore. The hull slipped onto the wet sand and lurched to a stop, almost knocking her off her feet. Her heart beating with the ferocity of a jackhammer, she cut the engine and jumped to the ground. Sand oozing between her toes told her that her cell phone was not the only thing she had neglected to grab on her way out the door.

She hunkered beside the boat, fully aware that her present position held a distinct disadvantage—anyone on the hillside could monitor her precise movements. Every cell in her body urged her to cut and run. Still, something was pulling her up the hill. She waded into the water and walked parallel to the shoreline until she reached the spot where she could see the same path she'd ventured up the previous day. Lucy cautiously approached the perimeter of the clearing, taking great care to avoid stepping on anything that might puncture the bottoms of her feet.

Angry voices filtered from the open window of the cabin. Crouching low, Lucy inched her way to it, then slowly raised her head.

A bickering couple sat at a metal table, their backs to her. The woman put her head in her hands and moaned, "I want out. This is more than I bargained for."

"We can't walk away yet," the man pleaded.

"It's too dangerous. This whole thing will backfire on us."

Lucy had scant time to absorb the discourse before the front door flew open. An angry squawk drove her to seek cover before she could identify the owner of the newcomer's voice. There had to be a mistake. It made no sense. She desperately wanted to take another look to confirm her suspicions, but the risk was too high.

Lucy sprang to her feet and ran to the boat as fast as her legs could carry her. The sun was now in full view above the treetops. She planted her feet solidly in the sand and heaved the heavy boat back into the water before clambering aboard. As the craft moved away from shore, she switched on the ignition and headed straight for home. A loose plan had taken form in her mind by the time she moored the boat at her aunt's dock.

She stood on the decking and glanced back across the lake. Lucy inhaled, counted to ten, and then slowly exhaled. She couldn't rationalize her passivity any longer. It was time to act. Lives were at stake.

Lucy solicited Jack's help. The fact that he agreed without any strings attached put her on guard. He called back within an hour. "I've got some interesting news for you."

"Great. What did you find out?"

"I'm in Minneapolis on business and kind of pinched for time. Any chance you can drive down and meet me for lunch?"

"Jack, just tell me what you know."

"It's sensitive information, and I'd rather talk to you in person. Why don't we meet at Little Italy? You remember the place. We used to hang out there back when we were in college."

"Yes, I remember it, but I'm not meeting you anywhere unless you give me some kind of information."

"I can't talk right now. Give me a couple hours and I'll call you back."

Lucy sighed deeply after they hung up. She seldom indulged in alcohol at this hour of the day, but a glass of chardonnay might help ease the anxiety she felt every time she confronted Jack.

CHAPTER TWENTY-FOUR

At a very young age, Jack Rydell's mother, Lesley, understood the power she wielded over men. Her China doll complexion and small, supple breasts had schoolboys scrambling to her side. She soon learned that grown men also found her attractive.

At eighteen, she caught the interest of Michael Rydell, a prominent executive from Minneapolis and the father of a young college boy she had befriended. Him being somewhat of a recluse after the loss of his wife to cancer the prior year, a whirlwind romance ensued when Lesley waltzed into his life.

Lesley had ambitious plans for their future, despite her agreement to their surreptitious meetings. Michael was an honorable man, and she was confident he would marry her if she were to become pregnant.

Things did not go quite the way she had anticipated. Sadly, Michael was killed in a car accident soon after she found out she was pregnant. Unable to face life without Michael—or, perhaps more importantly, his money—she turned her thoughts to Michael's son, James. She had known him throughout school, had even dated him before she set her sights on his dad. James was the sole heir to the estate, not counting, of course, the baby she was carrying. She and James were married two weeks later, with James none the wiser.

Lesley massaged her brow, recalling the day her baby boy had entered the world. When the doctor placed the infant in Lesley's outstretched arms, she had hungrily pulled him to her and swore that she would never let him go. This baby embodied the love she and Michael had shared.

James had approached her several weeks after Jack's birth and politely insisted she rekindle their sexual life. She threw him from their bedroom under orders never to return. In the end, he accepted her terms. They agreed to keep up a public front while he discreetly took other women to satisfy his sexual appetite. Eventually, young Jack became the sole purpose for Lesley and James's charade. They both loved the little boy who had bound them together. Lesley's love for her son, however, evolved into an obsession.

Lesley Rydell refused to think about the fact that her son was a product of her deceit. He was a gift from Heaven, and to that end, she sacrificed everything to ensure Jack would have a privileged life. Her undying affection cemented Jack's preconception of his own superiority.

He matured into a dashing young man, his charm and wit winning him favor among contemporary crowds. Lesley despised his outgoing personality and devil-may-care attitude, yearning for the little boy she could control. The day Jack left for college, Lesley locked herself in her room and didn't come out for days. When she finally emerged, her heart had gone from ice to stone.

Jack brought Lucy home to meet his parents shortly after their engagement. Lesley could not ignore the bewitching effect the girl had on her son. In her eyes, Lucy was commonplace and did not appreciate the finer qualities her son had to offer.

"Even a dimwit can see she's after your money."

Jack answered to no one. He chose Lucy above all else. "Lucy will soon be my wife. Get used to it."

"You know," Lesley said, "I know people."

"Are you threatening me?"

"Not you, dear. You know I would never do anything to hurt you."

"If you so much as touch a hair on Lucy's head, I swear, you'll live to regret it."

Lesley's tongue traced the edge of her teeth. "That's no way to talk to your mother."

"Mother? You call yourself a mother? You don't care about me. You're jealous because I've found true love." He swung around and stomped from the room.

<hr />

Lesley saw her folly the minute she sobered up. It took a considerable amount of time and effort to convince Jack that her predilection for alcohol caused her to say things she did not mean. She plotted her revenge from behind closed doors. Not one to accept defeat, she contacted a private detective. Every family has skeletons in the closet, and she would find Lucy's.

Two days later, Lesley entered a nearby coffee shop, stepped up to the counter, and ordered an espresso. She hadn't been seated long when Jill Adamczyk strolled in and joined her. Ms. Adamczyk was a tall, slim woman with long, silky hair that reached below her shoulders. Her piercing eyes exposed a keen intellect that made her one of the best detectives in the state of Minnesota.

This was not the first time Lesley had employed her services. They exchanged a few pleasantries and then got down to business.

Jill pulled a folder from her satchel and opened it. "I'll give you a quick summary. Lucy Rydell's father is Jacob Hershel, age 58. Her mother is Katherine Hershel, née Mason, age 57. Lucy also has an aunt: Sylvia Masterson, née Mason, age 58. Jacob Hershel was a decorated police officer with the Des Moines Police Department. Somewhere along the line, Hershel started using drugs. The department was unable to prove it, but there was chatter that he traded leniency for contraband." Ms. Adamczyk lowered her eyes to the bottom of the page. "Records show the police were called to the home of Jacob and Katherine Hershel on five different occasions for domestic violence." Adamczyk used her thumb and forefinger to flip the page. "The violence ended when Hershel walked out the door, never to be seen again. There is a warrant for his arrest for aggravated assault if he ever resurfaces.

"Soon after her husband's departure, Katherine took her five-year-old daughter and moved to Council Bluffs, Iowa. Interestingly, a search of the deed showed she paid cash. Where she got the money is anyone's guess."

Lesley leaned in.

"The police questioned Lucy's mother regarding her husband's disappearance at the time," Jill continued, "but found no evidence of foul play. They also interrogated Sylvia Masterson. Although they suspected she had a hand in Jacob's removal from the family, they had no proof."

The detective straightened the pages in the folder and tucked them into her shoulder bag. "It's not much. I'd be happy to search further. I can try to locate Mr. Hershel, but that will take time.

He's been missing for almost thirty years." Jill retrieved an envelope from her purse and handed it to Lesley. "Here's a detailed copy of the full report." She pushed her chair away from the table. "I might be able to find something on Sylvia Masterson. My sources tell me she has a nebulous past."

"No," Lesley said, "This will do for now."

"Contact me if you want more information."

They walked out together.

"I've got your number if I decide I need anything else."

Lesley was glad she had walked to the coffee shop. It gave her time to think on the way home. Her plans to draw Jack back into her web had sent her down the wrong path. Knowing her son, he had likely done his own research and discovered the same data she had. Nothing in the report would turn him against his future bride.

CHAPTER TWENTY-FIVE

Lucy was at a loss after her brief conversation with Jack. She took the time to catch up on a little housework. Bored with that, she retired to the deck with the book she'd been reading and another glass of wine, intending to relax until Jack called her back.

Three hours later, Jack's voice shook her from her catnap. "Here you are."

Startled, she turned to see him approaching the stairs. "What are you doing here?"

Jack stepped passed her, opened the patio door, and stepped into the kitchen. She trailed behind him, her mounting annoyance driving her blood pressure higher with every step.

Jack turned to her. "Give me a chance to catch my breath, will you? I've had a really long day. I dropped everything the minute you called. I've been on the go all day and haven't eaten since this morning. Can you whip me up something to eat?"

"You've got to be kidding. Why didn't you just call and give me the information over the phone?"

"Why are you being so difficult?" To emphasize the strain of his commitment, he massaged the back of his neck. "I'm here because you contacted me. I promise I'll fill you in on everything after I've had something to eat."

Experience told her that Jack would talk in circles until he got his way. Lucy puffed up her chest and marched around the kitchen island. Spaghetti from a jar was all he would get. She gathered ingredients for a simple salad. Noticing a bottle of wine on the top shelf of the refrigerator, Lucy grabbed it and filled two goblets half full.

Jack took one and lightly tapped his glass against hers. They each took a sip, savoring the robust liquid.

"Sylvia always did have a taste for fine wines. I'll give her that." He lifted his glass again. "Cheers!" He lowered himself onto a bar stool. "Now, isn't this nice? We'll sit, have a nice dinner, a couple of drinks, and relax a little. It's like old times. What was so bad about those days, Lucy?

"I don't understand why you left. We can work this little problem out. I'm willing." He let out a lengthy sigh as if to signal that her stubbornness was at the root of all their conflicts. "We've been through so much. Don't you think we should try?"

"Let's not get into that now." His reference to their little problem, meaning his affair, infuriated her further. He would never admit that he was the one who had caused the rift in their marriage, so why keep rehashing it? "Tell me how you ended up here today."

"That's my Lucy, always avoiding confrontation." He took another sip from his glass.

Lucy refused to let him bait her. She needed to keep the conversation on track, or he would spend the whole evening attempting to convince her to move back in with him. "I mean it, Jack. I don't want to discuss our personal issues tonight." Her scowl punctuated her resolve.

He relented. "I won't bring it up again if you promise to spend some time with me in the near future. I know I can prove to you that my love for you hasn't changed."

Of course, his love for her had not changed. That was not the issue. How many times did she have to tell him that? She was the one who had changed. She was not the same impressionable girl he had married. Lucy wanted time to discover her true self on her own, minus his constant interference. She'd tried countless times to explain that to him. Jack, as usual, had a hard time identifying with a viewpoint that differed from his own.

Lucy stirred the spaghetti sauce and conceded, groaning. "We'll set a time next week."

"I'm holding you to your word."

Lucy had no doubt that he would do just that. She finished preparing the meal.

"Let's eat on the deck," Jack said. The panoramic view, together with the gentle swish of the water lapping against the shore's edge, eased the tension between them, while the alcohol swirling through their veins added its own magic.

When they finished their pasta and downed the last of the wine, Jack scooted his chair around to gain a better view of the lake, sitting quietly, apparently trying to sort out whatever was milling around in his head.

"How about we go for a boat ride?" It sounded more like a demand than a request.

Lucy's mood nosedived. "Jack, why are you stalling?"

Jack got up and took both her hands in his. "Come on," he implored. "Let's cruise around the lake, and I'll tell you the whole story. I haven't been up here in several years. I forgot how beautiful it is. So peaceful." Again, that grin. "It'll be like old times."

Lucy didn't have the energy to say no. She loaded the dishwasher, punched the wash cycle button and pocketed her cell phone, while Jack gathered their glasses and another bottle of wine. They walked out the door and down to the dock. Lucy took the helm and navigated the motorboat along the south shoreline, Jack's attention lingering on the passing landscapes.

When they reached the middle of the lake, he asked her to shut off the motor. He refilled their glasses with wine. "This is perfect," he said glancing at the horizon. "Not another boat on the lake."

Lucy cringed at the odd tone in his voice.

"When I hung up from talking with you this morning, I called my buddy, Homer. Homer Wendt." He shrugged. "You remember him, don't you? I think you met him at one of my frat parties."

Lucy nodded. "I think I do."

"He and I have been friends since we were kids. We played baseball together in high school. That's where he got the nickname—Homer. Boy, could he hit that ball. He could have gone pro, you know. I found out later that he walked away from a lucrative proposition. It's really a shame. He was a natural."

Lucy took a deep breath. "Can you just cut to the chase?"

"Luce, when will you ever learn to lighten up? Look around." He waved his arm, glass in hand, to encompass the lake. "Where is there a more beautiful place in the world? Relish what you have today, because, like I've always told you, it can be taken away in a blink of an eye."

True to his nature, Jack cared about no one other than himself. He had plenty of freedom to relax and enjoy life. Lucy, however, had neither the time nor the inclination to sit back and enjoy the present. Somewhere, a clock ticked for the missing girls. Lucy fully understood the effect time would have on their safe return.

Jack persisted. "Like I was saying, I called Homer. In case you're not aware, he's the county attorney in St. Paul." Jack beamed with pride. "I actually facilitated his win in the election, so he owes me. He was more than happy to delve into a couple of things for me. Agents Hunter and Peterson are decorated FBI agents. They've been partners for more than five years. They're both single. Homer didn't have access to their current case, but nothing in their past files raised any red flags. Now, your friend, Rafferty—I think you referred to him as RJ—he's something else completely."

Lucy fidgeted with the top button of her shirt.

"You know how to pick 'em, Luce. Homer said Rafferty had several complaints filed against him. He beat up a girl about a year ago. They were living together at the time. Homer sent me photos of her." Jack raised his brows. "She was pretty bruised up."

Lucy's stomach tightened. She didn't want to believe RJ was capable of the charges Jack described. The conversation they had had at the bar had reflected a different kind of man. He seemed so devoted to his mother and his sisters. In contrast, he did deal with violence every day. Maybe he had succumbed to the pressures by becoming aggressive himself.

"Lucy!" Jack pointed. "Look there."

Their boat had drifted close to shore during their conversation. Jack's gaze stretched straight ahead to where a man ran across the sandy beach, his arms flailing. Another man broke from the cover of the trees. The loud hammer of a gunshot reverberated over the water as the first man fell to the ground.

"Duck, Lucy!" Jack screamed.

"Oh, my God," Lucy cried, "He's aiming at us!"

Jack grabbed her arm and pushed her to the floor of the boat.

A second bullet whizzed by their heads, propelling him to dive on top of her. "Stay down!"

Jack crawled to the captain's chair and switched the key to the on position. Keeping his head low, he seized the wheel and piloted the boat to the middle of the lake. The minute he thought they were out of range, he focused on Lucy, who huddled low in the corner with her cell phone clutched in her hand.

"What are you doing?" he yelled.

"I called 9-1-1."

His face twisted in disbelief. "Why would you do that?"

"Someone shot that man and then turned his gun on us. Why wouldn't I call the police?"

———◦◉◦———

Jack slid the Larson boat into the slip at the public dock just as two county deputies pulled into the parking lot with a speedboat in tow. One officer, and then the other, exited their SUV. They grilled Lucy and Jack extensively before backing their boat into the lake and climbing aboard.

"You two stay here 'til we get back," one shouted from the rear of the craft as it took off toward the scene of the crime.

Jack lingered at the fringe of the parking lot with his phone glued to his ear. Lucy sat quietly in her aunt's boat, now moored at the dock.

Jack joined Lucy, and they continued their vigilance. An hour crawled by before the purr of the deputies' motor announced their approach.

Creases lined the men's foreheads as the four congregated on the dock. The elder officer pulled a small can from his pants pocket and slipped a wad of tobacco into his mouth. The younger man glared at Jack and Lucy. "We didn't find evidence of a victim, nor was there any indication of a fight or scuffle."

Lucy took a step backward. "How can that be? We saw the whole thing. The guy shot at us, too! Did you check out the old cabin on the hillside?"

"Yup. We're familiar with that property. We inspected the entire area." This time the Scandinavian lilt came from the bigger of the two men. "Looks like someone's used the place within the past few days, but as far as we know, it may have been the owners. We checked, and there's been no complaint of trespassers. With regards to the beach, we found no blood, no footprints—nothing at all. We'll file a report. That's about all we can do. I hope you two aren't mistaken about what really happened."

Lucy winced. "Are you implying that we would lie about something as serious as murder?"

Jack shot her his mad dog expression, but within seconds, his face mirrored a clean slate. He addressed the officers. "We sincerely apologize if we misinterpreted the events. We honestly thought it was a real gun firing real bullets. Now that I think back, we weren't that close to the shore." He lied so easily. "Maybe it was kids horsing around. I guess they pulled a fast one on us."

The officers looked at each other as if deciding whether Jack was playing them for fools. "Stay here. We'll call in and see if anyone else reported shots fired in the area." They walked back to their SUV.

"What are you doing?" Lucy hissed. "Why are you telling them it was kids playing cops and robbers? I heard the bullet whiz by my head."

"Luce, you're always such a drama queen. Stop and think about it. If that guy could dispose of the body that fast, he must have had help. If they think we can ID the one on the beach, they'll come searching for us. If the police drop it, they'll think we have nothing to report. With any luck, they will forget we exist."

Lucy didn't care for Jack's theory. This, however, was not the time or place to debate the issue. Jack could take the lead for now. She would decide what to do after she had time to think about it.

The officers walked back toward them. The younger one nodded at Jack. "Someone did report gunfire. That doesn't mean much in these parts, though. Everybody 'round here owns a gun. Lots of hunters. You gotta understand: if we chased every call that reported gunshots, we wouldn't get anything else done. You see our dilemma?"

"What Jim is trying to say is that we can file a report if you want us to. Given the lack of evidence, not much will come of it."

"We'll trust your judgment," Jack said. "If you don't think it was anything more than some kids playing around, then that's probably what it was. Come on, Luce. Let these fine officers get on with more important duties."

Lucy doggedly shadowed Jack to the dock, where he took his time untying the boat. He slowly backed it out of the slip while the deputies efficiently loaded their speedboat onto their trailer and drove away. Jack peered over his shoulder one last time to make sure the coast was clear, shoved the throttle forward, and sped toward the crime scene.

"Where are you going?" Lucy yelled.

"I find it inconceivable that they didn't find anything to suggest foul play. Let's go back and see for ourselves."

Lucy leaned back in her seat and studied Jack's profile. He'd dropped everything to come to her aid. *Why am I always so hard*

117

on him? Her throat burned with the realization that her feelings for him hadn't completely disappeared.

When they neared the shoreline, Jack pulled on the throttle, shifted the gear into neutral, and let the watercraft coast up onto the sand far enough to anchor. To Lucy's dismay, the deputies' footprints covered the entire beach, eliminating any chance of detecting solid evidence to substantiate their story.

With his back to her, Jack's wry smile went unnoticed. He queried, "What do you think, Lucy? Could it have been a hoax?"

"It was real. I know it was." She glanced nervously up the hillside, terrified that the man with the gun might reappear. "It's too late to see anything more tonight. I think we should head back to the cottage. We can come here in the morning for a closer look."

Jack beamed from ear to ear. "Are you inviting me to spend the night?"

Lucy's cheeks reddened. "You can spend the night, but we're sleeping in separate bedrooms, so don't get any ideas."

"Luce, how long do you plan to punish me? I've told you repeatedly that the affair meant nothing to me. You're the one I love. I'm begging you to forget it and move forward." He drew her close to him.

With some uncertainty, she let herself lean into his hard body. The kiss began slow and soft. His passion fueled hers. When they finally separated, Lucy stepped back, barely able to keep her balance. Regaining her composure, she quickly moved to the boat. Jack's pace was slower.

They rode back under a veil of unspoken words, darkness settling around them. The rising moon offered little consolation. Lucy had no doubt that the kiss would complicate their relationship even further.

Once inside the cottage, Jack went to the kitchen sink and stared out the window at nothing in particular. "Why don't you go take a hot shower and relax? I'll finish cleaning up the kitchen."

She felt she should say something to open a dialogue between them. Maybe the right conversation could begin to mend some of the hurt they had caused each other. However, the words went unsaid.

Lucy collected a pair of clean sweats from her bedroom and proceeded to the bathroom. When she emerged, Jack was nowhere in the house. Looking out at the lake, she spied his dark frame at the end of the dock, backlit by the moon's fluorescent glow.

The impulse to go to him passed. She padded back down the hall, checked the bedding in Sylvia's room, and laid out clean towels for his use. Lucy then jotted a note and left it on the counter for Jack to find. There was nothing more for her to do. She went into her bedroom and closed the door.

<hr />

A steady breeze from the north allowed Jack to hang out on the dock without a scourge of mosquitoes attacking him. He bided time until he was sure Lucy had retired for the night before he took out his cell phone and made three short calls. He then lowered the boat into the dark water, jumped in, and started the motor.

Upon his return to the cabin, Jack let himself in and softly crept down the hallway, slipping into Lucy's bedroom. Standing beside her bed, he lightly stroked her hair. A tiny mew gurgled in her throat as she rolled over, exposing her back to him. Jack did not miss the significance of her body shift—she had been moving away from him ever since that fateful day when she had walked into his office and found him in the arms of another woman.

Jack had determined that his mother had sent Lucy on an errand to his workplace. His instincts told him Lesley had planned the whole thing. He would make sure his mother regretted the day she had elected to cross him. That, however, was not the only vendetta he had to settle. A slow fire burned in his soul.

CHAPTER TWENTY-SIX

L ucy awoke to the sound of clattering pans. The smoky aroma of bacon and eggs stirred her senses. When was the last time she had allowed herself to savor the decadent flavor of bacon? She donned her robe and proceeded to the kitchen to find the table set and Jack humming as he searched the kitchen cabinets for coffee mugs.

An alluring grin greeted her. "Do you remember the last time I fixed breakfast for you?"

She did. He had woken her early that morning with a gentle kiss that had led to hours of pleasure. The flashback almost pushed her to ask for the hundredth time why he had felt the need to seek out another woman, but Lucy held her tongue. No answer could ever rectify the heartache his actions had caused.

She pointed to the cabinet on the left side of the sink. Jack retrieved two mugs and filled them with steaming hot coffee. Taking one, she walked to the table and took a seat.

"I see you found some of Lloyd's clothes," she said. "For the life of me, I can't understand why Sylvia hasn't cleaned out his closet. He's been gone for over a year." It registered that she'd referred to her aunt's husband as *gone* rather than *dead*. She shuddered at the possibility that Lloyd might still be alive. After brief deliberation, she chose not to tell Jack about the information she had gained from the FBI regarding Lloyd Masterson.

Jack inquired, "Sylvia seems to be getting on with her life. I mean, she went to Europe. Is she traveling by herself, or did she go with someone?"

"She didn't really tell me very much. Like I told you on the phone yesterday, it's developing into quite the mystery."

Jack busied himself over the stove. "It's just like your aunt to leave a mess for you to clean up. I don't understand why you defend her. She doesn't deserve your loyalty."

"Why do you always want to drive a wedge between Sylvia and me?"

Jack turned and waved the spatula at her. "She left the country for nefarious reasons, leaving you with a hornet's nest."

"You don't know that. She could have a very legitimate reason for her overseas trip."

"You need to wake up, Lucy." He shook his head and directed his attention back to the stove.

"I don't have any answers right now, but I know my aunt would not intentionally put me in danger. Let's leave it at that. You can't convince me otherwise, and I'm not going to change your mind. You have never liked Sylvia, so let's stop right here. Please." She let a quiet pause hang between them. "Besides, we have to decide what to do next."

Jack finished stirring the eggs. "First things first." He filled two plates with generous portions of eggs and bacon, added a piece of buttered toast to each, and carried them to the table. "Let's set a date for when we can get together next week."

Lucy rolled her eyes. "I wish you wouldn't do this. I said I'd meet with you to talk about our marriage, and I will, but we have more urgent things to consider."

"I want to make sure I'm available when you are. If you give me a date, I'll mark it on my calendar."

Lucy looked down at her plate and counted to five before answering him. "I'm sure we'll be able to make time for each other."

He lowered his voice. "Yes, of course."

"I promise. When this is all behind us, I will make the time to talk things out to your heart's content." She took a bite of her eggs. "After breakfast, we can go explore the beach again. There's always a chance we'll uncover something we missed."

He massaged his lower lip with his forefinger and thumb. "I've been thinking about that. I'm sure the police would have noticed if anything looked suspicious."

"We really won't know until we see for ourselves."

"No, Luce. Something came up last night. I have to get back to the office."

"What is so imperative that you can't stay another day? You said you would help me, and yet you still haven't told me anything of importance—certainly nothing to warrant a four-hour drive from Minneapolis."

He ignored her slight and said, "Walking that beach will be a waste of time. You saw it. Those police officers destroyed any chance of us finding anything. It's to our advantage if I use my time to pull in a few favors and try to narrow down Sylvia's where-abouts. She's the one person who might have answers as to what is going on here."

"How do you plan to track down Sylvia if the FBI can't?"

"I won't know until I try, and I can't do it from here."

⸻ ◉ ⸻

After Jack left, Lucy took time to reassess her situation. Since their breakup, Jack had worked hard to put his best foot forward. However, the last twenty-four hours had painted him in a much different light. Yes, he came when she called. But the information he had relayed had nothing to do with what she had asked him to check out for her.

She summed up the facts in her head. The FBI alleged that Lloyd Masterson had ties to a human trafficking cartel and that he had played a vital role in the disappearances of five girls. They also indicated that he had survived the freakish boating accident. Even if all that were true, it was a big leap to conclude that her aunt was involved. It was ludicrous to think Sylvia would have participated in something so heinous as kidnapping; and it was insane to think that the voice Lucy had overheard from outside the window of the cabin on Kleins Point could have belonged to Lesley Rydell.

Lucy credited Jack for one thing: his assumption about the shooting on the beach. Rational thinking said it had to be a hoax. After all, the police saw no evidence to substantiate their claim. She had allowed her fears to override common sense.

She changed into a pair of shorts and a t-shirt. A good, hard run would clear her head further and relieve the residual tension from Jack's visit.

The intensity of the hot June sun fell squarely on her shoulders. Sweat poured from every pore in her body. Ignoring the discomfort, her feet pounded the road.

She rounded the curve and spotted a man walking ahead of her. Slowing her pace, she came up beside to him. "Hey, Sean," she gasped, sucking in depleted air. She matched his pace. She had learned that she had to draw him into a conversation. "Someone in town told me that a black bear with his head embedded in a bucket wandered into Frazee during the Turkey Day festivities."

Seans cheeks turned pink as he peeked at her from under his brow. "I heard about that. The poor thing was so disturbed. They had to put him down with a dart to remove the bucket and then let him loose near Tamarac Park."

Sean and Lucy continued walking side by side. He used the time to relate an incident he had experienced several years prior on his dad's farm, one that almost cost him his life.

Lucy came to a sudden stop. "A bear? In this area? Do you think it's safe for me to jog alone out here?"

"It wasn't the bear's fault," he said, halting beside her. "Bears usually shy away from human contact. If you meet up with one, don't panic. Calmly back away in the direction you came. I tried to get too close, and that was the wrong thing to do." Avoiding eye contact with Lucy, he said, "I can let you know if I see one anywhere near here."

Lucy lightly touched his arm. "Thanks. I feel safer knowing you're keeping an eye out for the neighborhood."

His ears beamed a bright red.

She drew back her hand. "I'm going to finish my run. Thanks again." She jogged another half mile, did an about-face, and headed home. Sean was nowhere in sight on the return run. That suited her just fine. Tired from the day's events, she looked forward to retreating behind locked doors and calling it a day.

CHAPTER TWENTY-SEVEN

D renched in sweat, Lucy jumped into the shower. In the kitchen, the answering machine showed that she'd missed three calls. RJ's voice, steeped in angst, beseeched her. "I called your cell phone several times and haven't been able to reach you. Call me and let me know you're okay."

Lucy frowned. What was it with her and her cell phone lately? With everything that was going on, the smart thing to do was keep it with her at all times.

She hit the button to hear the next message. Her shoulders snapped back at the sound of Sylvia's voice.

"Lucy, I presume you're enjoying your stay at the cottage. I'm having a great time here. Can you do me a favor? Be a dear and call Mr. Foley at the bank and ask him to transfer $50,000 into my travel account. I'd call him myself, but he'd ask too many questions, and I don't feel like talking to him at the moment. Oh, and if you run into Detective Rafferty, tell him that all bets are off. I left in a hurry and didn't have time to convey that message. Sorry I missed you. I'll call back in a few days. Love you much."

"Is she serious?" Lucy jabbed the replay button and listened for any hint of a secret code in her aunt's ramblings. If there was one, it was lost on her. She shook her head in disgust.

Lucy played the final message. Chris Foley's voice sounded strained. "I drove past your place last night, but you had company. I didn't want to intrude. It's crucial that I talk to you. Call me as soon as you get this."

The bank wasn't open on Sundays, and she didn't have Mr. Foley's personal number. She made a mental note to call him first thing in the morning.

She picked up her cell and punched in RJ's number.

CHAPTER TWENTY-EIGHT

W here the hell have you been all day?" RJ yelled into his phone, his concentration wandering from the road. When he brought his eyes back to the pavement, his truck had crossed the center line and was veering toward an oncoming car. RJ tossed the phone and grabbed the wheel with both hands as his truck nosedived down a ten-foot embankment and came to rest against barbed wire fencing.

The airbag failed to deploy. RJ clasped hold of the seatbelt stretched tightly across his chest. "At least you, my friend, did your job." He draped his arms over the steering wheel and bowed his head in gratitude.

A loud knock on the driver's window startled him into action. RJ twisted in his seat to see sharp blue eyes staring at him from amid acres and acres of wrinkles. The old man shouted through dentures too big for his mouth, "Are you okay?"

"Yeah, I think so." RJ groaned as he unbuckled the seatbelt. His body had taken quite a beating during the past twenty-four hours. The bruises on his chest would soon match the ones on his face. He wasn't complaining, though. He was lucky to be alive.

RJ opened the door and stepped gingerly from the truck. "Thanks for stopping. Were you the one I almost ran off the highway?"

"No, that guy kept going. I was behind him. You did some fancy drivin' to avoid a worse accident. I think he purposely ran you off the road."

Rafferty ruffled his hair with his fingertips. "What do you mean?" He tried to recall the exact sequence of events. "I lost control of my truck. I veered into him." He looked out his windshield and noted the matted grass from his skidding tires.

"Well, maybe that's how it happened, but from where I sat, it looked like the guy steered into your lane, like he was tryin' to hit ya."

"Did you get a good look at the car or the driver?"

"Sorry, but no."

"I appreciate you stopping and offering a helpful hand."

A smile crisscrossed the man's weathered face. "Well, my wife's gonna be worried if I don't git home soon. She'd want me to tell you to put a cold press on those bruises. It's already looking like a pumpkin."

RJ fingered his cheek. "Thanks for the advice."

"Let's make sure you can back your truck outta here. Then we can both be on our way."

RJ slid into his truck, shifted it into reverse, and backed up the embankment and onto the shoulder of the road. Rafferty watched the old man place each foot carefully in front of the other as he finessed his way across the ground. RJ waited for him to reach his old Chevy pickup and sidle into the driver's seat. They gave each other a nod before driving away in opposite directions.

His cell phone had landed somewhere on the floor of the truck. RJ didn't intend to tempt fate twice in one day. More to the point, his planned conversation required talking directly with Lucy. He had spent most of the morning rehearsing his speech. It had made sense at the time. Now, seeds of uncertainty pushed their way into his head.

RJ parked the truck in her driveway and retrieved his phone. He trudged toward the house, feeling a bit like a man heading to the gallows. Apprehension morphed into fear when his knocking garnered no response.

He tried the door; it was unlocked. Pushing it open, he called out Lucy's name. There was no reply. He unclipped the retention strap on his holster and moved through the cabin, room by room. Everything was in order. No hint of any foul play.

Once outside again, he cast his eyes around the yard and then scanned the road in both directions. On the lake side, he confirmed that she wasn't on the deck. Both boats were in their slips.

Footsteps approaching from behind brought back memories of the previous night. Acting in overdrive, he spun around and almost knocked Lucy to the ground. His hand brushed against her breast as he attempted to steady her. Its soft contour sent a rush through his abdomen and then bolted straight to his groin. What was it about this woman that rubbed his nerves raw?

RJ marveled at the fact that he even liked her. Lucy was contrary to everything he fancied in a woman. Be that as it may, he had to admit he enjoyed sparring with her. At every turn, she challenged him to be a better man. He dreaded the look in her eyes if he ever unmasked his dark side.

This was not the time to think about that.

Lucy took a step back and scowled. "What are you doing here? First, you leave me an urgent message to call you, and when I do, you hang up on me." She pushed past him. "Don't even bother to explain."

SOS

He grabbed her arm. "You don't understand."

She yanked free of his grip. "Keep your hands off me." Fire flashed across her features. "I'm not some young girl you can bully."

Her words pierced his heart. Did she know about Mindy? He fought the urge to explain the circumstances of his tumultuous interactions with his past girlfriend. Instead, he addressed his more recent gaffe. "In case you're interested, a car ran me off the road." His teeth clenched. "I had to ditch my phone. I needed both hands on the wheel to dodge a head-on collision."

The hostility in her eyes warned him that he would get no respite. "Do you know how many people are killed each year by distracted drivers on the phone? Imagine living the rest of your life knowing you were responsible for killing an innocent person because you couldn't put your phone down for just one minute."

RJ had no viable defense. An abstract thought popped into his head. Could her rebuke mean she cared about him? Her pinched expression told an alternate story.

Lucy's cat eyes scrutinized him as if determining the life expectancy of an annoying mouse. Her brows narrowed. "I've had enough of men for one day." She marched down to the dock.

"Lucy. I agree with what you're saying." He lagged behind her, pleading for her to listen to what he had to say. Although her independence intrigued him, RJ could not afford to play any more games with her. He had to find out if she had talked to her aunt, and if so, what she knew about the missing girls. He didn't have much time left.

CHAPTER TWENTY-NINE

From overheard conversations between his parents, Sean learned that Sylvia was out of town. That meant Lucy was alone in the house. He knelt in his usual spot behind the thick brush along the roadside. The view from there afforded him the opportunity to monitor Lucy's activities as she moved about the yard, pulling weeds from flowerbeds and sweeping the patio.

Lucy walked through a small opening in the hedge when a voice from the neighbor's yard summoned her. Sean got to his feet. The rumbling of a truck sent him scrambling back to his hiding place. The pickup, driven by RJ, swept into the driveway.

Sean gasped when Rafferty entered the house. He flipped his attention from the door to the hedge and back to the door. Finally, RJ exited and stepped around the side of the house. Sean checked the hedge one last time, sprinted to the porch, and slipped inside the house before Lucy returned from her visit next door.

He slunk through the small cottage, memorizing the layout of the rooms. His heart stopped when, through the kitchen window, he spied RJ and Lucy standing toe-to-toe. Sean wadded his hand into a tight fist and sunk his teeth into the fleshy part of his thumb. The taste of blood filled his mouth.

SOS

Throughout his life, Sean had worked to stay under the radar of do-gooders and busybody neighbors. School was a different source of pain. His height, weight, and clumsiness brought on brutal name-calling. Sean managed to muddle through his shortcomings until the day his only friend moved to Chicago. That's when Sean's isolation took on new meaning. The more he withdrew, the harder it was to fit in anywhere, including at home.

Sean dropped out of high school at the age of sixteen. With no means to support himself, he lived with his parents into adulthood. Their rules included mandatory attendance of Sunday morning church. Sean also had chores to perform around the farm and a strict curfew to keep him from wandering about at all hours of the night. He adhered to the directives for the most part, and for that, his parents acquiesced to his innate desire for solitude.

Despite his idiosyncrasies, Sean had the persona of a shy, gentle man incapable of harming anyone; but one fateful day refuted that assumption.

Sean snapped. No one in the family would speak again of that Sunday afternoon when Sean nearly strangled his mother to death. If his dad hadn't heard the commotion and come to her rescue, Sean would have succeeded.

He had never experienced anything remotely like the power that swept through him as his mother lay helpless, her protruding eyes begging him to spare her life. Often, late at night, when he couldn't sleep, Sean relived those moments up to the minute when his dad walked in and stopped him. Sometimes, he played it through, leaving out the part where his dad had pried his hands from his mother's bruised neck.

CHAPTER THIRTY

RJ prided himself on his ability to judge other people's motives. He had done his homework, and everything led him to believe that Lucy could and would advocate for him—if she trusted him. He hated himself for what he planned to do, but it was too late to alter his path now.

"Lucy, please let me explain."

"And why would I listen to anything you have to say?" Her hands went to her hips. "You've implicated my aunt in immoral activities, and so far, you haven't given me a single detail that would substantiate your assertions."

RJ nodded. "I hate to bring you into this, but Sylvia has left me no other choice. Before I tell you what I know, it's essential that I detail the dangers that lay ahead if you decide to get involved."

"Involved? I'm already involved." Her voice escalated with each word.

RJ's eyes narrowed. Lucy followed his gaze. Two fishing boats sat no more than a hundred yards from the shore. One boat trolled at a slow pace; the other sat anchored with a lone man positioned at the bow. He cast his fishing line, reeled it in, and cast it out again.

"Do you think he heard us?" Lucy mouthed.

"I should know better than to discuss private issues within earshot of someone." RJ's voice cracked under his breath. "Maybe we should go for a drive. No one can eavesdrop on us in my truck." Another X-rated picture popped into his head. *Dammit,* he thought. *Does she even know what she does to me?* If he wanted to remain in charge, he had to figure out a way to keep his emotions at bay.

Lucy arched her brows. Had she guessed his musings? Her words taunted him further. "I'm not sure that's a good idea."

RJ felt his cheeks flush. "I promise I'll be the perfect gentleman—scout's honor." He didn't wait for a reply before looping his arm over her shoulder and guiding her to his truck.

When they rounded the corner of the cottage, Lucy wiggled loose. "I have to grab my cell phone and lock up."

She secured the door on her way out. Neither she nor RJ had any idea that Sean Penalton was inside, hiding in the back bedroom.

CHAPTER THIRTY-ONE

S ean's knees buckled at the sound of the door closing behind Lucy. Peeking through the blinds, he watched her and RJ climb into the truck. Relief gave way to panic when Sean realized he had no way to go after them. Like a beacon, the tree-lined shore on the other side of the lake appeared through the windows, signaling him that everything would work itself out.

Fate had delivered Lucy to him, and he had no intention of losing her now. To soothe the darkness of abandonment, he fixated on the plan he had concocted to convince Lucy to run away with him. He had visited the local library in Detroit Lakes to research where they might live. His inclination leaned toward Colorado—possibly the Rockies—or maybe even Canada. It had to be somewhere secluded where no one would find them.

The memory of that plan jerked him back to the present. Sean settled into the recliner facing the lake. An hour came and went. He got up and wandered through the house, stroking Sylvia's collectibles before helping himself to a coke from the fridge.

He ultimately wound up in Lucy's bedroom. The dresser called to him. Sean eased open the top drawer to discover a treasure trove of intimate female apparel. Temptation spurred him on. The silky fabric felt cool against his cheek. A voice in the back of his head condemned his actions, and he swiveled ever so slightly, expecting to see his mother standing in the doorway, her wretched features dooming him to Hell. He sighed audibly, remembering that he was the only one in the house. Lovingly, he replaced the articles in the drawer.

The events of the day took their toll. Sean lowered himself onto the bed, rolled onto his side, and pretended that Lucy lay snuggled safely in his arms. He soon drifted into a peaceful sleep.

He woke with a start, confusion clouding his judgement until he realized where he was. The clock on the nightstand indicated that it was 1:20 a.m. Lying motionless, Sean listened for distant sounds to confirm that no one else was in the house. Hearing nothing, he rolled out of the bed and smoothed the covers.

Everyone knew what a man and a woman did when they were together all night. How could Lucy betray him like this? A fit of anger seized him. He lashed out at the faces of Lucy and her aunt, their smiles captured in a photo sitting atop the dresser.

The clatter of broken glass sent a jolt through him. He fled to the kitchen to find a trash bag and rushed back, carefully cleaning up the tiny shards. Sean couldn't bring himself to toss the picture. He gently tore it in half and threw Sylvia's image into the sack with the rest of the trash. He flattened the creases and torn edges of Lucy's image and slipped it into his pocket. With the bag tucked under his arm, Sean trudged through the cottage as if schlepping through thick mud. He lingered in the doorway for one last backward glance and then stepped outside. He didn't worry that his mother would have the house locked up tight at this hour. He had a key hidden for such occasions.

Heavy clouds hid any evidence of a moon. Sean relied on his instincts to guide him home on the pitch-black road. The cloak of night allowed him the anonymity he'd strived for his entire life.

In the sanctity of his bedroom, Sean sought the one place that provided him a semblance of security. It was the same place he had always escaped to as a child. On hands and knees, he crawled to the back of the closet, where he curled his large frame into a fetal position. It suddenly occurred to him what held him apart from everyone else. The vision sharpened. Why hadn't he seen it until now?

CHAPTER THIRTY-TWO

R J filled the time with idle talk as he drove around for an hour, endeavoring to bolster his courage.

Lucy gave him a nudge. "It's not like I don't enjoy hearing your little stories, but I thought you had something important you wanted to share with me. If not, I'd like to get back to my aunt's place."

"So I haven't bored you with my anecdotes?" RJ smirked.

She didn't let him off the hook. "You're stalling. If you can't bring yourself to tell me what's on your mind, please take me home."

He gripped the steering wheel against the likelihood of a backlash. "I've wasted enough of your time, so here goes. I assume you've been appraised that Lloyd was a prime suspect regarding the missing girls."

Instead of answering, Lucy interjected, "And, what exactly is your involvement?"

"As you know, I'm a detective with the Otter Tail County sheriff's department. My division is in charge of local cases." RJ went on to detail his duties and then brought the conversation back to the subject at hand. "I told you about my relationship with your aunt." The circumstances under which he'd met Lloyd Masterson wove their way into his story. He mentioned Lloyd's shaky money scheme.

"I swear, as soon as I became aware of the scam, I backed out of the deal. By that time, Lloyd had enough evidence to blackmail me."

Lucy gave an understanding nod.

Rafferty tilted his head from side to side, emitting an audible crack with each turn. "I felt like I'd dodged a bullet when I heard that Lloyd died in that boating accident. I met Sylvia for the first time at Lloyd's funeral." He swallowed hard to get rid of the lump in his throat. "It's necessary that I clear the air with you. I assure you, this fling with your aunt meant nothing to either of us."

If Lucy was curious, she didn't ask any questions; nor did she give any details as to what she knew about the case.

Daylight faded. RJ veered his truck into a roadside pull-off area equipped with a few picnic tables and killed the engine. He wanted to use what was left of the evening light to witness Lucy's reaction when he told her the rest of the story.

The sun sank beyond the horizon, and one by one, stars popped into view. RJ finally spoke again. "I have a contact in Arizona who claims he can arrange for me to meet with a man in Phoenix who deals in human trafficking. I'm almost positive he's the guy we are looking for."

"That's great news. If you can solve this case, Sylvia can come home."

"Hold on," RJ said. "Don't get ahead of yourself. Phoenix could be a bust."

"I know." Lucy frowned. "Does the FBI know about your man in Arizona?"

"I doubt it. Those agents are assholes. They couldn't find the broad side of a barn if it was right in front of them."

"You probably won't be surprised to find out that their opinion of you is the same."

"Yeah, I bet it is."

RJ had to find a way to keep Lucy from further contact with the agents. Several ideas occurred to him; one guaranteed success. It was risky. It might even cost him his career. Under the circumstances, that would be the least of his problems. He couldn't put if off any longer. "This case is personal for me. I'm determined to bring those girls home." RJ stared out the windshield. "I need your assistance."

"What can *I* do?"

"I'd like you to accompany me to Phoenix."

"Why me? Wouldn't it be wiser to take someone who's been trained for that type of thing?"

"Yes, it would, but my boss won't approve the operation. If I don't go now, it's likely we'll lose this lead."

"I don't think it's a good idea. I'm not qualified. Too many things could go wrong. What if I screw up and cause irreparable damage?"

"All you have to do is be yourself. We'll go in as husband and wife looking for a nanny for our kids. I'll go over all the contingencies so there will be no surprises."

Lucy shook her head. "I'm sorry, but this is way out of my league."

"Really, there is no need to worry. We'll be in and out so fast you'll wonder why you even questioned the plan. Fingers crossed, we leave with a girl; if not, we tried. That's all we can do."

The distance between them seemed to widen. "I need some time to think about it."

"My plans are to leave tomorrow. Why don't I go over all the details now and see how you feel once you know exactly what I'll need you to do?"

"I guess that won't hurt."

They discussed the pros and cons, charted the timing, and then laid out a plan that was agreeable to both. In the end, Lucy agreed to travel with him to Phoenix.

It was past midnight when they finally had everything in order. RJ suggested they run by his apartment, where he could grab an overnight bag, and then go back to her place. "This way, we can get an early start, drive to Minneapolis, and catch the first flight to Phoenix. If all goes according to plan, we'll be back by tomorrow night." RJ's heart hammered in anticipation of her reaction to a sleepover at her place as he strove in earnest to quiet his internal dialogue. This could all blow up around him if he let his desire interfere with his judgment.

He had gotten himself into this mess. He alone had to get himself out. He was about to tell Lucy that he was having second thoughts about taking her to Phoenix when a car pulled up behind his truck and flashed its headlights twice.

That was their code.

"That's Cassie Mitchell, my partner," he told Lucy. "Stay in the truck. I'll go see what she wants."

RJ got out and walked back to Mitchell's car. He leaned in to talk to her through the open window. "Kinda late for you to be out, isn't it?"

"I left four messages on your cell. Apparently, you're not taking my calls."

"I've been busy," he said evenly. Cassie had a habit of calling him at odd hours. There was a time when he had enjoyed their casual conversations outside of work, but somewhere along the line, she had become enamored with him, changing the dynamics of their relationship, and not for the better.

When her first call had come through earlier that evening, he had let it go to voicemail. The second call had come within seconds, prompting him to turn off his phone.

Cassie gave him a scorching look. "Didn't you get a call from Chief Miller?" She studied the darkness through her windshield. "Who've you got in your truck?"

RJ ignored her second question. "What's up with the Chief?"

"A body showed up in Becker County this afternoon. They suspect it might be one of the missing girls. The medical examiner from Minneapolis is driving up in the morning to perform the autopsy. Miller requested that we be at the station first thing in the morning to go over the details and any new evidence they find at the scene."

Alarms went off in RJ's head. "How did you find me way out here?"

"Dumb luck. I'm headed to a friend's house." Cassie glanced through the window again. "I recognized your truck and presumed you were probably parking here with the latest babe you've picked up."

RJ managed to keep his anger at bay. This wasn't the time to pick a fight. He had to send Mitchell on her way before she identified Lucy.

"All right," he said. "Thanks for tracking me down. I'll see you at the station, bright and early." He tapped the roof of her car, spun around, and walked back to his truck. He hoisted himself into the driver's seat and slammed the door shut, thankful that he had disconnected the inside dome lights. Always a quick study, he had figured that trick out back in high school.

Rafferty rubbed his chin. "We have to postpone the trip to Phoenix," he said to Lucy.

"Why? What was all that about?"

"Apparently, Cassie's been trying to reach me all evening. There's been a new development in the case. I have to report to the station early tomorrow morning."

Lucy's eyes widened. "What happened?"

"I probably shouldn't tell you, but they found a body."

"Oh, dear God." Her hands crossed her chest as if she were hugging herself. "Where?" she groaned.

"At the dump. Please don't share this knowledge with anyone else."

"Of course I won't."

"I ought to get going."

"When do you plan to go to Phoenix?"

"I don't know. It will depend on what we run into tomorrow. If the body belongs to one of the missing girls, we'll postpone the trip for now." RJ retrieved a Rolaid from the cup holder and popped it in his mouth to stem the acid working overtime in his stomach.

The drive back to Sylvia's place was quiet. Everything the authorities knew about the case led them to believe that the abducted girls were in Mexico. RJ hated to postpone the trip to Phoenix, but the identity and cause of death of the girl recovered at the dump could change the direction of the investigation.

He pulled his truck into the driveway and switched off the engine. Storm clouds had moved in, casting an eerie haze inside the cab. RJ sat back in the seat and briefly pondered how things might have worked out if he had met Lucy under different circumstances.

On impulse, he took hold of her hand. She hesitated before entwining her fingers around his. He leaned in and kissed her.

Their passion kindled for a moment until Lucy backed off.

Every time a favorable outcome seemed likely, she would throw a wrench into the mix. RJ had to concede that he was no match for her. She had cajoled her way into his head and played him well.

CHAPTER THIRTY-THREE

Lucy withdrew from his embrace and sank back into the seat like a giddy schoolgirl. The darkness beyond the windshield became her friend, wrapping her in a blanket of obscurity. RJ slid from the driver's seat and came around to open her door, and they walked single file up the dark cobblestone pathway. Inside, she pivoted to face him. Unable to resist his hunger, she melted into his arms. RJ pulled her tighter against his taut body.

Before she could stop herself, Lucy reached out and flipped the light switch. The harsh reality of the overhead bulb had a sobering effect. Lucy blinked. She had to maintain a platonic relationship if she intended to keep her wits about her. More to the point, she was legally married, which obliged her to consider her husband's mindset. If Jack got wind of her involvement with another man—especially if that man was RJ—all hell would break loose.

RJ leaned in and gave her one more passionate kiss. "Keep your doors locked at all times," he instructed as he left.

A strange sense of loss descended around her. She slipped the deadbolt into place and slowly walked to the bedroom, her fingertips gently caressing her chapped lips. His fervent embrace played over and over in her mind. Exhausted, she laid on the bed to catch her breath before showering and changing into her pajamas. Hours later, a loud rap on the door nudged her from a deep sleep.

CHAPTER THIRTY-FOUR

Hal Johanson spent days slipping in and out of consciousness. He didn't recall the fight he had had with Becca, nor did he remember the threatening call that had sent him racing to his uncle's farm in search of help. The terrible accident that had landed him in his present state remained a blank slate in his head.

Time seemed to pass through altered dimensions. One minute, he'd wake to demons hovering around in the darkness. The next, he lay in a dimly lit room, listening to unfamiliar voices talking about him as if he weren't there.

An eternity slipped away. The steady *beep, beep, beep* echoed in his ears as an IV tube fed liquid into his left arm. Parched, his throat constricted against the hard tube that rested on his tongue and stretched deep into his trachea. He gagged, causing unspeakable pain. Tears wet the side of his face. An angelic voice assured him that all would be well as he slipped back into a coma. His brainwaves clicked into action with the touch of something warm against his hand.

An inspiration grabbed hold of him. Maybe it was an angel caressing his hand. Yes, he was sure of it. She urged him to wake up. To his utter dismay, everything went black again. *No,* he cried,

I need to wake up.

A soft voice answered his unspoken plea: "If you can hear me, I love you. Please come back to me."

It wasn't an angel. It was Becca.

"Becca, I'm here. I can hear you. I love you. Please don't leave me, don't ever leave me," he screamed. At some level, he understood that no sound escaped him. He was stuck in a body that would not respond to his commands. He drifted deeper.

CHAPTER THIRTY-FIVE

Tears slid over Becca's cheeks and landed on the back of Hal's bruised hand where it lay clutched in her own. He'd been in a coma for almost four days, and the doctors gave no assurance that he would ever wake up. Despair bubbled within her. Hal was her soulmate. Without him, she had nothing to live for.

Becca rejected her parents' views of support. They counseled her to trust in God; He would guide her through this terrible time.

But she alone bore the blame for Hal's condition. Not even God could forgive her selfish mistakes. She should have told Hal what had been bothering her that day; they could have talked things out. Instead, she had stormed from his apartment, leaving him to think the worst. Her bigger sin was not returning his calls. If she had, he would have stayed in his apartment until she came back. The burning question that eroded her heart was why Hal had gone out to the farm. As far as she knew, he hadn't seen or spoken to his uncle for nearly a year.

Becca had no knowledge of the man who had tailed her for nearly a week. He had followed her to the mall the day she'd stormed out of Hal's apartment building and positioned himself in the food court, where he could conduct discreet surveillance.

From there, he had made the fateful call that sent Hal running straight to his uncle's farm for answers.

Clueless of those facts, Becca blamed herself. Her tormented sob tugged at the heart of the day nurse as she tended to Hal. After updating Hal's charts, Nurse Angela sat next to Becca. She placed her arm around the young girl's small shoulders and pulled her closer. Becca leaned in, finding comfort in the ample embrace.

"Please tell me he'll come out of this," Becca begged. "I have no reason to live if he's not here to share my life."

"Now, now," the nurse cooed. "You'll have plenty of time to think about that later. We must pray every day that he comes out of this. And when he does, he will rely on your strength. You have to take care of yourself."

Becca nodded. Hal was a fighter. He wouldn't leave her if he didn't have to. She wiped her nose with the back of her hand and inhaled deeply. She, too, was a fighter. She took a tissue from the nearby Kleenex box and blew her nose. "Thank you for your kind words. Just when I had given up on God, He sends you to me."

Smiling, the nurse enveloped Becca deeper in the warmth of her soft arms. "I didn't tell you anything your parents haven't already said to you." The nurse rose from her chair. She took Becca by her hands and pulled her to her feet. "Now, take a gander at yourself. How long has it been since you've had a good night's sleep? Hal isn't going anywhere soon, so I propose you go home, take a nice hot bath, put on your favorite pajamas, and crawl into bed. That way, when Hal wakes up, you'll have the energy to help him. Now, doesn't that make sense to you?"

"Yes, it does." Becca's eyelids drooped.

Her dad remained in the doorway. "I'll take you home, sweetheart, and I'll bring you back first thing in the morning."

Becca gave Hal a kiss and told him she would be back soon. She dragged herself across the room and into her dad's strong arms. Dan Banks mouthed the words *thank you* to the nurse. He guided his daughter along the corridor and into the waiting elevator.

CHAPTER THIRTY-SIX

The day Hal came to the farm, Wayne advised him to go back to his apartment and stay there until he contacted him. Wayne had barely returned to the house when he heard the squeal of tires and then a thunderous crash of metal on metal. He instructed the two men sitting at his kitchen table to call 911 before he raced out the back door and down the driveway.

His heart plummeted at the tragic scene laid out before him. It appeared as if the driver of a huge Hummer had attempted to park his vehicle on top of Hal's small, crumpled sedan. The driver's door of the sedan emitted a mournful screech as it rocked back and forth on its hinges. Wayne peered inside. "What the hell?" he screamed. Johanson tried to wrap his mind around what he was seeing. More to the point, he couldn't trust what his eyes told him. His nephew was nowhere in sight.

Confused, he wondered if there was a chance Hal had walked away from the mess. Wayne swung his gaze upward to the Hummer. Soot-blackened windows offered no comfort.

Suddenly, the driver's door creaked open. A young man in his early twenties pushed past the airbags and tumbled to the ground. He struggled to his feet, dusted the dirt from his clothes, and then surveyed the scattered debris dispassionately.

Johanson's fists knotted against his sides. Everything about the kid made his blood boil. Instinct urged him to transform that smug face into a punching bag, but distant sirens brought him back to earth. He'd deal with the boy soon enough. Wayne scanned the ditch in both directions. His focus finally rested on a mound of debris some thirty yards away. He dashed to his nephew's side as the first volunteer firefighter arrived on the scene.

"Over here," Wayne yelled, his voice hoarse with tension.

The volunteer hovered over Hal's limp body. An ambulance arrived, accompanied by two patrol cars, a fire engine, and two more volunteer firefighters. The police officers acknowledged Wayne with curt nods, aware of his reputation in the community.

Two EMTs assessed Hal's injuries. Another braced his neck and back. Together, they carefully buckled him onto a flat board. They lifted the board in unison, placed it on a stretcher, and wheeled it to the ambulance. The emergency vehicle pulled onto the highway with its lights flashing and sirens blaring.

Wayne called in favors during Hal's surgery. Once he was assured of Becca's safety, he recruited a friend to ensure her future welfare.

Hal's prospects, conversely, were not that well-defined. He had no broken bones or punctured organs. The collision's impact, however, had caused severe head trauma. The doctors could not predict his outcome.

Wayne had stayed by Hal's side throughout the night. In the wee hours of the morning, he choked back his fear of losing the only person who had ever meant anything to him. Leaning in close to his nephew, he murmured, "I know I haven't always been there for you. If you can hear me, I want you to know I have your back. Becca is safe. She'll be here soon." He glanced momentarily at the ceiling. "I promise I'll protect her until you're up and able to take care of her yourself." Wayne jotted Becca's name and contact numbers on a piece of paper and handed it to the nurse on his way out.

Four days later, Wayne Johanson pulled into the parking lot in time to see Becca and her father exiting the hospital. He laid across in the front seat of his blue pickup. When he was sure they were gone, he went inside.

Hal's condition hadn't changed in the days since the accident. Wayne sank into the chair next to his nephew's bed. He sat for a time, pondering his past decisions, many of which he regretted immensely. Amid the ceaseless beep of the heart monitor and the steady swoosh of the ventilator, he chastised himself for being so hard on his nephew. They had gone through some rough times. What family doesn't? He reminded himself that there had been good times, too.

One such event came to mind: the Park Rapids Rodeo. Hal's face had beamed with excitement as he'd watched the cowboys test their skills against angry bucking broncos. Wayne had taken him behind the scenes and introduced him to a couple of riders, who encouraged him to test his skill at mounting a somewhat tame bull that day. He had ended up in the hospital with a broken arm. The boy's joy in recounting the story at every turn only heightened the day's success.

Wayne's business expansions had presented new problems. He had recruited Hal without much forethought and secretly admired his nephew's courage to walk away from the illegal activities.

Wayne wished he'd had the conviction to do the same. If he had, Hal would not be lying unconscious in a hospital bed right now.

Wayne pushed himself out of the chair. Time to end the pity party. There was nothing more he could do here; it was up to Becca now. If Hal pulled through, it would be because of the love the two shared.

CHAPTER THIRTY-SEVEN

C hris Foley held the handset against his ear as he walked the length of his office and back to his desk. Why didn't Lucy pick up? Sylvia's voice came through on the answering machine. He paused, undecided as to whether to hang up or leave Lucy another message.

Lucy's breathy voice greeted him, interrupting his thoughts. "Hello. I'm here. I couldn't get to the phone in time. The machine picked up."

"Lucy, I've been trying to reach you. I left an urgent message on your machine yesterday. I got worried when you didn't call me back."

"I was out late. Besides, I don't have your personal number, so I couldn't call you."

"I assumed Sylvia had given it to you." He rattled off the number. "Is there any chance you can come to my office this morning? I spoke with your aunt yesterday, and it's important that I see you today."

"I can be there in an hour."

"Fine, I'll free up my schedule."

Chris ushered Lucy into his office the minute his secretary announced her arrival, his grim expression mirroring his thoughts.

"Thank you for coming." He closed the door, motioned to her to sit, and then took his seat behind the desk.

The dialogue he and Sylvia had exchanged the previous day resonated in his eardrums. "Chris, I have to go into hiding," Sylvia had said. "Everything has gotten way out of hand."

"I told you not to go looking for trouble."

"Let's not rehash old news, dear," she had countered. "I'll be out of touch for a while. I'll try to call in a few days, but I can't make any promises."

"What am I supposed to tell Lucy?"

"That's the real motive for my call. You have to convince her to pack up and go back to Des Moines. Things have gotten complicated, and I want her out of the line of fire."

"Do you really think Lucy will leave now?"

"I know this didn't work out the way we planned," Sylvia had said.

"Stop right there. I didn't plan any of this."

"What's done is done," she'd continued. "I can't change the past any more than you can. Your job now is to convince Lucy to leave Minnesota. In fact, tell her my life depends on her going home."

Static had interrupted the call. Chris swore he had heard a man's voice on the other end demanding that Sylvia hang up.

"Is someone there with you, Sylvia?"

"I have to go. I'll be in touch when things settle down on my end. In the meantime, you must persuade Lucy that it's safer for all of us if she goes home immediately."

The phone went dead.

Foley sat facing Lucy now, rebuking himself for not delving deeper into Sylvia's debacle. Sylvia's niece was not the type to abandon her aunt, and Chris could not walk away knowing the danger she faced.

Chris's life was a sham, and very soon, it would be aired publicly. The shame that would besiege his family weighed heavily on his conscience. He had nowhere to run and no way to derail the onslaught careening his way. His sole wish was that when it was over and the dust settled, he would have the opportunity to clear his name.

Lloyd Masterson had wreaked havoc on Foley's life, and although he wasn't proud of it, Chris had celebrated shamelessly when he received news of the boating accident that took Masterson's life. Hindsight revealed that it had been a fool's game to think his problems would evaporate with the man's death.

Chris saw no way to save himself. Committed now to correcting the damage he had caused, he rationalized that at least his family would know he died striving to do the right thing.

CHAPTER THIRTY-EIGHT

Five years earlier.

Art Mason struggled for years to overcome the lasting effects of his service in the Gulf War. He bounced from job to job. Nothing kept his interest for any length of time. He'd almost given up on ever finding a vocation that would stir his passion when his father's sudden heart attack forced him to step in and run the family business. Art flourished under the hard work required for the successful management of a bar. It gave him purpose, and for the first time in years, he was happy.

He had a natural aptitude for making people feel comfortable, and locals and tourists alike frequented the tavern regularly. Whether it was the food, the drinks, or the friendly service, everyone viewed Arthur's Corner Bar as the place to be.

Word of the bar's popularity slowly found its way to St. Paul, some 250 miles away, where Lloyd Masterson received the news with great interest. His experience had taught him that people from small Midwest towns were excellent recruits for his business, and he was always on the lookout for new ones. So when an associate invited him to join a small group of bikers heading to Vergas for a week of fishing and drinking, Lloyd accepted.

Heavy rain and summer traffic made the ride from St. Paul to Vergas a grueling trip. Even with the soggy beginning, the five men reached their destination, eager to let loose and enjoy the week's retreat.

The Lake's area had experienced more rain than usual that week, and by the time Friday rolled around, cabin fever had set in with a vengeance. Arthur's Bar was filled with people in search of good company and honest fun.

Masterson ignored the heads that rotated his way when he and his biker friends strolled into the establishment. The scowl of the bartender, on the other hand, rubbed him the wrong way as he led his party to the lone available table. He ordered a round of hot coffee for himself and his friends. Tonight, they would be on their best behavior.

Those who traveled in Lloyd's company abided by a strict code of conduct, and Masterson bought their loyalty by opening his wallet wide. Although his source of income was a mystery to most, he allegedly had plenty of money, and he took obvious pleasure in sharing it with others. The result was an entourage of out-stretched hands. Lloyd seldom declined any request for money. The goal was control. In his mind, he owned any recipient of his generosity, and Lloyd thrived on possessions, especially ones he could manipulate to his satisfaction.

One objective had motivated Masterson's trip to Vergas: he intended to con the locals out of their hard-earned money one way or another. His first evening there was a decisive success. He won a few dollars at pool, introduced himself to Art Mason, and gener-ated several new acquaintances for future business expansion. At eleven o'clock, he gathered his cohorts and headed to the Sweet

Pines Resort located on the west shore of Rose Lake, where he had reserved three cabins for the week.

They woke the next morning to a day that promised to be sunny and warm. Lloyd recommended that they try their luck at fishing. Several hours on the lake in a rented boat yielded a fine catch. They presented the cleaned fish to the owners of the resort. This gesture won them praise and an invite to a fish fry that night. With the rest of the day free, Lloyd took his entourage back to Arthur's Bar. No one objected to his lead.

Masterson entered the bar and immediately noticed the shapely brunette conversing with Art Mason. Lloyd nodded to Art on his way to the same table his associates had occupied the previous night. He ordered a pitcher of beer and then excused himself, sauntering up to the bar and greeting Art as if they were old friends. Masterson ignored the owner's blatant snub. Known to hold a grudge, he would deal with the barkeeper at a time and place of his choosing. Right now, he fixated on the striking woman who taunted him brazenly.

At almost his height, and a tad overweight by his standards, she was nothing like most of the women he spent time with. He started at her feet and moved upward. Finding such an exotic specimen in Vergas, Minnesota was like spying a ten-point buck on one of his hunting excursions. At this close distance, her scent drove him to distraction.

She exuded sensuality, matching his bravado and giving him an equal once-over before offering him her hand. "Sylvia. I haven't had the pleasure."

Her intense eye contact and firm handshake furthered Lloyd's intrigue. She seemed to savor the effect she had on him. He couldn't recall ever meeting another woman who so personified the true meaning of moxie. Strong, beautiful women were his nemesis. His experience told him he should run as fast and as far away from Sylvia as possible—but it was already too late.

Apparently not enjoying the heat emanating between the two, Art Mason excused himself and walked away.

Sylvia flirted with Lloyd for a few more minutes before taking her leave. "I have a prior engagement."

"Whoever he is, he had better give you the respect you deserve."

"I seldom meet a man who doesn't appreciate my merits," she mocked.

"I'm sure that's true."

Her supple mouth puckered to form a slight pout before spreading into an eye-catching grin. She spun around and ambled away, leaving him hungry for more.

Lloyd rejoined his friends. They ate lunch, and after a few games of pool, he decided to explore the area for business opportunities. Lloyd picked up the bill with the foresight that no one would chip in.

They exited the bar single file. A real estate office on the opposite side of the street caught Masterson's eye. "You boys go on ahead of me. I'll catch up with you tonight at the fish fry." He spent the next few hours viewing properties for sale in the area.

The rest of the week passed with little fanfare. Lloyd accomplished what he had intended to do. He spent several hours a day at Arthur's getting acquainted with the local people, assessing their position and mindset and tallying up who might be viable patsies for his new business deal.

He elected to spend more time in the area for a variety of reasons, one of which was a certain buxom brunette. Another was his business ventures. To that end, he bought a small acreage ten miles north of town. The place would require work, but overall, it was in decent condition. Situated deep in the woods, it met the requirements of his nefarious activities.

It was time for him to go home and tend to business in St. Paul. Masterson hadn't seen Sylvia since their first meeting, but he decided to swing by Arthur's bar for one last hoorah on the off chance that he might run into her. Lloyd parked his motorcycle perpendicular to the curb, next to the other bikes, and dismounted, placed his helmet on the seat, and stepped up onto the sidewalk.

She emerged from nowhere, her well-formed body swaying to the rhythm of unheard drums. He fell in step behind her, not missing a beat, her rocking hips propelling his imagination into overdrive. Lloyd lagged a few feet behind her to afford himself a gratifying view of her hips as she sashayed up the walkway and into the tavern—but too late, he realized that she had stopped. He plowed into her backside, almost knocking her off her feet.

Masterson managed to paste a smile on his face by the time Sylvia spun around to address him. Charm became his modus operandi. He sat across from her in the bar, drinking and laughing like a love-struck teenager. Sparks flew, overshadowing his concern over the FBI's scrutiny of his business affairs.

CHAPTER THIRTY-NINE

Through the mirror hanging above the bar, Sylvia witnessed a flash of rage flicker across Lloyd's face as he bumped into her. Somewhere in the vast corners of her scattered brain, she grasped that the episode opened a crucial window into the man's moral fiber.

Nevertheless, she let the incident slide. After a fast-moving, tumultuous romance, they found themselves in front of the Justice of the Peace, reciting their wedding vows.

Their first collaboration was remodeling her cottage. During this phase, Lloyd reveled in the strength Sylvia brandished. Sylvia, inversely, acquiesced to his authority in small yet telling ways. It all went south when their façades crumbled, exposing their true natures.

Sylvia soon tired of his indiscriminate tirades. She refused to let anyone bully her, least of all her new husband. Her response was to pack her bags and retreat to Des Moines, where she kept house at a condominium she had owned for years. Lloyd would usually regain his composure and show up on her doorstep with his tail between his legs, going to great extremes to woo her back. She repeatedly allowed herself to fall under his spell, and, confident that they would work things out, she hid their discord from family and friends.

His actions could be disturbing, even sinister at times. In the face of everything, Sylvia convinced herself that she had command of the situation. She had faith that he would make good on his promises to change. Together, they shuffled through the first two years of marriage, determined to make it work.

Her attitude changed during their third year as man and wife.

Lloyd feigned business and began to withdraw for days, leaving Sylvia to herself. The tension between them only heightened with her growing suspicions. Her first impulse was to hire a private detective; but she soon decided that a preliminary solo investigation remained the better choice. She counseled herself to be vigilant. His revenge would be a bitter pill to swallow if he ever learned of her deceit.

Sylvia bided her time until one morning when Lloyd announced that he had business to attend to and would be gone most of the day. She raced to his home office the minute he drove away and rummaged through every drawer and scoured every shelf. She flipped through books and files, always mindful to put everything back in its rightful place. Sylvia stayed alert for the slightest sound forewarning her husband's reappearance, constantly glancing over her shoulder.

The first notable thing she encountered was a receipt for a safety deposit box at the local bank. This sent her back to his desk, where a second search unearthed an envelope taped to the back of one of the drawers. Her face lit up as she extracted a small key. Finally: something that might prove useful.

She uncovered one additional item of interest: a black steel box about the size of a small suitcase. It was tucked behind several cardboard boxes on the top shelf of the closet. The weight was more than she could handle. It slipped from her grip and fell to the floor. She wondered if she would be able to get it back up on the shelf. She shrugged and resumed her mission, heaving the box onto a nearby chair.

The small keypad on the lid offered another impasse. Pacing the room, she wracked her brain for every combination her husband might use to secure the lock. She punched in his birthdate, her birthdate, and various other numbers. It was useless. The lock would not budge. She frowned. Now came the task of putting the box back in its original hiding place. Grunting and groaning, she labored. Finally, Sylvia collapsed in the chair and let out a sigh of relief.

Her ears strained for anything that might confirm danger. The coast appeared to be clear. She pushed herself to her feet and scanned the room one last time to make sure everything was back in its original place before shutting off the lights and pulling the door closed behind her.

She retreated to the bathroom to wash away her misgivings under the hot spray of the showerhead. Feeling no better, she toweled off, slipped into her thick, expensive terrycloth robe, and went to the kitchen to make herself a sandwich. She tossed it in the garbage after the first bite and settled into the comfy leather chair in the family room. TV was the only available distraction that might ebb the sense of anxiety building inside her. Still, it didn't work.

Sylvia moved to her bedroom and crawled into bed, ready to escape into the peaceful bliss of sleep. She tossed for an hour before finally dozing off. Lloyd woke her when he crawled in next to her. She rolled away from him and feigned sleep until she heard him snoring. Wide awake, Sylvia began plotting her next move.

When morning arrived, she announced that she was going shopping. Sylvia drove to the bank instead. The task of sweet-talking the teller into letting her have access to the safety deposit box was easier than she had anticipated. Feeling smug, she entered the vaulted chamber and placed her key into the little door. She waited for the teller to remove the selected box, carry it into a connecting room, and place it on top of a small table. The teller left, and Sylvia lowered herself into one of the two available chairs.

Her fingers tiptoed around the rim of the box. If damning evidence existed within, her life would never be the same. She slowly opened the box.

A gasp reverberated through the small room.

Sylvia counted $40,000 in cash. Among other papers were several bank statements reflecting large balances, plus two real estate deeds. The address shown on one of the documents disturbed her more than the money. Why hadn't her husband told her he owned property in Otter Tail County?

Sylvia's motivation shifted into high gear. She seized her cellphone and snapped pictures of the stacks of money and all the documents before placing everything back in the box and closing it.

The click of the door behind her seemed to confirm her suspicions: Lloyd *had* followed her. How else would he know where to find her? A dark shadow crossed the table in front of her. Her mind raced to come up with a plausible excuse for her duplicity. She pushed back her chair and prepared to stand. A strong hand on her shoulder settled her back into her seat.

"Please don't get up," Chris Foley said as he walked around the corner of the table. "I didn't mean to frighten you. It's just that when my teller told me you were here, I did a quick check of the documents and realized we made a mistake. I am sorry, Mrs.

Masterson. My clerk should not have allowed you access to that box."

"Please, call me Sylvia," she said with all the sensuality she could muster. "To be honest, Mr. Foley, I haven't opened the box yet. I know this sounds silly. I was reminiscing about the past." She swallowed hard. "Did you say I don't have access to this box? Don't I have marital rights?"

"No. For you to gain legal access, Mr. Masterson will have to add your name to the documents."

"I'm confused. He told me he was putting my name on everything. He must have overlooked the safety deposit box. You see, I planned to put my diamonds in there." She smiled up at him. "I guess I can come back after the proper paperwork is signed. Please forgive me. I didn't mean to cause you any undue problems."

"Don't worry about that, Mrs. Masterson."

"Again, please call me Sylvia."

"Sylvia, I think that since you didn't open the box, there's no need to mention this to anyone. Have your husband come in at his earliest convenience, and we can get this all worked out."

Sylvia rose. "Thank you for your discretion." She walked out of the bank on shaky legs, nodding to the teller as she left.

Driving back to the cottage, she berated herself for taking such a bold chance. Lloyd conducted a lot of business in town. What if someone saw her and reported her activities to him? Indecision clouded her judgment. Was it safe to go home? Maybe she should keep driving until she reached Des Moines. What then? She couldn't hide from him forever. Sylvia instinctively felt for the safety deposit key in her pants pocket. Her betrayal would have consequences she didn't want to face. She had to get that key back to its original hiding place one way or another.

The sight of Lloyd's car in the driveway curbed her courage. She sat in her car, inside the garage, and reconsidered every possible scenario. No matter how many times she painted the picture, returning the key to its hiding place was the prudent strategy. She got out of the car and went inside the house. To Sylvia's frustration, her husband had locked himself in his office. She leaned into the door. The sound of his flat, cold voice warned her of the dangers ahead if she kept on her current path. Time to revise her strategy.

Sylvia spent the next few days mentally poring over her options, keeping a low profile and avoiding Lloyd whenever possible. During that same time, her husband seldom ventured from his self-imposed confinement to his office. When he did, it was to use the bathroom, grab a beer or a sandwich, or fall into their bed late at night to catch a few hours of sleep. One rare evening, he showed up at the dinner table. She took a stab at small talk, but he wanted none of it. He ate what she served, mumbled what she took to be a thank you, got up, and went back to work. The harsh click of the lock on the office door announced the extension of her nightmare.

She revisited the plan to flee to Des Moines but again vetoed the idea. The key had to be replaced before her husband noticed it was missing.

Each night, Lloyd crawled into their bed hours after she had retired. Sylvia thought about sneaking into his office while he slept, but knowing he was a light sleeper, she thought better of it. Each morning, he'd slip from the bedroom without a word. Sometimes, she could hear him pacing in his office. Other times, a low drone drifted through the door. She had leaned closer on those occasions, listening for bits of a one-sided conversation. Sadly, nothing of importance revealed itself.

She finally woke one morning to find him nowhere in the house. His car was also gone. Sylvia stalled outside his office door, her heart pounding. Lloyd hadn't mentioned any planned trips. Then again, he wasn't in the habit of telling her much of anything lately. He had been locked in his office for days, barely speaking to her. Was it possible she had caught a break and he'd be out all day? Or had he simply gone on an errand and would return to catch her in a treacherous act?

Ordinarily a woman of impulse, Sylvia hated the fact that she had allowed her husband to reduce her to quivering jelly. "You've delayed this far too long," she chastened. "It's time to get this over with." She retrieved the key from her purse and placed it in an envelope. Marching into his office, she pulled open the drawer and taped it in the exact location where she had found it.

A sense of relief put her on cloud nine until the dull thud of a car door brought her crashing back to reality. She hastily pushed the drawer shut. It stopped halfway. Bending to look inside, she spied the problem. Sylvia hurriedly reached in with her left hand to remove the pile of papers bunched up in the far corner, her ears straining for the sound of footsteps in the hallway. She zeroed in on the office door, assuming the worst, and slammed the drawer closed with her free hand amidst the panic. She bit hard on her lower lip as waves of pain rippled through her. Tears filled her eyes. Easing the drawer open, she withdrew the injured fist, exposing deep gashes notched across three of her fingers.

She barely had time to retreat to the bathroom before she heard the back door fly open. Easing the bathroom door shut, Sylvia took a clean towel from the linen closet and carefully wrapped it around her bloodied appendages. She leaned against the shower door and slid to a sitting position on the floor. The room began to spin, making it impossible for her to think straight. It wasn't until she heard the back door open and close again that she realized she was holding her breath. Even then, she dared not move. Sylvia remained seated on the floor long after the sound of her husband's car tires receded down the gravel road.

At length, she pulled the towel away and flinched at the sight of the wounds. The cuts were more severe than she had thought.

Eight stitches later, Sylvia drove back home to find Lloyd still gone.

"This is insane." Her furor bounced off the walls. "I am not spending another minute living in fear of that man. I'm taking back my life."

Time for Plan B.

CHAPTER FORTY

Sylvia awoke in the morning, grateful to discover herself alone in the bed. She listened intently for telltale sounds—maybe the clink of a coffee mug or his muffled voice as he sat in his office talking on the phone. Nothing, except for the methodical tick-tock of the grandfather clock that stood solemnly in the hallway.

Sylvia buried her head under her pillow. Did she have the courage to confront her husband and demand that he tell her the truth? Would he give her an honest answer?

"Of course not!" she said, throwing the pillow across the room. Why did she persist in playing this game? All these idle thoughts were a waste of time. She showered, dressed, and breakfasted on a piece of toast.

Sylvia exited I-29 in Fargo, North Dakota and had no trouble finding the offices of the FBI. She strolled into the building projecting confidence, a valuable smokescreen she had developed through the years.

The minute Sylvia explained why she was there, Agent Hunter ushered her into a private office. A young woman appeared and introduced herself as Agent Margaret Peterson, Hunter's partner.

Sylvia had the full attention of both agents as she related her concerns regarding her husband.

"We have a file on Masterson that goes back six years," Agent Hunter asserted. "Every time we think we have enough evidence to nab him, he manages to evade our nets."

"He has an extensive underground network," Peterson said. "He always knows when we're closing in on him. More than once, he's pulled back his operation, only to start up again under a pseudonym in a different location. He's like a modern-day Houdini."

The agents listed a litany of offenses perpetrated by her husband, drug and money laundering being only two of the tougher crimes. Sylvia took it all in under the guise of calm acceptance until Peterson informed her that Masterson had now expanded his exploits to human trafficking.

Sylvia sat forward. "What are you talking about?"

"A young girl from Wadena went missing six weeks ago."

"I don't know anything about a missing girl."

Hunter took a commanding lead. "We have witnesses that put your husband in the neighborhood where the girl was last seen. You probably read about her in the newspapers. She was walking home from a friend's house, a block from where she lived. She never made it."

Sylvia crossed her arms in front of her chest. "Even if he was in the same vicinity when the girl disappeared, how does that tie him to the crime?"

"That in itself, of course, proves nothing—I agree. We brought Masterson in for questioning, and unfortunately, he supplied us with an airtight alibi."

"When did you talk to Lloyd?"

Hunter leaned back in his chair. "You mean he didn't tell you that we interviewed him?"

"No. No, he didn't," Sylvia admitted. "May I remind you that I'm the one who came to you?"

Agent Hunter ignored her retort. "Our sources tell us that Lloyd Masterson plays a prominent role in the management of the organization."

"You must be mistaken, I know my husband is not the most upstanding citizen, but your allegations can't be true."

"I wouldn't be sharing any of this with you if we didn't have a strong case against the man."

"You said he had an airtight alibi." Sylvia got to her feet. "Call me when you have proof."

Peterson interjected, "We know this is hard, but you have to keep your eye on the prize. You wouldn't be here if you didn't have major doubts about your husband."

Sylvia warily lowered herself back into the chair.

Agent Peterson continued, "We've given you a lot of information to digest. We suggest you go home and think things over. You've been living with this man for three years. Compare what you know about him with what we've told you."

The space between Agent Hunter's bushy brows narrowed. "We want you to understand that you have legal rights here. At this moment, we consider you an innocent bystander. But, let me be clear: if you assist Masterson in any way, we will prosecute you to the fullest extent of the law." He pushed his chair back with a loud thud and stood to leave. Halfway across the room, he whipped around and bore into her. "This is not a game. A young girl's life is at stake. Now that you know the facts, you are either part of the solution or part of the problem. You can't plead the fifth anymore. It's imperative that you understand the depth of your situation." With that, he walked out of the room.

The agents probably understood that their tough approach might easily backfire. Sylvia's anger about her husband's betrayal could spur her to look for ways to build a case against him, but it could also provoke her to call him out. Either way, no one could predict the outcome.

Peterson gave Sylvia a minute to think things through. "I'm sure you recognize that it is in your best interest to work with us."

Sylvia sighed, "I don't see what I can do."

"You can be our eyes and ears. Who better than you to keep us abreast of your husband's comings and goings?" Peterson outlined a detailed list of instructions for Sylvia should she choose to cooperate. When Sylvia agreed to the terms, Agent Peterson rose from her chair, indicating that the meeting was over.

"Thank you for your time." When they shook hands, the agent nodded at Sylvia's bandaged hand. "I've been meaning to ask you. What happened?"

Sylvia shrugged, "Oh, this. I slammed it in the car door yesterday."

"Hmmm. Sounds painful."

"I'll be fine."

"Yes. I suspect you will be." Peterson smiled. "I'll get someone to show you out."

CHAPTER FORTY-ONE

Sylvia exited the building with her head held high, despite her misgivings. She had dredged up more information about her husband's furtive activities than she cared to know. She also understood that the agents had not revealed everything regarding her husband's profile. But they weren't the only ones withholding information. Sylvia, too, had shied from telling the whole truth.

Her bravado weakened with each step she took. By the time she got to the car, her body bent under the strain of the emotional ride that had taken her to a very dark place. Her head felt like someone had beat her senseless. The inflamed flesh on her injured hand pushed against the bandage that was now much too tight for comfort. She rifled through her purse for two Tylenols and swallowed them dry, her throat gagging from the intrusion.

Sylvia leaned back against the headrest and sighed heavily. Agent Hunter's final words weighed profoundly on her mind. She hadn't let on at the time, but what he had said about the legal ramifications of her actions scared her. Maybe she should contact an attorney. *Why? I haven't done anything illegal.* Nor did she have any intention of crossing that line.

She took a backward glance at the federal building, started the car, and pulled away from the curb. During the drive home, a range of feelings further eroded her self-confidence. Three short years ago, her life had been perfect. She'd had friends and family, people she could depend on. Now, she had no one.

Her spirits lifted when she arrived home and learned that Lloyd was still absent. Ready to take a stand, Sylvia contacted the FBI to let them know that she was on board. Lloyd Masterson belonged in prison. That settled, she picked up the phone and called her niece.

Sylvia berated herself with the thought that she had allowed Lloyd to become the focal point of her life. Lucy was the apple of her eye—her only living relative. They had been through so much together. Sylvia had been the moving force that had removed Lucy's abusive father from the family. When Lucy's mother died, Sylvia had stepped in and helped her through her teen years into adulthood.

Delighted that their relationship was back on track, they chatted for a considerable length of time. Not one to share her problems with anyone, Sylvia kept a tight lid on the details of her own affairs as she soaked in renewed energy from Lucy's summary of events. Prior to ending the call, they agreed to a lunch date that weekend.

Sylvia stepped out onto the back deck and settled into the Adirondack chair. The expanse of blue water calmed her raw nerves. The skyline, streaked with vibrant shades of orange, joined her in bidding adieu to one of the worst days of her life. She prayed that the decisions she had made that day would not come back to bite her in the ass.

If Lloyd had really done the things the FBI accused him of, her loyalty to her husband was grossly misplaced. She had to stop making excuses for him. Sylvia couldn't claim to be any better than him if she did nothing to prevent him from carrying on with business as usual. She shifted her focus to the positive things in her life. She was a strong woman. She would get through this.

Her introspection ended when she caught sight of a bass boat heading in her direction. Something about the craft heightened her suspicions. Her apprehension worsened when it anchored twenty yards off the end of her dock and the men aboard tossed fishing lines into the water.

Sylvia rarely paid heed to boaters, but tonight, her vulnerability urged her to retreat inside. She wished now that she'd had the foresight to install curtains on the windows facing the lakeside.

Taking heart in the billowing clouds forming to the north, she went inside with the anticipation that the storm would move in fast, bringing a downpour that would send the anglers running for cover. The rain eventually rolled in. To her dismay, the men in the boat donned orange rain slickers and continued to sit anchored a short distance from her dock. The more she tried to ignore their existence, the more beleaguered she became. Had her husband sent them to spy on her?

The grandfather clock in the hall chimed nine, and yet the men showed no interest in abandoning their post. Sylvia turned tail. She extinguished all the interior lights and sought solace in the privacy of her bedroom. "If they're here come morning, I'll invite them in for breakfast!" she chuckled. "We'll see how that sits with them!"

In the middle of the night, she crept back through the house. The boat was gone. Relieved, she chided herself that paranoia did not befit a woman in her situation.

CHAPTER FORTY-TWO

The FBI's warnings rang loud and clear in Sylvia's head. Under no circumstances was she to do anything that would tip Lloyd off. She had been told not to follow him or interrogate him in any way. Her assigned task was simple: eavesdrop on his phone conversations whenever possible and report all irregular activities.

What did the agents expect from her? Sylvia had tried for months to discover what he was up to, to no avail. His dark moods and secretive activities made life with him unbearable. She couldn't even remember the last time they had been intimate. *That's it!* Her face lit up. *Why didn't I think of that before now?* If she could draw him into their bed and remind him of the good times they had shared, he might let his guard down, perhaps unwittingly mention a name or drop a clue that would land him in prison.

The FBI had explicitly cautioned Sylvia not to contact them from inside the house. They would exchange information at prearranged meetings. If she had to communicate with them at any other time, she had an emergency number where she could leave a pre-coded message.

Lack of sleep and the stress of another day passing with no word from Lloyd had Sylvia climbing the walls. The day dragged on.

The ring tone finally summoned her a little after 5:00 p.m. Her nerves wound tighter with each subsequent ring: two, three, four, five. She snatched up the phone.

His voice sounded almost giddy: "I have very good news."

Sylvia pressed Lloyd, but he cut the conversation short. "I have a few details to firm up. I'll explain everything when I see you. Meet me at Arthur's at seven," he urged. "And don't be late."

Sylvia arrived early. She took a seat at their favorite booth and ordered a glass of wine, then ordered a second drink before she finished the first. The alcohol swirled through her veins, working its wizardry, until Lloyd sauntered through the door and killed her buzz. He edged his way to the bar and ordered an expensive bottle of chardonnay on his way over to her. Sliding into the opposite booth, he peered at the two empty goblets on the table. "I see you've gotten a head start on me."

Sylvia had to keep reminding herself to breathe. Her third glass of wine did little to ease her uneasiness. They ordered dinner, but Sylvia barely touched it in fear of what was to come. She had betrayed him, and in her mind, he was there to settle the score. He appeared to draw things out to make her suffer.

The server removed the dishes and delivered another bottle of wine to the table. When they were alone again, Lloyd held up his glass and tapped it against hers. "Here's to my beautiful wife." He sat forward. "You never cease to amaze me."

Sylvia drank what was left in her glass and waited for the hammer to fall. It never came. Instead, Lloyd surprised her.

"I know I've told you this multiple times, Sylvia. This time, I mean it. I'm going to change."

Had she heard him correctly? He was not there to exact revenge, but to apologize for his past deeds. She brought her hands to the table, lacing her fingers together and inhaling slowly. Back in the driver's seat, she challenged him: "Why should I believe you this time?"

"I've decided to retire." His pearly-white teeth beamed at her. "My business takes up too much of my time. You, my girl, deserve better. It will be my life's goal to become the husband of your dreams."

She recalled the stack of cash in his safety deposit box. "You tend to be a big spender. Wouldn't retirement crimp your lifestyle?"

"Don't trouble yourself about money. That's my job."

"You told me you're an investment broker, but you've never explained exactly what you do." She tilted her head slightly. "How *do* you make your money?"

The lines at the corner of his eyes tightened ever so slightly. "You've never cared where my money comes from. Why are you inquiring now?"

"I'm inquisitive. You're a mysterious man." A demure pout curled her lip. "Normally, a wife knows these things about her husband. We've been married for over three years. Why don't you want me to know what you do?"

His expression narrowed as if to warn her she was going down the wrong path. Sylvia shifted uncomfortably in her seat and changed the course of the conversation. "I didn't know you arranged to be home this weekend. I planned to visit Lucy in Des Moines. I can reschedule if you want me to."

"Do you mind? I've been a huge ass, and I want to make it up to you. What do you say? Can we give it another try?"

Sylvia could spot a con a mile away. Like a cat, though, she let curiosity get the better of her.

Lloyd said, "I have to stop by the auto repair shop here in town and talk to the owner. I was in a minor accident yesterday, and my car is being repaired." He handed her his credit card. "Do you mind doing a little shopping while I check on it?"

Her hand instinctively reached for the card, and they exited the bar arm in arm. He escorted her to the gift shop next door and gave her a peck on the cheek. She lingered on the sidewalk until he retreated around the corner. Inside the shop, a fabulous Waterford crystal decanter beckoned from the display shelf. Sylvia bought two: one for herself and one for Lucy. A peace offering. After completing the paperwork for delivery, she opted to visit a few more stores on the street.

An hour passed, and Lloyd had not returned. Hesitant, Sylvia headed out to find him. She approached the body shop and entered through the front door. The lobby was empty. "Is anyone here?" No one responded. Distant voices filtered through a closed door at the back of the room, drawing Sylvia in that direction.

The door swung open. A tall, well-dressed woman exited and pushed past her. The woman glanced back and called out, "I think someone's here to see you, Lloyd." A trace of perfume wafted in her wake.

"How long have you been here?" Lloyd's voice was low and steady.

"I just walked in. The gift shop closed, so I came to get you." Sylvia gave him a stony glare. "Who was that woman?"

"It's late." He put his arm around Sylvia's shoulder and guided her out of the shop. "Why don't you give me a ride home, and I'll remind you why you married me."

Sylvia chose not to press the issue. Bigger things were in the making. She would cede to him now with the prospect of luring him into her web. When that day came, she vowed to take no prisoners.

CHAPTER FORTY-THREE

L loyd had every intention of starting anew with Sylvia. What he had neglected to tell her was that he had spent the last month tying up loose ends to ensure that no one could find them once they left the country. He had piled up enough cash to reap the benefits of a lifestyle that few achieved. Basking in the sun on a Greek island with his beautiful wife by his side was the happy ending he sought. It shouldn't be hard to convince Sylvia to ride off into the sunset with him.

The FBI had backed him into a corner. It wouldn't take much time for them to connect the dots and tie him to the missing girls. By his estimation, he had a few months left to make the final arrangements. That was plenty of time to bring Sylvia around to his way of thinking.

CHAPTER FORTY-FOUR

Lloyd made good on his promise with a concerted effort to win back Sylvia's favor. He wined and dined her, bought her expensive gifts, even took her on a couple of weekend getaways: one to Minneapolis and one to Chicago. She loved spending his money, and he had no qualms about giving her everything she asked for.

The FBI's warnings faded with each passing day. Sylvia lived in her own little world, oblivious to outside influences. She wanted what she wanted and would do anything to attain her goals.

The axe fell several months after they had renewed their vows. She picked up the phone on a warm October afternoon to hear Agent Hunter's stern voice: "Something important has come up. We need you to come to our office tomorrow."

Sylvia stalled. "I can't."

Hunter did not give her time to expound. "Don't give me any excuses. Be here by 10 a.m. tomorrow."

"You can't order me around."

"Don't test me. Be here by ten, or I'll show you exactly what I can do." The phone went dead.

Agent Peterson greeted Sylvia upon her arrival and ushered her into the same private office where they had convened during her previous visit. Hunter sat at the table, his visible contempt carved across his icy face.

No one engaged in small talk. Peterson hit the power button on the computer. With a few strokes on the keyboard, the overhead screen displayed a young girl. Hunter shoved a Missing Person's Report form in front of Sylvia.

"Can you account for Lloyd's whereabouts in the last forty-eight hours?"

Sylvia wilted in her chair. "Lloyd's been camping with his biker friends at White Bear Lake, north of St. Paul. He left four days ago. I haven't seen him since."

"I'm here to tell you that he was nowhere near White Bear Lake. We've had a tail on him. Four days ago, we lost him on Highway 34 heading for Park Rapids." Hunter tapped the report and said, "Park Rapids is where the girl went missing. Lloyd apparently suspected our tail, because he sped around the lowered guard arm at a railroad crossing. He barely got over the tracks before the train barreled through the intersection. My agent got stuck on the wrong side. When the train passed, Lloyd was long gone."

"Sylvia, if you know where Masterson is, it's essential that you tell us," Peterson demanded.

Facing the agents, Sylvia sagged further into her chair. Lloyd's ruthless undertakings were out there for the whole world to see. Anger seethed from within. How could she have fallen for him not once, but twice? He had played her for a fool. Well, she would beat him at his own game. He would rue the day he had crossed her.

Her hands fidgeted nervously in her lap. "I honestly don't know where Lloyd is. What I can tell you is that he is very smart. If he is who you say he is, and if he's done the things you say he's done, he's been able to conceal everything from me." Her guttural laugh filled the room. "I originally looked into his business dealings because I thought he was having an affair. Imagine that." She shook her head, more at her own shortcomings than for the evil actions of her husband. "What can I do?"

"All we need from you is for you to stay alert in case he slips up. We know he's planning something big. Exactly what, we're not sure."

Peterson leaned forward. "I don't think we have to remind you that you are living with a very dangerous man. No one would blame you if you changed your mind about helping us. It would be safer if you leave him." When Sylvia didn't answer, the agent countered, "We can put you in the witness protection program until this is over."

"No." Sylvia held Peterson's gaze. "I am going to see this through." A smart woman would walk away from the madness. Revenge, however, spoke to Sylvia's inner soul. "I'll do whatever it takes!"

Lloyd's fatal boating accident occurred six weeks later.

CHAPTER FORTY-FIVE

Present time

For the second time in a week, Lucy awoke to someone pounding at the door. Cobwebs clogged her head as she rolled onto her side and glanced at the clock on the nightstand. The haze lifted as the memory of RJ's sensual mouth against her own sent waves of heat through her body. She looked at the clock again. RJ had left only a few hours earlier. Maybe he had forgotten something. She hoped it wasn't anything more serious than that.

She slid out of bed, aware that she had on the same clothes she had worn the prior day. She must look a fright, but what did he expect when he kept her out until all hours of the night and then came knocking at her door early the next morning?

The memory that RJ had an early meeting at the office had her wondering if someone else was at the door. Through the windowpane, she spied the outline of a man's backside. She eased the door open. Malcolm Bremer, the man who'd shown up at her door the other night demanding that she tell him where Sylvia was, stood before her with a timid smile etched across his face.

"What are you doing here?" She couldn't hide the wariness in her voice.

"I came to apologize for my behavior the other night. I don't know what came over me. I promise I'm not here to cause you harm. I just have a few more questions." He inhaled. "Please, give me a chance to redeem myself. I swear, I am not a bad person."

Bremer wasn't a deviant. On the contrary, the circumstances surrounding his request tugged at her conscience. She didn't have the heart to reject him.

He pleaded, "I know it's early, but I assure you that I won't take much of your time."

"I don't know what I can tell you that you don't already know. Besides, it's very early, and as you might have guessed, you woke me." She fluffed her hair with her fingers.

He persisted, "Could I talk you into having breakfast with me at the cafe in town, say, in an hour? It's a public place. That way you know I won't do anything out of line."

How could she say no to this man? His daughter was missing, and her aunt's potential participation in the girl's disappearance deemed it a moral obligation that she do everything she could to facilitate his search. "Yes, of course," she said.

"This is very kind of you. I can't tell you how much it means to me." He glanced at his watch. "I'll meet you at the cafe at 7:15." With that settled, Malcolm walked back to his car.

Lucy took a quick shower and arrived at her destination well ahead of the agreed time. Mr. Bremer hadn't arrived by the time the server delivered the meal that she'd ordered. His absence certainly did not earn him points. Lucy ate alone, dividing her attention between the watch on her wrist and the door of the cafe.

He was still a no-show by the time she finished her food. The man obviously had no respect for her time. She paid the bill and drove back to the cottage.

Lucy had no reason to believe that anything was amiss until she pulled into the driveway and noticed that the side door to the garage was open. Her heart sank when she saw that the door to the house stood agape. She hastily released her seatbelt and ran up the walkway.

The utter destruction she witnessed when she pushed open the door sent shock waves spiraling through her body. Empty drawers lay askew, their entire contents strewn chaotically. Items pulled from the closets speckled the floors. Furniture sat awry. Area rugs were pulled back. Aghast, Lucy finally understood that Malcolm Bremer had never intended to meet her at the diner. He had tricked her into leaving the house so that he could ransack it. She wondered if he had found what he was looking for.

Although overwhelmed by the chaos, Lucy knew she should call the police, or at least contact RJ. Her compulsion to compartmentalize, however, trumped her need for help. Every component of her life was out of sync. If she didn't organize her living space, the chance of recovering from such a massive intrusion was questionable.

On autopilot, she went to work. She flipped the loveseat back onto its legs and shoved it in place. She picked up a drawer lying on the floor and repositioned it against the wall. Most of the dishes lay in pieces on the floor. Lucy got the broom and dustpan from the pantry and swept up the fragments of glass.

She worked uninterrupted for the rest of the morning until, depleted of energy, she stopped to assess her progress. At this rate, she would be at it all day. Slowly, she sank onto the sofa, tears threatening to overpower her.

Lucy panicked when she heard the back door opening. She

jumped up, expecting to see Bremer returning to the scene of the crime. Instead, she ran smack into RJ as he entered the room.

"I knocked, but I guess you didn't hear me. The door was open—" RJ stopped. "What in the world happened here?"

Lucy didn't know whether to fold herself into his arms for comfort or admonish him because she had to blame someone other than herself. Anger got the better of her. "Don't you dare yell at me. You said you would check out Malcolm Bremer and report back to me. Well, don't bother. He destroyed this place." Her arms flailed to encompass the room.

"What do you mean? How do you know he did this?"

Lucy explained what had transpired earlier. "If you had done your job, I wouldn't have agreed to meet him."

RJ snapped his head back. "Lucy, I'm so sorry. Did he tell you what he wanted?"

"No!" She sighed in disgust. "It must have been something significant for him to rip this place apart like he did. I've been working for hours and haven't made a dent in the mess."

"Let me make some calls. I'll get someone in here to assist you. In the meantime, keep an eye out for anything that might explain what he was after. It could be a notebook, even a piece of paper, or maybe a weapon. It could be anything. If you notice anything out of the ordinary, no matter how small, let me know. Did he go through the garage, too?"

She hadn't even considered the garage. Lucy moved through the hall and outside with RJ close on her heels. RJ protectively stretched his arm to stop her from opening the door further. He drew his gun and slowly pushed it inward. He flipped on the light. The garage had gone untouched. Either Bremer had stumbled upon what he was looking for, or he had run out of time and had to leave before he could search the area. If the latter was the case, he would likely be back.

RJ secured the garage and then escorted Lucy back into the house. He walked out onto the deck, punching numbers into his cellphone as he went. Lucy got back to work. This time, she approached the task more methodically. If RJ was correct, and Malcolm Bremer had missed something, she would find it.

RJ made good on his promise. A police officer and a cleaning crew arrived within fifteen minutes of each other. The house cleaners went about their job. At the same time, RJ, Lucy, and the additional officer searched every nook and cranny. By the end of the day, the cottage was back in order. Thus far, they had nothing to indicate the intruder's objective.

RJ lingered after the others had left. Lucy wished he could stay the night for a myriad of reasons, but her better judgment prevailed. She had to get a good night's rest, and that would never happen if RJ was in close proximity.

The telephone rang. Lucy and RJ just stared at the damn thing, but finally Lucy picked it up and cleared her throat before speaking into the receiver. "Hello."

"You sound terrible. What's wrong?"

She cringed at the sound of Jack's voice. "It's been a long day. Can we talk tomorrow?"

"I think you better hear what I have to tell you. It's about your detective friend."

"Okay. Please make it fast. I have a splitting headache."

Lucy twisted her back to RJ, seeking what little privacy she could. Jack's words still filtered through the earpiece. She faced RJ again. She couldn't begin to guess what was going on in his head.

Jack's belligerent oration persisted. When he finally finished, dead silence filled the airwaves between them.

Lucy pivoted away from RJ and spoke quietly. "I appreciate you calling me. I'll do some investigating on my own and call you in the morning." She disconnected and faced RJ head on.

RJ held his head high. "You have to trust me, Lucy. I'm one of the good guys."

Lucy prayed he was telling the truth, because as much as she wanted to deny it, her feelings for him were affecting her better judgement.

CHAPTER FORTY-SIX

RJ wanted to come clean with Lucy. Tell her straight up about his association with her aunt. Explain how Lloyd Masterson had drawn him into his web and played him for a fool. He wanted to confess all his shortcomings. Slow on the uptick, RJ elected to keep those thoughts to himself and see how things played out. With Lucy in his corner, he might be able to save his career and quite possibly come out of this a hero. He wanted to do the right thing for both of their sakes.

He glanced at his watch. "I have a thought. Why don't we run into town and get take-out from Arthur's? If I had to guess, I'd bet you haven't eaten much today."

"Now that you mention it, I am hungry."

He didn't give her time to reconsider. He pulled his keys from his pocket. "We can eat there if you'd like."

"No, I'm not in the mood for that. Let's get something and bring it back here."

Forty-five minutes later, they returned to the cabin. Lucy dug into her chicken salad while RJ chewed on his burger, his mind churning in overtime to come up with a stayover plan that Lucy would not reject.

"It's late. You need to get some rest. I can sleep on the couch if you're concerned about Bremer."

"No," she said. "That's not necessary."

"I don't think Bremer will come back, but if he does, I would never forgive myself if I left you alone to deal with him. I let you down before. I won't do it again."

"I'm a big girl. I can take care of myself."

He chuckled. "I have no doubts about that."

She cocked her head and grinned back at him. "I'm grateful for all you've done, but I don't think it's wise for you to spend the night." The determination in her eyes indicated that the matter was nonnegotiable.

"I guess I should get out of your hair, then, and let you get some sleep. I'll phone in a request to have a patrol posted outside for the night."

"Don't you dare. Mr. Bremer didn't mean me any harm. He was looking for anything that might lead him to his daughter. I understand that. You go home. We'll talk tomorrow." She walked him to the door. "Thank you again for everything."

He bowed at the waist. "All in a day's work, ma'am." RJ rocked on his heels. Unable to stop himself, he pulled her into his arms. After a long hug, he kissed the side of her face and whispered in her ear, "I assure you: everything will be fine. We'll figure this out."

RJ had no intention of leaving Lucy alone that night. Lucy was in this position through no fault of her own. He'd do everything necessary to keep her safe, including spending the night in his truck.

CHAPTER FORTY-SEVEN

Jack Rydell seized a nearby antique vase, a prized possession of his mother's, and flung it across the lavishly decorated living room. The resonating jingle of glass shattering against Italian marble only heightened the anger bubbling up from the pit of his stomach.

He had called Lucy with incriminating evidence on that bastard Rafferty with the sole intention of turning her against the detective. But the bitch hadn't believed a word he told her.

"The slut is sleeping with him." Jack's ugly growl echoed between the expansive walls. "What does he have that I don't? Nothing! That faggot has nothing over me."

Jack yearned to wrap his hands around his wife's scrawny neck and slowly squeeze them together until she begged for forgiveness. Grasping the phone in his left hand, he shook it as if the action itself would relay the rage she roused in him.

"Something wrong, dear?" His mother entered the room, ignoring the fragments of glass strewn across the tile.

Jack barked, "Where have you been? I left a message telling you I was coming over."

"I was busy upstairs." She went to the bar and fixed a drink for herself. "Can I get you one?"

"No."

"I'm glad you stopped by. We can have dinner together, and you can fill me in on what you've been up to lately."

Jack warily followed his mother into the kitchen and took a seat on one of the six barstools. He watched her effortlessly gather ingredients and prepare the meal.

His anger ebbed, and the conversation grew amiable through dinner. When they finished, Lesley said, "I'll put the dishes in the dishwasher. Go get the broom and dustpan from the pantry and sweep up the mess you made."

Jack bristled. The sultry tone in her voice suggested trouble to come. Upon completion of the task, he sat on the sofa. Deep in thought, he did not hear her approach from behind. He winced when her strong fingers pressed against his shoulders.

She leaned in and gave him a peck on the side of his face. "Sweetheart, what has you so upset?"

"I really don't want to talk about it."

She resumed the massage. "Your muscles are all in knots. Why don't you make us a drink, and we can talk?"

"I really must go. I've got some calls I have to make this evening."

"Oh, come on. Stay the night. Give your mother a little pleasure. We haven't spent much time together lately."

"I'll have one drink and then I'm going home." Relieved to escape her touch, he went to the bar. He returned to find her seated on the sofa. He handed her a glass, and she patted the cushion beside her. "Sit here." He declined and took the chair across from her.

Somewhere along the way, Jack had lost control. There was a day when his mother had doted on him and his every whim.

Lesley's current obsession with destroying his marriage and purging Lucy from their lives, however, made it almost impossible for them to occupy the same room. Every conversation evolved into a battle of wills. Jack saw no end to it.

Lesley finished her drink and stood. "Can I refresh yours?" Jack shook his head. She said from the bar, "I overheard you talking to Lucy earlier."

"I don't want to have this conversation with you." He got to his feet. It was time to leave.

His mother sauntered up to him. "Relax. I'm here for you."

"Are you kidding? You're doing everything in your power to ruin my life."

"The fact that you can't manage your wife has nothing to do with me."

Jack exploded, "It's all your fault! If you had stayed out of my personal life, I wouldn't be in this predicament!"

Lesley's lips folded back in a snarl. "That girl caused strife from the very start. I warned you not to marry her. Of course, you didn't listen to your adoring mother. Now you have to pay for your mistakes."

Jack took hold of her shoulders and shoved her until he had her backed against the wall. "You couldn't stand that I loved someone other than you. You're sick, you know that?" His spittle sprayed her face. "It's not right, what you did to me, your own son. How could you?"

"You mean everything to me," she screamed. "I devoted my entire life to you. And what do I have to show for it?" Lesley pushed her son aside. Pouring herself another gin and tonic, she drank it and refilled the glass once more. "Are you sure I can't fix you another one?"

"I think you drink enough for the both of us."

"Don't be such a sourpuss. Haven't I taught you that you get more bees with honey than with vinegar? None of this anger is helping to solve your woes. If you talk to me nicely—and I mean *nicely*—I will take care of all your problems."

"You disgust me!" Jack wrapped his hands around a Tiffany lamp that sat on a nearby end table and hurled it at her, missing her head by inches.

CHAPTER FORTY-EIGHT

When Malcolm Bremer's daughter Amber had disappeared three months earlier, Malcolm's life had spiraled into a tail-spinning abyss. One split second was all it took. Malcolm replayed that horrible night repeatedly, and each time, he grew more and more angry with himself and his inability to protect his beautiful little girl.

Prior to the incident, Amber's grades had slipped, causing substantial tension in the household. Malcolm and his wife, Delores, blamed it on her newfound friends Tabatha and Britney.

"It's not that we don't like the girls. They seem nice. But your grades have suffered since you started hanging out with them. You're spending way too much time on the phone and not enough time on your schoolwork."

"That's not true. I got all As except for one class. Why are you making such a big deal about one B?"

"This discussion is over. Your mom and I know what's best for you. You're grounded until you bring that B back up to an A." Malcolm went back to scanning the advertisement section of his newspaper.

Amber's adolescent face reddened with indignation. "Why are you doing this to me?"

Malcolm lowered the paper and eyed his daughter. "Don't raise your voice at me, young lady! You're a senior now. Your grades will play a vital role in determining which college you will attend."

"I don't think one B will keep me out of college."

"I'm tired of fighting with you. Go to your room right now, and don't come out until you've had time to think things through."

Amber stormed from the room, swearing she would hate her dad for the rest of her life.

By morning, she had cooled off. She apologized for her behavior and told her parents that she understood their concerns. Amber pledged that she would work harder to bring up her grades. "You know Nancy's birthday party is tonight. Can I go?"

Delores silently pleaded for her husband's consent.

Malcolm decided not to prolong a battle he wouldn't win. "All right—but you have to hit those books first thing tomorrow."

Amber let out a joyful yelp. She drew a cross in front of her chest with her index finger. "Cross my heart." She hugged her dad and flashed her mom a conspiratorial grin.

Amber spent hours primping for the party. As she headed out the door, her face aglow amid her soft red curls, she kissed her parents and thanked them for their love and support. She vowed she would be home by curfew and agreed to focus all her attention on her grades for the duration of the year. The special twinkle his daughter's eyes had held that night haunted Malcolm to this day.

When their daughter wasn't home by 11:15, Delores dialed her cell. She frowned when she got no answer. Malcolm trekked down the street to retrieve her. Nancy, the birthday girl, verified that Amber had left thirty minutes earlier. Several other teenagers confirmed that they had seen her leaving around 10:45.

To convince themselves that their fears were misguided, Malcom and Delores discussed how they would handle the situation when she returned home.

Anxiety grew as the minutes ticked by. Delores couldn't take it any longer. She grabbed the phone and called 911.

CHAPTER FORTY-NINE

There was no way Malcolm Bremer could have predicted the tragic event that befell his eldest child. He recognized that sometimes bad things happen to good people. Nevertheless, he blamed himself. A dad's primary responsibility is to keep his children safe. Malcolm had, in his own eyes, failed miserably.

Guilt consumed him in the days and months that ensued. He believed that he had a cosmic bond with his daughter. She had come from his loins. He should feel pain when she felt pain and perceive fear when she felt fear. It saddened him that he had sensed nothing of Amber's plight, neither before her disappearance or now.

As head of the family, Malcolm's obligation was to find Amber and bring her home. It became his sole mission. Delores pleaded with him to focus on his other two daughters. "Your love and attention are essential now more than ever."

Malcolm had a different mindset. "What they need to know is that their father would do anything and everything to bring *them* home if something were to happen to either of them." Malcolm was already late for an appointment with Timothy Walker, a private detective he had hired. He gave his wife a curt nod on the way out the door.

In the weeks following Amber's disappearance, Malcolm and Delores fought constantly. Malcolm lay awake at night listening to her quiet sobs. Her anguish, combined with his despair, opened a fissure between them that widened with each passing day.

Malcolm quit his job to spend every waking hour in search of Amber. He used a chunk of the family savings on the retainer charged by Walker and Associates. He consulted a professional medium who told him what he needed to hear: Amber was alive. That was all it took to fuel his resolve. Every clue received close examination. Leads took him to every corner of Minnesota, and on one occasion, he accompanied Detective Walker to Phoenix, Arizona.

Malcolm spent less and less time at home. Many nights, after a day of combing through police reports and chasing useless leads, he would curl up in the back seat of his car, too numb and weary to do anything except cry himself to sleep. Other times, when he had more energy, he'd find a secluded location and pitch the tent that he kept in his trunk. At least once a week, he checked into a cheap hotel to shower and sleep on a soft, clean bed.

Driving around one day scouting for a place to camp, he recalled an old, abandoned farmstead he had contemplated buying a few years back. The owners had informed him that the property was in a trust and that because of tax implications, they had no plans to sell. Malcolm drove by the place to see if it was still vacant. Tall weeds had command of the entire area, a plus in Malcolm's opinion.

Thankfully, Bremer had capable hands to take care of the necessary repairs. He stocked the cupboards with a few groceries and set to work. A little carpentry, a bit of plumbing, some elbow grease, and the house provided adequate shelter—better than a pitched tent and more comfortable than his car. Malcolm hated to think of himself as a squatter, but hard times deserved hard measures.

For the final touch, he added a few personal items, including a picture of his family: himself, Delores, Amber, and his two youngest daughters, Kate and Penny. The stark room reminded him of how much he missed his home, his wife, and his family. Nothing could console him.

Shortly after he started spending nights away from home, Delores had moved herself and their two daughters to Omaha to stay with her parents. Malcolm understood and agreed that it was the right thing for them. He cruised by the house periodically, to check on it and attend to any yard work when necessary. He couldn't bring himself to move back in. He wouldn't go home until he found his daughter and delivered her safely into the folds of her mother's waiting arms.

Malcolm contacted the FBI occasionally for perfunctory reasons and to keep them apprised of his findings. The agency generally took time to talk with him but seldom shared anything pertinent from their end.

Detective Walker, however, reported to him regularly. That's how Bremer connected Lloyd and Sylvia Masterson to one of the other missing girls. The discovery of Lloyd's fatal accident led him to Sylvia Masterson. Soon after, he learned that she had left the country earlier that month. Maybe her departure wasn't all that bad. With Sylvia out of the way, Malcolm was free to search her house. His excitement blossomed with the possibility of finding something, even the smallest clue, that would lead him to his lost daughter.

He drove past the Masterson house with the understanding that it was vacant, but lights filtering through every window told a different story. His reconnaissance over the next two days revealed that Sylvia's niece Lucy had taken occupancy for the summer. Malcolm spent another two days tailing Ms. Rydell to ascertain how she fit into the equation. He tailed her the night she met Deputy Rafferty at Arthur's, and on impulse, he followed her home and confronted her. She stunned him by inviting him inside.

Their conversation went well until his emotions took over and he became agitated, at which time Lucy showed him to the door.

Malcolm crawled into bed that night wondering if anything was ever going to go his way. The next morning, bright sunlight streamed through the bedroom window, welcoming him to a new day. A plan hovered in the recesses of his mind and developed throughout his morning chores. He drove away with renewed optimism.

Convincing Lucy to join him for breakfast in town proved a simple task. He then waited in a secluded place until he saw her drive off. Bremer entered the house through an open window in the bedroom. Nothing could stop him at this point. His search became more destructive with each passing minute.

Malcolm caught sight of the clock and let out a guttural roar, falling back into the La-Z-Boy chair. He had been there an hour and the hunt had revealed nothing.

His hungry eyes raked over the room one more time before coming to rest on a vent return in the side of the wall. Malcolm struggled to his feet, goosebumps sprouting across the back of his neck and down his arms as he approached. Standing on a chair he'd pulled close, he extracted a dime from his pocket, used it to remove the screws, and then pried the vent loose. His fingertips explored the ductwork until they folded around a small book. Removing it, he scanned the first pages.

Lloyd Masterson's journal lay open in his hands. "The man had to have an ego beyond all egos and a brain the size of a pea to document such atrocious activities. Could he be that stupid?" It didn't matter. For the first time in months, Malcolm felt a glimmer of hope settling around him.

He couldn't explain why, but he took the time to replace the vent. One more glance around the room filled him with remorse. What he had done to Lucy and this house was wrong in so many ways. He'd make amends in due time. He gripped the book in his hand and raced out the door to his car.

Malcolm sped back to the rundown shack, thankful to have a private place to examine Lloyd's journal. Did he dare contemplate the idea that his search for Amber might be coming to an end?

CHAPTER FIFTY

Malcolme Bremer pulled up to the house. The sight of the two Dobermans anxiously awaiting his return brought a smile to his face. Although they were not his dogs, he considered them his only friends. On their first encounter, Malcolm had been certain that they intended to tear him limb from limb, but he soon recognized that they were puppies at heart. Tweedledee and Tweedledum, as he lovingly referred to them, were named after characters from *Alice in Wonderland*, a favorite book of all three of his children. They ran to him jumping and yipping, begging for affection, hungry for any tidbit of food he might bestow on them. To ensure loyalty, he kept red meat in the refrigerator and fed them regularly.

"I'll feed you later. Right now, I have something much more important to do."

They pranced around his feet on the way to the porch, criss-crossing back and forth, seeking to charm him into changing his mind. The minute he entered the house and shut the door, the two took off for destinations unknown.

Malcolm tucked the journal under his arm and marched to the bedroom. He flopped onto the bed and spread the open book across the palms of his hands.

Two hours quickly passed. He closed the pages. Lloyd Masterson had been a very evil man.

Malcolm shook his head. "Too bad he's already dead. I'd take real pleasure in wringing his neck and sending him straight to Hell."

Standing in the shower under the hot spray of water, Bremer scrubbed furiously to wash away his feeling of utter disgust. He finally gave up, toweled dry, and donned a fresh shirt and a pair of clean jeans.

Malcolm briefly toyed with calling the authorities. "What good would that do?" he asked aloud. No one took him seriously anymore. When he stopped by the station, people tactfully avoided him. When he phoned, they put him on hold, probably wishing he would tire of waiting and hang up. Of course, he never did. Being the nice guy wasn't working. Time to take the bull by the horns.

He sat at the kitchen table and pored over the journal again. Masterson left very little to the imagination. The man clearly took deliberate pleasure in hurting others. "I can't let myself think about that. Amber and the other girls need me to stay focused."

Malcolm took copious notes during his second reading, including names and places that required reconnaissance. Upon completion, he examined his annotations. His eyes widened. How had he missed it? In horror, he snatched up the book and the sheets of paper and hightailed it to his car.

CHAPTER FIFTY-ONE

After spending the night in his truck, RJ woke to the chatter of birds. His aching muscles confirmed that age was taking its toll. A thin light trickled through the window blinds of the cabin, letting him know that Lucy was already up. He dialed her number. "Morning," he said cheerfully. "Were you able to get some sleep?"

"I am on my way out to bring you a cup of coffee—or would you like to come inside and wash up before you leave?"

"I'll be right there," he said.

He grinned sheepishly when she opened the door. "How did you know I was here?"

"I came out last night to make sure the garage door was locked and noticed your truck in the driveway. I walked up to it to see if everything was all right." She laughed, "I don't think you have a future as a security guard. You were sound asleep."

"I was playing possum."

She smiled. "I'm sure you were. And to answer your first question, I slept like a baby knowing you were out here keeping an eye on things. Do you have time for breakfast?"

"Thanks, but I have to get going. Care if I use your bathroom?"

"It's all yours. I'll get you a coffee to go."

"That would be great."

Back on the road, Rafferty had one thing on his mind. If his suspicions were correct, Bremer had intelligence that could cause him great harm. He had to get to his apartment, retrieve the switchblade he had taken from Sylvia's garage, and secure it in a safe place where no one would ever find it. He pulled up in front of his apartment building, the truck tires squealing against the hot pavement. RJ barely took the time to put the vehicle in park. He jumped out, ran inside, recovered the weapon, and sprinted back to his truck.

At this point, there were four people who knew about the knife. He and his partner, Cassie, accounted for two. Sylvia was the third, and the man who had used it to kill the young girl was the fourth. RJ absently kneaded the weapon through the plastic bag it occupied. Amber's father had become a bigger obstacle than expected. RJ had to locate Malcolm Bremer and uncover what he knew.

His phone buzzed. "RJ here. What's up?"

"The results from the autopsy on the young woman found at the dump just came through," Chief Branson said. "The deceased is estimated to be between twenty-four to twenty-eight years old. Cause of death is an overdose."

"Thanks for the info. I have another lead to check out. I'll report my findings as soon as I have something solid."

"Be sure you check in regularly. I don't like it when I have to go through Cassie to find you."

"Yes, sir. I understand."

The phone went dead.

This news changed everything. Rafferty would deal with Bremer later. Right now, he had to find a safer place to stow the knife. As soon as he completed that task, his number one priority was the lead in Arizona.

RJ punched in Cassie's number but disconnected before she answered. A sour taste filled his mouth. Lately, her mood swings made him dizzy. They had worked well together over the years, eventually becoming good friends. After a hard day on the job, they would sit over a beer and tease each other about their relationship. They had all the disadvantages of a marriage and none of the benefits: sex and more sex.

The vast amount of experience RJ had acquired in dealing with love-struck women couldn't help him here. Cassie was his partner. Shit, she carried a gun. She tended to overreact at the slightest provocation. When pissed off, she could likely take down an angry bear with a single blow.

He tried to see the positive side. They *were* partners. No, they were more than partners. They were friends, good friends. He had her back, and she had his. He hoped he wasn't giving her more credit than she deserved.

RJ hit the speed dial again and felt a wave of relief when he got her voicemail. "Hey, partner. Something's come up. I have to fly under the radar for the next couple of days. Cover for me and I'll owe you big time." He deliberately neglected to spell out the details. He would deal with the repercussions when he got back in town.

That settled, he put his truck in gear and drove away. With any luck, Lucy wouldn't have any second thoughts about their trip to Phoenix.

CHAPTER FIFTY-TWO

Becca had set her alarm early. She wanted to be at the hospital when Hal's doctors arrived for their 6 a.m. rounds. She awoke refreshed and whispered a *thank you* to the nurse who had kindly persuaded her to go home and get some well-needed rest.

But her presence at Hal's bedside that morning made no difference. Citing privacy rights, the hospital staff refused to talk to her about Hal's condition. Becca finally threw up her hands in despair and stomped from the room.

She had a back-up plan. She pulled out her cellphone and Googled "Wayne Johanson." The search yielded nothing. Becca gave a little shrug. *It's probably better if I do this face to face.*

She walked back through the brightly lit corridor to Hal's room. Inside, she closed the door and sat on the edge of the bed next to him. Becca took his hand gently in hers and squeezed it. "Hang in there. I'm going to get you the help you need." She bent in and kissed him lightly on the cheek. "I have to leave you now. I promise I'll be back soon."

Becca headed for her car. Questions filled her head as she pulled onto the gravel lane leading to Wayne's house. What would she say to Hal's uncle? How would he react to the news about his nephew's accident? And ultimately, what would she do if Wayne refused to get involved?

She parked next to an old pickup sitting near the house and took a deep breath before getting out of the car. "I can do this."

A deep baritone voice assaulted her from behind. "Can I help you?" The man stepped into view. Becca watched him cast his eyes across the driveway. His second question had more urgency. "Why are you here?"

Too nervous to say anything coherent, Becca let the words tumble from her mouth: "I have to talk to Wayne Johanson."

"You've come to the right place. I'm Wayne Johanson."

"I'm Becca Banks. I'm a friend of your nephew's."

"I know who you are," he snapped.

How did he know her? She glanced nervously around the farm-yard. Her eyes settled on a dozen chickens pecking at the ground near the barn. The clamor of the hens generated memories of her grandmother's quilting group. Her eyes watered. If she didn't pull herself together soon, she'd lose everything near and dear to her. How could she convince Mr. Johanson to do the right thing by his nephew if she acted like a crybaby?

She wiped her face with the back of her hand. "Hal's been in a horrible accident." Becca's heart thumped hard against her chest. "He's in a coma, and the doctors won't give me any information about him. They said they won't talk to anyone who isn't a family member. You're the only relative I know of." Her homily came faster. "The doctors are making decisions on his behalf because no one is there to speak for him. I'm not sure they're doing everything they can to make Hal wake up. Would you please talk to them?"

Wayne shook his head.

"How dare you say no? Hal's your nephew! Your blood! Hal told me you were a two-bit con artist. He also said he suspected you had a heart under your tough guy act. I guess he was wrong. You don't care about anyone except yourself." The glare in her eyes dared him to tell her she was mistaken.

A small smile lifted the corners of Wayne's mouth. "Well, I can see why Hal fell for you. You're a spitfire." He paused. "Let me tell you right off that I'll do what you ask. Come inside, and we'll talk about it. I don't like to discuss family matters in the middle of the driveway." His hand massaged the back of his neck as he scanned the yard one more time and then walked silently up the porch steps and into the house.

Becca stayed behind, unsure of what to do. Had she heard correctly? Fortunately for them both, she shadowed him inside.

He pulled out a chair for her and then opened the fridge and drew out a beer. Her fear nearly gone, Becca sat on the edge of the seat, her back straight as a board.

"You're mighty young to have such spunk. What are you? Sixteen? Seventeen? Hal's a lucky man." He took a pull from the bottle. "What exactly do you require from me?"

Becca had come prepared for a fight, but Wayne's eagerness confused her. Her grandmother's voice came to mind again: "Never look a gift horse in the mouth."

Becca proceeded to tell Wayne what little she knew about Hal's condition and recounted what she had overheard a doctor say— that Hal needed surgery to relieve the pressure building up inside his head. The hospital wouldn't allow the operation unless they had the necessary release forms signed by a family member. She stood and took a small step forward. "I need you to come to the hospital with me and fill out the forms. Maybe they could schedule surgery tomorrow if you sign the papers today."

"Shit," Wayne sputtered. "Hal doesn't deserve this." He walked to the kitchen sink, wiping something from the corner of his eye, and stared out the kitchen window with his back to her. "The weatherman predicted another hot, humid day. Every year, I swear I'm going to install central air in this old farmhouse, but it never gets done. On days like this, I kick myself for procrastinating. Maybe tomorrow I'll call an A/C guy."

Tires crunching on the gravel drive evidently sounded an alarm. Wayne turned back to Becca, droplets of sweat dotting his forehead. He blinked several times and then spoke in a soft, firm voice. At first, she thought she'd heard him incorrectly.

"I want you to do exactly what I tell you to do."

She shrunk back into her chair at the severity of his demeanor. "You have to leave now! I'll get to the hospital when I can."

Becca did not move.

He bore into her. "I said, get out of my house! Leave! And don't tell a soul that you were here today."

Becca scurried like a rabbit. From the front seat of her car, she glanced sideways and saw a man exiting his vehicle. She instinctively reached to lock the door and then shoved the key into the ignition and twisted it. The engine whined but did not start. She tried again. More whining. Becca looked over her shoulder and saw the man approaching fast. His hollow look chilled her to the bone.

The sedan's interior had reached sauna-like temperatures while it sat in the driveway. Even so, a shiver ran through her body. She turned the key one more time. Thankfully, the engine purred into action. Becca shifted the car into reverse and backed it up until she cleared the corner of the house. She sped away, gravel spitting at the man. Peering into the rearview mirror, she caught sight of him, alone in the driveway, staring after her.

CHAPTER FIFTY-THREE

Lucy didn't go back on her word to help RJ. They had flown into Phoenix Sky Harbor Airport the previous night and were presently at the Holiday Inn on 24th Street and McDowell Road. Her mind reeled from the events of the past several days.

A sliver of light seeped through the slit between the heavy drawn curtains, alluding to the start of a new day. She rolled over to see RJ asleep beside her. The clock on the nightstand glowed 5:24 a.m. Plenty of time to rehash recent events before their ten o'clock appointment. Careful not to wake him, she placed two pillows behind her back and propped herself into a sitting position.

There was no reasonable explanation for her aunt's digression, so Lucy focused on FBI agents Hunter and Peterson. If they still had her aunt's cottage under surveillance, the agents likely knew that she had teamed up with RJ, and that they had boarded a plane to Phoenix the previous night.

When she had told RJ that the agents were investigating him, he had scoffed. "Law enforcement agencies distrust each other by nature. All they had to do was ask me. I would gladly trade intelligence with them."

Glancing at him now, his hair matted from a night of restless sleep, Lucy wondered if she should contact Agent Hunter and update him regarding the events of the last forty-eight hours. She decided to table that call for one more day. If Rafferty's plan worked, they might be able to garner information that could bring this case to a close.

RJ stirred. Enough light filtered through the room to allow her to see the slight bruising on the side of his face. His eyelids fluttered open. Lucy reveled in the bright flecks of hazel and green that stared up at her. Soft brown brows and high, defined cheekbones formed a handsome frame. She could not help noting that the facial hair outlining his firm jawline gave him the '80's look of Don Johnson.

His warm raspy voice greeted her: "How long have you been up?"

"Not long."

"What time is it?" he asked before noting the clock on the nightstand. He held up an arm, encouraging her to lie next to him. "Let's snuggle a little before we get moving?"

"I know what you're angling for, and you're not getting it from me. We had a deal." Her words referred to the vow he had made the previous night. There would be no hanky-panky—at least, not on this trip.

They were in the same room because RJ had insisted it was for her own safety. "We're dealing with very dangerous people, and I won't get a minute's sleep if I have to worry about your well-being."

"You're definitely letting paranoia get the best of you."

"I won't back down on this," he had stated firmly when they entered the hotel lobby.

Lucy had waited to the side while he checked in and obtained an entry key. When they got to the room, he had opened the door and stepped back to let her enter. She had laughed, giving him the impression that she greenlit the room's furnishings—namely, *one* king-sized bed—but had dashed his spirits when she walked to the desk in the corner of the room, picked up the phone, and dialed the hotel receptionist. The one-sided conversation hinted that the changes she requested were not available. She replaced the phone in its cradle and aimed a formidable glare at RJ. "Why didn't you tell me the hotel was booked to capacity?"

He reacted with a slow grin.

Lucy feigned anger, but it wasn't RJ's fault that the room had just one bed. Besides, how could she stay mad at him when he smiled at her like a child on Christmas morning?

RJ shrugged his shoulders, suggesting that he was as much a victim as she was. "I didn't plan this, and you can't blame me if the thought of being in the same bed with you tantalizes me."

She didn't let on that the concept excited her as well. Instead, she declared a tad too loudly, "We are not sleeping in the same bed." She eyed the loveseat. "I'm sure this unfolds. You can sleep here." Lucy grabbed one of the cushions and removed it.

The sofa was not a foldout bed. And it was late. She was tired... and hungry. Her headache would worsen if she didn't get something in her stomach. "Let's call a temporary truce and find a quiet place to have dinner. We can figure out the sleeping arrangements when we get back."

"I'll go for that."

"Give me a minute to freshen up." She withdrew into the bathroom and re-emerged soon after. "I'm ready."

RJ proudly escorted her through the lobby and out the main entrance. Upon arrival, the desk clerk had handed RJ a list of nearby eateries, highly recommending a barbecue joint within walking distance. At Rafferty's request, the hostess at the restaurant showed them to a table at the back of the room, away from any windows. Ever the gentleman, RJ pulled out a chair for Lucy and then seated himself across the table, availing him a view of the front door. Lucy wondered if he was fearful or merely cautious. They perused the menu and ordered their meals and a pitcher of beer.

"I need to prep you for tomorrow."

"Before we get into that, I want to know about the body they found at the dump. With all the commotion over Malcolm Bremer and his break-in at the cottage, I forgot to ask you if there was any connection to the missing girls."

"There doesn't seem to be a link."

"I guess that's good news."

The waiter appeared with their food, offering a welcome diversion. Lucy pensively dipped her fork into her salad as she waited for RJ to expound on the evidence found. He didn't. Instead, he got to the business at hand.

"The meeting should be no more than a simple interview. It will take place in Eckhart Park, a thirty-minute drive from here." He opened a paper map that he'd acquired at the help desk in the hotel lobby and pointed out the park's location. "There will be a local farmer's market going on, which may or may not aid our mission. I want you to understand that with an operation like this, we can never cover every scenario. Be assured that I know what I'm doing. All you have to do if follow my lead."

When they got back to their room, neither had the energy to argue over who slept where. Lucy agreed to share the bed, and RJ grudgingly agreed to behave like a perfect gentleman. They laid next to each other, wrapped up in their own thoughts. RJ let out a sigh. "Please don't worry. This is my job, and I'm good at it."

"I'm not worried about you. I'm scared I'll be the one to screw up."

"I wouldn't have brought you if I didn't think you could handle it. It'll be a walk in the park." He snickered.

She smiled in the dark. "I'm glad you think so."

He gently reached for her hand. "Honest. Just be yourself. You've got this. Now try to get some sleep."

※

Having tossed and turned most of the night, Lucy was nevertheless ready to face the day when morning dawned. She reflected on the conversation she and RJ had had after they'd settled into bed. She had expected him to spend the time putting moves on her, but he didn't. He had been kind and thoughtful and had done everything in his power to convince her that she had what it would take to pull off today's undertakings.

She mused that she had rarely received any reassurance from Jack, and especially not any emotional support. She basked in the warm feeling that RJ believed wholeheartedly in her, so much so that he was willing to risk his livelihood and possibly his life. She smiled at herself. *Well, maybe not his life.* She didn't want to believe they were walking into something that dangerous.

Glancing back at the clock, RJ lifted himself onto his elbow and smiled down at her. "I hope you were able to get some sleep. Are you ready for today?"

"I am, thanks to you."

"I didn't say anything that wasn't true." He sat up and lowered his feet to the floor. "As much as I'd like to stay in bed with you, it's time we get rolling."

CHAPTER FIFTY-FOUR

They arrived at Eckhard Park forty minutes early to get the lay of the land. RJ hadn't expected the farmer's market to be so crowded. To fit in, he and Lucy checked out several booths, bought a few items and then made their way to a predesignated picnic table on the other side of the park where they were to meet with a man going by the name of Samuel Crane, a front man for the suspected cartel. Although RJ probably had enough evidence to put him behind bars for the rest of his life, Crane was only a peon in the organization. RJ had his sights on the kingpin.

Rafferty's contact had tried for more than a month to arrange the meeting. The goal was to get Crane to relinquish a kidnapped girl to an anxious couple in search of a live-in au pair. RJ and Lucy would play the leading roles. RJ trusted that once they had the young girl in their safekeeping, she could lead them on a trail that exposed the top men in the organization. He dreamed of the day when he would see every one of their sorry asses behind bars.

Barring any unforeseen circumstances, RJ planned to return to Vergas the following day with Lucy's part in his scheme remaining a secret. He shuddered to think what his superiors would do if his insubordination ever came to light. A demotion to a desk job was the likely outcome, but worse fates could be around the corner.

That said, Rafferty calculated that he could contact the FBI if he uncovered evidence that might lead them to the girls. He had no doubt that Agents Hunter and Peterson would gladly swoop in and take credit for his hard work, leaving him to return home with no one the wiser of his involvement.

As they neared the table, RJ eyed the pair of sunglasses sitting on the bench. This was the code letting him know he was at the right location. He scooped up the glasses and placed them on top of the table, his code letting Mr. Craine know that he was meeting the right contact.

Five short minutes later, a man dressed in jeans and a tee shirt approached. RJ made introductions and they all got right down to business. Everything went smoother than anticipated, with Lucy revealing herself to be the pro RJ knew she would be. Seemingly effortlessly, she played the doting wife and mother desperate for a nanny to help her with the housework and her two young children. They gave the story that they resided in Mexico due to RJ's job and that their nanny failed to live up to their high standards.

"We require a young American girl who won't expose our children to unhealthy foreign customs." Lucy's voice quivered with false disdain. "I cannot stress this enough. We expect someone who will abide by our rules. We're on a strict schedule, and she will not be allowed time on her own. We will not put up with another lazy girl coming into our home in pursuit of a paid vacation."

"I'll be in touch once I check your credentials." The man abruptly rose to leave.

"No, no, that won't work at all," Lucy insisted.

RJ gave Crane a subtle wink. "You see, we're flying back to Mexico tomorrow, and we expected to take a girl with us."

"We have cash," Lucy added. "There's a substantial bonus for you if you deliver us a girl by tomorrow." She gave RJ a woeful gaze.

"You'd be wise to remember that I'm the one in charge here," Crane growled.

"Please excuse my wife. We'll wait to hear from you. If it doesn't work out today, we'll be back in six months."

Crane started to walk away before turning back. "I'll see what I can do, but don't count on anything." His gruff tone belied the slight glint in his eyes. RJ suspected Crane would—and probably had multiple times already—sell his soul for a quick buck.

When they got back to the hotel room, RJ called the front desk of the hotel to extend their stay by another day and also called the airline to cancel their reservations. Unsure of what the next day would bring, Rafferty put off rescheduling a flight home. Lastly, he left a coded message with his underground contact. All his bases covered, he leaned back in the chair and laced his hands behind his head. "The rest of the day belongs to us. Any thoughts on how to spend the time?"

"Well," she said, "I've never been to Arizona. Didn't you tell me you used to live here? I would love it if you'd show me around town."

"That's not exactly the answer I anticipated, but if milady wants a tour of the land, a tour she will get."

He grabbed his car keys off the desk and stood. "It's too hot outside to take you hiking. I promise: when this is all over, I'll bring you back, and we'll go. There's no better view of the valley than the one you'll see from atop Camelback Mountain. For now, let's take in the sights from the comfort of an air-conditioned car."

"That sounds great—apparently, the high today will be 118 degrees."

RJ drove her to Scottsdale. They enjoyed a quiet lunch at Oliver's Bistro, a chic restaurant located on the water canal at Fashion Square near the downtown area. RJ took in the panoramic view. "Who wouldn't love calling this little piece of paradise home?"

Lucy agreed. Lofty palm trees and vibrant flowering plants offered a tropical feel. "It's very different from what I'm used to. It's not hard to visualize leaving your troubles behind and escaping to this alluring land."

The tour continued. Fountain Hills, a small town adjacent to Scottsdale's northeastern border, boasted the tallest fountain in the United States. The host at the Café de Fountain seated them on the patio where they enjoyed a leisurely glass of wine while taking in the spectacular view.

The last stop was Saguaro Lake. RJ drove north on Highway 87 through the Salt River Indian Reservation. A right turn onto the service road took them an additional twenty miles to the park entrance. Surrounded by the Goldfield Mountains, the lake's deep waters glistened in the afternoon sun. Aboard a rented speedboat, they spent an hour and a half cruising near the precipice as it rose from the water's perimeter, taking in the spectacular views. Later, they enjoyed a quiet dinner at a quaint restaurant overlooking the marina.

Neither had any desire for the wonderful day to end. They strolled down to the pier, where RJ instinctively encircled Lucy in his arms. The sheer beauty of the lake brought to memory RJ's query from earlier that day. Would she ever entertain starting a new life in Arizona? Even if the notion intrigued her, Lucy doubted she was the type to pick up and relocate, leaving behind everything she knew. Born a Midwest girl, she guessed she would always be a Midwest girl.

CHAPTER FIFTY-FIVE

Rafferty loosened his grip on Lucy. She'd come into his life and suddenly, his conscience kept him awake at night. The urge to redress his wrongs filled him with apprehension. Regardless, if he didn't change his present course, he could end up in prison, or worse.

RJ tossed his fears aside, leaned in, and kissed her. His emotions got the better of him. He drew back, his eyes seeking hers. What was he looking for? Acceptance? Not exactly. Permission? Maybe.

He drew her close again. He'd always been searching for the right woman: someone who brought peace and stability into his life. Someone to depend on when things got rough. RJ had no way to foresee the future, but Lucy was here now, and that meant the world to him.

It was foolish to ask her to blindly follow him—yet that was precisely what he planned to do. If he got it right this one time, Lucy could possibly be his salvation. He intended to take her on a ride through Hell and prayed to God that they came out on the other end alive and well.

"Come on," he said. "Let's get back to the hotel before we embarrass ourselves." They walked to the car arm in arm.

The drive back was quiet. RJ suspected they were both edgy about the path ahead.

Rafferty stiffened when their hotel came into view. Four police cars sat at the front entrance, their lights flashing.

"What do you think that's all about?" Lucy asked.

Through the glass doors of the lobby, they saw two officers positioned in the foyer. After circling the block twice, RJ pulled into an adjacent parking lot behind the building. "I need to find out what the police are doing here. If I don't come back in ten minutes, I want you to go straight to the airport and take the first flight back to Minneapolis. Lock the doors and stay alert."

"I am not going to leave you here," she barked, "so make sure you get your ass back here."

Rafferty didn't have time to argue, and from the look on her face, he would be fighting a losing battle if he tried. He left the keys in the ignition, got out, and watched her slide over the console and into the driver's seat before he took off toward the service entrance of the hotel.

Fifteen minutes later, RJ rapped his knuckles on the driver's window and beckoned her to open the door.

She jumped out and threw her arms around him. "I was about ready to go inside and see what was going on. What took you so long?"

He gently disengaged himself from her grip. "If I wasn't so glad to see you, I'd..." his voice trailed off. If she had left like he'd asked, he would be standing in the parking lot with no means of transportation.

The luggage sat on the pavement. "I think I got it all." He reached inside the car and pushed the button that popped open the trunk. "Let's get out of here."

Lucy lowered herself into the passenger seat and waited for him to toss the carry-ons into the trunk. RJ exited the parking lot and handed her his phone. "Call Delta and book us a flight to Minneapolis."

CHAPTER FIFTY-SIX

L ucy got little sleep on the flight back to Minneapolis, and the endless line at the rental car center heightened her fatigue. Weary travelers in front of her slowly dwindled to one couple. As the duo advanced to the checkout counter, Lucy's eyes wandered to the other side of the corridor, where RJ sat with his ear to his cellphone. He greeted her with a smile that melted her heart.

After she completed the paperwork and received directions as to where to pick up the rental, she gestured to RJ, rounded a corner, and encountered another infernal line. Her sigh echoed off the tiled walls of the women's bathroom.

Lucy took the opportunity to assess her current situation. Not long ago, she had discovered her husband's affair. Turn the page, and Lucy had become clandestine partners in an undercover sting with a man she barely knew—and who had, admittedly, had an affair with her aunt.

She speculated on Sylvia's lack of candor regarding her relationship with RJ. A twinge of betrayal churned inside Lucy, but she couldn't pinpoint exactly why. Sure, the two were close. That said, it didn't mean Sylvia had to keep Lucy abreast of her personal life.

Nevertheless, her aunt owed her the truth about the investigation. Especially when she had planted Lucy smack in the middle of it. *Did she really think I could move into her cottage for the summer and avoid getting mixed into the chaos?* "Did she even consider the danger she put me in?"

The sound of her own voice lifted the fog in her brain. Stares from the women standing next to her elicited a hangdog grin. Lucy reprimanded herself for squandering valuable time stewing over things she could not alter. No answers would be forthcoming until she spoke with Sylvia, and the prospect of that happening grew slimmer with each passing day.

Back in the terminal, she circled to where she had last seen RJ. A scowl knitted her brow when she saw his bag and her carry-on sitting on the floor adjacent to his empty seat. Why would he leave their bags unattended? Her first impulse was that he had also had to use the restroom. Minutes ticked by. When he didn't show himself, Lucy solicited the aid of an elderly gentleman to check the men's room for her. The man's stooped figure wobbled back to her. "No one answered to the name of RJ."

Lucy dialed RJ's cellphone. After several rings, his voicemail clicked on. She instructed him to call her as soon as possible.

Lucy scanned the crowd of people surging past her. No RJ. She didn't dare contact the authorities, because RJ's boss had not sanctioned their trip to Arizona.

She had few options. Strange as it may sound, she trusted RJ. He would not leave her without a good reason. Gathering their luggage, Lucy reluctantly glanced at the overhead signs and set out for the rental pickup area. RJ would know where to find her.

CHAPTER FIFTY-SEVEN

Rafferty had checked his emails and phone messages while Lucy waited in line at the rental car counter and breathed a sigh of relief. Cassie was the only one from the sheriff's office looking for him. He had one other message from his mother, inviting him to dinner that following weekend. He jotted a note to call her when he got home. The call from Cassie went unanswered.

He took his notebook from his carry-on and flipped through the pages. He glanced up to catch Lucy gazing at him from the other side of the terminal. God, she was beautiful. They held eye contact until someone nudged her and pointed out that it was her turn at the rental desk. The next time he saw Lucy, she gestured that she was heading to the bathroom. RJ went back to his notes.

Something drew his attention back to the crowded waiting area. An experienced cop, he knew not to ignore the bells going off inside his head. He furtively slipped his notes back into his bag and searched the crowd for Lucy.

A large man dressed in shorts and a Hawaiian shirt stood fifteen yards away. Those cold eyes irrefutably targeted Rafferty in much the same way that a big-game hunter surveys a trophy shot. RJ zeroed in on his scraggly hair and unkempt beard. The nasty sneer made his blood run cold. Lloyd Masterson, Sylvia's husband

and RJ's ex-business-associate, was alive and well.

Masterson approached and lowered himself into the chair beside RJ. "You look like you've seen a ghost. What's the matter, cat got your tongue?"

"Did you bring any of your goons with you?" RJ's eyes ran the length of the terminal.

"It's you and me, buddy. I can handle you all by myself."

RJ shifted uncomfortably in his chair. On his own, he didn't fear Masterson. His concern was Lucy.

Seeming to read his mind, Masterson responded, "First you ball my wife, and now you're shacking up with her niece. You're quite the rogue, aren't you?" Lloyd's laugh was loud and grating. "If you don't want to see little Lucy witness your demise, get up off your ass and come with me—now."

When Rafferty hesitated, Lloyd removed a small caliber handgun from his pocket. RJ rose, and together, they left the airport.

CHAPTER FIFTY-EIGHT

The initial shock of reading Lloyd Masterson's journal left Malcolm Bremer numb. The last entry was dated six months prior to Amber's disappearance. The book contained nothing specific that would lead Malcolm to his daughter or to any of the other missing girls. It did corroborate what Malcolm had suspected for months: Wayne Johanson was central to the search.

Malcolm had visited the Johanson farm multiple times during his hunt for his daughter. On one such occasion, he had discovered a unique hiding place, where he now often planted himself in the wee hours of the morning. Hunched in the dark space under the porch, he'd stay through the day and well into the night, retreating when he was sure everyone had gone to bed. These were grueling days—mostly useless. Even so, Malcolm pursued his periodic surveillance on the off chance he might gather something of value.

Now that he had proof in black and white, he intended to face Johanson and coerce a confession from him. His vehicle rolled down the long gravel driveway and coasted to a stop.

His blood ran cold at the sight of young Becca Banks rushing to her red Toyota.

During one of his stints under the porch, Bremer had uncovered information that Miss Banks dated Wayne's nephew, Hal. Why would any parent allow their daughter to date trash like the Johanson boy?

A door slamming behind him brought him back to the subject at hand. Wayne Johanson sprinted to the blue truck on the other side of the driveway.

Malcolm charged him, seized his arm, and whirled him around. "You're not going anywhere. The police are on the way," he lied.

The next thing Malcolm knew, he lay sprawled on the ground. He pounded his fists in the dirt as Wayne's truck drove away.

CHAPTER FIFTY-NINE

The meeting with Hal's uncle lifted Becca's spirits. A bile taste in her throat reminded her that the encounter with the foul man in the driveway had had an entirely different effect. Trying to calm her frayed nerves, she pulled into a fast food drive-thru on her way to a nearby park.

Seated at a lone picnic table, Becca drew comfort from watching a family out enjoying the warm, sunny afternoon. The mother never seemed to lose track of the two young children racing back and forth as she chatted with the man kneeling beside her, presumably her husband. Both youngsters ran headlong into outstretched arms, their gleeful laughter filling the air with sweet music. More than anything, Becca dreamed of recreating that exact scene someday with Hal and their future children. She got up and maneuvered her way up the walking path. Shade from century-old trees kept the hot sun at bay while the bird's melodic chirping quieted her nerves, strengthening her resolve.

Back in the hospital parking lot, she was primed to tackle whatever life threw at her. She drank the last of her cola, took a deep breath, and went inside.

Becca's mind raced a mile a minute as she advanced along the hallway. Two physicians walked several paces in front of her, their monotone voices drifting her way. Her ears perked up. Had she heard correctly? Had one of them said that Hal's uncle had been there an hour ago and authorized the paperwork required to give him the injection?

The men entered Hal's room. Nine staffers formed a semicircle around the bed. Hal lay motionless amid all the activity. The doctors eased their way through the crowd until they flanked either side of the bed. Becca remained near the back of the room, listening intently to every word said. Several times, she had to remind herself to breathe.

One of the doctors placed his stethoscope over Hal's heart. A nurse read his vitals from the chart in her hand. Another nurse prepared a syringe for the doctor as he addressed his associates: "We should know within a few hours if this works. Everyone, lower your heads, and let's pray together."

Becca panicked. What were these people doing to Hal that required prayer? Words flew from her mouth. "What are you doing?"

All heads bobbed to see who had spoken. The physician with the syringe took a step backward. "And who are you?"

A nurse intervened before Becca could respond. "This is Hal's girlfriend, the one I told you about." She draped a large fleshy arm around Becca. "She's been here day and night since Hal was brought in." The nurse smiled at Becca. "Let's go out into the hall."

Becca recognized her as the same nurse who had treated her so kindly the previous night. Confused, Becca offered minimal resistance.

The nurse explained in a hushed tone that Wayne had visited the hospital an hour earlier. "He and the doctors discussed the best course of action to help Hal regain consciousness," she said. "The drug they plan to inject into Hal hasn't been widely used, but it's shown a reasonable success rate in trial studies." She beamed. "The doctors believe the drug may bring Hal out of his coma."

Becca noticed the woman's nametag: *Angela*. How very appropriate.

Nurse Angela led Becca into a waiting room. "You can make yourself comfortable in here. I'll send someone to get you as soon as we know anything." She vanished before Becca had the opportunity to question her further.

Becca dropped onto the couch, barely able to contain her excitement. Hal's uncle had done what she had asked of him. Her enthusiasm faded with another thought. What if the drug caused more harm than good? Too exhausted to think anymore, she curled up on the sofa.

The touch of a man's gentle hand jerked her awake. "Are you Becca Banks?"

She rubbed her eyes and nodded.

"Please come with me."

She got up and trailed him to Hal's room. Hal lay quiet. Although they had removed the ventilator, the equipment surrounding him beeped as it had since his arrival. She stared blankly at the doctor.

He smiled. "Hal, someone is here to see you."

Hal's eyelids fluttered open.

The doctor addressed Becca: "He was adamant that he had to see you. Hal's very tired, so you can't stay long."

Becca flew across the room and into Hal's arms. His moan convinced her to back away. Tears showed her uncertainty.

"I'm a little sore." He shook his head. "I can handle some pain as long as you are by my side."

Becca gently climbed up onto the bed and they held each other for what seem to be an eternity. Finally, his grip loosened, and she sat back to appraise him.

Hal rubbed her cheek with the back of his hand. "Thank God you're safe! I was so afraid something bad had happened to you!" His arms closed around her again.

All she could manage to say was, "I'm sorry!"

Nurse Angela walked into the room. "It's time for you to leave. Hal needs his rest. You can talk tomorrow."

Becca crawled from the bed as the nurse attended to the bag suspended from a nearby pole. Hal's words began to slur, and soon he fell fast asleep.

Becca kissed him and then said to Nurse Angela, "Can I please stay? I'll be very quiet."

The nurse flipped through Hal's chart and then concentrated on Becca. "If you agree to let him sleep, you can stay."

Becca would consent to anything if it meant she could be at Hal's side. She scooched the chair up to the bed and settled in, her hand remaining glued to Hal's arm. For the next hour, a parade of doctors and nurses entered and exited the room, each presumably assigned to a specific task.

Dan and Mary Ann Banks dropped by a little after eight. They shared a congratulatory ceremony with their daughter and the medical staff before the professionals went back to their work.

"We're heading home now," Dan eventually said to his daughter. "You're exhausted. Why don't you come with us?"

Becca assured them she wouldn't be much longer.

"Okay, honey," Mary Ann said. "Call us if you're too tired to drive. Dad will be happy to come back and get you." Dan nodded in agreement.

Becca sank back into her chair, her eyelids growing heavy with the passing of time. She snapped awake to see Hal staring at her, his face etched in fright. Becca rang for the doctor in panic when she realized Hal didn't recall the car crash or any of the events leading to it.

"We expected this. It's normal memory loss," the doctor declared. "It's entirely possible he might never regain memory of the events of that day. Don't worry, though. Hal is doing fine in every other respect."

CHAPTER SIXTY

Becca's youthful optimism allowed her to leave the hospital on cloud nine. Hal's memory of the accident was a small price to pay considering the outcome. Earlier that day, she had assumed the worst. Now, they had everything to live for. Unmindful of the time, she decided to walk to their family church to say a prayer of gratitude and apologize to God for her lack of faith.

A vehicle approached fast from the north. Fear gripped her when it screeched to a halt in front of her. The man driving the car was the same man she'd seen at the Johanson farm that morning.

She stood like a deer caught in headlights. The man was out of his vehicle in a flash, wrapping his strong arm around her waist and shoving her through the open car door, his elbow propelling her across the seat as he slid in behind the wheel. Becca scrambled to exit the passenger side, only to encounter a mass of duct tape covering the door handle. She pivoted and attacked the man with a vengeance. She screamed. She spit. Her fingernails clawed at him.

The gun went unnoticed until he instinctively raised his hands to protect his face. Horrified, Becca stared in disbelief.

"Now that I have your attention, sit your ass down and stay quiet." Becca flopped back in the seat.

The man looked in every direction, checking for prying eyes. He lowered the gun to his lap and yanked the car door shut.

How could this be happening? Hal had finally come back to her, and yet now she was the one in grave danger. She rotated her head just slightly, thinking she might be able to crawl into the back seat and exit the car that way.

"Don't even try." His left hand swiped at the beads of sweat trickling from his receding hairline. He steered the car through the city streets, picking up speed when they got to Highway 15.

Becca searched the dark sky beyond. The North Star, visible through the passenger window, told her they were heading west, toward Vergas. When they took a right onto a paved road, she glanced at the clock on the dashboard. It glowed 10:19 p.m. For the first time in her life, she was thankful that her parents had set a strict curfew. They would come looking for her soon. *How will they ever find me, though?* Her lower lip trembled. *In the movies, the police track people through their cell phones. Maybe they can find me that way.*

Holding onto that thought, Becca eased her hands into her pockets. The phone wasn't there. Moving very slowly, she slipped her fingers between the seat and the console and then between the seat and the door. No luck. She slid her feet along the floorboard. Becca vaguely remembered having the phone in her hand when she left the hospital—she must have dropped it, along with her purse, during the struggle. Her windpipe constricted in panic. *Stop it*, a voice inside her screamed. *Don't you dare let him see your fear*. She had to focus on the details if she intended to dig her way out of this.

Memorizing their route became her top priority. Multiple turns, however, made that task impossible. To make things worse, a thick layer of clouds rolled in, blanketing the stars. By the time the car stopped in front of a large wooden gate stretched across a dirt road, Becca was completely lost.

"I'm getting out to open the gate," the man wheezed as he removed the car keys. "I suggest you stay put. You're much safer with me than you are out there." He waved the gun at the windshield. The vehicle's high beams revealed two large dogs pacing on the other side of the gate. Devil-red embers flashed at her.

"Those are my babies," the man gloated. "They respond to my command. If you don't want to be their dinner, you'd best sit tight. I'll just be a minute."

Leaving the driver's door open, he advanced to the fence.

Becca anxiously tracked his movements. He removed the padlock and jostled the gate open far enough to allow the car to pass through. To her horror, the dogs bounded through the opening and straight for her, skidding to a standstill within inches of the open door. In the dim glow of the dome light, she could see saliva dripping from their jowls. Growling menacingly, they took to circling the automobile, anxious for the command to enter.

The man did not oblige them. Instead, his terse order prompted them to sit. "Good boys!" His hands lovingly scratched each one behind their ears. "She's not yours unless she misbehaves." He lifted his head and grinned.

Overwhelmed, Becca could not hold back the tears any longer.

"You've scared her. Bad boys! Go find something else to entertain you." A shake of his hand sent the dogs bounding into the dark recesses of night.

"Don't forget: my boys are always around, and they'd love to bury their teeth in you!" An eerie sound whistled through the gap between his two front teeth. Trees overhead quaked in a gust of wind as if to affirm his edict, and a loud clap of thunder announced a fast-approaching storm. He drove his vehicle forward, got out to secure the lock, and then proceeded to drive deeper into the surrounding woods. Large raindrops splattered loudly against the windshield, blurring the image of an old, dilapidated house. The man parked the car, exited, and waved for Becca to do the same. She faltered momentarily before clambering through the driver's door.

"You go on into the house," his voice gurgled to the beat of the rain. "I'll be back shortly." He grabbed her arm. "Remember, the dogs are milling around, eager for you to join them for a midnight snack." The echo of his chuckle traced him back to the car.

Becca stayed grounded in the pouring rain, watching the tail lights fade into darkness. Resignation set in. She lowered her head and went inside the house.

There was an order to the sparsely furnished room. A thread-bare rug lay in front of an old, faded sofa. A rocking chair sat close by. Scuffed wood floors skirted the furnishings, and tucked in the corner of the room was a small desk flanked by a pole lamp, the sole source of the shadowy lighting.

She moved to the center of the room and turned in a full circle, memorizing the location of all the doors and windows. Each of the three windows had plywood nailed to the exterior frames.

Becca walked tentatively through the opening that led to the kitchen. Assisted by the glimmer of light escaping from the living room, she spotted a pull chain hanging from the ceiling. One tug snapped on the overhead fixture. Apart from a dirty plate and cup sitting next to the sink, the room was clean and tidy.

Newspaper covered the upper half of the back door. She slid the latch and gave the knob a twist, and the door swung inward.

Another sheet of plywood blocked her exit. Becca slammed the door shut. Her hand reached up and yanked the light chain on her way back to the front room.

A picture frame lying prone on the desk had previously gone unnoticed. Becca picked it up and flipped it over in her hands. A family, not unlike her own, posed for the unseen camera. Three young girls stood with their parents, each family member dressed in what Becca would describe as Easter Sunday attire. Broad smiles on everyone suggested a close, loving family. The image seemed eerily out of place in this house.

Recollections of previous Easters evoked memories of Becca and her sisters modeling new dresses and shoes bought especially for the holiday. The thought of her mother's pride as she gathered her family for a similar photo lit a fire in Becca.

I better check out the rest of the house before that man comes back.

Down a short hall, Becca discovered two small bedrooms, each fitted with a twin-sized bed, a dresser, and a wooden chair. Plywood covered the windows in both rooms. Becca advanced to the bathroom, a small, clean room with no windows. Two bath towels hung neatly from the towel rack. A hand towel hung beside the sink. The medicine cabinet was empty.

For the third time, Becca stepped back into the middle of the living room. The photo on the desk aroused her curiosity. She picked it up again, trying to wrap her head around its significance. Recognition dawned. The proud man in the snapshot, now gruff and haggard, was undoubtedly the same man who had accosted her on the street.

Engrossed in the family photo, Becca failed to hear the door open behind her. The man grabbed her from behind and tore the photograph from her hands. "You have no right to meddle with my things."

Becca backed away.

He walked into the kitchen, taking the picture with him. The light came on. Sounds of cabinet doors opening and slamming shut resonated through the doorway. Becca sank to the floor in the corner of the room, wrapped her arms around her knees, and pulled them close. The chill of wet clothing plastered to her skin finally permeated her body. She shivered uncontrollably, lamenting the pain she'd caused her parents. *All they ever wanted was the best for me, and what did I give them in return? Trouble. That's what.*

She hadn't done much better by her sisters. They were young; they idolized her. And how had she responded? She treated them like second-class citizens. How many times had she expelled them from her room, demanding they stay away from her and her stuff? A deep sob erupted. *If I ever get out of here, I'll make sure my entire family knows how much I love them.*

Thankful that Hal was on his way to recovery, she longed to be in the safety of his arms. They had been through so much together. Becca leaned her head against the wall.

Upon awakening, she found a blanket draped over her. Becca cursed herself. She didn't want to consider what the man could have done while she was asleep. He approached from the kitchen and knelt beside her. "I'm sorry I was gruff earlier. I don't mean you any harm."

"Then why did you kidnap me?"

He coughed. "I saw you at the Johanson farm today. I know you're dating Wayne's nephew. Do you know what they do to young girls?" Choking back phlegm, he wagged his finger at her. "I insist you stay away from them. Do you hear me?"

"Who are you? And what makes you think you can—"

"Don't give me any more of your excuses. Go wash your face. I hung some dry clothes in the bathroom. They should fit you." He rose. "Go! Now! Then we'll sit and enjoy a nice dinner. You're safe here. You'll see."

Becca shuddered.

His voice hardened. "I said go change your clothes! You'll catch a cold if you don't get into something dry."

She pushed herself up off the floor and backed out of the room. Her body leaned heavily against the closed bathroom door. "This guy is a certified nut job," she whispered.

Becca splashed warm water on her face. She spied clean jeans and a shirt hanging on the back of the door as she toweled off. The picture on the desk came to mind. These clothes probably belonged to one of his daughters. The photo suggested he had a loving family. What did he want with her? She slipped into the dry clothing, and a frown creased her face. Nothing made sense. She studied herself in the mirror. Whatever his motive, it didn't matter. She would find a way to escape.

Becca's parents had taught her to think for herself. She was smarter than the lunatic on the other side of the door. *I can do this*. Holding her head high, she nodded to her reflection. Time to face her demons.

CHAPTER SIXTY-ONE

Dan and Mary Ann Banks had rushed to the hospital to be by their daughter's side the minute they learned Hal was awake. When they left later that evening, they made Becca promise she would be home by ten. Ten-thirty came and went. When Becca didn't answer her cellphone, they called the hospital. Hal's nurse assured them that their daughter had headed home a little after nine.

A knock at the front door sent Dan hastily to see who was calling at this late hour. Mary Ann stood back a few feet, her normally rosy cheeks turning a pale white. The sight of the sheriff's deputy on their doorstep elicited a fear so deep it rendered her mute.

"Mr. and Mrs. Banks?"

Dan blurted out, "Oh, God! Please don't tell me something has happened to our daughter."

"I'm Officer Quincy." He was a tall man with light brown hair trimmed close to his head. His square frame and firm jawline personified his all-business approach. "May I come in?"

Dan shuffled backward and motioned him to the living room. "Is Becca Banks your daughter?" the officer inquired.

"Yes." Dan fought to breathe.

"Do you mind if we sit?" Officer Quincy seated himself on the edge of the side chair, his back straight as a rod. Mr. and Mrs. Banks took their places on the sofa. "I take it Becca is not here?"

Dan eased his hand from Mary Ann's death grip and put his arm around her shoulders. "We were about to call the sheriff. Becca should have been home by now. She was at the hospital. Her boyfriend was in a serious accident, and she was visiting him. We just got off the phone with his nurse. She informed us that Becca left the hospital sometime after nine."

"A jogger spotted Becca's purse and cellphone lying in the middle of the street in front of the hospital."

Mary Ann gasped. "Oh, dear." She grabbed hold of Dan's free hand. "Becca's okay, isn't she?"

"We don't know, ma'am." The officer checked his notes. "The jogger reported his findings at about 9:25 this evening."

"That was over an hour ago," Mary Ann cried. "Where can she be?"

"We're not sure at this point. Let me get the operator on the phone and file a report." Officer Quincy talked quietly on his radio. He then addressed Mr. and Mrs. Banks again: "We've issued an All-Points Bulletin, and the department is sending two men to knock on doors in the neighborhood surrounding the hospital. With any luck, we'll find someone who saw Becca in the vicinity." He glanced at his notepad. "Do you have a recent photo of your daughter?"

Mary Ann left the room and returned with Becca's yearbook picture. She handed it to the officer. "Please, Officer Quincy, find our little girl."

"We're doing everything we can to make sure your daughter is found quickly."

What everyone suspected, but no one dared say aloud, was that Becca was the newest victim in the never-ending string of kidnappings.

CHAPTER SIXTY-TWO

Lucy was scanning the overhead signs for directions to the rental pickup area when a hand with the strength of a vise grip clamped down around her arm. Expecting to see RJ, she couldn't hide her displeasure when Jack hooked his arm around hers and steered her to the escalators. Jostling her bags, she struggled to free herself.

Jack's strength held firm. "Lucy, I'll explain it all when we're out of the terminal. Please trust me. Our lives could depend on it."

"What in the world are you talking about?" She yanked her arm free and planted her feet. "Why are you here? And why would you assume I'd go anywhere with you?"

"Lucy, we've got to keep moving!" Jack didn't wait for her response. He grabbed one of her bags and pressed her closer to the escalator.

Although his claims sounded absurd, they frightened her enough to persuade her to relent. She scrutinized the area one more time, eager to spy RJ rushing to her aid. Seeing no sign of him, she looped her fingers around the handle of the other carry-on and let Jack take the lead.

Neither of them said another word until they were inside Jack's Mercedes and merging onto I-94. Her phone chirped. Lucy viewed the screen, hoping it was RJ, and gingerly tapped the answer button. "Hello?"

"Let me speak to Jack."

Lucy turned and demanded, "Why is some guy calling *my* cell to talk to you?"

Jack took the phone from her hand and put it to his ear. "This had better be important." He listened intently as the bumper-to-bumper traffic inched forward on I-94. When he disconnected, he handed the phone back to Lucy. "I assure you, Luce, I'm looking out for your best interests."

"And what makes you think you know what's best for me?" She shook her head. "This has always been the sticking point. It's not your place to make decisions on my behalf. Tell me what you know, or I swear I'll get out of the car this instant!"

Jack swore when the van in front of him came to a complete stop. Lucy's hand rested on the door handle. "Quit stalling!"

"Lucy, you truly don't know how much danger you're in!"

"Then why don't you enlighten me?"

Jack chewed on his lower lip as he stared at the taillights ahead of him. "It's not that easy." He paused. "I got word from a very good source that someone has a contract out on you." He glanced sideways at her. "It's the truth. I'm trying to keep you safe until I can have it neutralized."

"What are you saying? Who would want me dead?" Her head bobbed from side to side. "I don't believe you."

Lucy was vaguely cognizant of the activity beyond the confines of the automobile. Barricades had narrowed the traffic to one lane. A man in an orange vest waved for Jack to proceed slowly onto the shoulder and shadow the line of cars in front of him. Too soon, the Mercedes merged back onto the interstate and picked up speed. Her opportunity to jump safely from the car had passed.

Jack's voice drifted her way. "Someone is out to get you."

Bits and pieces of what she had uncovered in the last four days circled in her head. Until now, she had thought of herself as a bystander, a cameo appearance in a true-life drama. Jack's revelation awarded her a significantly bigger role.

"Jack, I don't understand. I haven't done anything to warrant this kind of response from anybody."

"I really can't explain it to you now. You'll be safer if you don't know the specifics. I know you, Lucy. Trust me: I will get you out of this."

Lucy let his words sink in, "You didn't accidently run into me at the airport, did you? How did you know I was there?"

Jack pushed forward, "You've always underestimated my love for you. I give you my word that I had nothing to do with any of this."

"Any of what?"

"I'm referring to Sylvia and Lloyd. I think you probably know by now that Lloyd is alive."

Unwilling to reveal what the FBI had told her, Lucy countered, "I've heard the rumors." She kneaded her hands in her lap. "No one can confirm it one way or the other. What makes you think he's alive?"

"Because I've seen him."

"Seen him! Where?"

Lucy detected a slight hesitation before he said, "At the airport, a few hours ago." Her stomach did a cartwheel. "I heard about all this the day I wanted you to meet me in Minneapolis. That's why I ended up at your aunt's cottage. I told you I called my friend, Homer Wendt, the county attorney in St. Paul? Well, he told me about the kidnapped girls. I immediately feared for your safety, so I drove straight to the cottage."

"Why didn't you tell me any of this before now?"

Jack glanced at Lucy and smirked. "Because I knew you wouldn't believe me if I didn't have proof. Also, I had to see for myself that you'd be safe if you stayed there."

"So, tell me, how did you end up at the airport today?"

"Now, don't get mad at me. After I left you that day, I contacted Homer again and asked him if he had the name of a private detective I could hire. I wanted someone to keep watch over you; someone who was qualified to render protection if necessary." He looked at her and shrugged his shoulders. "I really do love you."

Lucy ignored his assertion. There was more to the story than he was letting on. "So how long has this detective been watching me?"

"Since that day. He had a hard time tracking you in Phoenix. Out of curiosity, why did you go there with Rafferty?"

"RJ is trying to track down the missing girls. He had a lead in Phoenix, so he asked me to go with him."

The vein on the side of Jack's neck bulged outward. "I see. So, you're sleeping with him, even though you're married to me?"

"It wasn't like that. I went with him because his partner couldn't go." Lucy cringed when she realized she had let him bait her into answering the question. *He* was the one who cheated on her.

Jack raged, "He was on police business, and he dragged you into something extremely dangerous. Surely you can see it was a ploy to get you into bed." His voice escalated. "Did you sleep with him, Lucy?"

"I'm not debating this issue with you. It was a legitimate trip. We met with a man named Crane and posed as a couple in search of a nanny. We were supposed to meet with Crane again today to see one of them…" Lucy abruptly ended her homily, fearing that she had said too much.

Jack's knuckles whitened against the steering wheel. "Don't stop now." He clenched his teeth. "Did he put you in danger for nothing, or did your little escapade confirm the girls' whereabouts?"

She stared at her hands laying open in her lap. *Why did she continue to question Jack's motives*? They were husband and wife. He'd already explained that he was there to support and protect her. Maybe Jack would answer in kind if she initiated trust.

Her gaze wandered out the side window. "It's possible that something happened after we left Crane." She brought her eyes back to the road in front of them. "The police showed up at our hotel last night. Fortunately, we avoided them. RJ concluded that it would be safer if we dropped everything and came back here."

"Are you falling for this guy?" Jack said, his jawline rigid as granite.

Lucy honestly didn't know the answer to that. The one thing she knew was that she had no intention of discussing her feelings for RJ with her soon-to-be ex-husband. "We have more important issues at hand."

Jack's nod of agreement surprised her. "The first thing we do is make sure you're safe," he said. "After that, I can get in touch with a couple of my contacts to locate Sylvia. Has she been in touch with you since she left the country?"

"No, but she gave her attorney a number where he can call her."

"Then you have it?"

"No. Apparently, Sylvia gave him strict instructions not to share it with anyone, including me."

CHAPTER SIXTY-THREE

C hris Foley had graduated with his law degree from the University of Illinois before clerking for Judge Henry Schmidt in Chicago during his first year out of school. His ambition was to be the first in the Foley family to relocate more than a hundred miles from their hometown.

Despite the lucrative prospects a big city career offered, he found himself missing his family and friends. One year and four months after graduation, Chris was back in Minnesota, studying for the bar exam.

The family banking business in Vergas fell on the willing shoulders of his older brother, Matt. This allowed Chris to pursue his own dreams by expanding the business to include an Attorney at Law. He passed the exam on the second try and set up shop next to his brother's office at the bank.

Married to his high school sweetheart within two years of his homecoming, he was blessed with a bouncing baby boy the following year. He and his wife's second son arrived eleven months after their first. Chris loved his family beyond words and couldn't imagine life without them. Nevertheless, he often pondered where he would be if he had stayed in Chicago.

Tonight, he lay in bed for hours, going over the conversation he'd had with Sylvia two weeks earlier.

She had started with, "I need your help."

"I'll do whatever I can," Chris had replied innocently.

"It's regarding Lloyd's business before he died. I have no evidence, but a reliable source told me that Lloyd was involved in trafficking children."

"Whoa. I knew about Lloyd's shady reputation, but this sounds a bit overboard. Who's your source?"

"I'm not at liberty to say, but I can't let this go. I need to know if it's true or not, and I have an idea of how to prove it one way or the other."

Chris had tried to convince her to contact the authorities, but she'd refused. Sadly, he let her persuade him to support her in her plot to seek retribution. She jetted off to Europe a week later, leaving him holding the bag. On top of that, she had invited Lucy into the mix.

By morning, Foley convinced himself that he had to confirm Lloyd's guilt or innocence in the charges weighed against him. Remembering the isolated property he'd helped Lloyd take title under a pseudonym, he decided to check it out on the off chance that someone might use it for a business such as Sylvia had described. He kissed his wife goodbye, gave his boys a hug, and left for the office. If all went well, he would be back in time for dinner, with no one the wiser when it came to his day's activities.

Chris left home and called Cathy, his secretary, to let her know that he wouldn't be in the office that day. The attorney gave no reason for his absence, and if Cathy had concerns, she kept them to herself.

At the edge of town, he continued east on Highway 60, his eyes doggedly trained on the road ahead.

He passed the turnoff that would lead him to Masterson's farmstead and continued down the highway for two more miles before veering onto a dirt road lined with tall fir trees. Further up the lane, a wooden gate barred his entrance. Foley knew this property, too. He had no idea that Malcolm Bremer had taken residency in the small house that was now part of an estate scheduled for auction at the end of the month.

Fresh tire tracks embedded in the muddy dirt didn't go unnoticed. "Damn kids have too much time on their hands these days." Chris had a habit of talking aloud to himself under stressful circumstances. "No telling how much damage they might have done."

He locked the car door and navigated west through the dense undergrowth. "I'd better check on the house tomorrow." If he had taken the time to check the property today, he would have discovered Becca inside the house.

The distant sound of barking dogs brought him back to the impending task. A thirty-minute hike led him to his destiny. Out of breath and covered with dust from head to toe, Chris positioned himself on the north side of Masterson's property. Voices coming from behind the house sent a cold shiver down the length of his body. If there had been any doubts before now, they vanished.

"He didn't die in that freak boating accident." His hand flew up to stifle further utterances. *Did Sylvia know that he was alive?*

He automatically reached inside his pocket. An excellent shot, he welcomed the feel of cold metal. Chris Foley hoped it wouldn't come to that, but if it did, he would use the weapon.

CHAPTER SIXTY-FOUR

A sleepless night left Becca stiff and sore. She lay quiet, listening for any sounds on the other side of the door. Detecting none, she padded softly across the floor and laid her ear against the panel, wary that her captor was ready to pounce the minute she showed herself.

The night before, he had banished her to this room shortly after they'd finished eating the sandwiches he had prepared. Finding no lock on the door, Becca jostled the back of the chair to fit under the knob. She knew her efforts would not block his entrance, but she expected the clamor of the chair being knocked from its position to alert her if she dozed off.

She couldn't stay in the room forever so she slid the chair out of the way and eased the door open, poised to retreat if necessary. All was quiet. She tiptoed along the hallway. Everything appeared to be the same as it had the previous night. Becca moved into the living room and then proceeded to the kitchen, only to discover that he was nowhere in the house.

She made her way back to the bathroom. Although Becca longed for a hot shower, the image of her captor's reappearance made her shiver uncontrollably. The girl in the mirror firmly shook her head. That settled it. There was no shower in her immediate future.

Hunger pangs sent her back to the kitchen. A bowl and spoon sat atop the counter alongside a box of Cheerios. A hand-written note lay nearby. *Sorry, I can't have breakfast with you this morning. Make yourself at home. Don't forget: the dogs will be on the lookout for you if you decide to venture outside.* He signed it, *Malcolm.*

She didn't know what to make of this guy. One minute, he gave her the impression that he thought of her as a daughter. The next, he threatened to feed her to his vicious dogs.

Becca retrieved the milk from the fridge and poured it on top of the cereal. From where she sat, she was at a crossroads—one of which was hanging around until Malcolm came back. Or two, she could walk out the door and take her chances with the dogs. Neither sounded appealing. Undecided, she got up, placed the dirty dishes in the sink, and put the milk back in the refrigerator. On the bottom shelf, near the back, was a package of steaks. Finally, something was going her way. She had her ticket past the dogs.

CHAPTER SIXTY-FIVE

Rafferty walked stiffly in front of Lloyd through the terminal and out to the parking garage. They took the elevator up to the third floor, where a vehicle waited with the engine running. The driver got out and marshalled RJ into the back seat. Another man sat inside with a gun pointed at Rafferty's head. When they were all inside, the Dodge Ram lurched forward.

RJ had to remain vigilant. Lloyd clearly needed him alive—for now. In the end, Rafferty knew Masterson could not afford to let him live. He had less than five hours—the time it took to drive from Minneapolis to Vergas—to come up with an escape plan.

CHAPTER SIXTY-SIX

C hris Foley knelt on the ground and felt for the derringer. His blood pressure skyrocketed when he considered the events that brought him to his current setting. It had started nearly three years earlier.

He and his family had spent a relaxing weekend at their summerhouse on Lake Lida. That morning, they'd cleaned, fastened down the boats, and completed the essential chores to secure the cottage until their ensuing visit. With the work done, they had two hours until they had to make the drive home. His two sons tossed the Frisbee on the beach. He and his wife sat in chaise lounges, his head buried in a spy novel, her interest fixated on the pages of the current edition of *Homes & Gardens* magazine.

For months, Eleanor had tried to talk Chris into updating the kitchen at the house. Thus far, Chris had declined her pleas. They danced the dance, but in the end, they both knew she would get what she wanted. He recalled looking at her and smiling to himself. He was indeed a lucky man. As he sat counting his blessings, a boat pulled up close to their dock. Recognizing one of the two men on board, Chris walked out to greet them. Boris Krause was an investment broker from Minneapolis. He'd recently retired and opted to spend summers at his home on Lake Lida.

Boris and Chris were members of the same country club, and the two men golfed in the same league. Other than that, Chris knew very little about him.

Extending a firm handshake, Lloyd Masterson introduced himself. Not long into the conversation, Boris suggested that Chris accompany them in a round of golf. Foley's love of the game had always provided him an excellent opportunity to promote his business and the interests of the bank, and he agreed to meet the two men at the club the following Friday.

That meeting altered Chris's life forever.

It wasn't long before Chris figured out that Lloyd Masterson was the type to prey on people's weaknesses, manipulating them until he got what he wanted. Chris naively reasoned that two could play that game. A smart man, he deemed himself capable of staying one step ahead of Masterson. He proposed that Lloyd invest some of his purported money at Midwest Bank.

Lloyd Masterson did exactly that, showing up within days to open an account. His first deposit came as a bank transfer in the amount of a hundred thousand dollars. He also hired Chris to draw up legal papers. He used the pretext that he was looking to purchase a nearby piece of property and sought Chris's expertise on how to take title. That night, Chris patted himself on the back as he bragged to his wife about the success he had reaped from a few games of golf.

Their golf games resumed in early spring. Masterson invited Chris and Boris to meet him for a drink at the clubhouse after the season's first round.

Lloyd spent an hour flaunting his investment skills. The subsequent proposition came with a guarantee that his new friends would soon be very wealthy men. Chris didn't concur with Boris's enthusiasm. His gut reaction warned him to decline. Lloyd persisted, and by the time they had knocked back their fourth drink, Chris's resistance waned. He finally agreed to think it over and confirmed that he would get back to Lloyd by the week's end.

Boris contacted Chris afterwards and asked to meet for lunch, hoping to hash out the pros and cons of Masterson's deal without Lloyd's undue influence. Sitting in a corner booth at Arthur's Bar, Boris could not contain his enthusiasm. "I'm very excited about the prospect of making a large profit in a small amount of time." His teeth clicked together. "Besides, in the scheme of things, even if we lose our initial investment, it wouldn't be the end of the world for either of us. We can afford it," he said with a wink.

Chris sat back on the Naugahyde bench. "I don't know about you, but twenty thousand is a lot of money for me." He leaned forward again, his heavy brows forming a sharp vee. "Doesn't this sound too good to be true? It's been my experience that anything that seems this easy can spiral into disaster at a moment's notice."

Boris didn't backpedal, and his eagerness effectively countered every objection Foley threw at him. By the end of their lunch, Chris had agreed to go along with the deal.

True to his word, Lloyd invested their money, and within thirty days, he presented each of them with a check for double their invested amount.

"It's that simple, boys. Stick with me, and I'll make you a lot of money." He looked from one man to the other. "I'd like to present you with another proposal." Foley felt the heat of Masterson's glare. "You can take your profit and do whatever you like with it. *Or*, you can give it back to me and let me double it again."

Chris exhaled. He had decided to give his wife the go-ahead to draw up plans for a new dream kitchen. He ran the new numbers through his head. If he doubled the forty thousand, she could remodel the entire house. An image came to mind: Eleanor throwing her arms around him, insisting he was the best husband in the world. It didn't take long for that bubble to burst. What was he thinking? He could easily lose the money the second time around. In that case, he'd be in the hole. No, it would be smarter to take what he had and be thankful for it.

Boris, in opposition, did not hesitate for a single minute. He ceremoniously handed his check back to Lloyd. "I trust you, buddy. I'm in. And if you lose it, so what? I'll only be out the original twenty. No sweat, right, Chris?"

Krause and Masterson turned to Foley. The check in Chris's hand wrinkled under his grip. He wasn't a gambler by any stretch of the imagination. Forty thousand dollars was a lot of money. Hell, the original twenty thousand was more than he could afford to lose. Eleanor would kill him if she ever learned that he had invested their hard-earned money with a man they barely knew.

Again, though, Chris allowed Boris's zealous behavior to influence him. He slowly loosened his clasp and handed the check back to Lloyd.

Krause slapped him on the back, raised his drink, and made a toast to Masterson and their future: "Here's to the man who is going to make us rich."

The next two weeks wreaked havoc in Chris's life. Convinced he had made the wrong decision, every day became a long, drawn-out marathon. Chris was away from his office when the call from Lloyd finally came. The message directed Foley to meet Masterson at Arthur's at five. It was already five-thirty. He grabbed his keys and headed out the door.

Chris wove his way through the crowded bar until he caught a glimpse of Lloyd in deep conversation with a man Foley didn't recognize. His pace slowed until Lloyd glanced up and waved an arm, beckoning him to the table. A hidden foot shoved an empty chair outward toward Chris.

"Here's the man of the hour," Lloyd boomed. He signaled the server to bring another pitcher of beer. Boris Krause joined them a short time later.

"Boys, I can't stay and drink with you tonight." Masterson nodded to the man on his right. "There are two canvas bags under the table. One for each of you," he said. "I'll be in touch." He pushed back from the table. The other man followed suit, and they strolled single file to the exit.

Chris and Boris remained at the table. Chris donned his best poker face, glancing up for a take on his accomplice. Boris struggled to make small talk, and Foley couldn't focus on the conversation either. He drank the last of his beer, excused himself, and fled with the satchel draped over his shoulder.

Once outside, he inhaled deeply. He didn't dare go home in his current state of mind. Eleanor would know something was wrong. She saw through him at every turn. He had to settle things in his head before he confronted her.

Foley walked a block up the street to the bank, strolled around the corner, and let himself in the back entrance. Fortunately, everyone had left for the day. Chris flipped on the lights in his private office, closed the door, and slipped the lock into place.

Seated at his desk, he placed the knapsack squarely in front of him. He rolled his chair backward and forward again, guardedly fingering the package. His hand jerked back as though it were filled with Kryptonite. Too bad he didn't have x-ray vision. Whatever the satchel held, Chris's instincts told him he wouldn't be the winner if Lloyd Masterson had anything to do with it.

"Might as well get this over with," he muttered. He spilled the contents onto his desk. Chris counted eight straps, presumably containing $10,000 each, totaling $80,000.

Foley knew that the money had to come with a price—a price that, in all likelihood, he would find difficult to pay. Whatever had possessed him to invest in Lloyd's money scheme in the first place? He had only one recourse: he had to give the money back before it ruined his life.

Chris placed the straps in three large envelopes and stored the canvas bag in the coat closet. He scanned the office for a hiding place. The bank vault? No. That would create an entirely new set of potential problems. If someone were to happen upon it and inquire where it had come from, he had no viable explanation.

His private safety deposit box was the best place. No one else had a key. Careful to skirt pass the surveillance camera, he put both combinations into the vault door, and it opened quietly. He unlocked his safety deposit box and placed the cash under a stack of files before relocking it.

Chris had made a huge mistake, no argument there. He would contact Lloyd in the morning and inform him that he had no interest in this type of business. That settled, he locked up the office and set a course for home, where he would surround himself with his family's love.

CHAPTER SIXTY-SEVEN

The sound of Masterson's crackling voice echoing through the thick, humid air brought Chris Foley to the present. Foley scanned the farmyard from his hiding place. Then, keeping low to the ground, he crept through the brush until he reached the east side of the house.

The man on the receiving end of Lloyd's anger was none other than Boris Krause. *What was he doing here?* The two men continued their heated dispute as they entered the barn. Chris darted to the back of the building, scaled a wooden fence, and hid behind a stack of hay bales inside the large structure.

From that angle, he had a clear view of the barn's interior. What he saw inside opened a kaleidoscope of feelings that assaulted Chris's moral core. Sylvia's accusations regarding Lloyd's involvement in child abuse was correct. Sickened, Foley crumpled to the ground in defeat.

CHAPTER SIXTY-EIGHT

Becca rinsed her breakfast dishes as she weighed her choices. She didn't relish the notion of confronting the dogs. It was, nonetheless, better than waiting around for her captor to resurface. She grabbed the steaks from the refrigerator, removed the plastic wrapping, and proceeded to cut the meat into several smaller chunks. She portioned the pieces into separate baggies she found in the pantry, put everything back in its place, and wiped the countertop.

On a whim, she walked anxiously through the house one more time, starting in the living room and advancing to his bedroom. She ferreted through Malcolm's belongings like a squirrel rooting for food, her internal clock ticking throughout the search.

The one significant item Becca unearthed was an empty backpack from the rear of the closet. Placing it on the floor, she scanned the room one last time before walking to the bed and cautiously kneeling to peek underneath. Nothing there—not even dust bunnies.

"This is ridiculous! I need to get out of here before he comes back."

Rocking on the heels of her feet, Becca noticed that the top mattress on the bed sat slightly off-center. She slipped her hand under it and discovered a handgun. She whispered a thank you to her dad for taking the time to teach her how to shoot.

If Malcolm had a gun in the house, there had to be ammunition. Her dad had taught her that an intelligent person wouldn't store cartridges at arm's length from firearms, especially when children were in the house. Holding the pistol in her hand, Becca grabbed the backpack and went back to the kitchen. She positioned a chair near the sideboard and used it to hoist herself onto the counter-top. Her arm stretched to its max to reach the top shelf of the cupboard. The precarious balancing act garnered nothing. She hopped down, shifted the chair to the other side of the sink, and repeated the task. It took three tries—but the payoff was worth the time spent. A half-empty box of ammo occupied the top shelf of the cabinet above the refrigerator.

Becca jumped to the floor, opened the box, and withdrew six rounds. After loading the revolver, she stowed the remaining rounds, along with the baggies of raw meat, in the backpack, placing the firearm in the front zippered pocket.

"It's now or never." Becca inhaled deeply and blew air from her lungs. Her fingers had just clutched the doorknob when she froze. Her eyes widened with fear.

CHAPTER SIXTY-NINE

L ucy leaned back on the headrest. Even if Lloyd was alive, why would he wish her harm? Jack sat with a frown painted on his face, apparently expending every effort to jockey his car through the heavy traffic.

Lucy sank deeper into her thoughts. Several days earlier, she had driven this same stretch of highway on her way to housesit her aunt's cottage. She'd looked forward to the change, anticipating a quiet and peaceful summer. The trip had brought change, that was for sure, but there had been nothing peaceful or quiet about it. She had longed to simplify her life, put things into perspective, and make the necessary decisions to move forward. That was proving impossible. Jack had outmaneuvered her at every corner she rounded. Now, smack in the middle of an FBI investigation, he was telling her that someone had a contract out on her.

Jack was capable of many things, but would he lie about something as sinister as that? How would she know? "Who would profit from my death?" she asked.

Taking time to form his words, Jack spoke solemnly: "I want you to know that I won't leave a stone unturned until I find the person who did this to you. For your part, you have to promise me that you'll stay away from RJ—at least, until I find out how he's linked to this. If he is one of Lloyd's lackeys, he's a very dangerous man."

Lucy bristled at Jack's words. The ensuing silence opened a wide range of emotions deeper than Niagara Cave.

She had known RJ Rafferty for such a short time. She traced their time together, the conversations they had had. He wasn't a threat. In fact, her gut told her an opposing story. She didn't doubt that RJ wrestled with some past regret. Despite that, or maybe because of it, it was clear to Lucy that he was one of the good guys.

Lucy had reacted to her husband's affair by building a defensive wall, and the discord had intensified when RJ had come into her life. Each passing mile of endless farmland made it painfully clear that she had to keep moving forward. Fragments of the puzzle lay scattered on the table, and all she had to do was piece them together to gain sight of the full picture. She didn't dare turn back now.

Lucy finally spoke: "I think it's time we talk with the FBI."

"I don't see what we'll gain from that. Regardless, if they'll keep you away from RJ, I'll agree to meet with them."

She refused to let Jack's words convince her to stay away from Rafferty. In fact, she meant to do the exact opposite. She suspected RJ was in serious trouble. If she didn't advocate for him, who would?

Lucy didn't give Jack a chance to change his mind about the FBI. She dialed Agent Hunter's number. He agreed to meet with them at Sylvia's cottage in two hours.

CHAPTER SEVENTY

C rouched in an uncomfortable position behind a stack of hay bales, Chris Foley wished he was anywhere other than his current location. Bile burned the back of his throat. He had witnessed an unspeakable act without raising a hand to stop it. What did that say about him? Abundantly sure that he would never survive a face-to-face confrontation with Masterson, Foley had to come to grips with the fact that he didn't have the courage to make the ultimate sacrifice.

In his defense, who would help the girls if he died a martyr in his battle to set things right? He toyed with the pistol in his pocket and brooded over the dilemma. The fact that he recognized one of the girls in Masterson's barn tormented him beyond solace.

Amber Bremer was the daughter of Malcolm and Deloris Bremer. Chris did not know her or her parents personally, but his eldest son had attended school with her. If memory served him, Amber had gone missing about six months earlier. Rumors had it that the Bremer family had exhausted every resource to find their daughter.

The possibility of reuniting the Bremer family restored Foley's confidence—and to that end, the sooner he acted, the faster he could get back here with the police.

He focused on the occupants of the building, sizing up his chances of a clean getaway. Masterson toyed with the girls while Boris Krause sauntered to the other end of the gaping room. Now was the time for Chris to flee this hellhole.

Adrenaline carried him to the edge of the woods, where he stopped to catch his breath. Wheezing, he grabbed for his cell to call the police. The clip on his belt was empty. He patted himself frantically, to no avail. The phone had undoubtedly come dislodged when he had made a run for it.

Foley sank to his knees in defeat. "How could I be so stupid?"

His hollow lament underscored his peril and that of the girls. He gasped for air, his hand grasping his chest. What else could go wrong? Did he dare go back to find his cell, or would it be better to forge onward?

Chris chose the latter, and in his state of confusion, he hiked more than a mile in the wrong direction. He doubled back, regretting the time he had let slip through his fingers. He finally got to his car, sweaty and out of breath, and climbed in. His mind switched courses to the tire tracks he'd seen upon arrival. Ever the businessman, Foley made a mental note to check out the property in the morning. That is, his cynical side countered for the second time that day, *if I survive at all*. He tugged the car door shut, slipped the gear into reverse, and backed out onto the dirt road.

A movement to his left triggered Foley to stomp his foot on the brake pedal. To his astonishment, Lloyd Masterson walked straight toward him, his arm raised, a gun pointed at his head. In that instant, Chris Foley saw a bright flash. After that, everything went black.

CHAPTER SEVENTY-ONE

Marveling at his fortune, Lloyd Masterson lowered his firearm and walked decisively back the way he had come. Foley had sealed his own fate. Masterson smiled, remembering the sound of an intrusive ring as he had finished lecturing the two girls. The unmistakable tone of a cellphone ringing had prompted looks from all three.

"What the hell?" Masterson had screamed. He turned. "You two stay here," he commanded. "Don't move a fucking inch."

He ducked behind a tractor parked near the north wall and haltingly moved toward the chime until he was close enough to see the phone lying on the dirt floor behind the bales of hay. He approached with caution, anticipating a trap closing in around him. With nerves stretched taut, he snatched up the cell, only to drop it when it started up again. Masterson pivoted his head from side to side, making sure no one was playing him for a fool. He retrieved the device, read the screen, and waited for the person on the other end to say something.

"Hello. Hello? Can you hear me?" a female voice said. "Chris? Are you there?" Lloyd hit the *end call* button. It rang again.

This time it went unanswered. He shoved the cell into his pocket and faced his current prey. As ordered, they were exactly where he had positioned them. Masterson yelled for Boris to watch over the merchandise and then swiftly exited through the back entrance.

It didn't take long to pick up Chris's trail. When he ascertained that the attorney was the sole perpetrator, Masterson eliminated the problem. He wouldn't normally abandon a dead body in the open, but he wasn't afforded the luxury of time to dispose of this one. Lloyd figured it would be weeks, possibly months, until someone stumbled upon the scene. He aimed to be on some foreign beach, basking in the sun, when that time rolled around.

Masterson accelerated his stride on his way back to the farm. There were a lot of loose ends to clean up before his rendezvous with RJ. His throaty laughter filled the air. RJ's reaction when the two squared off would make his day.

The minute he completed that job, Lloyd intended to board a plane to Italy and settle a long-overdue score with his infamous wife.

CHAPTER SEVENTY-TWO

Becca's panic attack soon subsided. She opened the front door to the little house and sprinted down the road. Her heart leapt with joy when she saw the wooden gate her abductor had driven through the prior night. A parked sedan on the other side gave pause until it occurred to her that maybe aid was within her grasp. She scaled the fence in high spirits.

As she approached the empty vehicle, her exuberance faded. Fretful that the owner of the car could easily be a foe rather than a friend, she took cover behind a nearby tree to regroup and determine her next move.

Not much time had elapsed when the sound of the car door opening and then closing pricked her ears. Peeking around the weighty trunk, Becca was about to run to him until another man emerged from behind the thick brush on the far side of the road. The man raised his arm and fired a round into the car's windshield. Becca parted her lips to scream and then intuitively clasped her hand over her mouth. She dropped to the ground, praying that he hadn't seen her. Minutes ticked by until she finally got the courage to gaze back at the ghastly scene.

She surveyed the area from her vantage point. The man with the gun had disappeared. Becca retrieved the handgun she had stowed in the backpack and advanced. Painted with bright red streaks, thin spiderweb cracks stretched from one end of the windshield to the other. No sense in going any further. Nothing would help Mr. Foley now.

Becca froze at the sound of barking dogs fast approaching. There was no other option. She ran to the vehicle and jumped into the back seat, yanking the door shut seconds before the dogs smashed into the side of the car with a thunderous thud. Saliva dripped through their threatening teeth as they bashed into the glass. Fortunately, the dogs had a short attention span. They eventually bestowed Becca with one final growl and trotted off.

Fearing the dogs would reappear, Becca slouched in the back, prepared for an indeterminable delay. She bolted upright when a low moan filled the car's interior. Surprised to learn that she wasn't alone, she extended a shaky hand over the seat and felt for a pulse at the nape of the man's neck. Blood oozed from the side of his head. She peered closer and saw that his chest rose and fell slightly.

"Can you hear me?" she whispered.

He seemed to try to nod. Becca jumped out of the back seat and opened the driver's door.

"Can you move at all?" she implored.

She pushed and he painfully dragged his body to the side until Becca had room to fit behind the steering wheel.

She sped down the dirt road. When she got to the highway, she frantically scoured the area for hints that would tell her where she was. Nothing looked familiar.

CHAPTER SEVENTY-THREE

Agents Hunter and Peterson sat in their government-issued sedan in Sylvia's driveway, windows up, air conditioner purring. Jack parked his Mercedes beside them. Everyone exited their respective vehicles, and Lucy made introductions. "Let's get out of this heat," she said, taking the lead. Once inside, she ushered everyone into the kitchen.

Stress and lack of sleep had taken a toll, but a strong dose of caffeine would carry her through the meeting. Lucy filled the pot with water and added the appropriate amount of ground beans, followed by an extra scoop to achieve the desired jolt. She distributed the beverages and took the empty seat at the table.

Lucy got straight to the point. "In case you're not aware, I've delved into some investigating on my own since we last talked."

The agents' stoic faces revealed nothing. "Why don't you tell us exactly what you know, and then we'll fill you in on what we've compiled," Peterson said.

Lucy snuck a glance at Jack. "I flew to Phoenix with Detective Rafferty." When neither agent spoke, Lucy resumed her summary. "RJ told me he had information that could lead him to the missing girls. In anticipation that our endeavor would lead us to their whereabouts, I consented to travel undercover with him."

Agent Hunter's sober stare over the rim of his mug rattled Lucy. After a brief hesitation, she continued, giving the agents thorough details about her trip. Jack's furrowed brows made her skip the part where she and RJ went sightseeing and had dinner.

"When we got back to the hotel, uniformed officers filled the lobby. I sat in the car while RJ entered through a service door and collected our luggage. From there, we went directly to the airport and booked the first available flight home. We landed in Minneapolis early this morning, at which point I slipped into the bathroom for a few minutes. When I came out, RJ was gone."

Lucy glanced at Jack, unsure of how he'd react to her next statement. "I fear for RJ's safety. I've gotten to know him during the last few days, and his intentions are good. I don't think he would have left me stranded if he had a choice."

Jack's hands formed a steeple. "Did you ever find out why the police were at your hotel?"

"No." Lucy took a moment to reflect. "If RJ knew, he didn't tell me, and I didn't ask. Everything happened so fast."

Peterson interjected, "You said you last saw Rafferty at the airport. Thinking back, did he say or do anything that might give us an indication of where he might be?"

Lucy shook her head. "No. Nothing at all."

"Did you notice anyone in the terminal acting suspicious in any way?"

"No. I've gone over it a million times in my head. He was there one minute and gone the next. I don't have a clue what happened to him."

"Maybe he met someone there," Jack baited.

Lucy narrowed her gaze. Was he suggesting she tell the FBI that RJ may have met Lloyd at the airport? That detail would only give Agents Hunter and Peterson more ammunition against the detective. "I guess anything's possible," she said, avoiding a candid answer to Jack's query.

She turned to Agent Hunter for answers. "Can you tell me anything that would help me understand how all this is connected?"

"No. Not with regards to Rafferty. Do you remember the name of the man you met with in Phoenix?"

"I think he called himself Samuel Crane."

"We'll get our men on that right away. There could be a connection between him and RJ's vanishing act." Hunter nodded to Peterson, who rose, picking up her cellphone as she walked out the front door.

"On a different note," Hunter said, "your aunt got word to us that Kelly Grant, the girl who accompanied her to Europe, was on a return flight to Fargo. We picked up Ms. Grant at the airport yesterday. She claims she willingly left the country with Sylvia and that the police had no reason to look for her. The FBI has issued an arrest warrant charging Sylvia Masterson with kidnapping. Until we confirm otherwise, we're proceeding on the assumption that your aunt is involved in her husband's racketeering and human trafficking schemes."

Jack interrupted, "Do you have any leads on Masterson?"

"Interesting you should ask." The two men stared at each other. After an uncomfortable delay, Hunter said, "I can't discuss Lloyd Masterson with you. Why don't you tell us what you know?"

Jack shrugged. "I am acquainted with someone at the county attorney's office in St. Paul. He told me the authorities think Masterson is alive. Can you confirm that?"

"Like I said, we're not at liberty to discuss Masterson." Hunter pushed his chair back from the table and stood. He gave Lucy a surly smile. "We'll be in touch. Please contact us if you learn anything new." He walked out the door, leaving no room for further discussion, as Lucy followed him in a daze.

"That was strange," she said when she rejoined Jack in the kitchen. "Do you think we should have told them that you saw Lloyd at the airport?"

"I gave you a window," Jack challenged. "I assumed you kept quiet because you didn't want the FBI investigating deeper into Rafferty's connection in this mess." Lucy glared at him. Jack cocked his head. "Those agents weren't going to share anything with us anyway. They're not your friends, Lucy. They're appeasing you because they think you're their ticket to Lloyd, via Sylvia."

"I've told them everything I know."

"Yes, but you'll be the one Sylvia contacts when she figures out that she's at an impasse and needs help."

"What makes you say that? How can you be so sure that Sylvia has anything to do with any of this?"

"Wake up, Lucy. Lloyd is her husband. Not only does that connection incriminate Sylvia, but it also makes you a possible suspect in the eyes of the FBI."

Lucy sucked on the tip of her index finger. What if Jack was on to something? What if Sylvia was on the wrong side of the FBI investigation? She scrambled to come up with a logical explanation for her aunt's actions. *No,* she thought, *I refuse to let Jack manipulate me this way.*

Her stomach growled. She found the makings for sandwiches in the refrigerator. Happy to have a diversion, Lucy plastered mayo on the bread and added lunchmeat and a slice of cheese to each. A mound of chips completed the meal. They ate in silence, each cautious of the other's motives.

Jack ultimately spoke first. "It's been quite a morning, huh?" His voice lightened. "Since it's too hot to spend much time outside, how about we get in the car and drive up to Itasca State Park? When was the last time we did something fun together? A little down time might be exactly what the doctor ordered."

How could Jack switch gears so easily? Lucy reeled with the notion that someone wanted her dead. The possibility that she might be a suspect in the FBI's investigation made her head spin. And if that wasn't enough, RJ was MIA. What made Jack assume that she would put all that aside and enjoy an afternoon gallivanting with him?

He'd managed the unthinkable, though. If she believed his story that someone had a contract out on her, protection, in the form of a conspicuous companion, could be wise. Armed with a small cooler filled with bottled water and a few snacks, they headed east on Highway 10 to Lake Itasca, a small glacial lake notable for serving as the headwaters of the Mississippi River.

The afternoon worked out better than expected. There was no fighting, no disagreements. Jack said nothing to antagonize her. They stopped at a pizza joint on the way home and arrived back at the cabin a little after eight. Lucy startled herself by suggesting wine on the deck. Once they were seated, she casually asked Jack about his mother.

Jack's fingers wrapped around the stem of his wine glass. "She's fine," he said. "Why do you ask?"

A cool breeze slipped across the lake's surface, bringing a much-needed relief from the day's heat. Lucy gave him a slight nod. "No reason, really. You haven't mentioned her the last few times we've talked, and I was wondering what she's been up to."

Jack rubbed the back of his neck. "I don't see much of her since you and I split up. To be honest, she's been drinking a lot these days, and I don't care to be around her."

"I'm sorry to hear that. You two are close. I'm sure she hates to see you unhappy, and I know she blames me for that."

Jack leaned forward and reached for Lucy's hand. "You could make us both happy if you'd give up this charade and move back home with me."

Lucy pulled her hand away and snapped, "Jack, stop it. You won't like the results if you continue down this path."

Jack went crimson. "I'm so tired of walking on eggshells around you. I've done everything I can to show you how sorry I am, and yet you sit on your high horse and condemn me relentlessly."

Lucy's anger flared. "How dare you judge me! You brought this on yourself. You were the one who had the affair. I'm trying to get my life in order and figure out where I go from here. I need more time."

"More time. More time for what?" His voice escalated. "More time to chase after that detective guy? You get my hopes up and then you say things that make my blood boil."

Lucy got up and walked to the railing of the deck. Hoping to ease the mounting tension, she said, "We've been through a lot today. I'm tired. I'm sure you are, too. We can talk about this more civilly tomorrow."

"Lucy, you're always putting off this discussion." He stood with his hands on his hips. "If we don't ever talk about it, it will never be resolved."

"Honestly, I can't think about it now. Several girls have gone missing. They're out there somewhere. Surely you can't put yourself ahead of them—can you?"

Their eyes locked, his dark and foreboding, hers defiant. She held her ground. Jack altered his face to mirror a blank slate. He walked past her and down to the dock. Lucy picked up the glasses and the half-empty bottle of wine from the table and carried them inside.

She hated to end the night this way. The wood planks on the dock creaked, alerting him to her approach. He kept his back to her.

"I understand you're hurting," Lucy said, "but I can't help that." She took a moment to gather herself. "I'm trying to be as honest as I can with you. You can't push me on this."

When he didn't respond, she decided to cut her losses and go back inside. Glancing back over her shoulder, she noted his back was rigid against her rebuke.

"I'll put a clean towel in the bathroom. You can sleep in Sylvia's room again."

CHAPTER SEVENTY-FOUR

Driving east along the highway, it didn't take Becca long to figure out where she was. By her calculations, they should arrive at the hospital within twenty to thirty minutes. The pale, ghostly skin of the man slumped beside her sent shivers through her rigid body.

"Hang in there," she pleaded, "We're almost there."

When his bloodied head swiveled to face her, the ghoulish sight caused her to recoil, sending the car veering off the road. Becca swiftly regained control and forged on.

Flashing red lights appeared out of nowhere. Relieved, Becca quickly pulled to the side of the road and was out of the car before the police cruiser came to a complete stop. Becca inhaled sharply when the woman officer barked the order for her to get back into her car. Standing her ground, Becca shouted, "Please, you have to help me! Mr. Foley is in my car. He's been shot. He's in bad shape."

The police detective walked past Becca and leaned into the car. "Who shot him?"

Becca lurched backward at the officer's tone. "I don't know. A man came out of the woods and shot him. He's bleeding really bad. We need to get him to the hospital."

"Stay here, where I can see you."

Becca watched in disbelief as the officer walked back to her car, seized her cellphone and spoke into it. Too far away to hear any of the conversation, Becca remained alone on the side of the road, repeatedly glancing at the injured man inside the car. The officer approached her. Becca shrank when the woman pulled a gun and leveled it at her.

"You need to come with me."

"What are you talking about? We need to get Mr. Foley to the hospital."

The woman didn't hesitate. She swung around and fired her weapon into the car. Becca screamed and took off running. A second shot buzzed within inches of Becca's ear.

"Freeze, or the next round will penetrate your pretty little head."

Becca's feet slid out from under her. Shaken, she managed to get to her knees and pivot to face the woman, unable to tear her eyes from the silver nametag: Detective C. Mitchell.

The detective snatched handcuffs from the back of her belt. "Get up and turn around." Hard metal encircled Becca's wrists. Mitchell took hold of her elbow and propelled her to the patrol car. The key fob clicked, and the trunk popped open.

"Get in."

Nothing in Becca's short life had prepared her for this. Everything was a tangled mess. The police were supposed to be her friend. If she couldn't count on the men and women in uniform, who could she trust? She numbly hoisted herself over the rear bumper and briefly thought about the gun she had had in her possession when she had come across Mr. Foley. A sharp blow to the head rendered her ruminations moot.

Becca woke to find herself lying on her side on a dirt floor, her hands still cuffed behind her back. Waves of nausea surged through her body.

CHAPTER SEVENTY-FIVE

L ucy checked the bathroom to make sure there were clean towels for Jack and then, happy to have some time alone, collapsed onto her bed. Life was spinning out of hand, and try as she might, she had no way to stop it.

Large raindrops slapping against the windowpane roused her. Lightning slid through the sky and illuminated the small bedroom in step with a thunder clap that shook the cottage.

Lucy buried her head under the pillow and tried to go back to sleep. Wide awake an hour later, she crawled out of bed and proceeded to the kitchen, where she brewed herself a cup of hot tea. She contemplated Jack, asleep in the next room. What was it about him that set her nerves on edge? He had always been obstinate. Lately, however, his behavior had showed signs of paranoia. If she were honest, she'd admit that his father's death had potentially triggered an abnormal transformation in his personality.

The hard question was, did she still love him? Holding her cup with both hands, she took a slow sip. No. The answer was a resounding no. She doubted that she had ever loved him.

The bitter taste of failure almost overwhelmed her. She swallowed hard, conceding that she had no desire to spend another day married to Jack Rydell. Lucy blinked several times to erase the unpleasant thoughts in her head.

The image of RJ warmed her like bright sunshine on a cool autumn day. "Oh, God, please keep him safe."

She was finally ready to admit that her feelings for RJ ran deep. He was different from any man she had ever known; everything about him seemed contrary. Outwardly, he displayed roguish, errant traits, and yet he treated Lucy with the utmost kindness. She loved that he lit up when he talked of his family. And the pride he showed for his parents. The fondness he displayed when sharing stories of his sisters. The impish sparkle in his eyes when he flirted with her. His strong arms, which when wrapped snuggly around Lucy made her feel safe, even amid all the turmoil simmering around them.

The reverse side had her second-guessing his true character. The bar fight came to mind. Then there was the issue that someone hated him enough to take a bat to his head. The idea of the police report filed by his ex-girlfriend made Lucy squirm. She also struggled with the matter of his vocation. She admired his aspirations to "protect and serve," but was it possible that the job brought out the worst in him? Setting all that aside, his absence and potential peril was an anchor dragging her underwater.

Lucy imagined her fingertips brushing aside the tuft of hair that usually curled across his forehead. Her entire body ached for his touch. The physical attraction between them clouded any logic she could possibly bring to the table. No other man, including Jack, had ever elicited such feelings from her.

She doubted that she had the ability to identify a good man even if one waltzed into her life. Nothing in her upbringing had shown her the way; there were no role models. She didn't have to look any further than her aunt and her mother for proof that the fault could lie in the family genes.

Lucy's spine stiffened at her mother's pick for a husband, her head shaking vehemently to loosen the memories of her father's brutality.

Sylvia's record wasn't much better. Her picks hadn't been the greatest even before she met Masterson. Was Lloyd as bad as they said? Admittedly, Lucy had never trusted him. That, however, didn't necessarily mean he was capable of the heinous crimes outlined by the FBI. On the flip side, if he had committed the crimes, he could be the one who had ordered a contract on her life. If not him, then who?

CHAPTER SEVENTY-SIX

Sean Penalton woke to find himself curled in a fetal position on the time-aged hardwood floor of his bedroom closet. He had often sought solace there—the small cocoon offered him shelter from the outside world.

Surrounded by dark shadows, Sean could only guess the time of day. He put his ear to the floorboard and lay motionless, listening for anything that would indicate whether or not his mother was up and about. He didn't care to suffer another one of her incessant lectures this morning.

Hearing nothing, Sean untangled his stiff limbs and straightened his back, dwarfing the space he occupied. A spasm seized his left shoulder and spread to the left side of his head. He struggled to shake the image of Lucy and RJ entwined in each other's arms. Self-pity was something Sean delved into often. It dug deep into his psyche, twisting and pulling until he didn't know what to make of anything.

Lucy was nothing but a tease, no better than all the other girls he'd known. In grade school, they'd kicked and punched him, then ran away giggling. In high school, they had shown him their boobies. When he had tried to touch them, they had run away laughing. He cried silently.

With new insight, a hint of composure resurfaced. Lucy was a kind, loving soul. Rafferty was the problem. If Sean removed the detective from the picture, Lucy would be his.

Destiny called. With that in mind, Sean got to his feet, packed a few necessities in his duffle bag, and left through the back door with a bounce in his step. It would be hours before his parents learned something was amiss.

Sean set off on foot, pleased with his plan to capture Lucy's heart by any means necessary. Shoulders back, head high, he moved down the long walkway to the beach, his lips pursed with a jaunty whistle.

He glanced down to the water's edge. His father's fishing boat would certainly make the trip to the other side of the lake faster and easier. On the other hand, it would leave a trail for someone to follow. He had the time and was up for the long trek: Sean set out for the woods that ran parallel to the farmyard.

At the end of his dad's property, he hiked across the neighbor's land and then back along the road until he got to Highway 4. He crossed the roadway and cut through more grassland, jogging a couple of miles out of his way to throw any would-be trackers off his course. He doubled back and arrived at his destination five hours later. If he had used the boat the trip would have taken a mere thirty minutes.

Sean had discovered the neglected log cabin when he was a boy. In his youth, he'd played there with abandon, letting his imagination run wild as only a child can do. As an adult, he came for solitude. Seldom did anyone interrupt his private retreat—that is, until recently. During the past two years, Sean had witnessed people—scary people—coming and going at all hours.

He approached from the east, carefully circling the area, searching for potential poachers. Finding none, he set up a few traps for any unwanted visitors. Sean slipped inside the cabin. It was in much the same condition as it had been on previous visits.

Often, he pretended this was his house. The tattered sofa afforded him a place to relax and take naps on lazy afternoons. The table and chairs lent credibility to his make-believe world. Months earlier, someone had placed a dirty mattress on the floor on the far side of the room. This addition baffled Sean. Again, he shrugged off the bad vibes and went back outside.

He walked the perimeter of the property and decided there was no cause for concern. A hike to the lake confirmed that the old fishing boat was where he had left it weeks earlier, well-hidden behind thick underbrush. On his way back to the cottage, he came across a small mound of freshly dug dirt. His brow furrowed. Someone must have decided that this would be a quiet resting place for a beloved pet. With that settled, he moved on.

CHAPTER SEVENTY-SEVEN

C hris Foley lay drooped across the front seat of the car, exactly where Cassie Mitchell had left him for dead. He edged back into consciousness. The temperature inside the car made him feel akin to a turkey baking in a hot oven. Beads of sweat trickled across his parched skin, soaking every inch of his clothing.

The gruesome scene replayed behind closed eyelids. He saw Masterson's gun zero in on him. Tiny sparks arced in slow motion as the bullet exited the barrel. Small cracks spread like wildfire when it passed through the windshield.

Something else came to mind, something almost mystical. When he thought he was about to take his last breath, a voice in his head urged Chris to duck out of the way. Miraculously, he managed to shift his weight enough to avoid a direct hit from the bullet.

His shaky hand traced the caked blood along his cheek, and a bout of dizziness sent him back into the darkness. Everything came rushing back to him the minute he opened his eyes. He had survived not one, but two attempts on his life. The second assault had come from a weapon brandished by a police officer. That one had found its mark in his left arm. It was nothing short of a miracle that he was alive. Determined not to waste divine intervention, Chris's resolve strengthened. He promised himself that if he survived this ordeal, he would do everything in his power to see that Masterson paid for his crimes.

Using his right arm to steady himself, Chris grasped the steering wheel and hauled himself into a sitting position. His jaw dropped when he saw the view through the shattered windshield. A long, narrow highway, lined with fields of corn on either side, stretched beyond his line of vision. The road had fallen into disrepair. It could be hours before someone came along to help.

Chris took on the daunting task of driving himself back to town. He wrestled to maneuver his body behind the wheel, then held his breath and reached for the keys. "I can do this," Chris said.

He shifted the car into drive and eased his foot up against the gas pedal. His left arm proved useless, making it impossible to pull the driver's door shut. Chris inched the vehicle forward at a slow, steady pace, with the door swaying back and forth on its hinges. Self-loathing consumed him with each passing mile. And he was so damn tired. He longed to lie down, if only for a minute. Foley let his head drop to the steering wheel, his eyes blinking back tears.

"Don't you dare quit now." Chris strained to right himself back against the seat. "You have to stay alert. She'll come back. And when she does, you'd better be far, far away."

Chris had recognized the woman who had left him for dead. Any idiot knew it was bad practice to leave evidence lying around that would guarantee a prison sentence. She would be back. And if not her, she would send one of her lackeys to clean up the mess. He needed to get as far away from here as possible and without delay.

The sun was now a bright red orb sinking behind dark billowing clouds to the west. The impending darkness filled Chris with dread. His chances of finding help would diminish miserably once night set in. Gripped by his own fears, he almost missed the strange headlights bearing over his left shoulder. The machine lumbering toward him from an adjacent field appeared to be a combine harvester.

Chris's muddled brain rebooted. He slammed on the brakes and rammed his fist against the car's horn, doggedly trying to catch the farmer's attention. Optimism faded when it became apparent that the roar of the thresher's engine blocked out any chance of the farmer hearing his pleas.

Chris summoned every ounce of energy he had left. He leaned out of the car and tumbled to the ground at the exact moment that the farmer's huge harvester came to a stop at the edge of the property, a mere twenty yards away.

CHAPTER SEVENTY-EIGHT

Malcome Bremer walked out onto the porch. Tweedledee and Tweedledum stumbled up the steps uninvited, begging for a piece of meat or at least a small treat. "A lot of good you two are," Malcolm reprimanded. "Go home, where you belong."

The sour tone of his voice did nothing to discourage their animation. They wagged their stubby backsides and circled him, trying to cajole him into a better mood. He ignored them and moved down the stairs. Much to the dogs' chagrin, Malcolm opened his car door, got in, and shut it without uttering another word. The dogs sat on their haunches; their big brown eyes wide with wonder.

Malcolm lowered the window. "Don't look at me that way," he grumbled. "You boys were supposed to keep her here! Now I have got to go find her." He shook his head in disgust and drove away. "Where to start is the million-dollar question," he said aloud, tempting the fates to present him with a clear answer.

Malcolm parked his vehicle half a block from the Bankses' family home. The house sat in a quiet neighborhood landscaped with large deciduous trees. Proudly placed flowerbeds exhibited periwinkle, daylilies, and peonies. A sickening feeling crept through him as he came to grips with what his actions had cost his family.

Bremer sidelined his thoughts and slouched in the driver's seat when a big blue pickup lumbered into view and pulled up to the curb in front of the Bankses' home. Malcolm watched as Wayne Johanson got out of the truck and sauntered to the front door. To Malcolm's utter disbelief, Dan Banks opened the door and ushered Johanson inside.

"What the hell? Why would they invite this guy into their home? Don't they know who he is and what he's capable of?" Malcolm gazed skyward as if expecting a response.

He had no solid evidence of Johanson's connection to the kidnappings. However, he had established a link between Wayne Johanson and Lloyd Masterson. In Malcolm's mind, that was all the proof he needed to confirm Wayne's character.

Malcolm got out of his car and headed to the house. His feet refused to go any further than the sidewalk leading to the front stoop. If Becca wasn't here, what would he tell her parents? How could he admit to them that he had been the one who had taken Becca? He certainly didn't want to chronicle the deeds that had led him to their doorstep.

Malcolm couldn't live with himself if he didn't make sure that Becca was safe, and to find out, he had to face her parents. He marched up the flight of stairs with purpose, only to drop back when he confronted the front door.

CHAPTER SEVENTY-NINE

Wayne Johanson heard about Becca's kidnapping several hours after the incident and spent the night calling in every favor he had. No one could, or would, divulge the circumstances of her abduction. With no other avenue available, Wayne needed to talk to his nephew.

He arrived at the hospital early the next morning to learn that Hal's bed had been stripped and the room emptied of all his belongings. Panicked, Wayne lurched back and almost collided with a nurse coming out of the bathroom, her arms full of dirty linens.

"Excuse me. Where's the patient who was in this room?" Wayne demanded.

"I believe he checked out this morning," she said curtly, backing out of the room. "Check with the front desk."

Wayne rushed to the nurses' station. "I'm looking for my nephew, Hal Johanson. He was in room 212. I was told he left the hospital this morning. I don't think that's remotely possible."

"Let me see what I have here," the nurse said. A few keys strokes on her key pad brought on a smile. "Yes," she said softly. "He checked out this morning at seven thirty-five."

"How can that be? He woke up from a coma yesterday." He continued his barrage. "Why didn't someone notify me of his release? Did Doctor Miller consent to his discharge?"

She batted her long eyelashes. "I'm sorry. I don't have more details for you. Dr. Miller is on the floor. I can page him if you'd like to consult with him."

"Yes. I need to talk to the doctor immediately."

She pointed to the open door across the hall. "You can wait in there. The doctor will be with you when he finishes his rounds."

Wayne walked into the room and took a chair on the opposite side. Willing the doctor to walk through the door, he glanced at his watch several times and then at the big clock hanging on the wall. Fifteen minutes crawled by.

Dr. Miller cleared his throat as he entered. "What can I do for you, Mr. Johanson?"

"Thank you for taking the time to see me, doctor. I came to visit Hal and discovered he's checked out of the hospital."

The doctor nodded. "Yes. Hal was very agitated this morning. He demanded to be released."

"Was that wise?"

"No, it wasn't. I made every effort to persuade him to stay, but in the end, I had to discharge him. I can't keep a patient in the hospital against his will."

"Is it safe for him to be walking around so soon after the accident?"

"I made it very clear how important it was that he remain under a doctor's care. There could be dire consequences if he ignores my advice."

"Did he leave alone? Did someone pick him up?"

"Hal checked himself out. I took the time to escort him to the curb believing that I could convince him to stay for at least another day or two. As you can see, I didn't succeed. And no, I didn't see who was driving the car he got in." Doctor Miller gestured to the door. "If there's nothing else, I have patients to tend to."

"Yes, of course. I appreciate your time."

The two men walked out of the room together.

"Please keep me apprised of Hal's condition, and convince him to check himself back in."

"I'll do everything in my power to get Hal back here, where he can receive proper medical attention." Wayne shook the doctor's outstretched hand.

He dialed the Bankses' number the minute he was alone. At the sound of Dan's voice, Wayne blurted, "Mr. Banks, this is Wayne Johanson. I need to talk to you right away. I'm leaving the hospital, and I'll be at your house within a half an hour."

He didn't wait for Dan's response.

CHAPTER EIGHTY

Malcome Bremer stood on the front porch of the Bankses' home, knowing in his heart that Becca was not inside. If he could go back in time, he would do so many things differently. Becca had faced unparalleled dangers due to his incompetence. Why hadn't he told her about Amber...about Masterson... and about the Johansons?

Malcolm gripped the handrail to steady himself. For all his good intentions, he had ruined everything. "My sole motivation was to protect her," he whispered. Nothing he did now could alter the anguish he had caused. Malcolm took a deep breath and let it out slowly. Maybe—just maybe—he was blowing things out of proportion. Perhaps Becca had made it home safely. He raised his hand and rapped against the wooden door.

His heart sank the minute Dan Banks opened the door. The vision of another father's grief told Malcolm everything he needed to know.

"Who is it?" Mary Ann called out from an interior room.

"I don't know," Dan answered.

Malcolm winced. "My name is Malcolm Bremer. Amber Bremer is my daughter. I need to talk to you and your wife. May I come in?"

A part of Malcolm wished they would turn him away. At least then, he could say he had tried. His hopes that he'd find Becca inside vanished when Dan motioned for him to enter. Steeped in trepidation, Malcolm crossed the threshold.

He took a moment to absorb the cozy charm of the living room. Family pictures taken at various junctures adorned the wall to his left. He couldn't stop himself; he walked closer and studied each photo. The images told the story of an all-American family: two good-looking parents raising three healthy and happy girls. Also captured in several of the pictures were an older man and woman, presumably grandparents. Different stages, all projecting a long and happy life together.

Malcolm recalled a similarly adorned wall in the house he and Delores had shared not so long ago. He wondered if he would ever be part of a loving family again. For the first time, he questioned if he could win Delores back. Had she moved on? Had she found another man to take his place? He wouldn't blame her if she had. How long had it been since he had last talked to her? "Too long," he mumbled.

Suddenly, he froze. Seeing Wayne Johanson sitting calmly in a chair in the corner of the room made Malcolm's blood boil. The smug look on the bastard's face brought forth a rage that Bremer had held at arm's length for far too long. Something snapped. Screaming obscenities, he charged.

Wayne braced himself for the attack. He sprung up and out of the chair, thrusting his elbow into Malcolm's ribs. The scuffle ended within seconds, with Wayne pinning Malcolm to the floor in a half-nelson.

"What the hell is wrong with you?" Wayne yelled.

"Get off me or I swear to God, I'll..." Malcolm struggled to breathe.

Johanson rolled his antagonist over, doubled up his fist, and slammed it into the side of Malcolm's face. Wayne got to his feet and shook his head at the limp body sprawled on the floor.

Mary Ann and Dan stood in shock.

"Do you know this man?" Dan demanded. "Is he going to be okay?"

"Yeah, he'll be fine. I didn't hit him that hard." Johanson massaged his bruised hand, which belied his words. "He'll come to in a few minutes with one vicious headache. Serves him right. Why would he attack me?" Wayne faked innocence.

A moan bubbled up in Malcolm's throat. He managed to get himself into a sitting position, clutching his chest as if to say, *this is definitely not my day.*

CHAPTER EIGHTY-ONE

The handcuffs wrenched ruthlessly at Becca's wrists as she fought to free herself, both emotionally and physically, from the restraints. She lay helpless on the dirt floor, gasping for air. Heavy grit acted like sandpaper, grating on her teeth, tongue, and gums, making it impossible to swallow. A reflexive gag sent her body into convulsions. By the time the tremors subsided, she had no fight left in her. Becca slipped into a dismal void.

She woke with no clue as to how long she had been out. Determined to stay calm, Becca worked in vain to free her hands. Maneuvering her legs under her body and jostling herself until she was sitting upright, she pressed her back against the wall and shimmied up to a standing position. The 10' x 12' cubicle surrounding her suggested a barn stall. The walls were of old knotted wood, grey with age. She stared placidly at the double-hinged door, the top half slightly ajar—a possible means of escape.

Becca refused to give in to despair. Her parents had taught her to see a silver lining even when things were at their dimmest. She looked for the bright side of her predicament. *Being alive is a good thing. That's more than I can say for poor Mr. Foley.* She shuddered at the thought of him lying dead in the front seat of the car, at the hands of a police officer.

Becca's eyes moved to the door when the clang of metal on metal filled the small room. A young girl stepped inside. She stood a couple inches taller than Becca and appeared to be a few years younger. Thin as a reed, she had a full head of red curls that hung past her shoulders and bounced with her every movement.

The girl placed a small sack on the floor and instructed Becca to face the wall. The cuffs loosened. Becca brought her hands forward and gently rubbed the black and blue rings emerging around her wrists. She nodded a thanks to her new friend. Their mirrored expressions veiled the depth of their plight.

"I brought you something to eat." The girl picked up the sack and withdrew a sandwich wrapped in wax paper, along with a bottle of water. Handing them to Becca, she swiftly retreated.

"Wait!" Becca coughed. Searing pain stretched the length of her throat. "Who are you?" she sputtered. "Why am I being kept here?"

The girl shot back, "It's for your own good. Please don't try to leave this room." She vanished, leaving Becca feeling more alone than ever before.

She wanted to go after the girl, but her feet refused to move. Dim rays of light seeped through the crevices in the wall, making her wonder about the time of day. The last thing she had eaten was a bowl of cereal. Becca had no idea if that had been this morning or longer ago; it depended on how long she had been out. She took a big gulp of water, swished it around her dry mouth, and swallowed hard. She lowered herself onto the straw-covered floor, unwrapped the sandwich, and devoured it broodingly, chewing deliberately. When she finished it, she drank the last of the water.

With renewed energy, she got up and went to the door, shoved the top half open, and leaned over the bottom half far enough to catch sight of a man sitting on a bench a few yards away. He didn't have to say a word. Everything about him, including the ugly scar zigzagging across his cheek, told Becca he wasn't there to help her. She stumbled back into the stall. Her vision blurred. Seconds later, she fell to the ground.

CHAPTER EIGHTY-TWO

Sean spent the better part of the afternoon daydreaming about his future with Lucy. The need to stretch his legs encouraged him to grab the high-powered binoculars he'd purchased at an army supply store in Fargo and hike back down to the lake. He raised the field glasses and zeroed in on Sylvia Masterson's cabin. Sean did a double take when he spotted Lucy standing on the deck, staring straight at him as if she had passage into his soul. She didn't, of course, and with no binoculars of her own, there was no way she could see him.

"It won't be long now," Sean smiled. When the time came, he would use the hidden boat to retrieve Lucy. "You'll see," he said to the image in the lenses. "We'll be so happy together."

All he had to do now was bide his time, and if all went well, he and Lucy would be together before night's end. Sean walked back to his chosen hideout, which allowed him concealed surveillance of both the cabin and the path leading up to the road above.

Knowing he might be there for some time, he attempted to make himself comfortable. Heavy humidity and the strong, musty odor of damp undergrowth made it a tough go. Dark clouds filtered through the dense tree branches, forewarning a brewing storm.

Sean took time to review his strategy a third time and then a fourth for good measure. There was no room for mistakes. He would not get a second chance.

Time crept forward. Boredom set in, and Sean soon dozed off. Something jarred him awake. It took him a second to recall where he was and why he was there. He thought he heard car doors slamming shut. Whatever the sound, it came from the road above. He clamored to his feet and scurried to the top of the hill. From fifty yards away, Sean recognized the man and woman standing next to a newer-model SUV.

Would he ever catch a break?

He saw the man reach into the back of the vehicle and extract the limp body of a young girl. He hefted her over his shoulder, sending a mass of red curls cascading toward the ground. The man took the path that led to the cabin, leaving the woman to keep an eye on the SUV, and then returned and removed another limp girl from the vehicle. With his burden in tow, he retraced his steps. The woman followed this time.

Sean slunk to the vehicle, only to hurriedly duck for cover when a second woman eased herself out of the passenger seat. She slammed the door shut and pressed her hand to the handle to lock the car. Dressed in tight-fitting jeans and a pale blue rain jacket, the woman lowered her dark sunglasses and descended the trail with confidence. He'd seen her before but couldn't place her.

Sean quickly moved to the vehicle after she passed out of sight. He curled his hands around the sides of his face and peered through the dark windows. Confident no one else remained inside, he went back to his hiding place.

CHAPTER EIGHTY-THREE

Becca surmised that the redheaded girl had drugged the food she'd given her. Though she was afraid to open her eyes, her sense of smell told her she was no longer in the barn. Musty air infused with an expensive perfume replaced the stench of straw and animals, and the surface beneath her was softer than the hard dirt floor had been.

Faint voices came from somewhere behind her, the tone argumentative. A woman's voice rose. "They should be awake by now. I hope you didn't overdose them. We don't need another dead body."

Becca held her fear in check at the mention of someone dying at the hands of these people. She keyed in on one specific word in their conversation: *they*. She was sure she heard it right: "*They* should be awake.*" Did that mean someone else was here with her? Becca listened closely to the ongoing discourse.

"I know what I'm doing," a man snapped angrily. "Watch them and call me the minute they wake up."

A second woman chimed in. "It's getting late. Where the hell is Lloyd, anyway? He should be back by now."

Becca detected footsteps moving in her direction. The steel toe of a cowboy boot nudged her shoulder. Holding her breath, she willed herself to lay perfectly still.

"She's still out," the man said. "I have to hike up to the road and make a call to confirm our drop-off site. This damn cell phone doesn't work down here."

"Well, hurry up. I want to be miles away from here by this time tomorrow. We're risking way too much making this transfer. You said we'd call it quits after the last delivery. I don't know what you were thinking when you agreed to this one."

"Stop whining, will you?" the second woman demanded. "You're driving me crazy with all your nagging. By the time this is done, you two will have amassed enough money to make a new start wherever you choose."

"It can't come soon enough for me. I have a really bad feeling," the first woman said. "Go make your call and get back here, pronto."

"Quit fretting," he sighed. "You two stay here. I'll be back in a few minutes."

"Yeah. Like where would we go, anyway?"

Becca waited until his footsteps faded away. She peeked through squinted eyes. Luckily, the women's attention laid elsewhere. From her position, she confirmed her earlier assessment. She was lying on a dirty mattress on the floor of a very old log cabin. The outline of an old table came into view. Three plastic chairs sat around it. Behind the table was a small kitchen area with a sink and a minifridge.

The two women sat silently, both staring at the man as he exited through the door on the other side of the room. Becca carefully stretched her left leg behind her until her bare foot touched something soft and warm. It was true. She wasn't alone on the mattress.

CHAPTER EIGHTY-FOUR

Malcome Bremer pushed himself into a sitting position, groped the left side of his head, and winced. Glancing around the room, his weary eyes narrowed on his attacker. Malcolm lunged, only to fall short of his target and collapsed against the nearby chair.

"Hold it, buddy," Wayne said. "I think you'd best stay put until you can see straight."

"Don't you dare call me buddy, you son of a bitch. I know what you've been up to." Bremer struggled to his feet. "You had something to do with my little girl's disappearance." He dove for Wayne again. "I'm going to kill you!"

Wayne stepped to the side, propelling Malcolm into the arm of the sofa. "I don't know what you're talking about," Wayne jeered. "I know nothing about your daughter or what happened to her."

Malcolm sank into the folds of the couch.

Dan intervened. "I've had enough of this. I don't know what's going on between you two, but that's not important now. We need to find Becca."

Wayne and Malcolm nodded in unison, neither expounding on his intentions. Malcolm gently rubbed the lump on the side of his head. Wayne massaged his hand.

"Well?" Dan screamed. "Are you here to help us? If not, you need to leave, or I'm calling the police." He reached for the phone, signaling that he meant business.

Malcolm's voice cut through the tension: "Time's running out, Wayne. Tell us what you know."

Wayne Johanson used up precious time to account for his past. It was vital that everyone in the room know his history if he expected to gain their trust.

The entire time, Malcolm hovered in place, his head down, his hands shoved deep inside the pockets of his worn blue jeans. Johanson hesitated periodically to calculate the effect his saga had had on Becca's parents. Dan's rigid posture remained constant. Mary Ann's hands were restless in her lap. At one point, she reached up and wiped away a tear.

The narrative quickened as Wayne wound to an end. He was the first to admit that he had done a lot of things that didn't make him proud. He was not asking them to forgive or even understand him. He was only looking for acceptance. Their trust was vital—if they trusted him, they might be willing to stand with him.

Wayne noticed Dan's focus suddenly melt somewhere behind him. Mary Ann and Malcolm adopted a similar countenance. Wayne turned to see what had them so mesmerized. Hal stood in the foyer with his arm draped around the stair banister for support.

Uncle and nephew locked eyes. Neither one said a word. They didn't have to.

CHAPTER EIGHTY-FIVE

Hal had awakened to a loud knock on the front door located right below the Bankses' guest bedroom. Soon thereafter, his uncle's voice had drifted through the small Cape Cod home. Slipping out of bed and tiptoeing from the room, Hal perched on the top step at the end of a short hallway. Wayne Johanson's ballad-like narrative floated up the stairway. When it ended, Hal hobbled down the stairs and into the living room. His interest fell squarely on the man who had been the one constant drive in his life. The lined face stared back at him showing no indication that he had fabricated the story.

How had Hal not known about his grandparents' abusive behavior? Flashbacks from his childhood shook him to the core. His grandmother, dressed in her worn, flowered housecoat, fidgeting as she sat in a rocking chair. Her stare narrowed on the grimy windowpanes as if expecting an unwelcome guest to materialize in the door frame at any moment. Another glimpse found her kneeling beside an unkempt bed, her sobs assaulting young Hal where he lingered in the doorway.

He saw his grandfather at the kitchen table, guzzling a beer. Empty containers were strewn across the table, one laying on the floor. A hefty man sat with him, a bottle in his hand. Hal shivered despite the room's tepid temperature. Were these actual recollections or merely invented images? His grandfather's cruelty could explain his mother's desire to escape. Even if that were true, it would never excuse her for leaving her baby boy behind.

The pity etched on the faces of Dan and Mary Ann Banks elicited mixed emotions for Hal. Life with Wayne at the farm hadn't always been good. Nor had it been all bad. None of that made any difference if Wayne was telling the truth about his departure and subsequent return to the homestead. Had he indeed come back for the sake of his young nephew? If that were true, it changed everything. In Hal's mind, the information elevated his uncle to a new dimension. They were family, the only family either of them had. The past offered nothing to them. The future held everything.

Hal would go forward knowing that he was not alone. Wayne would always be there for him. And Hal intended to be there for his uncle.

CHAPTER EIGHTY-SIX

Wayne Johanson took full responsibility for the current situation. Becca Banks would be safe at this very moment if he'd had the courage to say no to the influences that had sucked him into Lloyd Masterson's web.

He would not admit it at the time, but he was glad that Hal had opted for a better life. He'd wished his nephew the very best, especially because he had always done everything in his power to keep his seedy business from affecting his nephew's well-being. Yet, he had missed the boy, missed his antics, his passion for life, and now, he had the chance to set all that straight. His nephew was safe and back in his life. Bringing Becca home to her family and to Hal would be his salvation.

A loud growl filled the room, ending Wayne's revelations.

"Arrrgh."

Everyone's attention pivoted to Malcolm Bremer. Now ghostly white, he dug his fingers into his temples, unable to look any of them in the eye.

Bremer drew a deep breath. "Since we're all confessing, it's time I admit something." The words stuck in his throat. "I—" he coughed, "I was the one who picked up Becca last night in front of the hospital."

Dan gasped breathlessly, "Then she's safe. Where is she?"

Mary Ann pleaded, "Please tell us where she is."

The air in the room grew heavy. "You don't understand. I was trying to protect her. You have to believe me." Malcolm took a step toward Becca's mother. "My sole intent was to hold her for a couple of days until I could convince her that Hal and his uncle were dangerous people." He looked sheepishly at Hal.

Mary Ann's legs buckled. Dan leapt to her side and held her in his arms. She pushed him away. "I'm okay," she snapped. She glared at Bremer. "What do you mean, you don't know where my baby is? You took her. You damn well better know what happened to her!"

Malcolm sputtered, "She got away from me this morning. I came here, hoping she had made it home. This is all my fault."

"Damn straight it's your fault! What made you think you could just *take* our daughter?" Dan raised his fist.

Hal grabbed hold of Dan's arm mid-swing. "Placing blame now won't solve anything." His dark eyes challenged Malcolm. "Do you have any idea where Becca might be?"

"I'm afraid I do."

"Dammit!" Dan's upper lip curled inward. "We've wasted all this time when we could have been out saving her."

"Let's hear the man out," Hal advocated.

"Two days ago, I found Masterson's diary. I was..."

"Masterson kept a diary?" Wayne tried to mask his discomfort. "How did you come across something like that?"

"It doesn't matter. You should be more worried about what he said regarding you. Your name was mentioned on numerous occasions. That's why I had to steer Becca away from you and your nephew."

The blood drained from Wayne's face. Malcolm continued, "We're all here for the same reason. It's imperative that we find Becca before it's too late." He took in the room again. "In his diary, Masterson detailed a lot of his dirty little secrets. He is one evil man." His voice quivered. "He took my Amber." Malcolm grappled with his emotions. "Masterson took her. And I think he's still alive."

Hal couldn't hide his anguish. "If he's still alive, he might have Becca."

Malcolm nodded. "That's what I'm afraid of."

"Do you know where he's holding the girls?"

"I'm pretty sure he's keeping them somewhere local for a few days. He referred to it as his 'little hideaway.' At some point, he'll move them across state lines, destined for either Canada or Mexico."

"I think I know where his hideout may be," Wayne said.

Together, they raced to come up with a plan. When all the facts were on the table, Dan picked up the phone. "Who're you calling?" Wayne demanded.

"The sheriff," Dan answered as he punched in the number.

Wayne snatched the phone from his hand. "You can't do that."

"The hell I can't! That's my daughter out there!" Dan reached for the phone.

"There are deputies in the area who will tip off Masterson if they get the chance." Wayne studied everyone in the room to gauge whether they really understood the danger. "Masterson is getting ready to pull up stakes. This has to be done right. There won't be a second chance."

Dan ran his hands through his hair. Dan and Mary Ann nodded in solemn agreement. It appeared that everyone was on board. Too ill to travel, Hal agreed to stay at the house in case Becca made her way home. Dan and Mary Ann, on the other hand, refused to be left behind. They followed in their minivan while Malcolm and Wayne led the small caravan in Johanson's truck. They drove off under ominous clouds that cast an eerie green hue along the horizon.

CHAPTER EIGHTY-SEVEN

RJ lay tied and gagged in the same barn stall Becca Banks had occupied hours earlier. His blurred vision was the result of Masterson swinging a two-by-four at his head. It was the second blow he'd received within the last few days. He would have to seriously consider a career change when all this was over.

Lying prone on the dirt floor, he detected a man's voice issuing orders above an undistinguishable noise, possibly a running engine. Footsteps approached from behind. A well-placed kick to the kidneys expunged any doubt about the severity of RJ's predicament. Boris Krause laughed. "Not such a tough guy now, huh?"

Rafferty held his breath, waiting for the second blow. When it didn't come, he lifted his head and glowered at the man.

Krause sneered. "Had to see how much fight you had left in you!" He stepped over RJ's body and ground the heel of his boot into Rafferty's ribcage. The unyielding gag stretched across Rafferty's mouth suppressed a gut-wrenching moan before he slipped into unconsciousness.

A douse of cold water brought him back. Krause had disappeared, replaced by Masterson.

Lloyd tossed the empty bucket aside. "I was afraid Krause had ended your sorry life." Lloyd twirled a large knife in his hand. With one fell swoop, the bindings that tethered RJ's ankles crumpled to the ground. "When I'm through with you, you're gonna wish he had. Now, get up off the ground!"

RJ struggled to his feet. This time, the blade carved through the dirty cloth that served as a gag, its sharp edge slicing RJ's cheek as it went. Blood oozed from the wound. Masterson shoved Rafferty through the stall door and into the expansive space of the barn's main room. "Keep walking. We're going for a ride," Masterson shouted.

Lloyd fell into step behind RJ and hustled him to the driver's side of a parked truck. He cut RJ's wrist binds and instructed him to get behind the wheel. Lloyd heaved himself into the passenger side of the cab, placed the key in the ignition, and told RJ to drive.

RJ shifted the gear stick and drove the vehicle up the lengthy driveway and away from the farm.

"You should have known better than to cross me, RJ. We had a nice arrangement until you messed it up." Masterson sheathed the knife and stuck it under the seat, replacing it with a pistol. He waved the gun in a circle. "You cost me a lot of money. Not to mention the trouble of wrapping up my business here and forcing me to start someplace else. You will pay for all of it."

RJ used his left hand to wipe dripping blood from his chin. His body ached from the beating he had taken, and his ears buzzed. He needed a miracle if he had any chance of prevailing over Lloyd's vengeance. "How'd *ya shurvive?*" RJ's tongue felt like it was twice its normal size.

Masterson laughed. "It was a stroke of sheer luck when that lightning hit my boat. By then, I was long gone. It worked out better than I'd planned. You should know by now that I live an enchanted life." The demonic snort erupting from Lloyd reminded RJ that it would be a mortal mistake to underestimate the man.

"Mind telling me where you've been all *yeshs* months?"

"I don't mind at all. Of course, you have to promise you'll take the information to the grave with you."

"My life's in your hands. I guess you get to make *dat* call."

"While you were screwing my wife, I was drowning my sorrows in the arms of our dear Lucy's mother-in-law. Lesley's quite the woman. By the way, you might be interested to know that the senior Mrs. Rydell loathes Lucy. Has from the first moment they met. Now, me? I can take or leave Lucy. She's not my type. I understand you've crawled into her bed, too." His teeth bared behind a wicked snicker. "Jack doesn't confide in me, of course, but my sources tell me he's not at all happy that you're banging his wife. You've managed to accumulate a lot of enemies. You better be careful. Someone might put a bullet in your head." Lloyd laid the barrel of his pistol against Rafferty's temple. "Bang!" he bellowed.

RJ didn't flinch. "*Sho* who knows you're alive?"

"Only a few of my trusted associates, and I intend to keep it that way. That's why I need your assistance."

"What *maksh* you think I'll help you?"

"Well, you don't have a choice."

"What do you expect *me* to do?"

"You, my boy, will be my decoy. By this time tomorrow, everyone will think you were the mastermind behind the kidnappings."

"No one will believe that." He feigned disbelief. Masterson was an egotistical maniac. Challenge his abilities, and he would go overboard to convince you of his superiority.

"Oh, no? Remember back when I had you pick up that stolen car a year ago, at the rest area on Highway 10? Remember what was in the trunk?"

The image still haunted RJ. Against his better judgment, he had let Cassie Mitchell talk him into keeping quiet about the body. A fatal mistake.

Masterson grinned. "Cassie did you in that night, and you never suspected a thing, did you? You think you're so smart." Rafferty's jaw tightened. "She got tired of you chasing every skirt in town except hers. A scorned woman and all. Didn't your daddy ever teach you anything about the birds and the bees? Never piss off a female, especially one that has the power to shoot you in the back."

"So I made a couple of mistakes. There's no evidence to pin this on me."

"That's where you're wrong. Your fingerprints are all over the car you picked up that night, inside and out. The girl's DNA is in the trunk, and Cassie has the knife that killed her. Your prints are on that, too."

Masterson was bluffing. Or was he? RJ's head reeled with possible scenarios. He had always worn gloves when he did jobs for Lloyd, to make sure no incriminating evidence put him at the scene of the crime. And as for the knife—Cassie never had possession of it. He did. He ran through what had transpired the day he and Cassie had procured the knife from Sylvia's garage.

Masterson appeared to be reading his mind. "You think you have it tucked away in a safe place, don't you?"

"What are you talking about?" RJ asked innocently.

"Don't play coy. Think back. It was Cassie who convinced you to search the garage. She's the one who found the weapon. That's because I told her where I hid it. Now, think hard. She handed it to you, and you put it in an evidence bag and then put it in your briefcase. Later that day, when you broke for lunch, she told you she had left her cell in the car. When she went to get the phone, she switched the knife with a dummy."

It finally registered. RJ had been the fool from the beginning.

"And now she's planting the real one in your apartment as we speak. Even though they'll never find the girl's body, the evidence will convict you of the killing. The authorities—your peers—will deem it an open and shut case."

Rafferty held himself in check. Masterson had been one step ahead of him the entire time. But the game wasn't over yet. They were in Otter Tail County now, where RJ had grown up. He knew every street, road, and highway like the back of his hand. "Where're we going now?"

"You'll find out in good time. Now shut your trap and drive."

RJ didn't think things could get any worse until he noticed dark olive clouds mushrooming along the western skyline. Rafferty knew the makings of a bad storm, and by his calculations, the one moving their way was going to be one for the history books.

CHAPTER EIGHTY-EIGHT

Paramedics arrived at the scene soon after the farmer witnessed Chris Foley's collapse on County Road 51. After stabilizing him, they transported him to St. Mary's Hospital in Perham.

Foley was in bad shape, but the doctors said he would survive. He was in surgery for more than four hours to remove the bullet lodged in his shoulder and repair the wound to the side of his head. The FBI agents were there to question him when he regained consciousness. Against the doctor's advice, Chris agreed to talk to them.

Within an hour, a team of agents surrounded the Masterson farm, but it was too late. Masterson had cleared out, leaving little evidence to indicate where he'd gone. Once again, he had revealed himself to be a worthy opponent.

CHAPTER EIGHTY-NINE

Sean Penalton crouched low to the ground as the first drops of rain marked the leaves above him. Seeing his plans to run off with Lucy dashed before his eyes, he pummeled his large fists against the dampened ground beneath him. Life was so unfair. He got to his feet, ready to retreat, until a troubling thought occurred to him: could he live with himself if he didn't do everything in his power to help the two girls trapped inside the cabin? He doubted he could overpower three adults on his own. His conscience, however, would not let him walk away. He had to try.

Sean analyzed different scenarios and finally came up with a strategic scheme. The best approach was to draw the kidnappers away from the cabin. If he could distract them long enough, he might be able to sneak inside and get the girls out. He knew these woods better than anybody. It would be a simple task to lead them to safety once he got them away from the shack—that is, if nothing else went wrong.

Drenching rain pushed through the canopy of tree branches. It was time to show everyone, including himself, that he had the brains and courage to see things through. Sean grabbed his backpack and moved quietly up the hill. When he got to the top, he went straight to the SUV.

He reached into his bag and pulled out a small hose, stuffing one end into the gas tank. Siphoning fluids was a function often utilized on the farm, mainly to tap gasoline from one piece of equipment to use in another. Sean also commonly harnessed the technique to pilfer gas from boats moored along the shoreline, using that fuel to power the small motor boat he kept hidden for his own use.

Today, the art served him well. Gasoline soon flowed from the tank. Sean bent the hose and directed the liquid under the SUV, where the ground was dry. He groped for a book of matches with shaky fingers.

When the gas ignited, he wouldn't have much time to distance himself from the vehicle. On the third attempt, the match caught fire, but the falling rain swiftly extinguished it. Sean cupped another match in the palm of his hands and tried again. The precious flame burst into life. He tossed the match under the car and retreated as fast as he could to the safety of the trees, where he held his breath and waited. Nothing happened. Seconds ticked by, and nothing. He gingerly made his way back to the SUV.

This time, he used a single match to set the entire book afire. Extending his body to shield the flame, he deftly stretched his hand beneath the car chassis and lowered the fire to the puddle of gasoline. It ignited with a flash. Sean jumped up and raced for cover. He was sure he had made it until a deafening blow hurled him to the ground. Intense heat scorched his clothing and singed exposed hair. He lay flat on his back in the mud. Valuable time slid by. Then, without warning, a spasm lurched through his body. His mouth opened, gasping greedily to replenish the air expunged from his lungs.

Sean struggled to stand, his head and shoulders trembling. He limped down the hillside and schlepped his way back to his original hiding place, where he flopped onto the muddy ground and let the cool rain wash over him. The beat of his heart was so loud that even the hammering rain could not drown it out.

This was no time to sit idle. Sean pushed himself up and ran toward the cabin. He crossed his fingers and pleaded to the powers above that the three people inside had found their way up the hill to investigate the cause of the explosion, leaving the girls alone inside.

Sean crept to the window and peered in. The two girls sat huddled together in the center of the room. Rain poured through an open door on the opposite wall.

Sean cast his eyes around the room. No one stood in his way. He glanced back to the girls, his gaze lingering on the one with a mound of red curls spilling around her head and shoulders. Shaking himself from a trance, Sean circled the cabin and swooped through the door. "I need to get you two out of here right now!" The authoritative tone he affected surprisingly galvanized his resolve.

"I can't get her to wake up," Becca sputtered. "They drugged both of us." She shook the other girl. "She won't wake up."

Sean gently brushed the mass of red hair aside, exposing soft, pale features. His deft hands lifted the girl's lithe body up and over his shoulder and lumbered out the door. Becca shadowed close on his heels, so close that she bumped into him when he stopped abruptly at the bottom of the steps.

He had planned to take the path that led to the lake, retrieve his hidden boat and pilot all of them to the opposite shore. The weather, however, rendered that trip impossible Instead, he led them to the tree line to the west. Low branches and thorny shrubs pulled at their clothing, snagging their hair and scratching their skin as they ran. When they reached a small clearing, Becca screeched to a halt beside Sean bending at the waist and gasping for air.

Sean felt every beat of Amber's heart as she lay still against his shoulder. It restored his spirit and gave him strength to carry on. He squinted through the heavy rain catching a glimpse of the lake fifty yards beyond the trees to the south. Sean needed to get to the water's edge to gain his bearings. He gestured to Becca to stay close behind.

As sure as he had been that everything would fall into place once they got to the beach, one look at the horizon told him the worst was yet to come. As if on cue, a streak of lightning fell from the dark clouds and hammered into the water's surface several hundred feet from their current position. The bolt appeared to sink deep into the water. As quickly as it entered, it rose back up to the sky, forming crystals in shades of pink and red as it went. The ensuing thunderclap shook the earth beneath them. Amber stirred as Sean's eyes widened with wonder. Becca stared, spellbound. When it was over, an eerie sense of dread descended around them.

They had to keep moving. Sean navigated the way until they came to a set of wooden steps leading up the hill away from the lake. He knew what awaited them at the top: a small summer cabin owned by Chuck and Natalie Moritz, friends of Sean's dad. The elderly couple seldom came to the lake anymore, and the place was likely unoccupied. The best he could wish for was a working phone that he could use to call for help.

There was no phone, no electricity and no running water in the cabin. It was, however, a dry, safe place to take refuge, at least for now. Sean gently laid Amber on the old couch while Becca rummaged through the dwelling for towels and blankets. She dried

Amber off and tucked a blanket tightly around the girl's shoulders before draping one over her own shivering body.

Raindrops slapped the metal roof with a deafening clatter. Sean covered his ears to drown out the distraction. Nothing had prepared him for this. He was scared. Really scared.

Amber's stricken gaze broke his heart. As with any other defenseless being, he could not ignore her plight. He upended his knapsack and emptied its contents onto the floor. Becca watched for a moment, then moved to sit next to him, and together, they went through everything in front of them until Amber joined in, her fingers wrapping around the flashlight. She turned it on and then switched it off, then on and then off once more.

She visibly fought to hold back tears. "I think I know how we can get help."

"What's wrong?" Becca pleaded.

Amber's shoulders sagged. "There was another girl. She taught me how to send an SOS signal with a flashlight. I'm afraid I don't remember how many times you're supposed to flash the light."

"I think I know how it's done." Becca held out her hand. Amber handed her the light. "I learned it in Girl Scouts. You blink the light three times fast and then three times slow." She demonstrated.

Sean took the device and tried it. "Like this?"

"I think that's right."

"Okay, I'll hike to the beach and try it. Hopefully someone on the other side of the lake will see it and come to our rescue." He rose to leave.

Both girls jumped up in unison. "We're going with you," Becca insisted.

"You'll be safer if you stay here," he said. "I won't be very far away." His expression left no room for argument.

Both girls grudgingly conceded.

Gale-force winds rushed through the door as Sean stepped out and struggled to pull it shut behind him. The storm hurled everything it had as if its sole purpose was to alter his course. He forged onward, his head lowered against the onslaught of nature's anger, fear growing with every step. Dark clouds blocking the evening sun dropped visibility to almost nil. Sean knew it was highly unlikely that anyone would see the SOS even if they were staring directly at it. Regardless, he had to try.

He stumbled to the beach, found a place that offered him a bit of shelter and pointed the flashlight at the opposite side of the lake. Mimicking Becca's example, Sean flicked the light on and off rapidly three times, then slowly three more times. He continued until a muscle spasm forced him to stop. He switched to his left hand and followed through with the same sequence.

CHAPTER NINETY

L ooking back on the events of the week, Lucy saw incongruity in the way everything had come together. Unknown forces had assembled all the players. Was it reasonable to think that the outcome would have been different if one person along the way had chosen a different path? For instance, if Sylvia had not met and married Lloyd, would he be terrorizing someone other than the good people of Vergas, Minnesota?

Lucy couldn't pinpoint exactly what was bothering her. Her anxiety increased with each passing hour. This morning, she was happy that Jack had slept in late. It had given her the opportunity to reflect. Jack, however, had never been one to waste mornings lounging in bed. At ten, she went to his room and knocked lightly. Receiving no response, she pushed the door open and peeked inside calling his name: "Jack?" He didn't answer. She stepped in. The bed had not been slept in, and his overnight bag was gone. There was no indication he'd ever been there. Lucy stomped from the room, slamming the door as she left. "Jack," she yelled, knowing full well he had skipped out on her yet again. "You've cajoled your way into my life for the last time."

Through the living room windows, she saw dark, billowing clouds rolling in from the north. She grabbed the phone, did a quick search for the Hennepin County Attorney's office in St. Paul and dialed the number. An answering service picked up. She explained who she was, left a detailed message, and requested a call back as soon as possible.

Lucy worried about RJ, fretted over the safety of the missing girls, and fumed at the fact that she had allowed Jack to manipulate her in so many ways. Add the knowledge that someone might want her dead, and plainly, she was in over her head. Self-pity was getting her nowhere. *I need to take back my life.*

The phone rang. She took a deep breath to calm herself. "Hello?" Her voice echoed caution.

"This is County Attorney David Wendt, returning your call."

Lucy spent several minutes detailing who she was and reiterated the message she had left with his answering service.

"First off, I want to let you know that I am not involved with the case you're referring to, but I am aware of what is going on. I talked with Jack a few days ago," Homer told her. "He did request information about the on-going investigation. I assure you I did not divulge anything relating to that case."

A long pause prompted Lucy to ask, "Are you there?"

"Yes," he replied. "I think Jack implicated himself during his conversation with me. Is it possible that he and Masterson run in the same circles?"

"Jack is acquainted with Lloyd through family. I'm sure you know Lloyd was—or should I say, is—my Aunt Sylvia's husband. As far as I know, there's no other link between them. Jack and Lloyd never cared for each other. In fact, Jack habitually lectured me to stay away from Lloyd. Said he was the biggest prick he'd ever known." Lucy heard a light chuckle on the other end.

There was another pause. Lucy held her breath. Homer finally let out a sigh. "Although I can't prove anything thus far, I think there's more context to their relationship. Lucy, I hate to put you in the middle of this, but I think you could be in grave danger. Have you talked to Jack today?"

"He spent the night here. In the guest room," she added with emphasis. "Anyway, I think he spent the night. He was gone this morning. I can't tell you when he left or where he went. He was upset with me. He's probably sulking somewhere."

"Do you mind telling me what you two talked about yesterday?" Lucy explained that Jack had showed up at the airport in Minneapolis not long after RJ's departure.

"You were with RJ yesterday?"

The tone of his voice caught Lucy off guard. "Yes, we flew to Phoenix to follow a lead RJ had on the missing girls." Lucy filled Homer in on the details of their undercover sting and RJ's vanishing act at the airport.

"And you don't have any idea what happened to either RJ or Jack?"

"None."

Lucy heard muted voices, as if Homer had placed his hand over the receiver. When he came back, he said, "I hate to cut this conversation short. I am late for an important meeting. Can I get back to you in a couple of hours? In the meantime, it is imperative that you stay where you are. I should be able to be there by mid-afternoon." He added solemnly, "Lucy, promise me you'll stay put. I'll contact the local authorities and get a policeman out there to ensure your safety."

"Now you really are scaring me."

"I'm sorry for that. Trust me: it's for your own good. You've got my number. Call me immediately if you hear from Jack or RJ. I'll be there as soon as I can." He disconnected, leaving Lucy with more questions than answers.

Lucy gathered her trusted pad and pen and settled into the La-Z-Boy, where she combed through the detailed notes she had previously outlined. She factored in what she had learned in Phoenix and what Homer had shared with her. Gnawing on her fingertip, she contemplated Jack's interest in Homer. Jack had used the word "owe" when referring to his friend: Homer *owed* him. That, evidently, was not how Homer Wendt saw it.

She brought her attention back to the text in front of her. Lucy had doodled three names on the bottom half of the sheet: RJ Rafferty, Jack Rydell, and Lloyd Masterson. What did these men have in common? She laid the pen on the side table and closed her eyes. The pads of her thumbs pressed her temples and moved in a circular motion. "Sylvia," she said aloud as her eyes popped open. "Aside from myself, they all know Sylvia."

She stared again at the names stenciled on the paper. So what if they all knew her aunt? It proved nothing. The FBI had implicated Masterson in the kidnapping charges. Homer had inquired as to whether there was an alliance between Jack and Lloyd. She doubted it, but what did she know? Lucy had been wrong about Jack in so many ways. Still, she didn't think he would associate with a man he ostensibly disliked.

And what about RJ? Had she built him up in her fantasies? Maybe he wasn't the man she thought he was. "Don't go there," she counseled. Lucy leaned back in the chair and quietly watched the storm clouds rumble closer. She got up and went to the dock to ensure that both boats were securely moored. Large drops of rain dotted the wooden deck as she hastily retreated inside.

The clock on the wall read 3:15. Where had the time gone?

Lucy willed the phone to ring. Where was Homer and where was the police officer he had said he would send to the house? She lifted the handset. The steady drone in the ear piece assured her that the phone was in working order.

A loud thud against the window sucked whatever resilience she had left from her body. She reeled around to see a dusty outline of a bird's wingspan stretched across the glass pane. The carcass of a blackbird lay sprawled on the deck like a bad omen.

If that weren't enough to send her blood pressure into the danger zone, the sudden streak of lightning slithering from the sky did the trick. It slid into the lake's water not far from the opposite shoreline. Red and grey shards danced through the air. At the very same moment, a deafening clap of thunder shook the house and everything in it. Interior lights flickered and then blinked off plunging the room's furnishings into the darkness. The final assault was the refrigerator motor clunking to a stop, resulting in an eerie silence.

Lucy scrambled to the kitchen to retrieve a flashlight. Rifling through drawers, she collected several candles and placed them throughout the cabin. Time dragged on, with no word from Homer. She couldn't stave off the hunger pangs. She fixed herself a sandwich and pensively carried it to the table. Wind whipped up buckets of rain and hurled it against the side of the house as lightening zigzagged across the sky with regularity. Nibbling her sandwich, it took a few minutes to understand what she was seeing. There it was again! That crazy light, barely discernible. She counted three short bursts of light and then three longer ones. No mistaking it this time. It *was* an SOS signal.

She couldn't ignore it any longer. Lucy lifted the phone to call Homer, only to discover it was dead. She dialed Homer's number on her cell and left a message when no one answered.

The signal flashed from the other side of the lake. There was no time to second-guess herself. If she didn't act now, she would live to regret it.

Lucy slipped into her rain slicker. Sticking the cell phone into her pocket, she grabbed the flashlight and the key to the boat before quickly extinguishing the candles. After one last glance around the cabin, she raced out the door.

CHAPTER NINETY-ONE

Malcome Bremer sat quietly in the passenger seat while Wayne Johanson concentrated on navigating the truck. Both peered through their respective side-view mirrors and noted headlights glistening on the wet pavement behind them. Dan Banks, with his wife seated beside him, kept a safe distance.

"I wish they hadn't insisted on coming," Wayne said.

"Their daughter is missing. Possibly in the hands of a monster. Nothing could keep them away," Malcolm countered.

"Yeah, I know, but they'll be more trouble than help, that's for sure. No telling what we'll run into when we get to where we're going."

"What would you expect from them? Sit back and wait? No, they're doing exactly what they need to do."

"If Masterson is still at the farm when we get there, all hell will break loose. And they'll be in the middle of it. How do we keep them safe?"

"We'll deal with it when we get there. In the meantime, can't you go a little faster? We can't let him get away."

"Don't tell me how to drive." Johanson's knuckles bulged, the result of his iron grip on the wheel. "The last thing we need is to end up in the ditch. Besides, we're coming up to the turnoff, and we can't afford to miss it." Squinting between each swipe of the wiper blades, he eased off the gas pedal. "Here it is." He veered onto a gravel road. "The farm is a couple miles up ahead. I'll pull over when we get closer and tell them to stay back. Masterson won't go easily, and I don't want them caught up in the crossfire."

"We've got enough gun power to send him to purgatory," Malcolm said, referring to the cache of arms they had compiled before setting out on the mission. Johanson's contributions were the three weapons he kept in his truck: an AK-47, a Remington 12-gauge shotgun, and a Smith & Wesson military .38 revolver. Bremer had the Glock he had purchased shortly after Amber's disappearance, and Dan's offering was a collection of firearms intended for hunting and target practice.

As they drove, Bremer scrutinized the red and blue specks shimmering in the distance. "What's that?" he quizzed, gawking at the display.

Johanson stomped on the brakes. "Shit!" he snarled in disbelief. Without thinking, he thrust the gearshift into reverse and pressed hard on the pedal. The truck came to an abrupt stop, throwing the two men against their seatbelts. Wayne's fists pummeled the steering wheel. He had unwittingly backed into the Bankses' van. One stupid mistake after another.

Blinding lights assaulted them on all fronts, giving them no time to regroup. Through the downpour, the shadows of a dozen armed men and women surrounded both the truck and the minivan, their weapons trained on the occupants.

Barely audible above the slapping rain, a female voice reverberated through a bullhorn. "FBI!" she shouted. "Put your hands out the windows where we can see them. Now!"

Malcolm and Wayne gingerly obeyed. Two agents swooped in, yanked open the doors, and hauled them from the vehicle. Jostled to the ground and forced to lay prone in the mud, they had no defense as the agents searched them, handcuffed them, and then jerked them back to their feet. Johanson gratefully noted that the authorities spared Becca's parents the bullying act. Dan and Mary Ann still sat warm and cozy in the confines of their automobile, several men standing guard.

Agent Hunter's gruff voice brought Wayne back to his own problems. "This is one for the books. I never envisioned you two joining forces." The agent confronted Bremer. "What in God's name are you all doing here?"

"Funny you should ask," said Malcolm. "You guys finally pulled your heads out of your asses and followed through on one of the leads I gave you."

"Don't get cute with me. I'm not in the mood tonight. Let's get out of this rain, and you and your new friend can tell me exactly what brought you here."

The agents steered Bremer and Johanson into the old farmhouse. After facing separate barrages of questions, Malcolm and Wayne rejoined Dan and Mary Ann Banks. The four of them sat together in the living room, silently waiting to hear their fate.

CHAPTER NINETY-TWO

"Pull over to the side of the road," Lloyd Masterson roared. They had reached their destination: a small log cabin located about fifty yards down the side of the hill. Sylvia had introduced him to the property with the idea of opening a bed and breakfast. Lloyd had convinced her that it would be a bad investment, leaving him to use it for his own use.

All Lloyd had to do now was finish off Rafferty, make sure his associates knew exactly what was expected of them regarding the safe transport of the merchandise, and then he would be on his way. A team was ready to swoop in and erase all evidence that Lloyd was ever there.

Thrashing rain made it almost impossible to see beyond the hood of the pickup. Masterson yanked the keys from the ignition and ordered RJ out of the truck. Lloyd slid across the seat and exited through the same door with his revolver raised, ready to take out Rafferty if he was stupid enough to make a run for it.

They stood motionless in the pouring rain, their mouths agape at the sight of the charred SUV in front of them.

"I get the feeling something went terribly wrong," RJ taunted. "Are there any bodies in there?"

The minute Lloyd bent to get a closer look, Rafferty pounced.

The handgun flew skyward as the men wrestled to the ground. Lloyd promptly got the upper hand and pinned RJ under the weight of his body, an elbow crammed into the back of his neck. Using his free hand, Masterson twisted Rafferty's right arm behind his back, almost pulling it out of the socket. A painful yelp gurgled from RJ's throat. Masterson snorted in triumph when the body beneath him went limp, released his hold, and struggled to stand erect. He took aim with a well-placed kick into RJ's already bruised ribs and then scooted to his truck, where he grabbed the flashlight from the glove compartment.

He spent the next five minutes searching for his revolver. Unable to locate it, he seized RJ by the collar and pushed him forward and down the path. RJ limped ahead while Lloyd trailed close behind. The flashlight offered little benefit as they negotiated the wet, uneven ground.

Masterson's uneasiness intensified as they advanced on the cabin. His concerns escalated when he realized there were no lights emanating from inside the small shack. Maybe RJ had been correct in his assumption that the SUV harbored the bodies of his comrades.

A streak of lightning lit up the dark sky. The deafening clap of thunder further eroded Masterson's confidence. His shaky hand aimed the flashlight at the cabin. The dim light bounced around until it finally rested on a ghostly figure framed within the small window. Lloyd recoiled. His foot tangled with a broken limb dislodged by the storm and sent him head first to the ground.

RJ reacted without a second's hesitation. He cleared the tree line and was out of sight by the time Masterson regained his balance. Lloyd spun around a hundred and eighty degrees before hearing the door creak open behind him.

The man standing in front of Masterson always reminded him of the *American Gothic* painting portraying the pitchfork-wielding guy in overalls. A visible twitch in the man's eye added to the grim nuance. He lowered his weapon and stepped back. Masterson pushed past him and entered the cottage.

The soft glow of a Coleman lamp perched on the table high-lighted the cast of individuals glaring back at him. The man and woman he had hired to transport the girls lingered by the door, fear simmering behind their pathetic faces. Lesley Rydell sat on the far side of the room, disheveled and yet stunning as ever. She was towel-drying her hair, her grey silk blouse clinging to her ample breasts. Lloyd mentally curbed his arousal. "Would anyone care to tell me what's going on here?" After another scan of the room, he screamed, "Where the hell is my merchandise?"

The couple near the door cowered.

"Don't you come in here and start bullying us." Lesley's voice matched Masterson's tone, with an extra touch of bravado. "You saw what's left of the SUV, didn't you? We heard the explosion and rushed up the hill to see what was going on. One look and I knew it was the work of a couple of felonious kids with too much time on their hands. Law enforcement is a joke out here, and you know it."

Lloyd didn't argue that point. It was the very reason he had chosen this location.

Lesley grumbled, "The short and long of it is...when we got back to the cabin, the girls were gone. We couldn't reach you by phone, and with our only mode of transportation destroyed, we had no option except to stay here until you showed up."

"Are you telling me all of you went up the hill and no one stayed to keep watch over the girls?"

Lesley tossed the towel over the back of one of the plastic chairs.

"They were still out from the drugs," she shrugged. "We weren't gone more than ten minutes. There is no way they woke up and had the strength to walk out of here by themselves."

"And yet they did." Masterson glared at his three comrades in crime as if they were prey ready for the taking.

He called out the man with the rifle. "Did you even try to follow them?"

The man stepped backward. "In this rain? It would be impossible to track them."

"You idiot." Lloyd snatched the firearm from the man's hands and smashed the butt of it against his skull. The man slumped to the floor, blood oozing from a gaping wound. The cowering woman screamed. Lloyd swung around and caught her jaw with his left elbow, and she crumpled like a deflated balloon next to her husband.

Masterson charged with the rage of a bull. Lesley swooped in and grabbed his arm, almost knocking him to the floor. "Lloyd, killing these two won't do us any good. We need to get out of here. The explosion was very loud. And if that didn't sound an alarm, sooner or later, someone will come across the SUV and contact the authorities. I'm surprised they're not here already."

Tension in the room rose exponentially with the clatter at the front door. Masterson raised his rifle but, lowered it when he identified the newcomer.

Lesley's jaw dropped. She glanced at Lloyd and then back at the young man standing in the doorway.

"At last," Lloyd gloated, "someone I can trust to get the job done right."

"What do you mean by that?" Lesley demanded.

"Lesley, dear, you forever underestimate my reach." His glib expression did little to cover the hatred running deep in his veins.

He'd met Lesley Rydell at a quasi-family reunion. Sylvia had insisted that he meet her niece, Lucy, Lucy's husband, Jack, and Jack's mother. Lloyd's first impression of Lesley was that she was overbearing and a bit of a prima donna. That assessment changed after several more encounters. It wasn't long before he was entangled in an affair that spiraled into a maddening rollercoaster ride that constantly tossed him between the highest peaks and the lowest depths of despair. By the time he figured out that Lesley could cause him serious trouble, he had inadvertently involved her in his business.

He had to rid himself of her. Thus far, he hadn't come up with a plan. Now, true to his luck, an opportunity presented itself. "Didn't you tell your mother that you work for me, Jack?"

Jack's somber countenance morphed into a ghoulish grin. "I guess the subject never came up. She knows now, doesn't she?" His words hung thick in the air. "Weren't you supposed to be gone by now? And what's with the torched SUV up the hill?"

Lloyd's anger came full circle. His arms flailed, inviting Jack to take in the perimeter of the room. "These idiots lost my merchandise!"

Void of emotion, Jack's eyes fell on the couple sprawled in front of him.

Chunks of Lesley's calm façade fell by the wayside. "I was trying to explain to Lloyd that it's crucial that we cut our losses and get out of here."

Jack angled his head as if to evaluate certain odds. Ignoring his mother, he said to Masterson, "They couldn't get too far in this weather. How long have they been gone?"

Lloyd plainly expected the answer to come from Lesley.

Another bolt of lightning slid through the sky, lighting up the room in a spine-chilling manner. Lesley consulted her Bulova watch. "If I had to guess, I'd say they've been gone less than an hour." Her eyes narrowed on Lloyd. "I insist we forget about the girls and get the hell out of here."

Lloyd paid her no heed. "Jack, do you have a weapon?"

"Of course." He opened his jacket to reveal his holstered Smith & Wesson .357 Magnum.

Masterson's smug expression dared Lesley to defy his authority. "You stay here. Jack and I will see if we can locate any sign of them." Lesley visibly fumed over her son's betrayal.

Lloyd wanted nothing more than to watch the family drama unfold, but there wasn't time. He had to find those girls. He bolted through the door, with Jack close behind him, and headed straight toward the lake under the assumption that the girls would flee in the opposite direction of the explosion.

Masterson hesitated as they neared the shoreline. "Keep an eye out for Rafferty," he hollered over the howling storm.

"Rafferty? Why would he be out here?"

"Don't ask. Just be aware." Masterson scanned the surroundings. "No point in looking for tracks. You take the path. I'll go this way. There's no phone reception out here, so let's meet back at this location in ten minutes. If you find anything, fire your gun to signal me."

They headed out in different directions.

Lesley's words circled inside Lloyd's head as he walked the beach. Was it possible the charred vehicle had been a decoy? That would mean that someone had facilitated the girls' escape. Masterson did an about-face and hustled back to find Jack.

He halted abruptly and tilted his head to one side. The sound of a boat motor chugging parallel to the shore didn't make any sense. No one in their right mind would be out on the lake in this weather. *Unless:* someone had summoned them. Lloyd broke into a trot as the humming noise progressed along the shoreline. He caught up with Jack, and together they ran parallel to the drone of the phantom boat.

Lloyd pushed Jack behind some nearby trees when the watercraft drew closer. From that vantage point, they witnessed the vessel come ashore. A hazy outline of the sole occupant came into view as another man ran up to the craft and pulled it out of the water. The man and the occupant appeared to exchange words before scrambling out of sight together.

"You stay here," Lloyd ordered as he crossed the puddle-filled beach. Masterson had identified the craft as it came ashore. Since Sylvia was in Europe, he surmised that Lucy had piloted the Larson. A wicked smile crossed his face. Masterson rolled his head skyward and bared his teeth, inviting the heavens to deny his superiority.

He leaned over the boat and glanced inside. Assured that no one else was onboard, he linked up with Jack again. "Let's go get them."

A set of stairs led them to a small cottage nestled amid ancient oak trees. Lloyd stormed through the front door, raised his rifle and discharged a round into the ceiling. The two young girls screamed as they huddled together, arms wrapped tightly around each other. Masterson recognized the dim figure moving protectively in front of them and throaty laughter filled the room. "Well, isn't this a sight to behold." Lloyd stepped closer and gawked at the young man shielding the girls. "You're that retard that lives up the road from Sylvia." He slid his fingers into his pocket for cartridges. Staring, he reloaded and leveled the rifle at Sean.

Sean's resolve held fast.

Lloyd admired the young man's boldness. "You're not a coward, I'll give you that." Masterson tightened his grip on the trigger.

"Your bravery won't help you now."

Slipping from the shadows, Lucy threw herself at Lloyd. The gun exploded, the bullet grazing Sean's left arm. He fell backward, his head connecting with the rim of the table as he went down. Amber rushed to his side, only to have Masterson's strong arms whisk her off the floor. She fought back, kicking and screaming with the fierceness of a rabid dog.

"Grab the other one and let's get out of here."

Jack stood grounded, staring at his wife. "What about her?" Lucy lay unconscious on the floor, her condition the result of the hit she had suffered when Lloyd swung the rifle around to fend her off. "Do you think she saw me? She'll know I'm involved with you if she saw me," he moaned. "This is not good."

"That's not my problem. I told Sylvia no harm would come to her niece at my hands, and a promise is a promise. What you do is up to you." Lloyd moved to the door. "Tie her up and come back later. Right now, we need to get these two up to my truck and on their way to their new home." He trusted Jack would kill Lucy if she became a liability. He chuckled. Good fortune had not forsaken him.

Masterson marched out the door with Amber in tow. The young girl's attempted attacks on her captor had not diminished. "Dammit," he yelled. "If you don't knock this shit off, I'm going to give you what you deserve."

CHAPTER NINETY-THREE

After dodging Masterson, Rafferty circled back up the hill. Unfortunately, the pouring rain had reduced visibility to a minimum. He scoured the soaked ground for the handgun Lloyd had dropped during their earlier scuffle.

When his efforts went unrewarded, he moved a little to the left and proceeded in the same manner, shuffling his boots a few inches at a time, determined to find the weapon against all odds. It had to be here somewhere.

The rain continued with a vengeance as he slogged through the mud. Back and forth. Back and forth. Ready to give up, he was doing one more pass when his left foot nudged something hard. He barely had time to congratulate himself before a pair of oncoming headlights threatened to blind him. He kneeled, grabbed the pistol, and ducked behind Masterson's pickup for cover.

The dark sedan parked on the side of the road and a man exited. RJ watched him approach the torched SUV for inspection and then advance down the trail as if he knew where he was going. Rafferty followed in hot pursuit.

The man entered the cabin.

After a short time, he and Masterson exited, moving at a fast clip. RJ sat tight until they were out of sight and then stepped up to the window, sneaking a look inside. Three people occupied the small room within. Two sat propped against the far wall. The third, a striking woman with coal-black hair, sat stiffly in a chair, staring at the door. When none of them appeared to pose an immediate threat, RJ hurried after Masterson and his cohort.

He caught a glimpse of them conferring on the beach. When they parted company, RJ adopted a wait-and-see tactic. One or both, he imagined, would eventually make their way back to the place of separation.

Again, it didn't take long. The distant purr of an outboard motor accosted Rafferty's ears at the same time Lloyd skated past him. Anticipating that this was Masterson's plan for a clean getaway, RJ closed in. The onslaught of rain hampered his vision. When the motor went silent, Rafferty assumed it had come ashore.

Approaching the unattended craft several minutes later, RJ lurched backward when he recognized Sylvia's boat. Why would Lucy be out in this weather? And if not her, who had piloted the boat? Rafferty didn't have time to consider the possibilities. He had to find Masterson and bring an end to this madness.

Fresh footprints led him to a set of stairs. As he ascended, a rifle shot reverberated through the air. Training had taught him to assess every angle before rushing head-on into a dangerous situation. He slowly advanced toward the darkened cottage until he spotted Lloyd's unmistakable outline standing in the doorway, a large object draped over his shoulder.

It was painfully obvious what was happening. A young girl, screaming at the top of her lungs, kicked and punched at Masterson. The rain eased somewhat. Left behind were gale-force winds that threatened to level even the sturdiest of trees. RJ positioned himself ten paces beyond the porch steps, the weapon in his hand aimed and ready to kill if necessary. "Drop the rifle and put the girl down!"

Lloyd Masterson froze. Anger seethed under his eyelids. "Is that my handgun?" He took a step forward, testing his opponent's doggedness. "I should have put an end to your worthless life when I had the chance."

RJ gripped the pistol tighter. "That's far enough. Drop the rifle, or I swear I'll bury a bullet in that thick head of yours."

"You won't shoot," Masterson jeered. "You might hit the girl." He pivoted slightly to offer her as a shield.

"Don't count on it. You said it yourself. You've got me backed into a corner. I have nothing to lose."

Hearing that, the adolescent renewed her efforts to break free. Rafferty didn't hesitate. He fired a round that buzzed within inches of Lloyd's left ear. At the same time, the girl slipped from her perch. On her feet in no time, she attempted to sprint past RJ but his outstretched arm wrapped around her and drew her close behind him.

"I'm not going to hurt you. I'm here to help." His steady voice had a calming effect on both of them. "Listen carefully. Take the path behind us. It leads to steps that will take you to the beach. About a hundred yards to the left, you'll find a boat moored on the shoreline. Go there and wait for me."

When Amber hesitated, RJ drove home his directive. "Go. Now!"

She needed no further encouragement. RJ listened to the sound of her retreating steps on the sodden ground, all the while keeping a steady watch on the man writhing at the top of the stairs, his left hand cupped to his ear. "Tell your partner to get out here or you're a dead man!"

"You son of a bitch. I'll get you for this if it's the last thing I do," Masterson barked.

Heavy rain resumed. RJ stood beneath the umbrella of tree branches, soaked to the bone. He fought the urge to wipe the pelting drops from his face and eyes as he studied Lloyd, ready to counter the slightest provocation.

Seconds ticked by, rounding to a minute. Another minute passed. Rafferty swore under his breath. He had made a grave mistake. In all probability, the man inside the cabin had bolted when he heard the commotion out front. If that were the case, he had either fled the area or had a gun aimed squarely at RJ's head.

Rafferty didn't waste any more time. He fired a second round, this time grazing Masterson's leg. The man fell forward and tumbled down the steps, his guttural growl lost in the wrath of the storm. RJ stepped closer and leaned in to examined Lloyd's wound. It wasn't lethal. Rafferty reached for the handcuffs that usually hung from the back of his belt. "Shit." The cuffs were on his dresser at home, where he'd left them prior to his trip to Phoenix with Lucy. He frantically scavenged the immediate area for anything that would secure his prisoner. An old, frayed rope lay under the porch. It wouldn't hold Masterson for very long, but it was all he could find.

Masterson hissed, "You better wish to hell that I don't get out of this, 'cause you're a dead man the next time I see you."

Rafferty yanked on the rope once more, extracting a deep grunt from his prey. He picked up Masterson's discarded rifle and cautiously entered the cabin. A second girl, huddled in the corner, came into view. RJ lowered himself beside her. "Are you okay?"

She nodded timidly and pointed to the other side of the room. RJ crossed the span in four strides and knelt by the man who lay there. After a quick assessment, he concluded that the wounds were superficial. Rafferty consulted the girl. "Where did the other man go?"

"Through that doorway."

RJ moved to the opening with his gun drawn. He slid around the doorjamb, half expecting a bullet to pierce his body. The kitchen was empty, the back door wide open.

RJ retraced his steps to the living room and sat on the floor close to the teenager.

She nodded at Sean. "Is he going to live?"

"Yes," RJ told her. "What's your name?"

"Becca. Becca Banks."

"I know this is all very scary, Becca, but I need you to concentrate. The man who went out the back door, was he alone?"

She shook her head.

"Can you tell me who he left with?"

"The lady." Her soft voice forced RJ to lean closer.

Her sobs quickly filled the room. "Sean, the man over there... Are you sure he's going to be okay?"

"Yes," RJ replied calmly. "He'll be fine. Now, can you explain exactly what happened here?"

Becca hiccupped several times. "He used a flashlight," she said, referring to Sean, "to send an SOS. That lady brought her boat to save us. We were leaving when that horrible man found us again. He took Amber. The other man was supposed to take me. When he heard voices outside, he grabbed the lady instead."

RJ's worst fears threatened to overpower him. "Was the lady hurt? Did she go with him willingly?" He held his breath, unsure if he could bear to hear the answers.

"The mean man hit her with his gun. She was lying on the floor until the other man dragged her to her feet and insisted she go with him. Even though she knew him, she didn't want to go."

"How do you know she knew him?"

"She knew his name. She called him Jack."

"Shit!" He slammed the heel of his foot onto the floorboard. It broke RJ's heart to see Becca shrink with renewed fear because he couldn't keep his anger under check. He wrapped an arm around her. "You're safe now. I'm going outside for a brief look." He dipped his head toward Sean. "I want you to talk to him, see if you can coax him awake. When he wakes up, try to get him on his feet. Can you do that for me?"

"Yes," she said. "Please promise me you'll come back."

"I swear. I'll only be gone a few minutes."

RJ inched through the back door and surveyed the immediate area. The last trickle of daylight would soon fade under the heavy façade of clouds. At that point, it would be impossible to track anyone in these woods.

RJ scoured the ground for signs indicating which way Jack had taken Lucy. Footprints left in the soggy mud led him around the side of the house and up a separate path leading east. With that information, he raced back inside the cabin. "We're getting out of here, now," he told Becca. "You take this." He handed her the rifle. "Do you know how to use it?"

"Yes," she said firmly.

They got Sean to his feet and then hustled out the front door and down the wooden porch steps, careful to keep a safe distance between themselves and Masterson as he lay squirming, trying to escape the bindings on his hands and feet.

CHAPTER NINETY-FOUR

R J's confidence rose as they neared the shoreline. He jogged up to the Larson and exhaled sharply when he saw Amber huddled inside. She shivered from head to toe, probably as much from fear as from the cold, wet wind. The fact that she was out of harm's way was all that really mattered. Rafferty helped Sean and Becca into the boat, pulled a tarp from one of the storage bins under a seat, and used it to shield the three from the further onslaught of rain.

"I'll be back as quick as I can," he assured them.

Rafferty presumed that Jack would head for his car, which was parked on the road at the top of the hill. He moved swiftly, hoping to stay one step ahead of the waning light. The front door to the cabin stood wide open, a dim light outlining its frame, reminding him of the Terry Redlin painting his parents proudly displayed on their living room wall.

RJ recalled the three people he had seen earlier in the cabin. He had to confirm whether Jack had hooked up with the group or gone off on his own. He unclipped his gun and found it had four rounds left. He prayed that would be enough.

Voices drifted from inside. A man and a woman were in a fevered argument.

"I can't believe you'd go that far!" the man said.

"I never understood what you saw in her, Jack," the woman shrieked.

The man countered, "We're running out of time!"

The escalating pitch of their voices warned RJ of the insanity he was about to encounter.

"Don't you see, dear?" The woman cackled like a witch. "She's the cause of all our problems. Our lives were perfect until she came along."

RJ carefully eased himself through the doorway. He quickly scanned the room. Lucy sat on a chair in the middle of the room. The man, who he now recognized as Jack, had a revolver trained on her. The woman Jack was arguing with was the one RJ had observed earlier, the one with the coal-black hair. She had positioned herself near Jack. RJ also noted that the other couple in the room showed no inclination toward intervening.

"Drop the gun!" RJ ordered.

Startled, the woman pivoted. RJ frowned at the derringer in her hand. Another stupid mistake on his part. She fired it at the same time RJ discharged his weapon. He heard the bullet from her pistol slam into the door jamb above his head. RJ's bullet, however, hit exactly where he had aimed it. Lesley fell to the floor.

Lucy jumped up and darted across the room, but Jack didn't miss a beat. He grabbed her arm and wrenched her close to his body. "I win," he gloated. Drop your weapon unless you plan to watch me put a bullet in her head."

Rafferty slowly raised his hands in defeat.

"Drop the gun," Jack reiterated.

RJ bent forward and laid his gun on the floor in front of him. "Now back away."

Lesley moaned. A bright red blotch colored the right shoulder of her silk blouse.

"You'll be fine," RJ intoned. "I advise you to stay still. Otherwise, the wound could bleed out."

"Shut your fucking mouth!" Jack roared. "You better be able to walk out of here on your own," he demanded of the wounded woman, "because there's no way I am carrying you."

Lesley endeavored to right herself. "Don't worry about me. I can take care of myself. What are you going to do with her?"

"Lucy is going to help us get out of here alive. Can you get that gun?" Jack motioned to the weapon on the floor in front of RJ.

Lesley moved on unsteady legs. RJ readied himself and lunged as she bent to collect the pistol. She staggered backward and fell into Jack. RJ snapped up the gun and rolled behind the couch.

Jack managed to keep his balance, with Lucy still firmly under his control. "That was stupid." Saliva spewed with every word. "Toss the gun toward the door and stand up slowly. Both hands above your head, or else Lucy here is a goner."

"Don't do it, RJ." Lucy's voice was surprisingly calm.

"Shut up! I know you've been sleeping with him." Jack tightened his arm around her. "I mean it, Rafferty. Do as I say, or she's dead."

RJ placed his pistol on the floor and kicked it toward the door, raising his hands over his head. Taking in the room one more time, Rafferty noted that the man and woman seated against the wall on the far side of the room had not moved an inch.

The woman with the black hair had regained her footing. Jack's arm wrapped tightly around Lucy's neck, but her resolve showed in her stance.

An eerie quiet fell over the room until Jack boomed, "Move out from behind the sofa."

RJ stepped into the center of the room.

"Jack, what are you waiting for?" Lesley interjected. "We need to get out of here! Shoot him."

"Jack," Lucy yelled. "Don't do this. He's a cop. If you kill him, you're signing your own death warrant. You'll go to prison for the rest of your life."

"This is all your fault," Lesley shrieked. "If you hadn't sunk your claws into my son, we wouldn't be in this mess."

RJ's eyes widened in disgust. "This is your mother?" he said in disbelief.

"All of you. Shut the fuck up." Perspiration dotted Jack's upper lip.

The hairs at the back of Rafferty's neck prickled. Jack was reaching a breaking point. RJ had to do something to defuse the situation, fast.

A loud thumping noise thundered from above. Jack and Lesley instinctively spun their heads around to see if they could identify the source. RJ locked eyes with Lucy, willing her to break loose of Jack's hold. Reading his meaning, she brought the heel of her shoe down hard on Jack's foot.

RJ rushed in as Jack's gun roared to life, pushing Rafferty backwards with a bullet lodged in his shoulder. Marshalling all his strength, RJ charged Jack. They wound up in a bear hug with the gun wedged between them. Jack pulled the trigger.

CHAPTER NINETY-FIVE

The sight of Jack wrestling to free himself from under the dead weight of RJ brought Lucy to her knees. One more shove from Jack, and Rafferty's limp body rolled over onto the floor, revealing the crimson stain discoloring the front of his shirt. Jack got to his feet, backed away from the ugly scene, and subtly used the towel hanging on the arm of the nearby chair to wipe the pistol clean.

In another world, Lucy saw a steel door slam shut. She heard what she thought was a lock clicking into place. A vague feeling of déjà vu settled around her. The nightmare she had experienced several days earlier crystallized, that same distant thud pounding relentlessly. She longed to rewind the clock and go back to where it had all begun—her in her aunt's guest bedroom, snuggled amid soft linens, before RJ had awakened her with his ceaseless hammering at the door.

Truth edged into her brain. The past was not hers to change. She could, however, do everything in her power to assure that today's outcome was the one she wanted. Gasping for air, Lucy fought her way back to reality. She crawled to RJ's lifeless form and placed her hand over his heart. "Please, I need you to wake up. I need you to know I love you."

Jack stepped forward and yanked Lucy to her feet.

She clawed at his fingers as they tightened around her forearm. "Get your paws off of me."

"Lucy, listen to me. He's dead. There's nothing you can do for him now."

"No. We need to get him to the hospital."

Jack slapped her hard across the face. He held her hand as he pressed the handle of his firearm firmly into her palm and worked her fingers around its grip. "Lucy!"

"What did you do?" she moaned.

"What did I do? I didn't do anything, Luce. You shot RJ!"

"You're crazy. We both know you shot him."

"No, Lucy. See, you have the gun. It's got your prints on it."

The unexpected heat of the weapon in her hand clouded her thoughts as it slipped from her grasp and landed with a dull thud.

"Luce, listen to me. Pull yourself together. If you come away with me now, I can keep you safe. We'll find a way out of this together."

"You've got to be kidding," Lesley screamed. "You still want her after everything she's done to you? You're a fool. You can't let her live."

Jack shook his head vehemently. He shoved his mother's words aside and confronted his wife again. "Lucy, look at me. Tell me you love me, and I'll make this all go away."

Lucy couldn't believe her ears. Did he really think she could ever love him again? She felt pure, unadulterated hate for him. RJ was the man she loved, and he lay bleeding to death right in front of her.

"No! He's not dead; he can't be." She clambered back to RJ and laid her hand on his chest. "Please wake up," she whispered. "I love you. Don't you dare leave me now!"

Jack's nostrils flared. "You stupid whore." He grabbed Lucy by the hair and jerked her up to him.

Her eyes darted chaotically, searching for anything that could help her. Where were the man and woman who had sat on the sidelines during the debauchery? Had they dared walk out and leave her to face this lunacy alone?

The thumping sound Lucy thought she'd imagined before vibrated from somewhere outside. *Thump... Thump... Thump.* She tilted her head to the ceiling. What would cause such a ruckus?

"It sounds like a helicopter," Lesley interjected. "Why would a helicopter be out in this weather?"

Lucy smiled wryly. "It's Homer." The mere thought seemed to light up the entire room. "I called him this morning. He told me he was flying in from Minneapolis." She twisted in Jack's arms, glowing with victory. "He's here for you."

Lucy glanced back at RJ, and to her amazement, she saw his finger twitch. "Hang in there, RJ," she whispered. "Help is on the way."

"I told you she was bad news from the beginning." Lesley's coldhearted laughter sent a chill through the room. Jack's focus suddenly became laser sharp. He raised his fist and viciously punched his wife, then knelt beside her where she lay in a stupor. "This is your last chance. Either you come away with me now or face the consequences." When she didn't respond, he snatched up the dirty pillow off the sofa and covered her face with it. A tear trickled from the corners of his eyes as he pressed harder. "If I can't have you, no one can."

Lesley screamed, "What are you doing? If she's telling the truth, Homer will be here any minute." Lesley moved to the door. "I'm not going to jail because of her. It's time to leave. Jack, please come with me!"

"Go on up to the road. My car's up there. I'll join you shortly."
Jack went back to the task at hand.

Lucy fought with every ounce of strength she could muster, but
in the end, she lay motionless. Jack eased his hold on the pillow
and gazed at his lost love, his eyes now devoid of all emotion.

There was one more thing he had to do. His revolver lay next to
Lucy—he didn't dare use that one. He zeroed in on RJ's handgun
lying on the floor near the sofa.

CHAPTER NINETY-SIX

Lucy awoke to a muffled thumping sound. The ringing in her ears made it impossible for her to distinguish whether it was real or the result of the punches she had taken.

Gradually, her senses came alive with the memory of the day's events. If that wasn't enough to motivate her, the sight of Jack hovering over RJ's prone body with a gun pointed at Rafferty's head spurred her to action. She tackled Jack, dislodging the gun from his hand, and dove straight for it. Jack scrambled over her, grunting as he stretched his hand, inch by inch, ever closer to the weapon.

Lucy jammed her elbow into his ribcage, causing Jack to waver, and, giving her the edge. They struggled for the gun until a deafening blast caught them both off-guard. Jack donned a cynical smile, pushed himself off her and fell back against the couch. Wide-eyed, they stared at each other. Lucy gawked at the weapon in her hand. That was when she noticed the hole in the floorboard where the slug had entered. Neither of them had taken the bullet.

Lucy didn't waste time contemplating her luck. Still in possession of the gun, she crawled over to RJ, never letting Jack out of her sight. Her free hand fumbled for a pulse. It was slight, but it was there. In her joy, Lucy lost track of Jack for a mere second.

He pounced. Lucy didn't hesitate.

Jack fell backward, screaming at the top of his lungs. "You shot me! You actually shot me!" He grabbed his knee and tried to stifle the blood flow. "I may never walk again."

Lucy had only one thing on her mind: getting RJ the medical attention he needed. "I swear to God, if you touch a hair on his body, your knee will be the least of your problems." At the last minute, she remembered that RJ had had a gun when he had entered the cottage. Spying it across the room, she seized it and rushed out the door, hurling threats of further mutilation at Jack.

The overhead thumping grew louder—it hadn't been a dream. The foresight to leave a message in Homer's voicemail prior to setting out had paid off.

The whirling sound came from somewhere near the lake. Oscillating lights shone from the sky, illuminating the way. Lucy reached the shoreline to witness a helicopter settling on the beach about fifty yards in front of her. Fighting the windy force of its blades, she trudged over to the two men disembarking.

"Lucy Rydell?" Homer didn't try to hide his relief. "I'm David Wendt."

Lucy labored to catch her breath, "You have to hurry!" she pleaded, "RJ's in the cabin up the hill. He's been shot. He's lost a lot of blood."

"Is there anyone else up there?" Wendt asked. He gave quick instructions to the man in the cockpit and turned back to Lucy for an answer.

Lucy yelled over the deafening noise of the rotors, "Yes. Jack's up there. I shot him in the leg. I don't think he'll get very far if he tries to make a run for it. His mother's waiting for him at the top of the hill." She sucked in air. "You were right about Jack. He's not who he pretends to be. He and Lesley are both part of the kidnapping ring."

Homer shouted orders to his companions: "Cal, you and Jessie get up to the cabin. Rafferty's been shot. Be careful. Jack Rydell is up there, too. Wounded, possibly armed."

"He's not armed. I have his gun. I also have RJ's." She handed both to Homer and then jogged after the men as they headed up the hill.

"Lucy," Homer called after her. "Those guys will take care of Rafferty and Jack. I need you to tell me what happened here."

Lucy hesitated as the men disappeared along the path. Every part of her yearned to be by RJ's side, but Homer was right. RJ would be in good hands.

Homer approached. "Concentrate, Lucy," he said, giving her no time to change her mind. "Tell me exactly what you heard and saw."

Lucy closed her eyes to regroup. "I came across the lake in my aunt's boat because I saw an SOS signal. When I got here, all hell broke loose." She frowned. "I saw Masterson. He *is* alive. We were in a cabin up the beach."

"Can you show me where it is?"

"Yes," Lucy answered with renewed energy. "And we found two of the missing girls. I pray they're all right. And Sean Penalton—I completely forgot about him." Lucy took off running.

Homer addressed the man in the cockpit. "Stay here in case someone circles back this way."

"Got it covered, boss."

Homer sprinted after Lucy as she ran past her aunt's beached boat. Homer stopped for a brief inspection.

"Lucy," he yelled. "Wait up. They're here."

She halted and rushed back, increasing her pace when she saw the two girls and Sean huddled safely in the hull. As soon as

Homer assured himself that the three did not require immediate medical attention, he and Lucy made their way to the Moritzes' lake home.

Masterson was nowhere in sight. A search of the area turned up drag marks and blood spatter, hinting at what had taken place outside the cottage. Nearby was a discarded piece of rope. Homer radioed the colleague he'd left manning the helicopter and asked for assistance. The voice on the other end reported that they had apprehended Jack Rydell and his mother.

Homer beamed at Lucy. "I'm going to love seeing that smug son of a bitch try to squirm his way out of this one."

"Me, too," Lucy agreed.

CHAPTER NINETY-SEVEN

H omer Wendt looked skyward. The storm had moved further to the east. Calmer weather would certainly make
everyone's job easier. "You were great tonight," he said to
Lucy. "No matter how this turns out, know that lives were saved
because of what you did."

Unable to muster an answer, Lucy shook her head. "What about
Lloyd?"

"I've been informed that thanks to you, the FBI is hot on his
trail." Homer smiled. "Come on," he said, "let's get back to the
others."

Standing beside the boat with Lucy, Wendt opined, "The storm
seems to have passed, but the terrain here makes it difficult to
get all of you up the hill. One of my men will transport you to the
other side of the lake in this boat. The local police will be there to
escort everyone to the hospital for a checkup."

Lucy protested, "You can send them back. I need to go with RJ."

"RJ is already on his way to the hospital," Homer lied.

"Is he going to be okay?" She raked her trembling hands
through her wet hair.

"The truth is, he's in pretty bad shape. It's touch-and-go at
this point. Lucy, the best thing you can do now is go with these

girls. They're young. It's essential that they're with someone they trust until we can get them to a safe place. I'll catch up with RJ and meet up with you at the hospital."

Lucy nodded and reluctantly boarded the small boat, where she received a heart-warming reception. Homer was a smart man. The girls did need a familiar face. With arms stretched wide, they embraced her. Sean sat alone across from them until Lucy invited him to join their huddle.

His brow knitted together—the simple gesture appeared to baffle him. Shunning a lifelong pursuit of isolation, he stood, visibly overwhelmed by their open affection.

CHAPTER NINETY-EIGHT

A gents Hunter and Peterson were at the Masterson farm when the call came from District Attorney Wendt. Peterson took obvious pride in relaying the news to the four people whose lives had been on hold for so long.

When the agent walked into the room, Mary Ann Banks immediately misread the expression on her face. "Oh, my God," she screamed, "I can't take any more bad news."

Peterson quickly apologized. "I didn't mean to scare you." She swiped at her tears of joy. "Don't mind me." She inhaled deeply and resumed her speech with the professional decorum it deserved. "We have just received news that your girls are safe." Peterson's complexion flushed with shared joy as cheers erupted and the group clambered to their feet, locking arms with each other.

The agent cleared her throat. "I have an update. The doctors at Mercy Hospital have given the patients a thorough examination. They've been through a lot, but everyone is optimistic that with your loving care, they will make a full recovery."

Pandemonium erupted as all four of them shrieked with utter joy, huge grins pasted across every face in the room. Dan grabbed Mary Ann and twirled her in circles. Malcolm Bremer gave Wayne

Johanson a slap on the back and then pulled him into a bear hug, confessing, "I've dreamt of this day for far too long." Addressing Peterson, he prompted, "Can I have my phone back so I can call my wife in Omaha?"

"I'd like mine, too," Johanson added. "I have to call Hal. I'll swing by the house and pick him up on the way to the hospital."

Mary Ann approached Agent Peterson with her hand tightly clasped against her chest. "We can't thank you and your fellow agents enough." Her eyes glistened. "We need to be with our daughters now."

"Of course. An escort is waiting to take all of you to the hospital."

CHAPTER NINETY-NINE

A procession of cars snaked through the parking lot at St. Andrews Funeral Home, extending along the street and around the corner. Most displayed Minnesota license plates. Some, however, exhibited official government identification. Behind the privacy of tinted glass, federal agents scrutinized everyone within view, their eyes skimming over the somber show of flags flying at half-mast.

It was midsummer, the air warm and heavy with humidity. Beneath the idling vehicles, puddles of water collected on the hot concrete, while the air conditioning units worked overtime to keep the passengers cool as they waited to embark on the last leg of the journey.

Lucy sat in the back of one of the limousines, alone and grief-stricken, a handful of Kleenex grasped in her fingers. She used one to dab her eyes, hoping to stem the flow of tears that had threatened all morning to be her undoing. She doubted that she would ever come to grips with the aftermath of recent events.

All her life, she'd weighed every key decision, knowing that each one had the ability to change the future. Most had no lasting effects. Others propelled her closer to the desired objectives. Some forced her to take two steps backward before moving ahead again. And then there were the ones comparable to those she had contended with over the last couple of weeks: ones that evoked devastating consequences.

The steps that had led her to this ominous day were unmistakable. It was so unfair that one person could erroneously shape the lives of so many. Logically, she couldn't blame herself, even though she had every reason to. Sadly, justification did not quiet her on nights when the *what if*s ran amok inside her head. If only she had said no to her aunt's proposal.

Hindsight made her question the wisdom of working with the FBI. Her biggest regret was bringing Jack into the equation. RJ would be alive today if it weren't for him. Regrets tormented Lucy during every waking hour and often crept into her dreams late at night. If she could turn back time, she would do everything differently. That, of course, was impossible. She prayed that time would ease some of the pain etched deep in her heart.

Jack's betrayal was an entirely different pill to swallow. Lucy had completely missed the clues that signaled his psychopathic nature. He was in jail now, which was exactly where he belonged. She dreaded his trial and wasn't looking forward to testifying against him. The experts at the FBI had explained that Jack's delusions of grandeur were likely the result of his mother's adoration. Their opinion was that Lesley had created his psychosis. Even so, the woman refused to accept any responsibility, for either herself or her son. She proclaimed their innocence over and over, insisting that Masterson had set them up to take the fall.

In spite of everything, Lucy had insight that there was a positive side to all of this. Although many things had gone wrong that night, she was grateful to Sean Penalton. He had risked his own life to save those of Becca, Amber, and her. He was a true hero. Soon, everyone would know it.

Lucy would be indebted to Sean forever. It had saddened her to break his heart that day at the hospital. It must have taken every ounce of his courage to propose marriage to her, and Lucy had tried in earnest to let him down easily. She wished him a speedy recovery both from the wounds he'd received that night and from the heartbreak she had reluctantly dealt him.

Lucy smiled. Sean had a strong spirit, and with Amber by his side, he wouldn't languish very long. Lucy warmly recalled watching Amber attend to him at the hospital. It was apparent that the two had a compelling connection that would last a lifetime.

The limo Lucy occupied eased forward, forcing her back to the present and illuminating her path ahead. RJ was dead. He had died trying to protect her. The image of his body lying on the floor, blood oozing from his wounds, plagued her at every turn. She would always be grateful for him and his sacrifice.

Lucy was also thankful to the family RJ had left behind: his mother, his father, and his sisters. Even in their loss, they welcomed her with open hearts. She wondered why she had ever disputed RJ's integrity. For that, she blamed Jack. Everything Jack had told her had been a lie.

Lucy gazed through the tinted window of the limousine, gaining strength from the big oak trees lining the edge of the parking lot. The car had just begun to move when someone rapped on the glass and startled her out of her reverie. The limo rolled to a stop and the door beside her opened. A man leaned in. Bright sunlight backlit his features, making it impossible for her to see him clearly. As recognition dawned, she quietly asked, "What can I do for you, Agent Hunter?"

"We have to talk."

"Now? Can't it wait until tomorrow?"

"It probably could, but I think you should listen to what I have to say."

"Fine. If you must. Please get in."

He climbed in and closed the door. The driver sought direction from the agent, and Hunter signaled him to continue forward. He said to Lucy, "I want to bring you up to date on a few things, and then I'm going to ask you for help."

Always the professional. Even at this particularly sad time, even during a funeral procession, he behaved like an FBI agent. Did he ever let down his guard?

Getting right to business, Agent Hunter proceeded to update Lucy on what the FBI had learned regarding Lloyd Masterson and Cassie Mitchell, RJ's former partner. "With what we gleaned from Chris Foley, we have a warrant to tap Mitchell's phone. Masterson had called her three times that day: twice from his cellphone and once from a land line. He apparently freed himself from RJ's bindings and made it to a neighboring house, where he gained entrance and used the phone. It was sheer luck that the owners weren't home. There's no telling what Masterson would have done if someone had confronted him.

"Mitchell tossed her cell after she and Masterson hooked up, and we recovered it from a trash bin at one of the nearby parks. Masterson likely required medical attention, with the bullet lodged in his thigh. We've contacted every hospital within 100 miles, but our search has come up short so far. There is a good chance they've parted company by now, so we've alerted airports and border patrol to be vigilant. It's only a matter of time. We will catch them," Agent Hunter said with confidence. "Thanks to your description, we tracked the couple you saw in the cabin with Lesley to Minneapolis and arrested them before they boarded a flight to Miami. They're cooperating with us. Between them and the lead Rafferty had in Arizona, we've traced the whereabouts of one other missing girl. She will be back in the States and reunited with her parents later today. We have viable leads on the other three."

"That's wonderful news," Lucy agreed. "Did you find out anything about my aunt?"

"We'll deal with Sylvia Masterson in due time."

Lucy folded her hands softly in her lap. "Isn't it possible that my aunt had nothing to do with Lloyd's criminal activities?"

"I don't doubt that Sylvia is involved up to her eyebrows. Why else would she leave the country? Why would she go into hiding?"

"Maybe she's afraid of Lloyd," Lucy interjected.

"We've considered that possibility."

Lucy wanted to delve deeper into the agent's cryptic words. Gathering her thoughts, she glanced out the window. To her utter shock, the limo had left the procession and was now heading out of town in the wrong direction. "Where the hell are we going?" Her voice shook with anger. "I need to be at the gravesite when RJ is laid to rest. Turn this car around," she screamed at the driver.

"Take it easy, Lucy," Agent Hunter demanded. "Everything will be fine."

"What the hell does that mean? Nothing is ever going to be right again. Don't you get it? I loved RJ. He shouldn't be the one we're burying today. It should be me. Jack killed RJ because he couldn't stand the thought of me being with another man. Don't you see? RJ wouldn't be dead if it weren't for me!"

Obviously uncomfortable with her outburst, Agent Hunter slid an awkward arm around her shoulders.

Lucy shrunk from his embrace. "Don't you dare try to placate me. I demand you turn this car around right now."

A deep flush colored his cheeks. He pulled back. "Lucy, I know this is hard for you." The driver veered into the parking area of a roadside park. "Look. David Wendt is here, and he has something important to share with you."

Hunter's noticeable relief confused Lucy. "I don't understand. Why are you playing games with me? Just tell me what's going on."

"It's complicated, Lucy. Please trust me on this. Before I turn you over to Homer, I want you to know that he was one of our best agents before he decided to go back into law. On his climb to county attorney, he kept his contacts at the FBI. When he told me he and a couple of his marine buddies were in a helicopter on their way to assist you, I knew you were in good hands."

With that, Agent Hunter opened the car door and got out. He extended his hand to assist Lucy as she exited the car and stood by his side. As Wendt approached, Hunter leaned in and whispered, "His devotion to your happiness proves that you are one special lady." The agent nodded to Homer. "I'll leave you two to talk."

"Hi, Lucy," Homer said warmly. "Sorry for all this cloak-and-dagger stuff. You will understand in due time. Please come with me." He took her arm and led her to his car, opened the passenger door, and motioned for her to get in.

Glancing backward, she hesitated when she spotted the limousine that she had arrived in exiting the lot, presumably with Agent Hunter inside.

"Please, Lucy, we don't have much time."

Lucy sighed wearily and climbed into Homer's vehicle.

Neither said a word for the duration of the drive. Something was amiss. Homer repeatedly surveyed activity in his rearview mirror. Mimicking his paranoia, she checked the side mirror multiple times, half-expecting another vehicle to come racing up behind them. They drove on.

Homer's cellphone beeped at that exact moment. He spoke into it: "We're almost there." There was an extended pause. "Got it. My ETA is less than five minutes." He checked the mirror one more time before disconnecting.

A few miles further, Homer swerved off the highway onto a gravel road, advancing a short distance and parking behind a black SUV. Homer exited the car and walked around to the passenger side to open Lucy's door. She got out and silently searched the surroundings for clues that might explain Homer's behavior. The only thing that came to mind was that they *had* found Sylvia, and for reasons unknown, they deemed it necessary to keep this meeting under wraps. Still, that didn't give them the right to hijack her on this day of all days. "Homer, please stop this charade. I'll never forgive myself if I don't get back to the cemetery in time."

"Don't worry. You know I have your back. Please, just see this through."

Lucy allowed Homer to lead her to the SUV. When they neared the vehicle, the driver got out, came around to her side, and opened the back door. Lucy peered inside. Despite the physical changes, the figure sitting in the back seat took her breath away. She slipped inside. The click of the door lock sent shivers down her spine.

She stared blankly at the ghost of a man beside her, wanting desperately to believe that it was really him. Tragically, it had to be an illusion. Too much had happened in the last ten days. She couldn't trust herself anymore.

She glared at Homer through the side window, where tinted glass denied him a reciprocal view of her. She watched him check his cell phone multiple times as he paced back and forth.

"Lucy? Please look at me," the man beside her pleaded.

His voice sounded authentic; still, she refused to believe any of it. None of this was real. Every night was the same. In her dreams, RJ was still alive. The second she awoke every morning, reality pierced her heart. The dark SUV closed in around her.

A reassuring hand pressed against hers. She fought the desire to affirm his presence, knowing that the minute she acknowledged him, he would fade away like the ghost he was. She slowed her breathing and willed herself to wake up.

His hand was on her cheek now, brushing aside the tears. She turned, resolved to end this charade. Little by little, the haze lifted. It had all been a horrible nightmare. He was here, by her side. His arms encircled her as she leaned in. Their lips met, meshing into a passionate kiss. If this was a dream, she prayed she would never wake up.

<hr />

After turning Lucy over to the capable hands of Homer Wendt, Agent Hunter sped down I94 on his way to Hector International Airport in Fargo, where he would join Agent Peterson and board a private jet to LaGuardia Airport. From there, they would fly to London's Heathrow Airport.

When they reached their destination, they would take custody of Sylvia Masterson and escort her back to Fargo, where she would face charges of abetting a criminal, racketeering, and human trafficking.

A smiled touched his lips. Today was, indeed, a good day.

EPILOGUE

Lucy awoke in a cold sweat and reached for RJ. He nestled her in his arms. "Another nightmare?" he queried, holding her tightly. "Hmm," she confirmed and snuggled deeper into the warmth of his body. "But they're getting less intense."

"I hate that I can't protect you from your dreams. I feel so helpless."

"I know what you can do to reassure me." She ran her fingernails across the small of his back.

"Now that's the kind of rehabilitation the doctor prescribed."

They moved into each other with the familiarity of a lifetime together, and yet there was always a nuance of the first time for both. Maybe it was because there was always the threat that it might be their last time.

They spent an hour thoroughly exploring each other's bodies. With a flushed face, Lucy slapped RJ firmly on the butt and ordered him up and out of bed. "You're going to be late for work if you don't get moving."

"Jeff will be there. He can handle things 'til I arrive." He glanced at the clock on the nightstand as he grabbed her arm, tugging her gently back on top of him. "We have time for one more round," he said, nibbling her earlobe.

"You may have a responsible partner to cover for you. Sadly, I don't." She laughed as she pulled away and headed to the shower.

"The shower it is, then," he agreed. "We can wrap this up in there. Kill two birds with one stone, as the saying goes." He padded behind her. She could not, nor was she inclined to, resist him.

An hour later, dressed and ready to go, they walked out the door.

"You can drop me off at the office and have the truck today."

"Are you sure?" he asked.

"Yeah, I have enough to keep me busy all day. The Casagrandes requested serious changes in their kitchen design, so they asked me to put together a couple of ideas for them. How's their house coming along?"

"We're on schedule to pour the basement floor before the frost sets in. We start framing within the next thirty days. We won't need your completed plans for the kitchen until then."

"That's true, but I'd rather be ahead of schedule than behind."

"That's why I love you, Mrs. Demarco."

"Right back at you, Mr. Demarco." They both laughed.

"I don't think I will ever get used to my new name," Rick Demarco said.

"I hope they catch Lloyd soon so we can go back to our normal lives," Patty Demarco soberly replied.

"They will, darling. All in good time," RJ said. "In the meantime, I rather enjoy our new life here. Construction was always a second career choice for me. I think I prefer it over law enforcement. And you're a natural at home design. You know, you could always go back to being a freelance writer if you wanted to. Maybe you should think about writing a novel."

"I don't think so. And for your information, I don't care where we live or what we do, as long as we're together."

Smiling, he leaned in and gave her one last kiss before they headed off to work.

AUTHOR'S NOTES

To learn more about preventing human trafficking, go to **dea.gov/resources**. Remember: no one chooses to be exploited. Abusers use threats, violence, and manipulation to control their victims. *If you see something, say something.*

If you think someone is a victim of human trafficking or if you want to report suspicious activity, call the National Human trafficking Hotline at 1-888-373-7888.

"This hotline connects victims and survivors of sex and labor trafficking with services and support to get help and stay safe. It also receives tips about potential situations of sex and labor trafficking and facilitates reporting that information to the appropriate authorities in certain cases."

See **humantraffickinghotline.org/en** for more information.

Lucinda Michalski and her husband, Jerry, currently reside in Arizona. During the summer months, they enjoy spending time at their lake home in Minnesota. Late one night, Lucinda witnessed an electrical storm perform a mesmerizing dance against the backdrop of the vast, dark waters of the lake. It sparked her imagination. A story emerged and continued to evolve over the years, and SOS eventually took on a life of its own.